HALF A RING

HALF A RING

Part II of the HAFRÖN series

Cary A. Conder

iUniverse, Inc.

New York Lincoln Shanghai

Half A Ring
Part II of the HAFRÖN series

Copyright © 2004 by Cary Anne Conder

iUniverse books may be ordered through booksellers or by contacting:

iUniverse
2021 Pine Lake Road, Suite 100
Lincoln, NE 68512
www.iuniverse.com
1-800-Authors (1-800-288-4677)

ISBN: 0-595-33758-9

Printed in the United States of America

Dedicated to my favourite muse, Andre Norton.

Also to David Brin and David Cherry, Bob Eggleton and Bob Silverbeg.

And with special thanks to Michael Sheard.

Unexplored
Region

Glacier

Glacier

Northern Wastelands

Southern Wastelands

Unexplored Region

Neranik Sea

Kandyn
Islands

Púdorná of
WÓBINY

Wób
River

Iny River

Irvó

Iny
Marsh

Rimtön of
EKÖZAV

Zaval
River

Hycót
River

Colony

Port

Colony

Revil

Averan

Pindkol

Rashordi Mountains

Korid
River

Rash
River

Vyhal of
NÜHYKAR

Frigid Sea

PROLOGUE

▼

Twenty Years Post Insurrection

Jikpryn

Scrolls and the detritus of several snatched meals flew in all directions as Jikpryn, Usurper Alaiad of Fimiah, cleared his desk top with a violent sweep of his right arm. In the neighbouring chamber, his page started and peered fearfully in the direction of his liege. Jikpryn ignored the boy. Today the clawed fingers of his crippled right hand throbbed a counterpoint to the pain stabbing at his skull behind his ear. Eyes screwed shut he waited for the moment to pass.

He should have been confirming the schedules laid down by his advisor for audiences with the senior lords of his realm. Every time he attempted to concentrate on mundane matters, however the pain returned, vengeful in its assault, forcing him to break off what he was doing. Once bark-brown hair was now heavily grey-streaked, a legacy of the twenty plus years since he had taken and held Fimiah's high seat. There were deep lines around his eyes. More dragged down the sides of his mouth, and there were furrows across his brow that had not been there before his assault against Iryô's hereditary ruler.

Dragging his chair around to face the window, Jikpryn contemplated the view beyond his turret study. Even at this distance, the ravages of the past spring were evident to any with eyes for the obvious. Stunted crops struggled to produce sickly foliage in drought-stricken fields, despite the constant care diligently applied by the farmers and their families. Pastures were yellow-brown where they should have been a lush late spring green.

Dôzhik Koryn had begun with heavy snowfalls and five wicked cold snaps. An unexpected early thaw had filled the rivers and streams beyond their capacity.

Several massive blocks had broken off the ice sheets in the far north and south. One had sent a huge tidal bore down the Iny River, washing away entire villages, killing hundreds of unsuspecting inhabitants and their livestock, and finished up by destroying the docks in Pûdornâ, capitol of his home province, Wôbiny.

Also damaged were a number of prized orchards. The early thaw had coaxed far too many crops to an early start, only to be frost bitten or killed. Now what, to all reports, looked to be a strained production of edible commodities would be stretched beyond reasonable capacity by the necessity to send food north to stave off starvation over the next winter.

"And then there's Vyhal's fleet."

Nearly one-third of Nûhykar's fishing fleet had been damaged or destroyed. Just as they had sailed on the late spring tide a towering wall of water had surged across the frigid in-land sea. The massive wall of water had caught the fleet at anchor and vessels, large and small, had been tossed onto the shore. Several houses had been flattened by debris, their inhabitants crushed. There would be no fish to spare this year.

"Nor roe," reflected Jikpryn.

Like many Fimiahri, he enjoyed the tasty delicacy whenever it was available. Tolbôun might insist it was his due to order up such titbits with which to entertain his guests. Yet despite his disdain for anyone who was not Wôbiny-born, Jikpryn had no desire to risk insurrection by starving his people while dining in luxury.

Again, a stab of pain pulsed. Nostrils flaring, his eyes teared. Quickly pressing two fingers against the spot, he rode the assault until it had crested and faded away. Once more, he reflected upon the capitol spread beyond his fortress' walls. There should have been far more people about. Hardly anyone dallied in the markets. His spies brought him such gossip as they managed to reap, but the bulk of it was unreliable at best, gleaned in the taverns from those too deep in their cups to hold their tongues. The more reliable rumours were those gathered in the markets. This spring, however the only thing that really seemed to preoccupy the residents was the prophecy.

They had tried, he and Tolbôun, to prevent it escaping the fortress. Oh, how they had tried. But, escape it had. That damned benighted prophecy. It chased his dreams at night and haunted his waking hours until he thought he would go mad trying to understand it. Even now, it chattered through his brain.

'Black on black, they saw him,
Half a ring of the Warrior's shield,
Bearing the blade of hope
And Star blood at his side.

Black on black, he will come
And with him, justice will ride.
Half a ring, half a rune,
And Star blood at his side.'

CHAPTER 1

▼

Marrek

Hands pushed and shoved with relentless determination. Fortunately, what Hafrin was packing did not consist of breakables. Otherwise, Marrek would have set him to another task. Marrek watched his foster son from the corner of his eye but refrained from voicing his concern or advising caution and less force. This was their first trip onto the trade route since Nichole's departure.

Departure? Hardly, thought Marrek. Head down, he concentrated on padding the breakables before carefully fitting them into the smaller packs, which would sit on top of the pack rynad's load. *Why not just admit it. She was kidnapped, and by our own people.*

Across the cabin sitting room, Hafrin's hands paused in the midst of work. Forewarned that his shields were leaking and Hafrin was reading those stray thoughts Marrek quickly reinforced his mental shields. A slight flush crept up the back of Hafrin's neck. The young Alaiad Presumptive knew Marrek had noticed his breach of psi etiquette.

Hold your tongue, Marrek ordered himself. He took a slow deep breath, counting, and released it. *Give him space. This will pass.*

It had to pass if Hafrin was to survive. Months of frayed nerves, short temper and recalcitrance were wearing on Marrek. Not even Kili had been spared Hafrin's barbed tongue. Yet, Hafrin's milk mother had been the only one to seriously champion his cause when the Hynarkin had initially insisted Nichole leave.

And it's all your fault, Marrek grumbled, *You should have taken her with you when you went up to the colony, injured or not. If you had...*

The other half of his subconscious countered, *And risked her dying en route. Idiot.*

With a sigh, Marrek closed the clasp on the last satchel and straightened. A shock of black hair had fallen into Hafrin's eyes. Impatient, he shoved it back off his face. But the lock fell forward again. As he angrily pushed it once more out of his eye, Marrek sensed he was on the verge of exploding.

"Dammit," Hafrin snapped in Hynarkin, following up with a Fimiahri oath, "Serpent take it. Stay there!"

"You need a haircut," Marrek quietly observed.

"Then cut it," Hafrin retaliated, his eyes flashing with thinly restrained fury.

"Sure," said Marrek, trying to make light of the situation, "if you don't mind looking like a sheared tilkrin."

Hafrin opened his mouth but nothing came out. Settled back on his heels, surrounded by the last of their trade goods, he rested his hands on his thighs. The fire quietly crackled in the hearth.

"Why don't you take a break? Ride down to Ziv's with the last of the things we need them to store while we're gone. Ask Kili to cut your hair."

Unprepared for Marrek's reasonable response to the situation, Hafrin glowered at his foster father. Tight-lipped he asked, "Do you want the rest of this stuff packed for tomorrow or not?"

For a second time that day, Marrek took a long slow breath and released it, silently counting until the press of pent-up anger dissipated. "I'm not going to get into a fight with you over this, Rin. Go get Kili to cut your hair. While she's at it, ask her to run some more of the dye through it. It's grown out over the winter and we've been remiss about keeping on top of it."

Anger sparked the air between them. It turned Hafrin's eyes dark behind the contacts that altered his startling blue eyes to a safe neutral brown. For a minute, Marrek thought Hafrin would continue to balk at the suggestion. Then Hafrin shoved one pack aside, stood and grabbed at his heavy jacket. He stormed out of the cabin, slamming the front door shut behind him. The tiny building shook beneath the assault.

Eyes fixed on his hands now resting on the small packs in front of him Marrek shook his head. Rubbing the back of his neck where a tension headache was beginning, Marrek went to the stove and poured himself some ale from the warming pot. He took it with him when he went to the sitting room window. Outside, Hafrin appeared from behind the small stable, mounted on his magnificent black rynad stallion. Bïzhan Koryn barely broke stride as he took the pasture fence.

Marrek muttered, "I really wish you'd use the gate, Rin."

He sipped the ale and watched until rynad and rider disappeared into the forest. By their elected direction, they were not headed directly to Zivvoz's hold. Rather, Hafrin was more than likely going to take a more roundabout route to blow off steam. Thankfully, Hafrin still had sufficient presence of mind to know he was being unreasonable. It would not stand him in good stead if he arrived at Zivvoz's still seething, and take out his frustrations on those who had raised him for his first ten years of life.

Despite his early childhood, during which Hafrin had believed Zivvoz's family was his own, the Alaiad Presumptive had quickly adapted to the knowledge that he was an orphan. In fact, he had readily and, it seemed, eagerly turned to Marrek to provide the father figure he craved. That was not to say everything had gone smoothly. Truth be told, there were numerous times when Marrek had despaired the boy would survive to adulthood. Throughout the winter seasons, Marrek had expanded Hafrin's tutoring beyond what any other Fimiahri would learn, including Hynarkin dialect and trade practices in his instruction.

Bright and inquisitive, Hafrin had striven to be the dutiful son. He had seen his introduction into Hynarkin life as a secret to be protected and had revelled in being privy to that introduction into such aspects of Marrek's people. Like most intelligent children, however, he had proved a handful.

"Like the first time I took him on the trade route. Christ, he scared the life out of me."

Settled on the hearth, his goblet with the dregs of the ale cradled in his hands, Marrek set his mind on his life after Hafrin had moved in with him. There had been a day during Hafrin's initiation on the trade route when he had wanted desperately to go to the aid of a furrier's wife and daughter when several bullies attacked them. Hafrin had come incredibly close to ending his short life that day. Fortunately, he had chosen to heed his foster father's advice.

Throughout all of those years, however, they had built a solid, close relationship, one as strong as any between a father and his natural son. Even after Hafrin had discovered the truth of his ancestry: Royal born and sole true heir to the Fimiahri high seat. In the same evening, he had also stumbled upon the truth behind the Hynarkin. Alien to Fimiah, they were embroiled in an interstellar war. Moreover, just as surely as a bit of driftwood in a spring flood, Fimiah was caught up in those same currents.

It had been Nichole's unannounced arrival in their midst which had altered everything. Not that it was her fault. Marrek had to admit he should have seen the warning signs: the closeness between Bïzhan and Hafrin from the stallion's birth, and the manner in which Vrala Harz had trusted Hafrin the day he had discovered her, a fledgling trapped in a thicket.

"Yes I should have seen it. But no native Fimiahri has ever displayed signs of psi talents. And no one thought to warn me about our blood in his genes."

You should have guessed, insisted the treacherous voice of his subconscious. *All the warning signs were there. You just didn't want to admit the possibility existed.*

Instead, he had put it down to a sympathetic nature, which animals sometimes sensed. "And I still haven't asked him when he first became aware of the voices in his head. Damn."

Getting to his feet, Marrek headed back into the kitchen nook. After putting his mug on the counter, he gathered up the stachels of breakables and moved to the bench beneath the sitting room window. Trapped on the horns of a dilemma for which there was no solution Hafrin would accept, Marrek set about packing the remainder of the trade goods.

Dusk had fallen by the time Hafrin returned. Marrek looked up from sealing a pack. Hair, now a nut brown, was trimmed straight across his forehead. Layered down the sides so that it was several lengths, it was shorter in front of his ears, tapering to a tail at the nape of his neck. The sides neatly blended into the beard Marrek had forced him to grow to help conceal his identity. Marrek blinked and frowned.

"You look different," he told Hafrin. A smile suddenly caught his lips. "She's dyed your moustache as well."

A hint of a smile flickered in Hafrin's eyes. For a brief instant, Marrek hoped against hope that his charge's mood was finally softening. His optimism was dashed. Hafrin grunted and shrugged his shoulders. Resigned, Marrek gestured to the five packs surrounding him.

"If you'll put these behind the door for tomorrow morning, I'll start supper."

Headed for the kitchen, Marrek ran his fingers through his own hair, organizing it and drawing it back. Once satisfied he had almost all of the strands, he wrapped a thin hide thong around it and tied it back out of his eyes. With vegetables set to steam, he slipped down into the root cellar beneath the kitchen to collect some of the smoked meat. What they did not eat for supper they would pack as the next day's trail rations.

Across the cabin, Hafrin dutifully stacked the packs against the wall beneath the coat pegs behind the front door. That done he disappeared into the loft where they slept. Marrek's paring knife paused in the midst of slicing slivers of meat into a pan of leftover drippings.

Up there was another sore point for contention, which, regrettably had not come to light until the first night after their return from the Wanderer way station. In a snit, Hafrin had yanked his pallet across the loft to the farthest corner. Unfortunately, he had revealed something that had been hidden for years. At some time after discovering he was Alaiad-in-exile, Hafrin had carved the Alaiad's rune into the loft boards beneath his bed. A childish prank, Marrek might otherwise have been simply annoyed because it had damaged the carefully smoothed boards.

It was the second carving that had nearly stopped his heart, however, and sent him into a lengthy tirade at his fosterling. Meticulously picked out in the wood beneath the Alaiad's rune was the Royal family's lineage. Last on the list were the words: Hafrin af Fanhri va Rityöm, or Hafrin son of Fanhri out of Rityöm.

"God in heaven, Rin. What were you thinking? If your uncle's men had ever come here, either in our absence or while we were here," Marrek paused to recover his composure. Voice dropping he had continued, "Didn't you think what would have happened to us? To Ziv and his family because of their close association to us?"

Sullen and silent, Hafrin had withstood Marrek's railing. Then he had stoically fetched two sanding stones, one coarse, the other fine, and set to work erasing the carvings. It had taken three days of concerted elbow grease, but he had succeeded. They did not speak of it again. If Hafrin had inflicted further damage of similar nature he never said, but Marrek suspected he probably removed all other traces.

Already stinging from losing Nichole, Hafrin withdrew further from Marrek. Sullen, recalcitrant, he performed his chores as an automaton. Only the wicked weather had kept him immured in the same building as Marrek, aside from sojourns to the stable to care for their rynada, plus the few rakkïal Marrek possessed.

On the first day of good weather, Hafrin saddled Bïzhan and disappeared. A quick investigation revealed he not taken camping supplies or his small stash of funds made over years on the trade route. Before he could completely panic Vrala Harz flew in with a message from Zivvoz. Hafrin was at their cabin. Hafrin had remained with the hold family for three days then returned as though nothing had happened.

Which brings us here, thought Marrek. Aloud he called, "Supper's ready."

While Marrek had been preoccupied with making supper and recalling the past, Hafrin had brought down four sleeping rolls for their trip from the loft. He had also fetched four tarpaulins and six water flasks from the storage shed and set them with the packs.

Marrek served up supper. Seated at the kitchen nook table, they ate in silence that was anything but companionable. Without being told, Hafrin cleaned up the dishes. In unspoken accord, they prepared packages of travel rations and returned them to the cold cellar. That done Marrek headed for bed.

From his pallet, he listened to the silence that fell over the cabin. In the stillness of the night's early hours, he wondered if Hafrin was mentally conversing with his rynad and orved. Born latent, his psi-talents had been inherited from a Hynarkin ancestor several generations back. At least, that was what the Wanderer colony scientists believed. It was only after meeting Nichole that Hafrin had discovered he was not going mad. Worse, his abilities were unique and in desperate need of training. Nichole had done what she could in the short time they were together.

Which is undoubtedly why he misses her so much, Marrek considered. Staring out the tiny loft window at the night sky he silently asked, *What have we done, Vern? Was it the right decision?*

There was no answer to that and it was far too late to change any of it. Nichole was gone, light years away, living and training at the Fleet and Colony Training Academy. Something downstairs scuffed the floorboards. Fire irons softly clanged against one another. Hafrin was banking the fire. They would not build it back up in the morning but would let it die out. Breakfast would be a cold meal, taken in the dark of pre-dawn.

So life goes on.

Footsteps tapped the loft ladder rungs. Restless, Marrek rolled onto his side, facing the loft entrance. In the limited light provided by Dôzhik's quarter crescent in the night sky, Marrek made out the outline of Hafrin entering the loft. His foster son's head turned briefly in his direction, indicating he knew Marrek was still awake. Without speaking, Hafrin washed and stripped. Crawling into his bed, he turned his back to Marrek and composed himself to sleep.

CHAPTER 2

▼

Hafrin

Eleven days on the trail and Hafrin still could not shake the black cloud hanging over him. He repeatedly re-ran Bïzhan's comments made the day of their departure. The stallion and his dame had accompanied them as far as Zivvoz's hold where they would remain until the end of the trading season. En route, using images, since animals did not possess an understanding of speech such as sentient species employed, Bizhan reasoned that as he saw it his rider and friend had two choices. He could continue to accept Marrek as herd boss, not an altogether unacceptable position, or Hafrin could strike out on his own and start a herd of his own: succinct and to the point.

As if I could, thought Hafrin. One of his trail gelding's grey ears twitched back then pricked forward once more.

Over the past three years, Marrek and his fellow traders had been actively cultivating likely leaders amongst the residents of the wilds. All were men who were dissatisfied with the insurrection the day of Hafrin's birth. A good percentage of them professed loyalty to the original royal family and expressed regret that none remained.

That they know of.

Doubtless they would be shocked when they discovered one of the bloodline had survived and that one was the son and heir. Those men whom the traders found to be the most reliable and trustworthy were being groomed towards the eventual retaliation and insurrection. It was a delicate task at best. At worst, it was dangerous. All it needed was one wrong move. An ill-spoken word in the wrong quarter would dash all of their hopes and, in all likelihood, result in their deaths. Until the Hynarkin had established a satisfactory base for a rebellion to retake Iryô's high seat, he was constrained to rely upon them.

And unlike my parents, I have no heir to carry on should anything happen to me.

That knowledge darkened his mood still further. At the same time, he could see the folly of directing his anger at Marrek. His foster father had had as little say in Nichole's fate as Hafrin and Nichole had.

It's really Vern's fault, Hafrin reasoned. *Marrek was just following orders.*

Following orders, his subconscious sneered. *Right. It's not like he made a conscious effort to stand up for your rights, or hers, for that matter.*

He had no choice, Hafrin argued. *Vern made it clear they would have taken Nikki by force no matter what.*

You don't know that.

"Oh shut up," he snarled under his breath.

Guilty, he glanced up. Fortunately, Marrek had failed to overhear. He had already had this particular discussion several times with Zivvoz and Kili, and once with his shield brother, Indoro. Each time he had come away with a healthy dose of wisdom, words of sympathy and a headache. Whether he was in the right or not, there was nothing he could do to change what had happened. She was gone so far away that, not only could he not mind-speak her, he could not sense her.

"We'll camp the other side of the Alier," Marrek suddenly announced.

An unwelcome intrusion into his privacy, the statement shook Hafrin out of his misery. He glanced around, surreptitiously surveying his surroundings. On the trade route, it was vitally necessary that both of them remained alert against any and all potential hazards. Aside from inherent natural dangers, there were a number of bandit bands in the area preying on the unwary.

Not to mention Wôbiny soldiery, he reminded himself.

In this, he had been incredibly remiss. Half the afternoon had passed. While indulging in self-pity, any number of things might have happened and he would have been woefully unprepared to defend himself or assist Marrek. To his surprise, he had also dropped far to the rear. They had reached a forest clearing while he had been caught up in reverie. Marrek was almost completely across the clearing while he was just entering it. As usual, their pack rynad, Neranïl plodded stoically along at nearly the full extent of its lead behind Marrek. Sunlight winked off the white bluffs that paralleled their route no more than a half-day ride to the west. Limestone, the Wanderers called it, useful in all manner of things.

"As if my people aren't aware of that," Hafrin muttered.

Annoyed with himself, Hafrin tapped his heels against Shalinô's flanks to urge the gelding to quicken its pace. Muscles bunched beneath the saddle and Shalinô abruptly shied sideways. Alert to possible danger, Hafrin checked his surroundings, first on the visual and audible levels, and then sweeping the area as Nichole had taught him employing his psi senses. Nothing.

Now aware Hafrin was no longer accompanying him, Marrek reined in. A short distant to Hafrin's right, a tiny copse of four three-year old deciduous saplings and two shrubs swayed even though there was no breeze. A jagzic, one of the small avian creatures that Vrala Harz found so tasty, took flight.

"What's wrong?"

To Marrek's question Hafrin replied, "I don't know, but Shalinô doesn't want to cross the clearing."

Even as Hafrin spoke, their pack rynad reared back hard. Neranïl's actions were so unexpected and violent he actually snapped the lead rope close to Marrek's saddletree. Having no wish to chase Neranïl through the forest, Hafrin flung himself out of the saddle and ran forward to round up the pack animal. Strangely, even though he was now free, Neranïl made no further attempt to escape. Instead, all four feet firmly planted, the pack gelding rolled white-rimmed eyes in Hafrin's direction and refused to move even when Hafrin used mind touch to encourage him.

Marrek asked, "What's wrong with him?"

"He's terrified but he can't explain why," said Hafrin. He tried to soothe Neranïl, to no avail. "Soo. Easy boy."

From the periphery of his eye, he saw Vrala swoop low, while Shalinô darted back into the trees. Unable to shift the unusually stubborn pack animal, Hafrin turned to summon Shalinô.

"Come on now. It's okay," he told Neranïl, but it was anything but all right. The ground suddenly dropped away beneath them.

"Rin, leave him. Rin!"

Before he could consider obeying his foster father, the earth inhaled Neranïl first and then Hafrin. Setting his full weight against the rope, Hafrin did his best to encourage Neranïl to move towards him. Still hanging onto the pack animal's lead, Hafrin concentrated on keeping his feet in his headlong slide into a huge black hole. The gaping maw ingested them with an accompanying rush of semi-liquid soil, rocks and choking clouds of dust. Down they plunged. Neranïl screamed in near-human terror and fought to remain upright in the unstable mass. Then everything was still. Deafened by the overpowering roar of moving earth, half blind from the dust, Hafrin clung to the pack animal's lead as a drowning man clutched a river-washed tree branch.

"Rin? Rin."

Muffled as much by the mound of debris as it was by distance, Marrek's voice reached him from above. Hafrin scrubbed a hand across his face, coughed to clear his lungs and peered upwards. Several rynad-lengths away, blue sky filled a ragged, almost oval, opening. Bits of earth continued to trickle down from the rim on all sides.

"Rin."

At Marrek's frantic shout, Hafrin finally responded, "I'm okay."

A quick glance at Neranïl confirmed their pack animal had also survived the horrific plunge into Fimiah's bowels. What terrified Hafrin the most was sight of the incredible, seeming infinite black maw some distance behind the rynad.

"We're both okay," he managed, his voice shaking.

Time was slipping away while he remained inactive. Carefully making his way down the unstable slope, Hafrin reached Neranïl's side. The pack rynad blew repeatedly. His ears flat against his skull, the gelding stood frozen with terror. Working quickly, Hafrin removed the packs but left the harness in place. He located the ball of tenting twine and one of their two contingency ropes.

Still out of visual range, Marrek called down to him. "What are you doing?"

Evidently, Marrek was afraid of getting too close to the rim. Hafrin shouted back, "I'm lightening the load."

"Okay. Let me know when you're ready."

Working the heavy line through Neranïl's harness and around his haunches, Hafrin tied it off in front of the pack animal's chest. To the free end of the rope, he tied one end of the twine. Then he summoned Vrala. She reluctantly responded to his call, planing down through the opening in the ground. Instead of landing, she spiralled around Hafrin's head uttering short, sharp complaints.

Okay Vrala. I know. Hafrin sympathised with her sentiments and concentrated on mentally sending her instructions. *I'm going to toss you this line. Take it to Marrek.*

He held up the free end of the twine. As Vrala came back around, he tossed it into the air. Claws extended, she neatly caught it. A short cry announced her success as she winged up and out of the hole, her flight somewhat impeded by the twine trailing behind her. Several minutes passed before Marrek took up the slack on the line. Marrek hauled on it. When the rope reached him, he called down to Hafrin.

"What's on the other end?"

"Neranïl," said Hafrin.

Nerves jangling, he waited. Neranïl snorted and shifted his weight. Beneath them, the ground moved slightly. Before Hafrin could cry out a warning, Marrek called back down to him.

"Okay, let's get you both out of there."

"Neranïl first," Hafrin insisted.

"Rin."

"No arguments, Marrek. I'm not leaving him down here. He's frightened but otherwise unhurt so let's just get to it, okay?"

There was a brief moment of inaction then the rope went taut once more. Neranïl grunted. He flung up his head and reared slightly in protest. Prepared for this, Hafrin brought the flat of his hand down hard on the rynad's neck.

"Hijah!"

Startled by the shout, Neranïl lunged forward. Once started, the pack rynad continued up the crumbling slope, urged on by Hafrin's shouts and encouraged by the compelling force of the rope beneath his rump. Clumps of earth flew downslope, striking Hafrin. Turning his back, Hafrin put his hands over his head and waited for the shower to stop. When he was no longer being peppered with earth, he looked back up the slope. Neranïl was at the rim, hesitating as his front hooves pawed for purchase on the crumbling rim. With a final lurch, he disappeared.

Pulse racing, Hafrin waited for the free end of the rope to return. Vrala reappeared above the hole. There was a thick knot in the free end of the rope, weighing it so that it dropped cleanly into his hands when she released it. A strange calm settled over Hafrin. Without conscious thought, he dragged the closest two packs towards him and lashed the rope around them.

"Okay, Marrek," he instucted. "Haul away."

The packs waddled a short distance up the slope, paused, and then completed the journey back into the light of day. As Hafrin expected, Marrek demanded an explanation.

"What are you doing? Leave them, Rin and get out of there."

"It's okay," Hafrin insisted, "Just give me the rope."

However much Marrek might object, he was in no position to force Hafrin to listen to him. Sensibly, he returned the rope and waited. Hafrin glanced at the other three packs. One of the large packs and the small top pack had slipped further down the slope. He went to the nearest one and tied it to the rope. With a tug, he signalled Marrek to haul it in. While his foster father retrieved the third pack, Hafrin inched cautiously down the slope to the nearer and, coincidentally, fourth of the large packs of trade supplies. Vrala 'creeled' to inform him she was back. He caught the rope and tied it to the pack.

Frustrated by the distance to the smaller pack, but equally wary of the impenetrable darkness a short distance beyond, he took a tight hold on the large pack. With his free hand outstretched, he eased towards the small pack. As his fingers touched it the ground gave way with a nearly sub-sonic groan. Pivotting, he grabbed for the big pack with his free hand.

The sound built to an overwhelming roar of cascading earth as the ground vanished. A bottomless void opened beneath his feet, leaving him and the last large pack dangling in space. Air rushed up from below, buffetting him with a gale's force. Dazed, eyes tight shut, Hafrin clung to the pack. Then all was still once more.

"Rin!"

Marrek's voice filtered back down to him, shrill with more panic than Hafrin could have imagined. Unable to immediately respond, Hafrin concentrated on maintaining a solid grip on the precariously swaying lifeline. Beneath him, the pack moved. He gasped and tightened his hold until his fingers began to cramp. Moving in fits and starts, the pack slowly rose. At the rim, it snagged on something and refused to budge.

"Rin? Are you there?"

Coughing to clear his lungs, Hafrin glanced up. Dirt spattered his face. He shook his head and scrubbed his face across the pack.

"Yes. I'm here."

"Can you see what the pack is caught on?"

"Just. There's a lot of dirt still falling off the edges of the hole. I think the pack's caught on a stone."

"Can you climb the rope?"

Hafrin thought about that and realised if he tried to release his hold at this time he risked losing his grip entirely. "No. Sorry."

"Okay." Marrek paused to consider the problem. "Can you rock the pack loose?"

Braving the dust and dirt Hafrin shot a quick look at the pack. A large boulder stuck out from the lip of the hold. Due his weight on one side of the pack, it had snagged underneath the protrusion.

"Rin?"

"Hang on. I'm going to try something. Keep some tension on the rope."

By throwing his weight to one side, Hafrin worked the pack until he was side-on to the boulder. The rope scrubbed back and forth across the boulder and

Hafrin's fear was that the sharp edges on the rock might chew through the rope. To his relief, the pack popped free with one more jerk. Simultaneously, it bounded upward. Even though he was in the open air once more, Hafrin clung to the pack while Marrek encouraged his rynad to continue pulling the load well clear of the hole. At length, all movement ceased. Boots thudded on earth. A shadow fell across him. Marrek carefully uncurled his fingers from the pack lashings and rolled him over. Then he expertly checked for any injuries.

"I'm okay," Hafrin told his foster father, croaking through the dust in his throat.

"Here."

Marrek passed him a water flask. "Drink and rinse off your head. Then we've got to get moving. The ground's still unstable."

"Serpent," Hafrin cursed. He took a mouthful of water, rinsed, gargled and spat. The next mouthful, he slowly swallowed while pouring more water over his head to wash away the muck from his adventure. Shalinô and Neranïl stood a short distance away, well within the treeline.

"How did that happen? What is it? Another Craneeno trap?"

"No," Marrek told him, his expression grim. "It's a sinkhole. I've never seen reports of one before. Not on Fimiah anyway. This can't be good."

"It's natural?" Hafrin found that difficult to believe.

"Yes. Can you get up?"

Slowly, Hafrin pushed himself upright. His fingers cramped. He kneaded them in an effort to loosen the joints and tendons. Silently, Marrek extended a hand. Hafrin took it and allowed his foster father to pull him to his feet. To his surprise, his legs were shaking. More tremors ran through his other limbs.

"That was foolish," said Marrek. Despite his words, there was pride in his voice. "You could have been killed."

"If we had lost the packs, we would have had to go home," said Hafrin, "or risk contacting the colony with a request for more. As it is, we've lost the primary medi-pack."

"No amount of trade goods or medical supplies are worth your life," countered Marrek. His arms enveloped Hafrin in a crushing hug. "God, Rin. If I had lost you…"

The rest remained unspoken between them. Shock coursed through Hafrin. His rage over Nichole's arbitrary removal ebbed. For several breaths he was content to let Marrek hold him, but as the shaking in his limbs increased, his foster father released him. He whistled to Shalinô. Reluctant, the grey rynad joined them. Marrek removed Hafrin's cloak from behind the saddle and wrapped him in it. An image filled Hafrin's mind, projected by his mount: the ground opened again to swallow all of them.

"Shalino thinks we should leave," said Hafrin.

"He's right," said Marrek. "Think you can ride?"

"Better that than hang around here," Hafrin managed. "Actually, I don't think I'll be able to do much walking for a while."

"Understandable," Marrek told him. "You had a close call."

One arm around Hafrin's shoulders, Marrek guided him to Shalinô and helped him into the saddle. He rounded up their pack animal and his mount, Krohl, and once more tied off Neranïl's lead to his saddletree.

Until now, Hafrin had avoided looking in the direction of the hole. As they turned into the woods to circumvent the clearing, he forced himself to survey the scene. All around the glade, the ground was disturbed. Close to the opening, huge fractures fanned out from the hole. Further away, the earth bulged in ragged ripples, open scars on what had once been a pristine landscape.

They circled the glade at what Marrek determined was a safe distance as he guided them back towards their original route. Ahead of them lay the river crossing. For a time Hafrin was content to be left alone with his thoughts. But eventually he had several questions for which he wanted answers.

"So, tell me about sinkholes. What exactly are they?"

"Hmm. That's a tough one. You'll have to bear with me because this is going to get a little scientific."

"Ah," said Hafrin, his mood genuinely lightening for the first time since winter. "Scientific."

Marrek glanced back and grinned at him. "Sinkholes are formed when subterranean water erodes the roof of a limestone cave."

"A cave. In the ground?"

Marrek chuckled. "That's what caves are, Rin, holes in the ground. You're just accustomed to seeing them in the sides of hills and mountains. Unfortunately, it looks like there are some underfoot as well."

Hafrin considered the information. "And streams actually run under the ground?"

"Yes. They make up what scientists refer to as aquafers," Marrek explained. "I suspect there'll be more of those holes before long."

"Why?" Hafrin wanted to know. "And why now?"

"Well," Marrek shrugged, noncommittal. "I'm only guessing, but it may be because we've had a couple of years of drought followed by a warming trend. The drought probably caused the subterranean water table to drop, which removed the cave supports and weakened them appreciably. Now the glaciers are melting. That's sending more water down through the channels, above and below ground."

Hafrin grunted as the pieces of the puzzle came together. "Which has carved out more of the cave roof supports."

Marrek nodded. "Yes. Of course, we won't know for sure how extensive the rot is until the colony climatologists and geologists have had a chance to study the phenomenon."

"Rather them than me," said Hafrin. "One experience inside a sinkhole is quite enough."

All three rynada snorted in unison and bobbed their heads. There was no need for Hafrin to translate. Marrek laughed. "Point taken. But it's unlikely the scientist will physically inspect the site. They'll use ground-penetrating sensors and robots to explore the system. Much safer. Machines can be replaced."

This was a litany Hafrin had heard often enough since the destruction of the Wanderer's cavern colony prior to Dôzhik Koryn. He refrained from pursuing that subject. His thoughts veered away, returning to the sinkhole.

"Marrek?"

"Yes, Rin?"

Afraid of the answer he was certain he would receive, Hafrin asked, "Just exactly how big can those things get?"

Blowing out his cheeks, Marrek kept his gaze fixed on the trail ahead. "Big."

"How big?" When Marrek remained silent, Hafrin pressed the issue. "Big enough to swallow a house?"

Voice strained, Marrek answered, "Big enough to swallow several houses."

That was the last thing Hafrin wanted to hear. They rode on in silence, each caught up in their own thoughts. The incident had drawn him close to Marrek once more. For the first time since Nichole's departure, she was the farthest thing from his mind. Here and now was a problem that required his complete attention. It eased his rage and pushed his frustration into a tiny corner of his mind. The pain in his chest finally eased to where he could deal with it.

CHAPTER 3

▼

Early summer: one year post Dôzhik Koryn

Hafrin

In spite of all of the innovations introduced by the Hynarkin, there remained pockets of decay about the countryside. Some of it was due to lack of funding for improvements. In other places, new ways were slower to be passed along. However, here it was a direct result of distrust. Distrust in new ways and change in general, and distrust in the motives of those who introduced those improvements.

Such was the case in this tiny hamlet. Situated on Ekôzav's north border, this minuscule outpost of habitation was considerably off the beaten track. It was however, one of Robar's rare stops, one he visited approximately every third or fourth year. Coincidentally, it was also the one spot where Marrek and Robar's routes overlapped.

The locals were not given to warmth towards strangers. They greeted all outsiders with equal helpings of wariness and suspicion. They bartered hard for trade goods, while volunteering little news. Soldiers were disliked as a whole. Hatred was reserved for those in Wôbiny livery. So traders and soldiers alike rode with extreme care, a hand to their weapons and nerves strung to battle readiness.

Hafrin had been through Thïol only once in the past: his first year on the trade routes, as it so happened. Even so, he recalled the inhabitants' recalcitrant nature all too well. Tonight he was acutely conscious of sour spirits. Conversations were unaccountably loud, with no care given to outsiders in their midst, eavesdropping on gossip that revolved around local business and private concerns.

Seated in a dark corner of the room, Hafrin struggled to keep from coughing as another gust of wind blew down the poorly constructed chimney. The gathering storm outside puffed more smoke into the room, compounding the haze already turning the interior air blue. Hafrin surreptitiously cleared his throat and sipped the ale. If Thïol offered nothing else, at least its common house sold good ale.

Unlike some places we've been, thought Hafrin.

"This should pass through tonight," Marrek softly stated, referring to the weather.

Head tipped slightly down, his partially shuttered eyes never left off scanning the room. Robar was late. Soon, the clientel would begin heading for home and bed. That would necessitate their seeking the stark loft room next door, for which they had pre-paid prior to supper.

Supper.

As his stomach gurgled a complaint Hafrin barely restrained an audible snort. What passed for food at this establishment was so poorly prepared, he was positive even a cur would have scorned it.

A curious juxtaposition to the quality of the ale, he reflected.

Indoro cooks better meals on the trail, thought Hafrin.

And that was definitely saying something, considering his Shield Brother had once burned a pot of water. Marrek's hand touched his. Drawn back to the room and its occupants, Hafrin shot a quick glance in the direction of the door. Three people had just entered. As most travellers did, they halted immediately inside and stepped aside to clear the doorway. Hairs on the nape of Hafrin's neck crawled as two more ruffians sought shelter within the common room.

Trappers or thieves? He wondered about that and decided they were more than likely both. *Wouldn't want to run into them on a bad day.*

Movement on the stairs caught his eye. Without turning his head, he watched two individuals descend the stairs. A nerve in the back of his left hand jumped as he identified both men.

Robar and Sandi; both of them?

If nothing else, Sandi was well off his trade route, and at a time when he ought to have been passing through Nûhykar's coastal village. Against his left shoulder, Hafrin felt Marrek's muscles bunch briefly as he recognised his fellow traders. Concern and bewilderment leaked through his mental shield. He had erected that protection after learning Nichole possessed untrained psi talents. Since discovering Hafrin also had psi abilities, Marrek had maintained his shield. However much Hafrin might feel that lack of trust was a slap in the face, he was forced to admit the necessity for it. He was only partially trained and given to unconsciously probing for answers from his foster father when under undue stress.

"Marrek."

Voice pitched low, Robar greeted Hafrin's foster father with genuine warmth tempered by caution. He and Hafrin exchanged polite, if strained greetings, which primarily consisted of a nod and an informal 'hi'. Then Robar and Sandi settled across from them. The lad who served the patrons promptly appeared, took their order and disappeared into the crowd and haze.

"Do you have a place for the night?"

To Sandi's question Marrek nodded. "The stable loft."

"Good."

The boy returned, interrupting them. Expression neutral, Robar waited while their server deposited two mugs with sufficient force to slop some of the contents down the outsides and held out his hand. Robar paid the boy. Once the lad had left, Robar leaned forward and cupped his hands around his mug. He sipped some of the contents, lifted an eyebrow in appreciation...whether feigned or genuine, Hafrin could not be certain. Unlike the other Hynarkin, Robar possessed a natural shield.

"We've found another three."

"That makes fifteen," remarked Hafrin to that announcement of new members solicited to their cause.

Marrek shot him a look that suggested he listen rather than participate, and asked, "All reliable?"

Sandi snorted, sipped his ale and set the mug aside. "About as reliable as we can be certain, short of a scan."

Images flitted about the periphery of Hafrin's thoughts; a man sat in a chair wearing a curious cap-like contraption. Thin wires led from the cap to disks. These were stuck to the man's head, arms and chest. Hafrin blinked, snatched his thoughts back to his surroundings and caught Sandi's gaze. From the other man's expression, Hafrin knew the images had been allowed to leak out.

"There may be a way," said Sandi, redirecting himself to Marrek and Robar.

A short pause ensued. In that moment, Hafrin deduced what Sandi was implying. It quite took his breath away. Abruptly Marrek shook his head, hard.

"No. Absolutely not." It was all he could do to keep his voice down.

"Why not?" Keeping his voice low and pleasant, Sandi jerked his head in Hafrin's direction. "He doesn't need to probe. Just listen."

"Out of the question."

"Why?"

"It's against regs," countered Marrek with such force Hafrin checked the surrounding tables to ensure no one else was listening. Fortunately, their neighbours all appeared equally engrossed in their own conversations.

"Ours," argued Sandi. "Not theirs. In fact, they don't have any."

"They should," said Marrek. "I've repeatedly explained to Hafrin about the necessity to honour the privacy of others."

Throughout the outburst, Robar plucked at his lower lip. Discretion foremost in his mind, Hafrin kept silent, letting Marrek and his cousin debate the issue. As heated as the argument grew, both men continued to temper their disagreement, conscious of the tavern's other patrons.

"Once you start down that route," Marrek continued, "it's all but impossible to stop justifying the use of such methods."

The proverbial slippery slope, thought Hafrin, and finally understood the full intent behind that Hynarkin expression.

"Once won't..."

Marrek remained adamant. "No, Sandi."

"He's got a point, Marrek."

Robar's unexpected disagreement crossed Marrek's stubborness so softly that it took Hafrin by surprise. Marrek was openly astonished. Clearly he had difficulty countenancing what he had just heard. None of them spoke now. Intrigued, Hafrin watched the silent battle of wills between his foster father and Robar. Marrek was determined not to embroil Hafrin in what he saw as underhanded, dirty tactics. On the other hand, Robar made no effort to conceal his lack of qualms over Hafrin merely eavesdropping on the thoughts of those individuals the Hynarkin were sounding out to support a prospective insurrection, whether as contacts or leaders.

Hafrin sympathised with his foster father's feelings. At the same time, he leaned towards what Sandi was advocating. The benefits would out-weigh the negativity of such actions. Yet Hafrin felt he should be the one making this decision.

"No," said Marrek again but this time his denial lacked solid conviction.

Hafrin touched his foster father's hand. "Sir, if you can't trust me to use discretion and self-control at this stage of the game when will you?"

This time he succeeded in catching Marrek's attention and holding it. In his foster father's eyes, Hafrin read his every indiscretion and failing of his twenty years: first and foremost was their quarrel over Nichole. Even now, Marrek had no idea just how deep his affections for Nichole ran.

For the first time in over a year, Hafrin discovered he could take that reminder, along with all its heartache and loss, and allow it to wash over him and away like so much rain. To his amazement, Marrek broke and looked away. In all of their years together, Hafrin had never witnessed his foster father trapped in a quandry of this magnitude. Just when he thought he could stand it no longer, Robar reached out and rested a hand over Marrek's.

"Marrek, you should know I've already spoken to Pete about this."

Justifiably irritated that Robar had spoken to the senior trader/scout before-hand, Marrek growled, "Thanks."

Unperturbed, Robar continued, "Pete said he trusted your judgement in this. However, he did ask me to remind you of two things."

"Which are?"

"One," hand held up, Robar rolled back one finger, "Hafrin is now Fimiahri majority."

Shock coursed through Hafrin. Because he was Hynarkin-raised, he had for-gotten his people reached majority at nineteen. Unlike the Hynarkin, or Wander-ers, who insisted their longer-lived offspring were not legally adults until they reached twenty-one years of age.

"Second," said Robar, "it's up to Rin to make this decision. Not us."

And live with the consequences, thought Hafrin.

He knew Marrek was thinking the same thing. Once again he and Marrek locked gazes. This time, however, Marrek's expression was one of concern and caution. Now aware they expected him to take his place within their circle as an adult, Hafrin carefully weighed the pros and cons of employing his psi gifts to further his cause, determining the loyalty of their contacts. Unlike the Hynarkin, Hafrin knew some of his people had natural barriers in their minds. He voiced his observation for the first time.

Eyebrows shooting up, Robar demanded, "You're sure, Rin?"

Hafrin nodded. "Ziv's got one."

"Why didn't you tell me?"

To his foster father's question, Hafrin replied, "I never thought it pertinent, until now."

Before Marrek could pursue the issue, Piltar said, "Take it easy, Marrek. The boy only just learned what he was a short time ago."

Reminded of the rift that had existed between them until the previous sum-mer's sinkhole incident, Marrek gradually unwound. Around them the locals were starting to leave. Several who were perhaps too deep in their cups were beginning to take far too much interest in them. He redirected the conversation to a safer topic.

"How are we doing getting the word out about the sinkholes?"

"Slowly. Fortunately the priests are accepting our warnings. It's a shame we were too late to save those two families in Mijonar, though," said Piltar, regret colouring his voice.

Mijonar, a tiny Ekôzav village whose primary industry was a gemstone quarry remained a sharp reminder to the perils of sinkholes and the Hynarkin's inability to disseminate information as quickly as they would have liked. One night, before any of the traders could apprise the local priest to warn the population, a sinkhole had opened on the perimeter of the village. It had swallowed two houses, killing eight of the nine inhabitants. Only a two-year old girl, asleep in the loft, had survived. And that only because her house had been the one upslope.

Nerves jangled a warning and Hafrin slid a surreptitious glance around the common room. More than half of the early crowd had already left. Several more were just departing. Corner on to where he sat the two groups that had entered just before Robar and Piltar had joined him and Marrek were deep in their cups. Repeated sharp looks from two of the group set the warning claxons vibrating through Hafrin. He let his gaze pass across them, allowed a small smile to touch his lips at something Robar said even though he failed to catch it. Temptation tickled him. His vision blurred. Slowly he dropped his mental barrier, delicately reaching out.

"Rin?" Puzzled, Marrek gently nudged him.

Startled back to his surroundings, Hafrin twitched violently. Before Marrek could question him concerning his distraction, Hafrin said, "I think we should leave."

Without appearing to, all of Hafrin's companions surreptitiously inspected the room. All of them made note of the group that had caught Hafrin's attention. Robar gave his head a brief twist, as though relieving a crick in the muscles, and pushed aside his mug.

"Well, I don't know about the rest of you but I've had enough. I think I'll hit the sack."

This particular Hynarkin idiom was a favourite of Hafrin's. He exchanged a grin with Robar as Piltar stretched.

"Good idea. It's been a long day, and tomorrow will undoubtedly be much the same, although I don't fancy the sound of the weather."

"Perhaps it'll push through overnight," said Marrek, emphasizing the right words to infer he knew it would.

"Hope you're right," said Piltar, and pushed back his stool.

In concert, they stood and headed off towards their respective destinations. By leaving all at once, they would temporarily confound those who had been studying them as potential targets. Why they should have attracted such adverse attention intrigued Hafrin, but he suspected there was no one particular answer to the riddle. Nor was he likely to get a satisfactory response if he had the opportunity to question their stalkers.

From Robar's thoughts, Hafrin picked up the suggestion that he and Piltar would not be remaining long in their lodgings. Foul weather notwithstanding, Hafrin suspected he and Marrek would likewise be moving this evening.

In the stable, Marrek scaled the ladder rungs more swiftly than safety recommended, telegraphing to Hafrin the necessity for speed. Thoroughly irritated, Hafrin lcoated his small personal pack and restored the few items he had removed from it when cleaning up before going to supper.

"Damn," Marrek gumbled under his breath. "I had hoped we'd get at least one good night under decent shelter."

"Aren't you the one who constantly reminds me about the best laid schemes of mice and men?"

Across the dimly lit loft, Hafrin caught the white flash of teeth. Marrek finished lashing his pack and gathered it up, along with his bedroom and personal tarp.

"Better wear your cloak," he advised.

With a soft laugh, Hafrin continued in Hynarkin, "Now who's teaching Grandmother to..."

He never finished. A raised finger warned Hafrin. Using Hynarkin handsign, Marrek redirected his attention to the rustle of straw in the stable below. Hafrin reached out to his gelding. Prompted by his rider's mind touch, the grey rynad inspected the stable interior. Through his curious ocular vision, Hafrin picked out three of the five men from the tavern. They were creeping cautiously up the stable aisle between the box stalls. Alert to danger, Shalinô stomped a hoof and snorted. Hafrin urged the gelding to be silent. Disgruntled, Shalinô set to work on unfastening his stall door. If need be, the gelding could well prove to be what Piltar referred to as their ace in the hold. At the time when Hafrin had asked what that meant, Piltar had proceeded to teach him the card game.

Hafrin flashed his foster father a warning and raised three fingers. Marrek nodded and gestured to the block and tackle system rigged to haul bales into the loft. Together, they each took a rope and expertly descended to the stable floor.

There was no cushioning the noise of their boots as they hit the planking. On his own initiative, Shalinô chose that appropriate moment to break from his stall and charge the nearest stalker. While he pursued the nearest attacker down the aisle and out the exit, Marrek and Hafrin took on the remaining pair. Thief or assassin, Hafrin could not care less as he drew his sword and advanced on his chosen adversary. To his surprise, both men fled.

Not about to be suckered into dashing out of the lit stable into the darkness, Hafrin halted just inside the entrance and stepped off to the side. Shalinô returned, snorting and tossing his head, immensely pleased with himself and disdainful of the ease with which they had routed the enemy. Slumped against a nearby stall door, Marrek wiped a sleeve across his forehead.

"Thank goodness for that," said Marrek.

Not quite willing to believe their good fortune Hafrin remained vigilant, studying the stable shadows. "Do you think they'll try again?"

"It's entirely possible."

"Do you still want to leave tonight?"

Outside the wind continued to rise. Gusts battled through the streets between the buildings and battered the stable. Exterior boards bowed beneath the onslaught. Debris, swept before the wind, pattered against the building. The stable door banged against its latch then flew open. Heads bent low, Robar and Piltar entered the building leading their two mounts and a pair of pack animals. Piltar forced the door shut behind them and secured it.

Robar gestured. "We decided moving on tonight might not be such a good idea after all."

"I'm not surprised," said Hafrin as their companions shook out their cloaks and checked for empty stalls in which to settle their animals.

"Any sign of the hostler?"

"No. But then, I suspect he's comfortably esconced in a nice warm bed at home," said Marrek.

While removing tack from his mount and pack animal Piltar asked, "Marrek, are you sure this storm's going to blow through overnight?"

"The Met's positive."

Robar grunted. "Well then, since our jolly guests have seen fit to depart the premises, perhaps we should all spend the night bedded down here."

"I doubt the hostler will care," Marrek observed.

Behind Hafrin, Shalinô snorted and returned to his stall. As the gelding settled in the straw, Hafrin laughed. "Shalinô says if we're going to stay here tonight, maybe we should sleep in the stalls."

"Now that's what we used to call horse sense," said Robar in Hynarkin.

Hafrin picked up the image of a creature very much like a rynad but with a full bush of tail, hooves that were all of one piece, and no horns. He unwittingly passed along what he gleaned to his mount. Unimpressed, Shalinô mouthed a bit of loose feed.

"Sleeping in the stalls makes sense," said Piltar. He settled his packs and both saddles on the floor just outside the pack animal's stall. "The rynada's sense of hearing and smell is far more acute than ours. With them keeping watch, it's unlikely anyone will sneak up on us tonight. Especially if Rin asks them to keep an eye out for any more intruders."

"So you say," said Marrek. With a sigh, he clambered back into the loft to collect their things. He called down, "Rin, I'm going to send down our packs."

CHAPTER 4

▼

By the time dawn broke, the storm was, as promised, well past. All of them rode out before the sun rose, Piltar and Robar heading east and south respectively, while Hafrin and Marrek headed north along the Rashordi foothills. In the storm's wake, the township was left with several shredded rooftops. A plethora of shattered branches and several downed trees marked the route north. The going was comparatively slow and Hafrin was left to reflect upon the changing weather patterns observed and recorded over the years since the birth of his natural father; a person whom he had never known, dead since the day of his birth.

Overnight, the temperature had dropped appreciably. Sleet and frost were out of tune with the time of year given the lateness of the season. Watery sunlight glittered from hoarfrost riming tree limbs. A thin film covered the road surface, clinging persistently to spots where trees and shrubs overshadowed the road. Stepping warily, the rynada picked their way with care. Satisfied to let their mounts set the pace, Hafrin and Marrek gave the animals their heads and hunched down in their cloaks.

Despite their rynada's vigilence throughout the night, Hafrin had slept fitfully. From the look of his foster father, Marrek was in much the same condition. He blew on his fingers through his knitted gloves, patted his hands together and stuffed them down between his thighs and the saddle.

Marrek glanced back. "Cold?"

"You could say that."

Neranïl shook his head repeatedly, so that his roached mane rustled. All three rynada abruptly halted even though neither rider had indicated they wanted to stop. Hafrin immediately scanned the woods on either side of the road.

"Nothing," he said.

Head tipped on one side, Marrek observed in clipped Hynarkin, "River sounds high."

By the landmarks, they were still a good distance from the crossing, yet the rumble of the river was clearly audible. Hafrin frowned. He urged Shalinô up alongside his foster father.

"That doesn't sound good, sir."

"No," Marrek agreed. "It doesn't."

From Marrek, Hafrin received a faint flicker of concern, quickly banished. This crossing was one of a rare few high in the wilds where the locals had taken the time and expense to construct a proper bridge across the river. In most areas, there was simply a fording place.

Probably because this river is fairly big in the spring, thought Hafrin. *Which isn't surprising, since it's a tributary of the Hycöt.*

With uncertain meteorological conditions over the years for almost a generation prior to his birth, a changing environment the Wanderers were diligently monitoring, rivers were consistently running higher throughout all four provinces. Additionally, there were several new rivers forming, plus a number of small lakes: all directly attributed by Wanderer scientists to global warming.

Well, Hafrin considerd the possibilities, *if it really is the end of the ice age, we should see more arable land in the near future. Of course, who will control it...*

"Did you hear that?"

Caught from reverie, Hafrin dutifully listened for whatever had attracted Marrek's attention. Shalinô's ears pricked forward, a sure sign he had heard something unusual too. An unintelligible noise penetrated the river's roar.

"That sounds like a cry for help," said Hafrin, and urged his gelding forward at a run.

Slowed by their pack animal, Marrek trailed Hafrin to the riverbank, arriving as Hafrin inspected their route and the river. At this point, the road emerged from the trees and paralleled the river down to the crossing. In all of his years, Hafrin could not recall anything quite so awesome as what they now faced.

Turbulent water, yellow-brown with silt picked up along the way, roiled between the banks. Rampaging towards the sea, the river was widening its course with uncustomary vociferousness. On either side, the water was undercutting the edges. A short distance downstream, a portion of the road had fallen away. Boulders grumbled as they ground their way along the watercourse, adding to the tumult. Trees and shrubs added to the awe-inspiring, fearsome sight as they jostled and tumbled, their roots and limbs entwined. From time to time, they momentarily snagged against some concealed obstruction.

"There. Look." Marrek pointed.

Drawn inexorably by his foster father's directive, Hafrin stared downstream. Where the bridge had once arched across the flow in three sections, only the central span remained. The collection of twisted lumber swayed precariously beneath the river's attack. What held their attention, however, were the two men clinging to the remnants of the bridge railing.

"Wôbiny," Hafrin observed at the flash of mauve livery.

"Does it matter?"

To Marrek's question, Hafrin shook his head. "No."

He was out of the saddle and digging through one of Neranïl's packs before Marrek could dismount. "What do you have in mind?"

"One of us has to take them the safety line," said Hafrin.

Marrek's hand clamped onto Hafrin's forearm. "Are you insane? There's no need for either of us to risk our lives to save them, Rin."

"Sir, it's you who taught me to value all life."

"I'm not advocating abandoning them, Rin. But throwing it away needlessly is no way to demonstrate your belief in my tutoring." Marrek dragged out the lighter line. "We can try a bow shot, or have Vrala drop the end to them, like we did at the sinkhole."

Even as he considered the options, Hafrin extended his mind. What he read made him shake his head. "One of them is badly injured and barely conscious, sir. His friend is all that's keeping him from being swept away."

"Rin."

"Sir," Hafrin rested his free hand over Marrek's. "You know I'm right."

"Then let me go."

Wry humour caused one side of Hafrin's mouth to twist up. "I'm the stronger swimmer."

"You nearly drowned as a child."

But Marrek's objection lacked conviction and, in the end, it was Hafrin who stripped off his cloak, heavy jacket and gloves. Marrek double-checked the slip-knot Hafrin tied when he secured the rope around his waist, before tying the free end to his mount's saddletree. High above them, Vrala Harz screamed a protest and Shalino shoved Hafrin with his nose, reinforcing the orved's objections.

"I have to do this," he told them, including Marrek in his declaration.

"I agree with them," said Marrek, resigned. "You're a young fool."

With those words ringing in his ears, Hafrin took a running leap out into the river. Ice stabbed into his veins as he went under, driving his breath from his lungs. It left him gasping for air as he surfaced, his muscles constricting. Determined, Hafrin struck out, his contact with Vrala directing him across the flow.

Without warning, his left hand slammed against a piling. Numb with the cold, Hafrin was scarcely able to feel the encounter. He clawed at the wood, fumbling for a hold. A hand caught at the shoulder of his vest, and Hafrin found the strength to clambered up onto the remains of the bridge.

"Hynarkin."

Astonishment filled the soldier's eyes as Hafrin looked up. "Yes."

"Why?"

"You're in trouble," Hafrin told him. "How's your friend?"

"Dazed. I think he may have broken a rib. When the bridge collapsed, we were thrown by our mounts."

"You're lucky," said Hafrin. "If they hadn't tossed you, you'd probably be dead."

"Perhaps," replied the conscious soldier. "But I think I'd have preferred a quick death to this. We've been here since just after dawn."

Legs wrapped around a bridge railing support, Hafrin stuffed his hands into his armpits in an effort to warm them. From the riverbank, Marrek watched him with unconcealed concern.

From the repeated shuddering of the wood, it was evident this section would not survive much longer. There was no sign of the soldiers' rynada. Dead, Hafrin suspected. Swept away when the bridge came apart.

"Who said anything about dying?"

Hafrin flexed his fingers and discovered some of the feeling had returned. He loosened the coil about his waist and slipped it over his head.

"What's your name?"

"Tynnim," the man told him. "Corporal in the Alaiad's guard."

"Well, Corporal, when my father gives me the signal we're going to help your friend jump out into the river. My father's rynad will keep the rope tight so the force of the water will swing your friend into shore."

Tynnim countered, "He'll drown."

Pragmatic, Hafrin replied, "You're right. If he jumps into the river he may drown. But if he stays here, he certainly will die. Make a decision."

"Tyn," said the injured soldier, "the trader's right. Better to risk the jump than sit here like a dumb jarryn sitting on a branch."

Myriad objections and excuses flowed through Tynnim's thoughts, but he sighed and nodded. With his help, Hafrin secured the line about his friend's waist and helped the injured man slither along the steeply tilted bridge deck to the edge. The remaining span continued to quiver and sway, threatening to pitch all of them into the ravenous torrent.

"Okay," said Hafrin, his gaze fixed on his foster father. "Jump!"

Despite his best efforts, the injured man lurched forward, more pushed by their hands than leaping into the flow. He vanished beneath the surface. The rope snapped taut and the soldier surfaced briefly, his mouth open in a silent scream of agony. Then he disappeared again. Desperate, Hafrin hung out over the current, watching while the line swung towards the shore. Tynnim's hand rested on his back between his shoulder blades; whether in dire warning or simply for support was problematic at this juncture.

Marrek had left Lasier, his new mount this season, ground-tried and was racing along the bank. Water slicked hair surfaced as the line and its weight contacted the shore. Impotent, Hafrin and Tynnim could only watch while Marrek struggled to retrieve the limp body of the injured soldier. Twice Marrek nearly fell into the river as the bank crumbled beneath his feet, but finally he had the unconscious man on solid ground.

"Is he alive?"

To Tynnim's question, Hafrin shook his head. "I don't know."

A lie, because he knew the man was dead. However, if Marrek could move quickly, and there was enough strength remaining in the injured soldier, Marrek might be able to revive him. When Marrek glanced over to check on his condition, Hafrin waved, then gestured towards his own ribs to indicate the likelihood of an injury.

Marrek nodded. Working swiftly, he rolled the soldier onto his stomach and crossed his arms beneath his head. Then he began a series of carefully timed compressions to the man's ribs, interspersed with arm lifts.

"What's he doing?"

Hafrin glanced at Tynnim. "It's a life-saving technique all Hynarkin know. It should expel the water in his lungs and help him to inhale good air."

"I hope you're right, Hynarkin."

No slur coloured Tynnim's words and, for the first time in all his encounters with his uncle's troops, Hafrin felt no animosity towards this man in Wôbiny mauve. In truth, by the man's appearance, he could not have been much older than Hafrin. For that matter, he might not even have been born at the time of the insurrection. To their relief Marrek settled back on his heels and carefully eased the injured soldier onto his back. The man weakly flapped a hand at Hafrin's foster father. Relieved, Hafrin triumphantly thrust a hand into the air.

"Yes," Tynnim cheered.

Acutely conscious of their precarious perch, Hafrin turned to his companion. "You're next."

"Okay," said Tynnim. "But exactly how is your Dad going to get the rope back to us?"

"Wait," said Hafrin.

Lips pursed, he released a high-pitched whistle. Vrala plummetted from the sky. She backwinged and hovered in front of them above the surging water. For Tynnim's benefit, Hafrin gestured as though giving her hand instructions. At the same time, he told her precisely what he needed. On the riverbank, Marrek was now working feverishly, tying off the slim line to the heavier rope. The orved banked away, landing at Marrek's feet.

"Yours?"

Surprised the soldier could find the courage to carry on idle conversation in their present predicament, Hafrin nodded. "Yes."

Soon Vrala was winging her way back overhead, the thin line firmly clutched in her talons. With unerring accuracy, she dropped it into their hands. Together, Hafrin and Tynnim hauled in the rope.

"Your turn," said Hafrin.

On the verge of securing the rope around his waist, Tynnim paused. "Are you sure?"

"Go," said Hafrin.

Stilling the self-preservation urge, Hafrin helped Tynnim balance on the edge of the bridge until Marrek gestured. Then he was alone. Out in the current, Tynnim struggled to keep his head above water as he was dragged inexorably across the flow in the direction of the bank. Once again Marrek assisted, this time having a slightly easier time of pulling the victim ashore as Tynnim clawed his way to safety.

Leaving the soldiers to look after one another, Marrek worked rapidly, retying the light line to the rope. Still circling overhead, Vrala swooped in to catch the line, which Marrek tossed for her. As she headed back out towards the crumbling bridge span, Marrek glanced upriver. His eyes went wide.

Hafrin turned to find the source of Marrek's terror. Rolling ponderously through the flood swells was the trunk of a tree. A giant of its species, it had probably been torn from the ground high on some mountain slope. Most of its limbs had been snapped off during its passage, but its sheer bulk made it a formidable assailant.

Vrala screamed again and dropped the line as Hafrin looked up. He grabbed for it, missed and barely caught the trailing end before it was dragged away by the river. Even as he hauled in the lifeline, he knew with unerring certainty that he would not have time to secure the rope around his waist. One eye on the oncoming tree, Hafrin worked hand-over-hand to retrieve the rope. His fingers contacted the heavier line just as the trunk encountered an obstruction and lurched into the air. There was barely time to thrust one arm through the loop before the tree smashed into the remaining bridge span.

As his footing crumbled, Hafrin inhaled and pushed off. In his mind, he heard the combined screams of his foster father, Vrala and the rynada. Water closed over his head. Desperate, he clung to the rope. Fibres burned his chilled fingers. He clutched at the strands, refusing to relinquish his grasp on his sole lifeline.

So intent was he on hanging onto the rope, he was unprepared for the force with which the river slammed him into a subsurface rock projecting from its bed. Hafrin gasped, inhaling a quantity of water. Choking and gagging, he flailed about, seeking the surface. Initially, his free arm was strangely numb. Then pain knifed through his body. Out of control, he carromed into the riverbank. Unable to defend himself, he was repeatedly battered against the waterlogged earth.

"Rin!"

Only partially conscious, he hung limp in the river's embrace while Marrek fought to recover him from its grasp. And then he was on solid ground. A blanket was wrapped around him. Hands fought to restore his circulation.

"Drink."

He automatically sipped from the flask that touched his lips and grimaced when he tasted more water. This time there was no grit in it however. Unaware of his injury, Marrek grabbed Hafrin's left arm before he could warn him. Hafrin screamed and passed out.

Day was well advanced when he woke to find Marrek bending over him. "What happened?"

"You did something incredibly stupid and very brave," his foster father told him.

When Hafrin struggled to sit up, Marrek assisted him. There was no sign of either soldier. In fact, there was no sign of the river. Puzzled, Hafrin wordlessly demanded an explanation.

"You lost a contact in the river. I thought it prudent for us to move on before you woke up."

Hafrin nodded, inhaled slowly and carefully exhaled. He was battered and bruised all over. Stiff muscles complained whenever he moved. More importantly, his left arm was strapped across his chest.

"Incidentally," said Marrek, his tone unconscionably pleasant, "you broke your arm."

CHAPTER 5

▼

Fleet Training Academy

Nichole

Dull metal corridors stretched ahead. Underfoot the spongy fire-retardant flooring cushioned Nichole's footfalls. Signs in red advised of escape routes and the importance of keeping clear of sliding bulkheads. Emergency alarm fixtures broke up the otherwise monotonous blue-grey continuity of the walls. Overhead light panels were interrupted at regular intervals by red emergency lighting bars.

Hollowed from a massive asteroid, then abandoned aeons earlier by an unknown alien species, what had remained of the infrastructure had been taken over shortly after its discovery by humans and their allies. Ideally situated out of range of their mutual enemy, the installation originally provided the allied species with a launch platform for their combined fleet of battle and exploration craft. Over generations, the installation had been repaired, upgraded and eventually expanded upon to house headquarters for the Patrol's deep-space and ESP training facilities, temporary housing and assignment offices for scout and patrol personnel, plus a way-station for friendly vessels passing through that particular region of space.

To each unit there were Out-Of-Bounds areas. Assigned personnel and travellers did not mix, nor were they permitted access to training facilities. Trainees from each section were permitted two visits to other areas, but they had to request permission. Quartered with other ESP trainees, Nichole was in a class of her own, housed with the seniors. Unlike the other senior cadets, however, she had a room to herself because of her field experience and the fact that she was a random quantity. Her classes brought her into contact with everyone from first-year students to those months off graduation. Once again, she was trapped into being classified a loner, unable to make friends even where she might otherwise have wanted or needed companionship. Her courses were a montage. Amongst them were those on alien species relations, telepathy, weapons training, and, most important of all, psychology of the scout selected to blend with an alien race. Not for her the extraneous courses, no electives. Just the bare bones, in most of which she was playing catch-up compared to her classmates.

Head down, she hurried to her next class. Along the way, she passed numerous hallways branching to the left and right. All led to different yet equally important rooms. This level housed the junior instructors while below were first-year students. Above this level, second and third year dorms sandwiched the instructors but made all attendees readily accessible to the tutors. The fifth and final level of the station housed Administration and those areas primarily concerned with graduate assignments; although not precisely out-of-bounds to students, Nichole had yet to screw up the nerve to visit that level. It sufficed that she was at the Academy and on her way to another class.

Three and a half months had passed since her arrival. In that time she had altered physically, developed a more robust figure. In fact, her waist and bosom strained the elasticised dark green jump suit. Little over a year before, her movements had been hesitant and self-conscious. Now they were less tentative, more graceful and lithe. Predominately green-brown eyes stared out at the world with curiosity and a zest for life that had once been sadly lacking. Red highlights in shoulder-length brown hair had dimmed under the constant barrage of artificial light. Her ponytail corkscrewed along in her wake, occasionally tapping the tops of her shoulders. She knew men's eyes drifted in her direction, sensed their interest, but held them at bay by projecting a purposeful, almost aloof air.

Thoughts buzzing with the survival training class just over, she eagerly approached the next period of instruction. A metal panel barred her way. History was probably her favourite time. After this, she had a free period in which she would take a quick shower to remove the sweat from her weapons training and perhaps visit the Hydroponics Park. From a breast pocket, she removed the personal access card attuned to her chemistry and slipped it through the swipe slot. The door slid aside and she entered the room beyond. Inside sat her course peers for this class, fourteen in all. Nichole readily took her seat. Another latecomer slid in behind her.

Not all esper talented Patrol personnel were comfortable in the G-3 conditions, which Nichole's people found acceptable. For that reason, the asteroid-based Academy had areas that were pressurised and maintained to permit a variety of other species. This day, however, Nichole's class was being tutored in the social science of the known sectors. The walls of this particular lecture room reflected a variety of small, three-dimensional images of the subject taught: zeno/human inter-related history. As always, Nichole marvelled at the individual who welcomed her with a universal wave.

Now that we are all present, Nichole glanced around at her tutor's 'pathed observation, and realised the class was minus one, *we will do a quick overview of our previous lesson before looking at our topic of discussion for the day.*

M'bracni flowed across the front of the class. His gelatinous form swirled with muted colours. Protrusions that might have been tentacles appeared and disappeared about various portions of his anatomy at what Nichole considered his waist level. In the time Nichole had known M'bracni, she had never discerned a reason for the majority of the tendrils. Occasionally, as with the wave, there was a purpose. For the most part, they remained a mystery.

Then again, she mused, taking care not to let her thoughts leak out, *I don't even know if M'bracni is male or female. Amoebas are asexual, so maybe he is too.*

Even so, it seemed somehow logical to refer to M'bracni in the masculine. Whenever Nichole and her classmates discussed a lesson that was how they identified their History tutor. Now M'bracni squished and oozed, shifting his position again. Because of his physical structure, M'bracni conducted his lessons entirely via telepathic communication, which suited Nichole.

Would someone please give us a quick overview of yesterday's studies? Without altering shape of position, now, M'bracni somehow conveyed the impression that he was examining each class member. Someone quickly raised a hand. *Very good, Alain, if you would. Please keep it brief.*

Due to the nature of the class, Alain, some twelve years Nichole's junior, concentrated hard and carefully projected his synopsis. It was also evident that what he projected to the class had been memorised from a textbook.

On our mother world, Earth a foreign nation invaded one of the North American countries known as Canada. Shortly thereafter three generation-ships left orbit. Somewhere en route to her initial destination, the PERIHELION encountered a spatial phenomenon and was transported into a foreign quadrant, near the orbit of the Uths-sitssi binary system. The survivors made first contact and soon afterwards found themselves involved in the ongoing conflict with the race we know as the Craneeno.

Very good, Alain. A pseudo-limb extended then retracted. M'bracni's next thought caught Nichole unprepared. *Now then, our topic for today is a world that presently is the centre of much controversy. Unfortunately, from playing a minor role, it has recently been thrust into one of some importance in our conflict with the Cra-*

neeno. Interestingly enough, the native race may not in fact, have originated there, but that is something for a later lesson.

Several of Nichole's peers stirred, so she was not alone when she started. One of the previous lessons had included a more in-depth history of her people's first extraterrestrial encounter with the lizard-like Uthssitssi. Now it appeared they would cover a subject very near and dear to her. Attention riveted on their instructor, she ignored the curses in two dialects muttered by a couple of her older classmates. One she recognised as a colourful, crude assessment of the enemy's lineage. Within M'bracni's gelatinous form, the palate of soft tones swirled. Red darkened. Blue and green muted. Orange points that Nichole began to suspect might indicate the location of his primary nuclei or reproduction centre alone remained steady. He made no allusions to the expletives.

As Fimiah is familiar to one of your classmates, Nichole's heart leapt into her throat, and then settled at that acknowledgement of her recent experiences, *I believe we ought to have her take us on a brief tour of her first-hand contact with the flora, fauna and lifestyles of the local inhabitants.*

Fear at being singled out froze Nichole in her seat. M'bracni moved towards her, halting in front of her desk. Although his gelatinous form could not produce a smile, Nichole nonetheless experienced the sensation that he was indeed smiling, encouraging her to share her thoughts.

There's no need to stand. He settled her nerves with that assurance.

In truth, Nichole suspected she would have had difficulty getting up at that moment. She took a deep breath to settle her rattled nerves and concentrated. Aware she was limited in what she could reveal to her classmates, Nichole slowly, carefully opened her memories to them.

Jagged grey-black mountain flanks rose to snow capped peaks. Green and mauve foliage mounted the lower ridges, while a massive rift valley sliced the land between the Rashordis and the foothills. This was not drawn from her personal memories, but rather was taken from her mind-meld with Hafrin. Treacherous emotions threatened to overwhelm her. Fearful of emoting, of letting her peers and tutor into her personal life, Nichole quickly switched to her first images of Zivvoz's hold as seen from the loft window.

Graceful tïlkrïn milled about several mounds of fodder strewn along the fence of a snow-covered pasture. Rakkïal...laying fowl...scurried around the yard, keeping close to the stable where their perches were. Next, she switched to an external view of the cosy hold. On the outside railing a jesset, or female orved, mantled. Wings unfurling, the Fimiahri raptor launched skyward with a high scream. Now Nichole conjured one final image. Two rynada stood in the hold yard awaiting their riders. A pied mare rested her lower jaw across the back of a large black stallion. Her jaw horn with its ring was clearly visible against the pale saddle pad. Two spiralled horns sprouted from her head in front of her ears and just above liquid brown eyes.

They look like horses. Someone inserted that observation.

Naw. More like Earth deer, another mental voice countered, referring to humanity's distant past, *but with three horns instead of two antlers.*

They sort of look like both, said a third.

M'bracni cut in with a soft warning, *Class.*

Momentarily thrown off-balance, Nichole unwittingly allowed herself to linger on the black. The stallion turned his head, and there was no doubting the intelligence behind his eyes. The image of Bïzhan Koryn conjured painful memories and Nichole snapped her link with the group before more private thoughts spilled over.

Well, M'bracni commended, indicating she had done well, *that was quite impressive. Thank you, Nichole.*

Classes with the Shrklattr were, by necessity, short. Nichole surreptitiously glanced at her wrist chronometer. Almost an hour had passed. Aware the younger students were tired from the session, M'bracni concluded the lesson for the day.

The majority of you have a free period, I believe. I suggest you spend some of it in the library, expanding on what Nichole has so graciously let us see second-hand.

All around Nichole the youngsters got to their feet, chatting and joking. A few glanced at her, intrigued and evidently tempted to question her further. But M'bracni moved around the desk. He watched Nichole sort through her study material.

Have you any plans for your free time?

Startled, Nichole glanced up. Beyond M'bracni, one of the departing youngsters shot her a poisonous look. Jealousy was an emotion she had, until recently, not had to deal with. For most of her life, she had been regarded as something bordering on a cripple. Someone pitied for her inability to read minds or levitate, far-see or foresee. The coloured spots inside M'bracni shifted slightly.

It bothers you, he observed.

"Sir?"

Several tendrils looped out and were retracted. M'bracni's disapproval of her dissembling stung Nichole. *I'm certain it's difficult coming late to the talents. More so because most of your classmates are not only four to six years younger than you are, but they've been together for two or more years already.*

To his statement Nichole shrugged. "They're children, sir."

I suppose. But it isn't a good sign that some are jealous of your good fortune. Now M'bracni's form squished down so he no longer towered over her. *Or do you consider your time on Fimiah fortuitous?*

Memory flooded back, painful with the intensity of accompanying emotions. Her pleasure at being on a strange world had been offset to some degree by being relegated to Records keeping. Then the wonder of caring for native stock, and finally, perhaps best, as well as worst of all, the Craneeno attack on the primary community and her time with Hafrin.

In spite of her resolve, Nichole felt him close to her. She hurriedly buried her thoughts. Awareness of her surroundings returned. In front of her, M'bracni had gone absolutely still. No colour shifted through him. The nuclei at his core had perceptibly darkened.

Well, he said after a long moment of silence, *I can see why I've been cautioned against pressuring you. To let you chose when to participate.*

Uncertain where his conversation was leading, Nichole pulled her small satchel from under her seat and deposited the study disks inside. They clicked against those already inside. M'bracni flowed back, allowing her room to stand.

You're something of a loner, said M'bracni as Nichole checked to see she had everything she needed.

"Most of my life," she told him, and snapped shut the seal on her satchel.

Which isn't always a bad thing.

Perhaps, thought Nichole, but she kept that to herself. Over her years, while fostered with her cousins and then again at the Fimiah community, she had had no friends. Only at the hold had she learned the true meaning of what it meant to meet people who readily accepted her as a friend. Who treated her an equal, laughed with her and took no exception to her being an outsider.

If M'bracni picked up on any of her ruminations he did not allude to them. *I understand your weapons instructor is quite pleased with your progress. Particularly with knife and rapier.*

Still unaccustomed to open praise for her limited achievements, Nichole blushed and ducked her head aside. She stood. In truth, she had told the Weapons' Master that she had received initial instruction in combat with a duelling knife at the Fimiah Wanderer community. Then, later, at Zivvoz's hold.

You must get past this self-effacing manner, M'bracni gently chastised her. *Or is it that you simply are unused to being commended for your accomplishments?*

To that Nichole hesitantly admitted, "A little of both, I suppose, sir."

A tendril rested lightly on one shoulder. The sensation was similar to a comforting hand. A little smile tugged one corner of her mouth. Rose tinted M'bracni's body, displaying the blue and green.

Pleasure, she thought.

So, here I am taking up your free time. Off with you. I'm sure you've got more than enough studying to catch up on.

"Thank you, sir."

We really must get together one day when we've both got some free time, said the Shrklattr. *I would like to hear more about your time on Fimiah.* When amazement rushed through her, two more protrusions were extruded. The one on her shoulder retracted. *It's all right, Nichole. I have the necessary security clearances. All your instructors do. Didn't they tell you?* She shook her head. *Well then, at least you know to whom you can unburden yourself whenever you need someone to talk to.*

"Thank you, sir," Nichole repeated.

Dismissed, she left. Outside the classroom, the corridor was empty. The quiet ring of the five-minute warning for the next sessions echoed along the passage and died. Unconcerned, Nichole wearily traipsed back to her quarters. She craved solitude. Her stomach growled at her. Even though she had foregone breakfast, thought of food sent bile up her throat. Instead of heading for hydroponics, she hurried to her quarters, silently praying she would not spew all over the hall. She barely made her room. Dropping the satchel just inside the door, she dove for the bathroom. Head swimming, she knelt in front of the toilet and waited for the sensation to pass. Fortunately, nothing came up. She gradually recovered. Carefully getting to her feet, she returned to the bedroom and collapsed on the bunk.

There was a multitude of things she really should do. Language instruction topped the list. Somehow the idea of forced instruction was just as attractive as food, but without the accompanying nausea.

Maybe I should just go to hydroponics for an hour.

On the heels of that, her door-com buzzed. Not expecting anyone, Nichole went to the panel. "Who is it?"

"Nikki?"

CHAPTER 6

▼

Without conscious thought, Nichole's hand hit the door release. As the panel hissed open, she caught sight of the person on the other side. Tall, lanky, with dark hair and grey eyes that sparkled at her surprised expression, the man in the passage waited patiently for her to catch her breath.

"Victor!"

Her younger brother extended his arms. "In the flesh, little sister. Congratulations. Let me look at you."

Since she had last seen him, he had muscled out. Tall, always lean, Victor's biceps and chest now bulged, straining the fabric across his front. More fair highlights than usual intruded into his hair, hinting he had recently been in a particularly warm climate. Laughter lines and worry creases seamed the corners of his eyes, his brow, and tugged at the sides of his mouth, lending his oval features a craggy aspect.

He surveyed her critically, nodding at what he saw. Blushing to the roots of her hair, Nichole flapped a hand at him, then gestured, inviting him into her quarters. Victor stepped in, swept a glance around the room that inferred he thought she ought to have done something to make the place more agreeable and settled on the chair by her desk.

It's true, Nichole thought.

Unlike her contemporaries, she had not bothered to put up simula-screens of other worlds to brighten the walls. Nor had she acquired any ornaments to scatter about the two shelves and desk. However, unlike her peers she knew she would not be here very long. One way or another she would be moving on to another location within the year.

"So tell me," Victor interrupted her train of thought, "what happened? When did they find out you were a telepath? I thought you tested negative on your last session?"

"I did." Nichole answered his last question first. "But when I was selected to backfill a vacancy in Records at one of our colonies on a contested world, I was put through sleep training."

"Everyone gets that in school," countered her brother.

Nichole shook her head. "I never did. Probably because my initial test scores were so low."

"Damn." Victor's expression intensified. "Someone's going to wear it back home. Wait until the cousins hear about this."

"Yeah, well, I'd just as soon they didn't," Nichole replied.

"They should. Especially from what I heard about the way they treated you," Victor growled. "If I had known, Nikki, I'd have done something about it, I swear."

"How could you?" Ever the realist, Nichole reminded him, "You were off world on assignment. Besides, where else was I to go? An orphanage? Perhaps some foster home?"

"You might have been better off with complete strangers who had no preconceived notions about what you should or shouldn't be able to do."

"On Baccaria?" In that short phrase she reminded him of just how global the village mentality was on their birth world. "You know that old saw back home."

Without further prompting, he responded, "Sneeze on the plains and everyone gets a cold."

For several minutes they sat in silence, staring at one another. Eventually, Nichole began to feel uncomfortable beneath her brother's penetrating gaze and rubbed her sweating palms down her thighs. Aware he was making her uneasy, Victor forced a smile. He gestured expansively.

"So what do you think of the place?"

Obviously, he was expecting her to expound on the facilities, that she would express her enthusiasm about being at the Academy, training under some of the best alien and human instructors drawn from the known worlds. Instead, Nichole unwittingly released a rush of homesickness. In that brief instant, he must have felt just how much she missed the open air, the closeness of animals, a blue expanse of sky overhead, and the wind in her hair. Then she clamped down.

"Sorry," she muttered.

Sympathetic, Victor lifted a hand. "It's okay, Nikki. There's no doubt you'll be a field operative. You have the knack. You'll go native so easily, no one on the ground will ever suspect you aren't one of them."

"One of whom?"

A brief puff of air escaped him. "The natives of whichever world you're assigned to. It's usually a lifetime position, you know."

Fully conversant with field operatives, Nichole nodded. This encounter with her brother was not going as well as she had dreamt such a meeting would. Too much had happened to her on Fimiah. He was patrol. She was destined to be, in fact had unwittingly already been, a field operative. The distance between them yawned like the gulf of space between Academy and the planet she wanted so desperately to return to.

"Hey," her brother broke across her thoughts. "Where are you?"

"Sorry," she apologised again.

"You looked like you were parsecs away."

I was, she thought, but simply smiled and gave a tiny shake of her head.

"Well, how about we slip down to the observation area? I could do with something to eat. Isn't it lunch time?"

To Nichole's relief, her brother's inquiry did not elicit a corresponding attack of nausea. She glanced at her satchel, automatically bent to retrieve it and unwittingly diverted her brother. He watched her set it next to her feet against the bunk.

"What do you have in there?"

"Lessons," she told him. As much as she enjoyed seeing him again after five, almost six years, she knew she really ought to apply herself to the disks.

"Would you rather I dropped back later?"

In spite of herself, Nichole shook her head. "Actually, I was planning on going over to hydroponics first for a break."

"Then let's go on up to the observation lounge. We can grab a quick bite. Maybe afterwards I can show you around Ops."

Operations; the word was magical and alluring to her peers, both those with whom she shared classes and those of her own age. Unlike Nichole, however, they had no actual field experience. She knew what it was like to be under fire, too.

"Maybe after supper," she deferred.

"Sure. Suits," he shot back.

The observation lounge was almost empty when they walked in. Victor paused as though undecided where to sit then drew Nichole across the room.

Giant potted plants were scattered about the floor area. Trailing vines covered the wall beams. Freestanding trellises prevented them reaching the great dome. Through the transparent ceiling, occupants had an unobstructed view of the vast expanse of space. At the nearby station, several docked shuttles and two ships were being serviced by a horde of worker drones. Pods flashed through the tubes connecting the station to the Academy. All this Nichole had seen repeatedly over the previous weeks, though less often of late.

"Here." Once she was seated, her brother gestured, "What would you like?"

"Just something hot to drink," she deferred.

"Hmm," Victor grunted. "You sure?"

"Yes."

While Victor went to the counter to get his food and her drink, she watched what little activity there was about the lounge. Several maintenance workers checked the hydroponics connections to ensure the plants were receiving the correct quantities of nutrients. Across the floor area, one of the Academy's custodial staff was passing a scanner across the transparencies and their seals. An auto-sweeper cruised the floor cleaning up dust, food crumbs and such dirt visitors left behind.

"Here you go."

Yanked from her reverie, Nichole started. Her stomach twisted as she inhaled the steam rising from his tray. She swallowed convulsively and looked quickly away. Something scraped the tabletop.

"Here's your chocole," he said. "Hey, are you okay? Is something wrong?"

"No. I'm fine," she lied, and instantly knew she had spoken too quickly, with an uncommon edge to her voice.

"Me thinks she doth protest too much," countered her brother. For all he tendered a line from a popular, ancient play, he spoke in ceremonial, high Baccarian. As he slipped onto the seat across from her, he continued, "You know, Nikki, the…"

For some unexplained reason his familiarity grated on her nerves and she pushed her seat back from the table a fraction. Nostrils flaring, she glared at her brother.

"Don't call me that."

Confused, Victor protested, "Nikki, what's wrong?"

"I said don't call me that. Ever. My name's Nichole. Nichole. Do you understand?"

Nerves frayed by the unexpected confrontation, she found herself unable to comprehend the sudden irrational demand for respect from a sibling. No less confounded by the turn of events that had altered a family reunion into a battle of wills, Victor capitulated.

"Sure, Nichole."

He gently eased her mug of chocole closer. His actions effectively diffused the moment. Even Nichole found herself wondering about her peculiar reaction. If anyone had the right to call her by her pet name, it was Victor. As children, they had been good friends. When Victor got into trouble, she had stood up for him when their parents had threatened to punish him. And he had supported her. Only Victor was aware of the soothing effect chocole had when she was upset or sick.

Embarrassed, she sipped her drink and watched her brother over the rim of her mug as he polished off his lunch. Although the chocole partially settled her stomach, it was not wholly effective. She was glad when he finished eating and took his tray to the dispenser.

Returning to the table, he leaned against it, waiting for her to finish her drink. Nichole set the mug aside and got to her feet. The auto-sweeper scooted under the table. A tiny smile caught her as she watched the machine's comical actions.

"So, why don't you show me around the place? I doubt things have altered that much. They never do, or so they say." Victor shrugged. "Except for the faces, of course. I wouldn't mind a guided tour for the hell of it, though, if you don't mind, that is?"

"Okay."

Anything to divert his suspicious mind, she thought. Despite the time that separated their last meeting, Victor still knew her better than anyone else. *Except Rin.*

Nichole slammed the door shut on memory. She fell in step with her brother, conscious when he let her take the lead by half a pace. He commented on the classes they bypassed and made tiny observations about those to which she indicated she was assigned. Out of habit, she took the grav lift up to the library. Silent, her brother accompanied her. Outside the library entrance, she abruptly turned aside and drew Victor down the long passage to the upper entrance of the great hydroponics atrium.

They emerged on the uppermost level of the three-story complex. With Victor now unconsciously leading the way, they sauntered down the nearest ramp that wound down to the floor far below. Nichole knew that the far end of the atrium was out-of-bounds to everyone except assigned personnel. It was there that special foodstuffs were cultivated both for the residents and to export as prized commodities to colonies and allied worlds. Additionally, there were specific areas set aside to provide specialised nutrients for the non-human species; humans considered some of them to be delicacies. Others were either distasteful or outright poisonous. All of this was included in Nicole's scout training.

That she had actually been selected for such prized status, after everything she had done contrary to regulations while on Fimiah still dumbfounded her. These were perilous times, however. The Craneeno, their enemy, were increasingly less covert in their assaults against those worlds which bordered their space and the region occupied by humans and their allies.

Wanderers: that was how their allies often referred to the refugee human colonists. Gypsies was what the humans generally designated themselves. Castaways who had fled a world whose economies and societies were collapsing in a deadly downward spiral. A little over four hundred years separated their initial settlement from her.

"You're miles away again," commented Victor.

His observation yanked Nichole back to her surroundings. Somehow he had known the precise spot to bring her. The pleasant tinkle of flowing liquid soothed her nerves. Although water was precious, a tiny waterfall cascaded down through four artificial pools to a small pond. It ran out over a low lip to meander across the floor of the atrium and finally vanish into a wall. There, it was recycled. Foliage clinging to the walls on either side and about the basin drew moisture from the spray. Water plants in the basin provided additional greenery and exotic blossoms. Real trees, flowering shrubs and ground creepers provided the Academy residents with a relaxing atmosphere. Meticulously selected because of their high oxygen production, they were carefully maintained by a host of highly trained botanists. Many of the species also supplemented the dietary needs of the station inhabitants. There were even real birds and insects, the whole providing a self-contained ecosystem that required constant monitoring to maintain.

This was where Nichole came to study, striving to refresh a sorely bruised spirit that refused to mend. Now she felt it was a mistake to bring her brother here. It was too late to turn back, however, so she settled on a bench near the waterfall.

Victor stared up the soothing cataract and reflected, "I used to come here a lot too, at first. Until I got more involved in my training."

"I find it easier to study here," Nichole admitted.

"Rumour has it you got a bit too close to the action," he said.

Unwilling to react to the question, Nichole watched her brother from the corner of her eye. He turned and stared down at her. With no one else in the vicinity, Nichole was trapped into a conversation she did not want to have.

"It's okay, you know. They told me you were injured in an attack on one of our colonies. It was pretty easy to put two and two together, Nik...Nichole. Besides," he sought to draw her out, "I am Patrol."

Unable to avoid responding, Nichole managed a short nod. "I was in the wrong place at the wrong time."

To that, her brother laughed. "Isn't it always the case?"

Now he had her unguarded attention. "Have you run into them?"

"Who? The Craneeno?" Victor shook his head. "Fortunately, no. Been close, or so I'm told, but nothing like you. Did you see any?"

This time she responded in the negative, even though she had Hafrin's memories of his close encounters. Not about to collapse into tears, which she felt close to the surface, Nichole glanced at her chronometer.

"Damn," she muttered. Victor looked at his own timepiece.

"Whoops. Sorry," he apologised. "You better get on to your next class. See you this evening?"

"Ah, sure," she reluctantly acceded to his request.

"I'll pick you up at your quarters, okay?"

For a moment, Victor stared at her, but to Nichole's relief he finally turned and left. She glanced once more at her chronometer and knew she just had time to make it to her final class of the day if she ran. And run she did, slipping into the room just ahead of her survivalist instructor.

CHAPTER 7

▼

Four hours later, refreshed after a quick needle shower, Nichole sorted through her few belongings, conscious of the time. Eventually, she selected a pair of slacks and a shirt with full-length sleeves. Her brother would be arriving all too soon. From the small wall safe, she took an armband. She turned it over repeatedly without looking at it. Fingertips traced the etchings on the inside of the cool metal before she finally clasped it around her left biceps. Once she had tugged the sleeve back down, the band was no longer evident. A tiny sigh escaped Nichole. Before she could close the safe, her door-com buzzed.

"Yes?"

Her voice activated the speaker. "Nichole, it's Vic."

"Come on in."

Unconscionable irritation rose at the intrusion, even though it was expected. A deep breath settled it. In its wake, her stomach remained sour. The door to her room slid open. Victor stepped in. He glanced at the wall safe and spotted the tiny box inside.

"Hey, is that a medal I see?"

Cheeks burning, Nichole nodded. Wordless, she handed him the small container. He snapped up the lid, revealing one of the Patrol's highest awards: a comet. Its ribbon, striped dark blue along its outer edges had a red stripe on a white background and three stars embroidered on the ribbon. There was no bar. Those were reserved for auspicious acts of heroism. This version of the comet was awarded to those seriously injured in combat while on assignment. In spite of everything, Nichole could not help feeling the award was something she did not deserve.

"Wow," breathed Victor. "Wish I had one." He glanced up. "Guess I wouldn't exactly want to go through what it takes to get one, though."

He passed back the box, and Nichole returned it to the safe and shut the door. A last check of her room confirmed everything was where it ought to be. Should the Staff spring a spot inspection, they would find her room in order. She headed for the exit.

Her brother asked, "Did they throw a big parade when they presented you with it?"

"No."

"Hell, why not? There aren't too many living heroes around the Patrol, you know. Maybe fifty living recipients at the three star level. And most of them are retired and over the hill."

"I wouldn't say that too loud." Nichole reminded him, "The Commander's got one."

"He's a five star with bar," countered Victor. "And personally, they can keep it. There's no way I'd risk what he did."

"You really are the limit," Nichole shot back, and released the door.

A snort of laughter escaped Victor as he followed her into the hall and fell in step. "So tell me, is old M'bracni still around?"

That was Nichole's first clue to the Shrklattr's age. She told him, "I study with him almost every day. But I thought you were telekinetic?"

"I am," Victor replied. "But M'bracni's a jack-of-all-trades, as it were."

"Really? He never tells anyone about himself. I don't even know if he really is a he."

"Outside his own race, I doubt anyone knows what sex he is," Victor told her. "So you're what…a telepath?"

Nichole nodded. Her brother glanced at his chronometer as they walked, ambling nowhere in particular. Victor announced, "I've got to drop by the Posting Office. Why don't we do that first? Then we can grab supper."

"Okay."

Supper was the farthest thing from Nichole's mind. Since arriving at the Academy, her appetite had been slowly diminishing. Not the best thing, given she required a high calorie intake in light of her strenuous workouts twice a day, three times a week. If her instructors were aware of her weight loss, she was certain they put it down to an expected drop due to her length of time in cold-sleep and being launched immediately into training. Undoubtedly they all expected her to begin bulking up soon. Unfortunately, her metabolism had other plans. The harder she strove to eat more, the less her body wanted. Or so it seemed.

"Here we are."

For once, Victor had elected to remain silent en route to their initial destination. Ahead, a sign warned of access to Authorised Personnel Only. On the sliding door, another sign indicated they were at the Posting Office. Never having summoned the nerve in the past to request permission to make the one expected visit to the upper level, Nichole realised she was grateful Victor was with her. He stepped forward and swiped his Ident Card through the code access panel. The door opened.

Suddenly Nichole was loath to proceed. Victor glanced at her. "It's okay. No one will mind. All the important stuff is in code anyway."

They stepped through and the door slid shut behind them. An inexplicable sensation of terror swept over Nichole. She was trapped in a hallway. Several other passages gave off it to her left and right. A glance down each revealed more rooms down either side with placards above for ease of identification. Several doors stood open: examination rooms, Medical inspection areas, and offices for instructors. Final year students and directors lined the way, a gauntlet through which she must pass. At the end of one passage, she caught sight of a pressurised hatch. Prominently painted on it was an environmental warning sign. Pressed close to her brother's side without quite touching him, she forced herself forward. Ahead lay an open bulkhead. Beyond, a long counter barred their way. Victor moved ahead, eagerly leaning up to the waist-high barrier. Nervous, Nichole halted a pace behind his left heel.

The duty person proved to be insectoid. Nichole had to agree that on first glance it looked like an out-sized bug. Green and blue lines wove intriguing, iridescent designs across the dull black thorax and abdomen.

Multi-faceted eyes stared, unblinking, at the newcomers. Four lower limbs splayed out from the thorax as it squatted on a stool. Its two upper limbs shuffled several data pads aside. Around the upper extension of its left uppermost limb, between two spikes, was the Duty Non-Commissioned Member's armband.

The largest pair of two sets of antennae twitched and dipped towards Victor. This, Nichole realised, was a greeting of one friend to another even before it spoke.

"Victor." Mandibles clicked, and a tiny translator affixed to the upper thorax rapidly translated, "How was your last tour? Uneventful, I hope."

"So, so, Zkritlac," Victor responded, and tipped his right hand from side to side. "How's it going with you, old buddy?"

Upper limbs spreading to either side in a very human approximation of a shrug as it indicated the desk job, Zkritlac replied, "What can I say?"

Victor laughed, turned to Nichole and drew her forward. "Zkrit, this is my kid sister, Nichole. Nichole, Zkritlac was my co-tutor during my final year of extraterrestrial studies."

"Nichole." The insectoid politely inclined his upper thorax.

"Zk…ritlac," Nichole stuttered hesitantly until she picked up the correct pronunciation projected by the alien.

That he recognised her telepathic abilities both disarmed her and worried her. Then she caught the correct greeting and extended the first two fingers of her right hand. The smaller feelers on Zkritlac's head lightly brushed her skin. As cold as this alien being's exterior appeared, he radiated respect, pleasure and welcome. Delight lightened her anxiety. She smiled.

"You are my friend's sister, so you may call me Zkrit, too."

Completely bemused, Nichole nodded. The more she gazed at Zkritlac, the more differences she noted between him and his miniature cousins. Rather than a hard carapace, Zkritlac appeared to possess skin through which musculature was evident. Its joints were clearly more flexible. On the other hand, its species had retained the ability to swivel their head about one hundred eighty degrees without apparent discomfort, something Nichole rather wished she could do.

Light glistened off the facets its eyes as Victor leaned on his elbows on the counter. "So what have they got me slated for next, old buddy?"

"Let me see."

Zkritlac ran an appendage across the keypad built into the desktop in front of him. Now Nichole could see how nature had adapted the claws into miniature, tri-jointed fingers. Impressed and intrigued, Nichole studied the alien as its head twisted from side to side.

"It says here you're on extended leave. Note to file suggests you visit your brother on Farthom." Thorax tilting back, Zkritlac exuded mischief. "So how come you rate that much leave?"

"Must be all that clean living," shot back Victor. It was all Nichole could do not to insert a repartee as her brother turned serious. "Does it say why?"

"Nope. As you're so fond of quipping to others, 'them's the exact words, boyo'," Zkritlac returned. "Were I you, I'd not be staring too closely at a gift from the parakol."

Parakol? Perhaps it's kind of like us saying, don't look a gift horse in the mouth. Frowning over the unfamiliar word, Nichole mentally filed away the puzzle. When time permitted, she would research the expression.

"If you say so. Thanks, oh scholastically inclined." Victor pushed himself upright. "Come on, sis."

"Fate treat you both kindly," Zkritlac called after them.

With Victor guiding her back along the main corridor, Nichole allowed herself to consider her encounter with her brother's friend. As strange as M'bracni had seemed on first encounter, Zkritlac had tested her ability to deal with alien life forms. Mankind had a built-in aversion to most insects. In fact, to any 'creepy-crawly' inhabiting every world they encountered. That a being embodying all those aspects in immense proportions should fail to arouse disgust left her mildly astonished.

At length she managed, "So where does he," she almost said it, "come from?"

"Who...Oh, Zkrit." Victor grinned. "Kind of gets to you, doesn't he?"

Nichole quickly deferred, "Oh, no. I think he's...beautiful. Those colours are incredible. Are all his people like that?"

"The chitin patterns vary slightly," he brother informed her, "But apparently the principle means for them to tell each other apart is the aroma they emit. Most of us can't tell one from the other, but then their olfactory senses are far more acute than ours."

"He's quite incredible," Nichole mused out loud.

Astonished by her unusual reaction, Victor stared at her for several minutes. They stepped back into the grav-shaft that had brought them up from her floor and began the descent. Finally, Victor spoke again.

"Zkrit is from Zkrixtalc."

"Now that's a mouthful," Nichole blurted.

"Sure is. Takes a bit getting around the 'zk' in their names."

Eyes wide, Nichole exclaimed, "Do you mean all their names start with zk?"

"Most of them," acknowledged her brother. "Only the hierarchy has a different honorific. It's something they have to earn."

"So then you really shouldn't call him Zkrit," Nichole admonished.

"I guess not."

When Victor stepped from the grav-shaft, Nichole automatically followed him. As they progressed along the hallway, passing junctions more people joined them, all heading in the same direction.

"Ah, supper," her brother exclaimed.

Caught up in her encounter with Zkritlac, Nichole failed to note where they were heading until her brother's enthusiastic observation. At the same instant, the combined aromas of a variety of cooking foods struck her. Fortunately, she spotted the female 'heads' and made a dash. Inside, she passed a third-level trainee. The other girl watched, curious, as Nichole dropped to her knees in front of a toilet and began to wretch. Dry heaves shook her repeatedly. After a couple of minutes, something cold settled on the back of her neck. Its presence eased her convulsions.

"There now," someone said, sympathy edging their words. Nichole turned her head a fraction. Her solicitous companion was the woman she had passed on the way in. "Is there anyone I should call?"

Nichole shook her head. Yet, even as she denied her need for further assistance, the bathroom door opened a fraction and Victor called, "Nichole? Nikki, are you okay?"

The woman glanced behind her. "Who's that?"

"My brother," Nichole muttered.

"Oh, well." Now the woman left her. She opened the door to the washroom and nodded over her shoulder. "Go on in. I'll stay here so everyone knows it's all right."

"Thanks," said Victor. He hurried to check on Nichole. Resigned, she slowly pushed herself back onto her feet and straightened. He peered at her. "What's wrong? Are you okay?"

"I'm fine," she deferred.

Victor shook his head. "I don't think so. You're as white as a ghost and shaking like the proverbial leaf. You need to see the MO."

To that, Nichole vehemently shook her head. The last thing she wanted was to draw unwanted attention. Just being here, and the manner in which she had been selected for training, was sufficient to raise eyebrows and a certain degree of envy and jealousy.

"I don't need to see a doctor."

Now the older woman caught Victor's eye as she addressed Nichole. "I really do think you should see the Medical staff, dear. You look awfully thin and pale."

To that, Victor added, "You really do, Nichole. Maybe the Medics missed something when they checked you over after you arrived."

Stubbornly determined not to go, Nichole shook her head and insisted, "I'll be fine."

"No, you aren't," countered Victor. Then he frowned. "Is there something going on I...we," he amended, inferring the Academy staff in general, "should know about?"

It took little imagination to understand his meaning. Trapped, Nichole shook her head vehemently. "No. There isn't."

"Hmm," mused her brother and re-quoted his favourite line from Shakespeare. "I really think the lady doth protest too much."

Beyond him, Nichole saw the other woman give a fraction of a nod. They were not about to let her off easy. She dug in her heels. Arms crossed, she glowered at her brother and the other student. Victor took a deep breath and slowly released it in a manner she knew from old was indicative of an older sibling struggling not to yell at his kid sister because she refused to comply.

"You have two choices," he declared, unrelenting. "You can come with me willingly, or I'll call Security and have you forcibly taken to Medical."

Terrified, Nichole acquiesced. The thought of being dragged through the Academy halls was too ignominious to contemplate. Resigned, her shoulders drooped. Victor stepped back to let her pass. Although Nichole refrained from glancing at the other woman, she felt the other student's sympathy as they left the bathroom. Thankfully, the food odours failed to cause a repeat of the attack of nausea. The infirmary was one level up. They arrived far too quickly for Nichole's comfort.

CHAPTER 8

▼

As fate would have it, the Medical officer on duty was Major Lothar, the same physician who had performed the scans on Nichole the day she had emerged from hibernation. The swish of the door opening and closing made him look up. Upon seeing Nichole and Victor, he tapped a key on the desk pad and sat back from his computer. His brow wrinkled as he studied them, then cleared.

"Trent, isn't it?" With a sidelong glance at her brother, Nichole nodded. "And who's this?"

Victor answered before she could respond. "I'm Nichole's brother, sir. Victor Trent, with Exploration."

"Ah, yes. I remember seeing your name in her dossier. So, what's this all about? Did we miss something in our scans? Or is it just a cold?"

"I'm not sure, sir," Victor replied. "My sister appears to be having repeated bouts of nausea. And I suspect she hasn't eaten a decent meal in quite a while."

Concerned, the doctor emerged from behind his desk. "Is this true, Trent?"

To lie was not in her nature. Again, Nichole nodded but refrained from speaking. Silent, the doctor led her into the examination room. At the door, he paused. "You stay here."

Separated from her brother, Nichole realised she was without what little moral support he represented. The Major handed her over to a female Medic. Obedient to instructions, Nichole settled on the examination table and lay back. Lights dimmed in the room. To her left, a terminal lit up. Before long, the lights came back up. Nichole was alone with the doctor.

"You can sit up, Trent."

Nerves fluttering, Nichole swung her legs over the edge of the examination table. Major Lothar leaned against the desk against the wall beyond the foot of the table and stared at her. Expression grave, he tapped his fingers against the underside of the desk edge.

"Care to tell me who the father is?"

Worried as Nichole was that she might disgrace patrol, that they would send her packing back to Baccaria, pregnancy had been the farthest thing from her mind. Shaken, she stared at the doctor. Everything coalesced in a crescendo of images and emotions. Tears pricked her eyes, set her nose stinging. Prepared for the reaction, the Major handed her a tissue to blow her nose.

"I can't be," she blurted. "My cycle..."

"It's been known to happen," the Major informed her.

While Nichole recovered her composure, he pulled out his chair and sat, watching her intently. At his elbow were the results of the examination. Nichole suspected they indicated her pregnancy was a little into her second trimester. That would explain why she was suddenly filling out, she belatedly realised. There was no doubt in her mind of the identity of the fetus's father. Her condition had continued to advance during her hibernation trip from Fimiah. Cold-sleep had slowed its growth to a crawl. Where, under normal conditions, she would be almost ready to give birth, in reality, her pregnancy was only four and a half months along.

"Correct me if I'm wrong, Trent," said the Major, "but weren't you in hibernation from Fimiah to the Academy?"

"Yes."

"Then would you mind explaining how you could be four months..." He stopped, glanced at the report on the desk screen. "You were living with the natives for what...three weeks after the attack?"

"Yes, sir."

A heavy sigh escaped the doctor. "Trent, Trent. Don't tell me you went native on us?"

With a shake of her head, Nichole tried to deny what she knew to be true. If anywhere had ever been home to her, Fimiah was. She ached to return. Around her biceps, the armband burned a reminder of her brief happiness. Just as inexorably, she knew there was no going back. At least she had something, someone that would be a constant reminder of those short months. If, that was they did not force her to abort the child. Her hands unconsciously settled over her flat belly.

"I understand the freedman's son," the doctor caught her gaze as she glanced up, "Indoro, wasn't it, is quite handsome."

Something in her expression froze the doctor. Trapped, unable to break free, Nichole squirmed. There was no doubting he was getting far too close to the truth. What the Patrol would do with her if it came out frightened her.

"So it wasn't the hold boy. Perhaps one of the colonists." Now the doctor considered the options. His conclusion evidently was on the mark. Nichole steeled herself for his next demand.

"Trent, tell me what happened. You weren't seduced by someone at the Colony?"

She shook her head vehemently. "No, sir. I was still considered an outsider at the time they discovered I was a latent. They yanked me out of Records and placed me with Master Herder Bartlett the month before the attack."

"Hmmm." The doctor mused aloud. "And Bartlett was pretty shrewd in his judgement of people."

Nichole caught on that. "Was?"

Shaken, she stared at the doctor. His expression told her everything. She burst into tears. Instantly contrite for the way he had delivered the bad news, the Major apologised.

"I'm sorry, Trent. I thought you knew." Mute, Nichole shook her head. While she recovered from the shock, he explained, "It happened soon after your injury, I'm afraid." Gratified for the opportunity to switch topics, he added, "I'm pleased to see you've healed so well. You could have suffered significant scarring. I understand it was one of the locals who treated you."

"Yes, sir. Unfortunately, I don't remember too much of the incident. Or the next day."

"Small wonder; people have been known to die from being grazed by a Craneeno weapon. So," he returned to his original line of questioning, "since you had to have become pregnant on Fimiah, and it wasn't someone at the community, it had to have been while you were staying with the natives."

Face turned aside, Nichole felt her cheeks burning. There were times when she knew she was an open book, and this was definitely one of them. Speechless, she fidgeted. One foot swung back and forth in a short, jerky motion. Her eyes remained fixed on the toe of her boot.

"Come, Trent. It's not unusual for young people to experiment."

That he considered her condition attributable to an ill-advised dalliance irritated Nichole. Embarrassment altered to indignation. "It wasn't like that. We're…"

"You're what?"

"Married," she finished in a whisper. Her right hand rose as if of its own volition to curl about the marriage band hidden beneath her sleeve.

Gaze fixed on her hand, the doctor nodded. "So the father isn't one of us."

"No...sir." Aware there was no escaping telling the truth, she added, "His name is Rin."

"Rin?"

"Hafrin."

"Not Mark's ward?" When she nodded, he swore softly, "God in heaven and lords of space protect us. Do you have any idea who that young man is?"

Obviously the Major did. Nichole nodded. "I do...now," she admitted, unable to look in his direction, "But not then. Not until the day after we pledged to one another."

"Were there any witnesses to this pledge?"

"Yes. Indoro."

"The Alaiad's shield brother." Eyes flicking about the room, the doctor asked, "Does his foster father know?"

"About us? No, sir, I don't think so. He's only aware that we love one another, not..."

"Not that you had sex. Christ, you don't believe in doing anything by halves, child. Are you familiar with how the Alaiad's heir is chosen?"

Guilt now flushing down her neck, Nichole replied, "There's a special sword. Somehow it knows and imprints the heir with a rune under the left arm."

"That's right." He fell silent, concentrating on the problem at hand. At length, a heavy sigh escaped him. "All right, Trent. Continue with your training schedule. I'll advise your fitness and weapons trainers to modify your workouts."

Startled, Nichole blurted, "Then you aren't going to make me give up Rin's baby?"

"No, I haven't that authority. But I am going to have to pass this matter upstairs." He looked at the computer screen set into the desktop and then up at her. "Go on. Get out. Tell your brother everything's okay. You'll be advised of the Commandant's decision in a couple of days. Take these if you continue to feel nauseous. You have to build up your constitution. Remember, you're eating for two now."

Nichole accepted the tabs he handed her. "Yes, sir."

Reluctantly, she headed for the door. As she reached for the pad, the Major added, "And I don't think you ought to speak to him about our discussion."

"Sir?"

When she turned, he was eyeing her gravely. "Of course, you may need some-one to talk to. I believe M'bracni is one of your instructors."

"Yes, sir."

"Good. Talk to him if you need to. He has top level clearance and is fully con-versant with your past."

He flipped his hand at her, shooing her from the room. She slipped the tabs into her pants' pocket and opened the door. In the outer room, Victor stopped pacing at the hissing of the door. Speculative, he studied her as she joined him. "Well?"

"It's okay. He gave me something to settle my stomach."

"That's all?"

"Yes."

"You're certain you're okay?"

"Victor!"

Exasperated, Nichole headed back to her quarters, not bothering to check if Victor actually followed her. He tagged along in her wake for several minutes before lengthening his stride to fall in step with her. Silent, they took the grav-shaft down to her floor. Outside her room, Victor caught her arm just below the band, unaware of its presence.

"I'm sorry for being so pushy, Nichole. Look, while you were with the Major, I received a heads-up on my transport. I'm out of here tonight."

"So soon?"

A rhetorical question, Nichole felt a stab of guilt at her relief that he was leav-ing. No more questions, no further risks of letting slip something that, as far as she was concerned, was none of his business. Even though she sensed Victor knew how she felt, he did not allude to it. Nor did he appear upset by her reac-tion.

"Let me know what happens. Okay?"

"If I can." She evaded making any promises she might not be able to keep.

"Of course." His head tipped as he checked the time. "Look, I know you're not hungry, but I'm starving. If I don't run, I'll miss the second sitting."

"Okay. Go," she ordered, and gave him a tiny shove.

Still, he hesitated. "It really was good seeing you, Nichole. I hope everything goes well for you."

"Thanks. You too. And say hi to Zkrit for me next time you see him."

"Yeah, I'll do that. Anyway," he grinned, "he'll probably know where your assignments take you before I do. Besides, you can always go up there again, you know. You were my guest this time around."

"Then it doesn't count as my personal visit?"

"That's right."

"Sneak," she countered.

"Hey, family should look out for one another. If we don't, who would?"

Her immediate response was, "Command."

A laugh escaped him. He turned on heel and disappeared up the passage, back the way they had come. With a shaky inhale Nichole entered her room. She halted immediately inside the door, feeling the panel brush her back as it slid shut, closing out curious pedestrians.

CHAPTER 9

▼

Retreating into the sanctuary of her quarters, Nichole considered her next actions. The tabs in her tunic pocket poked at her. She removed them, considered the package then pushed one from its blister and swallowed it dry. Her stomach was rumbling, demanding sustenance. A series of feathery flutters tapped across the inside of her belly. Something she had experienced twice over the past week, she now realised it was her baby.

Gently, little one, she 'pathed to it. *You're okay. No one's going to hurt you or take you away from me.*

Determined to test the properties of the medication the doctor had given her, Nichole decided to return to the cafeteria. By the time she arrived, only a few people were still eating. Victor was nowhere in sight. She slipped along the steam line, inhaling carefully and was pleased when her system failed to respond with a nausea attack. Even so, Nichole chose carefully, selecting a light salad, two pieces of baked poultry breast meat and mashed tubers. The lateness of her appearance elicited scowls from two of the assistant cooks, but she persevered. With a mug of chocole added to her tray, she settled to one side of the room and carefully worked her way through her meal. Everything went down and stayed put. Relieved, Nichole turned in her dishes and tray to the cleaners and returned to her quarters.

There were no messages waiting for her on her computer when she settled to her evening studies. All too soon, however, the day's events resurfaced to interfere with her efforts to apply herself to her homework. After an hour of rereading the same chapter twice and failing to absorb anything, Nichole closed the file in disgust. Her thoughts repeatedly replayed her conversation with Major Lothar. That a report on her physical condition would have to be passed on up to the Commandant deeply disturbed her. She keyed a request into her e-mail. Within minutes, she had a response.

"You wished to speak with me, Nichole?" M'bracni was incapable of audible speech, but his computer had been programmed to vocally respond to key input, if required.

"Please, sir."

"Where?"

"Hydroponics?"

"All right. I shall be there shortly. Is there somewhere specific in the gardens?"

"By the waterfall."

"That area may already be occupied."

"I realise that, sir. If it is, there are other places, but I'll meet you there."

"All right."

M'bracni broke the connections. Nichole shut down all unnecessary functions on her machine, left a message to anyone trying to contact her that she had gone out, and left.

As with most evenings at the Academy, the hydroponics dome was filled with couples and small groups, strolling the pathways or seated in quiet nooks about the shrubbery. The bench at the waterfall was indeed occupied. Nichole moved on and halted just the other side of the bushes screening the area.

The quiet hiss of shifting gravel announced M'bracni's arrival. Nichole stepped from the shadows to greet him. With a gesture and a silent confirmation that they would have to seek some privacy elsewhere in the grounds, she led the way along the path. They made a strange pair, the silent human female and gelatinous Shrklattr. Most residents did not frequent the company of Shrklattr, although Nichole was uncertain why this was the case. Heads turned slightly. Speculation lit many faces, but the curious politely redirected their attention.

Here.

M'bracni indicated a small alcove beyond a decorative humpback footbridge. While he settled himself into something that resembled fruit gelatine, Nichole sat on the edge of the bench. Instinctively she glanced about, but there was no one within earshot.

So tell me what was so urgent you needed to speak with me outside of classroom hours.

Prompted, Nichole quickly outlined what had transpired that day since her final class. Colours swirled through M'bracni's form. Blue ovals within his form darkened, while the delicate rose-tone visibly faded. When she explained about her relationship with Hafrin and its consequences, the rose turned almost crimson. Even the Shrklattr's pseudo-limbs froze.

You swore an oath of marriage with the heir to the Fimiahri throne? Shocked to near mental speechlessness, M'bracni shifted his bulk, thinning until he was nearly twice his usual height. The three primary colours inside his body stilled. *You bear his child?*

"That's what the doctor says," Nichole reluctantly admitted.

Gradually the Shrklattr slumped back into a pudding puddle in front of her. Two large spots of colour, one green, one blue, prescribed a pirouette within the lower right quarters of his body. This, Nichole suddenly realised, was the Shrklattr's equivalent to shaking one's head.

I must admit your bloodline has always been a rash one. Not dangerously so, perhaps, M'bracni advised her, *but definitely adherents to one of your species most sagacious axioms: fools rush in where angels fear to tread.*

His humour was obvious even to someone as unfamiliar as she was with Shrklattr body language. Several pseudo-limbs exuded from his form and were retracted. Areas within his form pulsed, the gentle rose tone once again prevalent throughout. Aware he had pricked her curiosity with that statement, M'bracni projected an image.

For one brief moment, Nichole felt she was elsewhere. Blank, dull grey metal walls surrounded her. She stepped through an open doorway and found herself up to her ankles in pink goo that stretched from wall to wall. Startled, she halted. Then she was back in the garden.

That was your several times great-ancestor.

"Where was that?"

On board the first Craneeno ship your people and the Uthssitssi captured intact. The auspicious moment of encountering another friendly species was somewhat marred by your ancestor's unannounced entry into the cell where my great bud-parent was being held.

"He stepped on…"

I believe 'in' is a more appropriate description. Once again, Nichole received the impression that M'bracni found the incident highly amusing. Had the Shrklattr been capable of the vocal reaction, he would undoubtedly be laughing. *May I?*

So sudden was his request that Nichole was wholly unprepared. With a hesitant nod, she watched as a thin limb extended from M'bracni toward her belly. A short portion of the tip rested lightly against her. Intrigued, Nichole looked up in time to see the blue and green nodes inside the Shrklattr deepen and pulse. A series of orange globes appeared lower down inside M'bracni then faded. His limb withdrew.

So, he 'pathed to her, *are you interested in the sex of your child?*

It's a boy, she sent back. That much she had deduced in the one brief contact she had had with the infant before meeting with M'bracni.

An heir for the heir, he continued. *Well, at least, we need not fear for continuation of the line.*

His words conjured images of her time with Hafrin. Anguish and loss welled up, overwhelming her, forcing her to break her link with her instructor. Prepared for the reaction, M'bracni settled two tendrils about her shoulders. A third caressed the crown of her head. Calm, patience, and understanding emanated from the Shrklattr, easing Nichole's pain and soothing the infant inside her.

If you wish, I shall speak for you, he told her.

"Is that wise?" Nichole meant that question for herself, but he picked up on it immediately.

M'Bracni's response was not only a relief, it took her off-guard. *I believe a neutral party would be advisable in any decision made concerning the future of you and this child.*

On either side of her, Nichole caught the movement of the foliage. At first she thought someone had been hiding in the bushes, but when the branches dipped around her she experience a surge of fear. She flinched and the greenery lashed about.

Calm yourself, M'bracni commanded sharply. Behind the Shrklattr, several small pebbles took flight. He flattened himself against the path just in time to avoid being struck. Terrified, Nichole leapt to her feet, but the plants appeared to reach out to her.

Nichole. M'bracni's mental shout jerked her back to her senses. *You must calm down.*

Nichole swayed dangerously, fearful of the strange events. Her breath shuddered through her as she struggled to take control of her emotions. Eyes closed, she took a deep breath and released it, then a second. Her heart rate slowed.

Good.

At M'bracni's declaration, she opened her eyes once more. With colours darker than normal expressing intense emotions, the Shrklattr squatted before her. He resembled a squashed ball with a small bulb at the top.

I can see you are in need of…other lessons, he observed.

Confused, Nichole stared about her, but the foliage had returned to its place. The only sign that anything untoward had transpired was the uncustomary presence of several small branches and a dusting of leaves lying about the bench.

"What happened? What did I do?"

Apparently there is more to your latent abilities than turned up on the initial tests. Tell me, what was the extent of the original results?

"I can far-see and use telepathy."

Far see. Hmmm. That's it?

"Well, they did say my ability to far-see was particularly strong."

Ah, then they ought to have tested you more fully.

"But that's why I was sent here," she objected. "Only…"

The attack must have caused someone to drop the ball, said M'bracni. His familiarity with human figures of speech effectively distracted Nichole. *This too must be addressed to the Commandant.*

In spite of everything Nichole blurted, "I don't want to be a problem."

A tendril appeared, touched her arm briefly and shrank back. *Most of this is not your fault.*

"Most."

Now the very tip of that tendril rose and gestured expressively. To Nichole, it reminded her of a parent waggling a finger at an errant child. Aware she was blushing, she ducked her head and stared at the ground.

Yes, well, that cannot be undone. We must live with the consequences. When Nichole glanced up at that, the Shrklattr continued. *All of us. And perhaps on closer examination, we shall discover the situation not altogether a bad thing.*

Desperate for direction, Nichole asked, "What should I do?"

Do? Continue your classes. Study hard. And eat. You are far too thin.

"I've been throwing up."

Morning sickness. I understand it's not uncommon among most humanoids.

"I guess."

Slowly M'bracni resumed his original form. Tendrils once more appeared and disappeared at seeming random intervals about his form suggesting their conversation was over and that he was satisfied with what he had learned. Nichole looked past him. For the first time she realised the artificial daylight was lowering, simulating nightfall.

Yes, it's time you returned to your quarters. Don't spend too much time tonight studying. Sleep is more important. I'll speak with the Commandant first thing in the morning after…how do your people call it…prayers.

"Morning brief," Nichole automatically amended.

M'bracni exuded humour. *Given the subject of many such gatherings, I prefer the former description. I shall endeavour to have some sort of answer for you by supper. All right?*

"Yes, sir."

Then go get some rest.

Dismissed, Nichole stepped past M'bracni and wandered back along the paths to the exit. Before reaching the short passage to the exit she glanced back, but there was no sign of the Shrklattr, which was not wholly unexpected since there were several exits around the three levels via which he could return to his quarters.

Sleep, she thought. *I'm never going to be able to sleep tonight.*

But sleep she did, deep and near dreamless. Morning came all too quickly. Even so, she woke fully rested and hungry and with sufficient time to peruse most of her homework before heading to her first class of the day. More importantly, she was no longer fearful of what the future held, even though that was far more uncertain now than it had ever been in the past year and a half. Determined not to be distracted she threw herself into training with renewed vigour.

CHAPTER 10

▼

Spring—two years post Dôzhik Koryn

Jikpryn

It was hours before midday and the sun was high and hot. Above, the pristine expanse of purple-blue sky stretched unspoiled, from horizon to horizon. No breath of wind relieved the stifling heat of the midsummer's day. Jikpryn strode along the inner passage of the ancient fortress and down a flight of stairs of age-worn grey stone, conscious of his constant shadow. At the correct distance behind his left heel trod his advisor, the Outsider, Tolbôun. Here within the timeworn pile of stone, there was a measure of relief from the oppressive temperatures.

Annoyed by what he could not control, the Wôbiny Usurper to Iryô's throne considered the prophecy cast at the turn of the New Year. Of itself, it was little more than a reinforcement of the one given at Dôzhik Koryn. Since then, numerous peculiar occurrences had upset what ought to have been just another uneventful spring.

Perhaps I shouldn't have summoned the seer.

He considered that and realised how custom had trapped him just as surely as his dagger had pinned Fanhri to the high seat almost twenty-one years earlier. The request had been a calculated risk. After all, it was customary for every ruler to have a seer perform a reading at the turn of the year. If nothing else, Jikpryn had struggled to ensure as many customs and laws had remained in place since taking control of Fimiah's people. In so much, he had succeeded in keeping rebellion confined to a few small pockets of trouble, and governed the otherwise sullen population as fairly as possible. But the cost had been extreme; the headaches were perhaps the worst, assailing him whenever he made decisions crucial to the lives of the people, whether it was an individual or the population as a whole.

And Hafrön had eluded his grasp. That benighted sword was well gone, thrown into the Neranik Sea by the Captain of his personal Guard. Thankfully, Hilcaz had not brought up the episode since returning from leave.

Just as well. He's too valuable to lose, Jikpryn considered, *and one of too few whom I can trust. If he simply vanished, I could well have a revolt amongst my loyal guardsmen.*

Spring had come too early, deceptive in its quiet intrusion. Massive glacial blocks had broken loose in the far north and south yet again, sending tidal bores racing down streams to catch the population along the riverbanks unawares. Villages had been inundated or entirely swept away. The docks in Pûdornâ had been ripped away as well, despite the broad delta at the point where the city sat. The freezing rains in late spring, followed by an early drought, and now this incredible heat wave, was sapping the resources of even the most reliable provinces. Spring seedlings withered to dust. The more daring of the population, determined to survive at all costs, were fleeing the populated centres and taking to the wilds.

There must be an answer, Jikpryn told himself as he entered the great hall. Once Jikpryn sat, Tolbôun gestured to the petitioners waiting patiently at the far end. The first to approach was Lord Baryan's ambassador.

"Ser," the man began cautiously. His gaze darted nervously from his sovereign to the Outsider and back again. "Lord Baryan has asked me to put this petition to you: Our people demand an explanation for the prophecy. They grow restless with expectation. Our history tells us to expect great things of these times, but this uncertain weather has done little to assuage their fears."

"Tell Lord Baryan," Jikpryn began, infuriated by this subordinate's audacity.

"Ser," Tolbôun whispered in his ear, "a word if I might."

Jikpryn raised a hand, freezing the ambassador. One eye fixed on the man at the foot of the dais, he half-turned his head and lowered his voice as he snapped, "What?"

"Perhaps you should re-summon Seer Triklâ. Order her to cast a more favourable reading which you can disseminate to the people."

Eyes veiled, Jikpryn considered the suggestion. *If rumours are true, she won't be able to. But I could order her to explain the previous one. And if she refuses, I could hold her until she does.*

Tolbôun continued, unaware of his lord's thoughts, "You know these seers. They delight in expounding riddles that only they understand. It might be wise to have one here to call upon as you require."

Thought of controlling a seer titillated Jikpryn by its sheer daring. History had never recorded any prior Alaiad achieving such a coup. Since Dôzhik Koryn heralded great events, perhaps this was one such. For all Tolbôun made light of such things, there were times when the Outsider produced timely advice. Where he might have been tempted to warn his advisor against intruding, this time Jikpryn felt inclined to agree. He gave a barely perceptible nod of his head.

"Have Hilcaz take charge of this matter personally. I want a patrol dispatched to the Temple. Tell him to escort her back here immediately."

"As you will, ser."

With a short bow, Tolbôun withdrew from the dais, turned and hurried from the hall. Patience itself, the Ambassador waited for his sovereign's attention to return to him. Slowly, Jikpryn permitted his gaze to return to Baryan's petitioner. For all the man appeared unaffected by the whispered exchange, curiosity and speculation were rife in his demeanour.

"Tell Lord Baryan I am examining the matter and have summoned the seer. Until then," Jikpryn dismissed the Ambassador the a flip of his fingers, "he, and your people, will have to wait on the Great Serpent's favour."

Pleased with his spurt of eloquence, Jikpryn lounged back in his seat as the Ambassador bowed and stepped back. From this point on, he was trapped by the vagaries of the Temple, and its priests and priestesses. What he considered now was perhaps his most daring move to date. Rarely had anyone in history ever threatened to imprison one of the Great Serpent's seers. On two such occasions, the individuals responsible had met with somewhat mysterious, untimely ends. The man withdrew into the crowd of courtiers and petitioners filling the hall. Other petitioners came forward, helping distract Jikpryn from the passage of time.

Am I doing the right thing?

More and more these days he found himself questioning his decisions. Sharp pain seared the base of his skull. It was all Jikpryn could do not to flinch as the invisible needle lanced up through his brain. He turned carefully and gestured to the page to the right of his seat with a lift of a finger. Tentatively, the boy edged forward, tray with flagon and goblet held before him. Slowly, the boy went to one knee his eyes fixed on Jikpryn's boots. Sight of the youngster conjured thoughts of his own son and Jikpryn paused, irritated.

Too young to bear children, yet forced into lying about her age by an ambitious family, his wife had bled to death shortly after their son's birth. Had he known just how young she really was, he would probably have looked elsewhere. At the very least, he would have opted for a protracted engagement. His stupidity had compounded an already difficult situation. Consequently, his only issue was condemned to life as an imbecile, hidden away in a back wing of the fortress. Not that he allowed his son to be abused or neglected, and Jikpryn visited him almost daily. For his part, the boy exhibited no more intelligence than did the idiot who was responsible for mucking out the fortress stables. Again, pain lanced through his skull. He stifled a flinch, waiting until it passed before carefully pouring himself a drink.

So you sit and brood, he berated himself, *and you drink too much, while making excuses and refusing to consider any future match. Who will hold what you've gained if you don't sire an heir?*

Feeling the flagon return to the tray, the page glanced up. Jikpryn gave a tiny jerk of his head and the boy withdrew. His thoughts continued to tumble about the matter of an heir.

But what woman would consider me a suitable mate?

Their revulsion had little to do with his age. True, grey intrusions in his nut-brown hair had increased three-fold since he had taken the throne from Fanhri. There were more lines in his features, but he maintained much of the tough, wiry physique of his youth. No. It was the result of his encounter with Hafrön, and his permanently crippled right hand that caused potential suitors to shy away. Propitiously he was left-handed and could still wield a sword. Unfortunately, despite every concoction and old wives' remedy he had tried, the flesh of his right hand continued to resemble broiled meat; wrinkled, an angry red claw he would as soon cut off were he insane enough to attempt the act. From time to time, the flesh quivered as though it possessed a life of its own. At certain other times, it cramped and ached so that he never forgot its presence.

CHAPTER 11

▼

Hilcaz

Off-duty, Captain Hilcaz af Orïl lounged on his bed, boots off. Never one to pass up the opportunity to catch up on sleep between patrols or manoeuvres, Hilcaz drifted on the edge of consciousness. On the periphery of sleep, he was aware of the common sounds that filled his days. Across the room, his secretary was sorting through the latest reports submitted by the city patrols, annotating something on another piece of parchment. The scratch of the quill tip affected a pleasing under tone to the shouted orders from the Drillmaster on the Parade Square just outside. Somewhere nearby, an unruly rynad squealed a complaint. Wooden sparring weapons clashed repeatedly.

Drill schedules were strictly adhered to under his command: running first thing before anyone broke their fast, then sword, battle axe and mace drill a candle mark after the morning meal. Mid-morning was principally for the Cavalry. They practised on one of the two fields below the fortress northeast of the city. In the afternoon, pikemen drilled in the same fields if the weather was good, or within the confines of the parade square when it rained. Foot soldiers drilled while the cavalry practised. Three times a week, they went on manoeuvres in the forests and fields, rain, snow or shine. Every second day, they held archery practice, outside or indoors depending upon the weather.

Hilcaz knew most of the schedules by heart, having dictated them himself. Occasionally his officers sprang special operations on the men, just to keep them in peak fighting form. Of course, there were the patrols responsible for law and order in the streets and along the main thoroughfares, dictated by his senior subordinate in charge of law enforcement. Men were systematically rotated through the various military waystations and the posts in outlying communities to prevent allegiances being formed.

A soldier's allegiance must, first and foremost, Hilcaz reminded himself, *be to his lord.*

And so, like many of his predecessors Jikpryn maintained his own army. At the same time, he reserved the right to call upon the lords of the land to provide additional help in times of crisis. Of course, soldiers did more than fight and enforce the law of the land. They were also expected to assist in times of natural disasters. At planting and harvest, they went out in shifts to help the farmers.

Which makes sense, if we expect to eat without it costing the Alaiad a small fortune, or causing resentment amongst the landsmen and holders by levying higher tariffs or confiscating produce.

Yet, the Alaiad's advisor, Tolbôun sneered at such activities. Numerous times, Hilcaz had heard the Outsider remarking to courtiers within earshot of guards that real soldiers never stooped to manual labour that ought to be left to commoners. On such occasions, Hilcaz could only grind his teeth. Thus, he took care to ensure daily briefings covered the importance of maintaining good rapport with the people. Nevertheless, there were the dissatisfied amongst the men who leaned towards Tolbôun's way of thinking, and Hilcaz knew he could do little to alter their mindset.

Sharp pain lanced through his skull behind his left ear. He flinched, pressing his fingers against the offending spot. Eyes squeezed shut, he waited for it to subside. Gradually, the stabbing eased.

What was I thinking? Why should soldiers work the fields like common labourers? Our duty is to maintain control of the population and fight. That is what we do.

He swung his feet off the bed and sat up all in one motion. Stocky like his forefathers, he was favoured with swarthy, broad features and alert eyes. Although he had never wed, Hilcaz seldom lacked for female companionship. Since being awarded Captaincy of Jikpryn's personal guard, plus a seat as one of three senior officers in control of the combined Wôbiny/Deccöt provincial armies, however, Hilcaz took far more care in selecting where he spread his favours. Generally, he tended to a solitary existence. He rotated his shoulders, felt tense muscles crunch. Outside, voices rumbled. A fist thumped the door. Hilcaz glanced over his shoulder.

"What is it?"

Tolbôun stuck his head in. "Captain."

"Lord." Hilcaz rose and turned.

"The Alaiad commands you take a troop to the Temple and escort the seer, Triklâ, back to his presence."

"Yes, lord."

"Post haste, Captain."

Before Hilcaz could question the Outsider, he disappeared. Muttering under his breath, Hilcaz tugged on his mail shirt and the surcoat with its coat of arms. Sword belted at his waist, he tucked his helmet beneath his left arm and went out to the Parade Square.

His bellowed command produced four men in short order. Even as they assembled in front of him, a messenger sprinted in the direction of the stables. Under normal conditions, his patrol would have marched to the Temple, secured the seer and escorted her back in a litter. These were not normal times, however. Nor were the people of Iryô his people. So it was that all special summons were delivered by fully armed and mounted escorts.

And with eyes all around one's head, Hilcaz reminded himself as he inspected his men.

Satisfied, he briefed them on their assignment and led them to the stable to collect their mounts. A spare rynad was brought out to accommodate the seer. Old and docile, the creature was useless under most circumstances. But it was ideal for conveying special guests to appointments with the Alaiad.

Most of those never make the return journey though, Hilcaz silently mused.

Shrugging aside that thought, he swung up and waited for his troop to fall in behind him before setting off through the portcullis and across the moat's bridge. A second portcullis, with its out-riding sentry post, cast its shadow across the party. Then they were in the open, trotting downhill in the direction of the Temple.

Located near the river docks, the Temple was as fortified as the Alaiad's home, complete with hefty metal portcullis to block the entrance and a ramp they could raise in times of trouble. Manned by guards who swore allegiance to the Great Serpent alone, they were, by necessity, the only military personnel the Alaiad could not command. He might request, but the Temple was within its rights, by law, to refuse. Throughout Fimiahri history, religious persecution had not been uncommon. So it was that the somewhat loose-knit sectarian members tended toward being safe rather than sorry, more often than not electing to remain neutral.

Comprised of Advisors, Seers and Healers, the sect was monitored and steered by Guides. Great Serpent Advisors for each provincial capitol were trained in Iryô by the Temple's Senior Guides. Other graduates were then sent out to the various hamlets, towns and villages. Only in Iryô were housed the rare seers. Healers had training centres of their own, but Iryô's Temple Prelates oversaw their instructors and curriculum.

Seers generally lived in the capitol, occasionally making excursions into the countryside as the Great Serpent instructed them. No one actually controlled the seers. They were nearly a power unto themselves, but their tendency to drop into trances at unexpected moments necessitated they never travel anywhere without at least one attendant to oversee their needs.

At the city end of the ramp, Hilcaz and his men reined in their rynada. Complying with etiquette, they kept their mounts just back of the ramp's leading edge. A Temple guardsman approached, spear carefully balanced in such a manner as to imply he would use it if necessary.

"What do you want here, men of Jikpryn?"

That the guard's address bordered on insult raised Hilcaz's hackles. But, the Temple acknowledged only one lord, the Great Serpent. Pressing down his anger, Hilcaz took a moment to compose his irritation before delivering his request.

"The Alaiad desires another meeting with Seer Triklâ. We've been sent to escort her, and have brought a mount for her to ride."

For all his forced politeness, the Temple Guards were not fooled. Eyes narrowing, the man in front of Hilcaz considered the thinly veiled demand. His spear butt came to rest on the ramp planking. Behind him, his three companions remained alert.

"Even Jikpryn must understand seers need time to rebuild their strength following a reading. Particularly if it's to be accurate."

In so many words, the Temple Guard informed Hilcaz that Triklâ had been working quite recently. The Captain of the Guard could not help wondering what she had seen, and for whom. Still, his lord had commanded he return with her and no one else.

"I have my orders," he replied. "We'll wait."

With a shrug that inferred they were in for a long wait, the Temple Guard turned on his heel and returned to his comrades. After a quick exchange Hilcaz could not hear, the guard vanished beneath the portcullis. The remaining three guards resumed their vigilance.

Rather than dismount, Hilcaz elected to maintain the visible position of authority by height. Reins in hands, he rested the heels of his palms on the raised fore skirt of his saddle. His gaze never left the three Temple Guards. Behind him, rynada snuffled to clear flies from their nostrils. Foetid air from the direction of the river assaulted him. The unusual heat had shrunk the river's flow. Barges and large boats were unable to proceed further than a half day upstream from Iryô, even with the assistance of tow-rynada. At the docks, the river stench was overwhelming. Worse, more trash than usual was accumulating in the streets.

No doubt it's a symptom of the populations' displeasure with the overthrow of Fanhri's dynasty. He blew through his lips, clearing a drop of sweat from the tip of his nose. *No pleasure cruises for the indolent this year.*

Behind him, Hilcaz caught the sound of a cloven hoof stomping the ground. Impatient to be out of the sweltering heat, the rynada were growing increasingly restless and difficult to curb. Sweat trickled down Hilcaz's face. As time passed, he felt increasingly more like a fish set to broil over an open flame. A maddening itch he could not scratch developed between his shoulder blades. Sweat stung his eyes. A surreptitious flick of his tongue, and he tasted salt. Blood flies were congregating. If they remained stationary much longer, the troop ran the risk of losing all control over their mounts.

Abruptly, a group of people emerged from the deep shadows beyond the portcullis. All were mounted, a contingency neither the Alaiad nor his advisor had foreseen. To the Captain's amazement, Triklâ sat a young, fractious mare. The animal, so masterfully controlled, was a direct contrast to the age and apparent decrepit appearance of its rider. Without a word, the seer bore down on the Royal troop, forcing Hilcaz to order his men to draw aside. He fell in beside the seer, while his men joined the vanguard of the Temple Guard.

With what could only have been complete malice of forethought, Triklâ led the group up the main thoroughfare. Along the way, they passed through two large markets. Due to the heat and time of day, there were few people about, merchants or customers. Of those present, many stared with undisguised curiosity. All the way to the fortress, frowns and furtive whispers noted their passage. Darting eyes and surreptitiously pointed fingers marked their progress all along the route.

At length, they reached the fortress and halted in the courtyard. As was her due, Triklâ waited for someone to take her mount's head before she dismounted. Hilcaz was at her side before her feet touched the ground. His bow was short but respectful. A gesture of his hand and he led her and the Temple Guards up the stairs, through the great doors. The Temple Guards halted just outside. Hilcaz continued through the open doors accompanied by the seer and her assigned accolyte. They traversed the aisle down the audience chamber, which was, by decree, kept free of impediment.

The instant the great doors swept open all conversation on the other side had died. Courtiers turned. Sight of the party aroused a flurry of whispers. Ladies fluttered fingers. Furtive observations passed amongst the gathering. As the group advanced up the hall, Hilcaz at the front, Triklâ half a pace behind, the gathering separated like grain before a racing rynad. Fabric whispered as the ladies shifted.

Full skirts brushed against the gowns or trousers of their companions. Heads dipped here and there, acknowledging the seer's presence.

Hilcaz glanced quickly towards the high seat. Eyes narrowed, Tolbôun was taking note of those few who silently admitted a closer affiliation to the Great Serpent's teachings than the rest of those present. Hilcaz halted a full body-length from the dais. To his consternation, Triklâ steadfastly advanced past him. Close at her heels followed the acolyte.

CHAPTER 12

▼

Silent, Triklâ gestured to her young companion. Stoic, eyes surreptitiously darting back and forth between the Alaiad, his troops and the seer, the young acolyte carefully unrolled a small rug and spread it on the floor. Triklâ settled on it. Instead of facing Jikpryn, she placed her right shoulder to him.

Not good, he thought, *but it could be worse.*

If it had been her left shoulder he would have known exactly what the outcome of her reading would be, dire manifestation and most likely death and destruction for more than himself and his family. The right shoulder indicated Triklâ already sensed imminent events on the rise. Whether for good or ill, it was yet to be seen.

Now the small fur stretched across the rug between its edge and the seer's knees. The bright blue square was closest to him. A murmur filtered through the audience. Annoyed, Jikpryn raised a hand.

"Clear the hall," he commanded.

Guards promptly left their posts along the walls, moving toward the crowd of courtiers. Women hurriedly gathered up their skirts and hastened from the vaulted room, their escorts at their sides. Stragglers grumbled but no one dared trifle with the guards' sharp lances. It was the Alaiad's right to hear in private what the seer said, and his decision whether or not to proclaim the news. At Tolbôun's nod, the majority of the guards likewise withdrew.

Head bowed, mildly amused Triklâ watched through the screen provided by her hair. Unafraid of letting him see her reaction, she tipped her head briefly in Jikpryn's direction, before returning her attention to her task. One hand on the arm of his chair, Jikpryn leaned forward to better view the hide. At his left shoulder, his Advisor remained aloof. Down the hall, Hilcaz remained carefully out of earshot.

One gnarled hand swept the air above the fur. Blue was immediately before Jikpryn. To its left was green then yellow, and beyond that, red. This was not the background with which Jikpryn was accustomed. White centred all. A chill finger walked up his spine. He shook it off. His eyes fastened on the hand that dipped into the hide bag resting against Triklâ's right thigh. She cast the fragile orved bones, her movement so swift Jikpryn started in spite of himself. Behind him fabric rustled as his advisor likewise twitched. It was strangely comforting to know even Tolbôun feared something.

Bones scattered across the square. Most landed where they had at turn of the year: four in the blue, five in the red, three in the yellow and one in the green. This time, however, an extra bone appeared to have been tossed, and it intersected red and white. Again a chill raced across Jikpryn's frame. His gaze darted to the seer's face.

Like an orved about to drop on unsuspecting prey, she gazed across the room. Hands cupped at her breast, Triklâ rocked back and forth. Trapped in the Great Serpent's spell, she crooned in time to her movements. The high keening vibrated painfully against the fine bone behind Jikpryn's ears and he pressed his fingers against the flesh in search of relief.

Inexplicably, the noise went on and on. Infuriated, he lunged to his feet. "Enough. Explain the reading."

Age had half-crippled Triklâ's fingers. Knuckles were little more than misshapen lumps of flesh. Blue veins traced each tendon from finger base to wrist as her clawed fingers pointed to each square.

"It is time."

"Time for what?"

"His time."

Fear chewed at Jikpryn's innards. He stalked slowly across the dais to tower over the old woman. "Whose time?"

> "Black on black, they saw him,
> Half a ring of the Warrior's shield,
> Bearing the Blade of Hope
> And Star blood at his side."

As the first stanza of Dôzhik Koryn's prophecy rolled off Triklâ's lips, Jikpryn stepped back. His right foot caught the leg of the high seat and lost his balance.

He grabbed for support and almost missed the chair back. Even as he sought to recover, the seer continued.

> "Black on black, he will come
> And with him justice rides.
> Half a ring, half a rune,
> And Star blood at his side."

Now Triklâ rested a cold, unforgiving look on Tolbôun. His expression remained hard, but something unreadable flickered in the depths of his eyes. In the brief exchange, Jikpryn saw a side of his advisor that he knew he ought to have suspected existed but had failed to take into account. Before the Outsider glanced his way, Jikpryn redirected his attention to the seer.

Triklâ had risen. Her assistant had withdrawn to the entrance, rug and tools of the seer's trade clutched against him. Hands pressed against her chest, expression devoid of all emotion her voice rose as a triumphant anthem.

> "At year's end will come half a ring,
> Stars within, beside and behind.
> Sky demon above, night runner below,
> And half a rune borne before
> To guide the destinies of all."

Rocked once more by the power of the prophecy, Jikpryn dropped into the high seat. Unaware the seer was now almost to the exit, he struggled to grasp the complexity of the reading. Fingers curled about the intricately carved chair arms. He called to Triklâ. Shaken as he was, he somehow managed the correct response of a petitioner.

"Seer, give me a key, a clue so I might understand the meaning of this reading."

Swaying, the seer hummed for a minute. Then, eyes fixed on the point above Jikpryn's head where his family's banner hung, she breathed deeply. Her lips moved, but it was a male voice, deep and rich that resonated about the walls to shake the tapestries, stir the flames in the hearth and set the torches dancing.

"Find the one with the Great Serpent's eyes, but harm them not. Therein lies your key, Jikpryn of Wôbiny."

In the silence that gripped the hall, seer and acolyte slid through the exit. The Temple Guards closed protectively around them. Trapped by that final warning, Jikpryn was unprepared for the rapid departure. For several moments he stared, unseeing, his gaze fixed on a point beyond the hall's glazed windows. By the time he recovered, his trap had been sprung and his prey had escaped.

"Find her," Tolbôun yelled at Hilcaz. "Bring her…"

Caught back to his surroundings, Jikpryn raised a hand. On the verge of complying with the Outsider's directions, Hilcaz obediently froze. "No."

"Ser?"

Startled by that contradiction, the Outsider stared down at his lord. Jikpryn slowly rose, paced down the steps and went to stand before one window. He stared out at the watery view it granted of the courtyard. Already the Temple party was disappearing beneath the portcullis.

They make excellent time. Their strategic haste could not be construed so much a retreat as expediency. Aloud, he told his advisor, "I am not about to make an enemy of the Temple. Not now. Not with this hanging over us."

For once even Jikpryn was uncertain whether he had spoken in the Royal 'us', or if he was unconsciously including all Fimiahri. A sharp stab of pain lanced up the back of his neck, probed his temples. He rubbed them, unconscious of the action. The headaches were far too frequent of late. This time, however, he refused to alter his decision.

"Twice," he muttered, "Twice the same prophecy. This time with a key."

"Some key," Tolbôun sneered. "Serpent eyes. I've never seen an account anywhere of a Fimiahri with green eyes."

"Yet there must be one somewhere," Jikpryn mused.

Down the hall, one of the door guards shifted his weight. His armour inadvertently rattled, drawing his master's attention. Stiffly correct beneath Jikpryn's gaze, the guard locked his eyes on a point directly above the Alaiad's head. Hilcaz had turned to stare at the offender, but Jikpryn's next words caught him back to the pair at the end of the hall.

"Send word to all of our patrols," Jikpryn snapped. "Put them on alert. I want this green-eyed person, male or female, young or old, delivered to me. See to this personally, Captain. And ensure that there's no doubt concerning latitude when dealing with the acquisition of this person. They are not," he heavily emphasised his instructions, "to be harmed in any way. If the troops encounter a problem convincing the individual, and their guardians if the person is a child, then they are to detain them at their home or quarters and send a racing orved with message directly to me."

"Yes, ser."

Snapping a salute, Hilcaz slid from the hall. The moment the door closed behind him, the Outsider leaned forward and spoke softly in Jikpryn's ear.

"No doubt this will be a fool's mission, ser. A complete waste of time. You know the Temple's angry because you don't pay tribute, as your predecessors did. They're trying to stir up unrest among the people, nothing more. Best, perhaps, to simply eliminate the source."

Hand jerking up, Jikpryn silenced Tolbôun. "That is not a course of action I shall even consider pursuing until I have definitive proof they are acting against me, Tol. In all of our history there has only been one recorded incident of anyone going against the Temple. After that, even when they fell from favour and were openly ridiculed in the streets, all subsequent Alaiad refrained from overtly or covertly attacking them. Before you make any further suggestions along that vein, I suggest you read the accounts in the chronicles."

Disgruntled, Tolbôun protested, "But, ser."

"Enough, Tol." Jikpryn raised his voice, thrust himself from his chair and stepped down. "I'm not about to start a religious uprising on top of everything else. The reading's been cast...twice. It's up to us to solve it."

For a brief moment, the horrors of war compounded by religious fanatics swept away all other consideration. Jikpryn gazed, unseeing, down the length of the hall. Pain speared his temples. He winced and waited for the moment to pass. Between one breath and the next, it faded. As his vision refocused, he discovered Hilcaz once more in the hall.

"Captain Hilcaz." At his lord's gesture, Hilcaz approached. "Summon my guard and assemble the rynada. We ride for Pûdornâ."

"Now?" At Tolbôun's inadvertent interruption, Jikpryn slowly turned. For all his correctness, there was no doubting Hilcaz's interest. For a long moment, Jikpryn held his advisor's gaze then turned back to the Captain of his personal guard.

"Captain."

"Ser."

Fist thumping the left side of his breastplate, Hilcaz acknowledged the command. He spun on heel and marched smartly from the hall. Irritated, Jikpryn returned to his seat. With a nod, he indicated the courtiers should be allowed to return to the assembly area. The great doors swung wide and those who had elected to wait on their Alaiad's pleasure flowed back into the hall. Women paused before him, crossed their arms over their breasts, heads inclined, before drawing aside. At their sides, their escorts pressed right hand to left breast and likewise inclined their heads before accompanying them back into the press of bodies.

A quick inspection revealed the crowd was thinner. Those who had already withdrawn were of lesser nobility, hangers-on with aspirations of attracting favourable attention in what remained of the day. Once the last courtier had made their obeisance, Jikpryn rose. The polite rumble of conversation promptly died.

"We shall be withdrawing," he informed them. "This oppressive heat irritates us and we are minded to close court until the fall. A cooler clime beckons us."

Their faces mirrored his treacherous thoughts, hinting they believed the seer's visit was driving him from Iryô. Goaded by their thinly veiled mockery, Jikpryn remained determined to withdraw to Wôbiny with his family. Born and raised in the north, close to the great ice barrier, he had scant liking or tolerance for the oppressive summer heat in Deccöt. With a flick of a finger to his advisor, Jikpryn descended the three low steps from the high seat and headed for his private exit.

As always, his son met him at the top of the stairs to the Alaiad's private apartments. A beautiful child with dark hair and equally dark eyes, Larnzan bounced from one foot to the other, hands up-stretched as he implored his father to pick him up. An otherwise healthy child, at four years old, he could utter no more than two distinguishable words at any given time. Generally, Larnzan mouthed gibberish, words that were normal speech apparently to his ears. Jikpryn swept his son off the floor and briefly held him high in the air.

"How's my boy?"

"Dada."

Jikpryn tilted Larnzan from side to side while his son spread his arms, pretending he was an orved in flight. "Show me what you've done today."

"Flith shratter," Larnzan cheerfully proclaimed, and struggled to be put down.

Once replaced on the floor he dragged his father to the desk by the window. There he proudly displayed a charcoal drawing. Momentarily bewildered by the mass of squiggles and lines Jikpryn turned the work of art this way and that. Suddenly the subject focused: Hafrön. It was all he could do to smile at his son, and set the drawing down rather than ball it up and throw it out the nearest window as instinct commanded.

How Larnzan could possibly have known what the bedevilled Star Given sword looked like was beyond Jikpryn, but he intended to find out who had been telling his son stories about Hafrön. There was no doubt in his mind that the sword was directly responsible for his son's mental condition.

It's your fault, not the sword's, his conscience pricked him. *If you had not been so determined to produce a child and attempted to force the sword to acknowledge him heir...*

He shook off the betraying thoughts, turned back to his son. "That's very good."

Larnzan grinned at his father. "Yours."

Determined not to permit his adverse emotions to take control, Jikpryn accepted the parchment, carefully rolling it up and sticking it in his belt. All the while, he was acutely conscious of Tolbôun waiting at the entrance to the nursery. Jikpryn addressed the nurse.

"Dress him warmly and see he has sufficient clothing for a long journey. We ride for Pûdornâ this afternoon. I would have him with me."

"Ser," the woman protested, "the warmth here is good for him. And he's so young to undertake such a perilous journey."

"Do as you're told, woman," Tolbôun snapped.

One hand lifted, Jikpryn silenced his advisor. "Tol, see to our fighting tail. We travel in comfort this trip: baggage wagon, plenty of food and my pavilion. Also, I would have the men properly billeted this time."

"A slow progress," Tolbôun observed.

"Yes," Jikpryn acknowledged. He waited until the Outsider had left before turning back to the nurse. "We want him with us. If we leave him behind, we suspect he would not be long for this world."

"Ser!"

Shocked by his brutal frankness, the nurse continued to hover while he hugged Larnzan once more and departed. Jikpryn professed no illusions about the safety of his son in his absence. His child was malleable and amenable by nature, fair game for court machinations. He was under no illusions in that, and had no intention of leaving such temptation in the path of plotters who, undoubtedly, would be only too eager to take advantage of such an opportunity.

They set out immediately after the midday meal. With Larnzan mounted on an old mare, riding at his side, Jikpryn took the road down into Iryô proper. Ahead of them rode five soldiers, one bearing the royal standard. On sky blue cloth, the rune of the Alaiad had been picked out in gold thread, commanding the centre of the banner. Mauve trimmed the square, brilliant flashes of colour on the insipid breeze. Sullen, the banner refused to do more than flutter, its leading edge teasing the viewer with suggestions of its magnificence. Directly behind Jikpryn rode his advisor. Tolbôun, by tradition, accompanied them for one day's ride out from the capitol. Then he would fall back to the fortress where he would sit as adjudicator until Jikpryn's return.

Along the route, Jikpryn observed his land. While his son chattered away, sometimes intelligently but more often than not speaking gibberish, he inspected his surroundings. Sun-scorched fields exhibited a straggling of miserly crops this year. Most growth was so stunted he doubted they would produce a crop. Children and the elderly hauled water constantly throughout the late afternoon, struggling to keep the new growth's thirst slaked. Due to the severe winter just past, many of the trees that normally provided some shade had been stripped or, in some instances, removed entirely.

Not a good sign, he mused. *I'll have to see about having those replaced. We need them.*

Pain. Fire behind his eyes. He swayed slightly in the saddle, clutched a handful of mane and managed to retain his seat. When he glanced around him, no one appeared to have noticed his momentary aberration. Thankful for small mercies, Jikpryn took several deep breaths until the pain subsided.

"Dadda?"

A small hand plucked at his tunic sleeve. He glanced down, grateful for the distraction Larnzan provided. The journey ahead would be long and he looked forward to the evening break.

CHAPTER 13

▼

Nichole

Early evening, late fall and dusk was giving way to darkness, the encroaching gloom was punctuated by the measured beat of two weary rynada making their way along the road. On either side of them, frost had hardened the ground to iron rigidity. Such crops as were not yet harvested or had been abandoned were wilting in the chill. Overhead clouds scudded in from the sea, colliding with the towering Rashordi Mountains. The wind bit through the riders' clothes and they shivered. Ahead, a sign at a fork in the road advertised lodging. The pair turned aside.

When they finally drew rein outside an inn well known to their people they were at the point where Wôbiny, Deccöt and Nûhykar provinces met. The region was hotly contested; a curious fact, given that there was little industry or large settlements to attract anyone save the brave, lost or outlawed. The riders dismounted. The shorter paused, leaning into the rynad.

"Are you all right, Nikki?"

"I'll be fine, Harry," she assured him. "I just need something hot in me and somewhere to sit, preferably on something that isn't moving."

"A comfortable bed wouldn't hurt either," he muttered. To himself, he groused, *Why did they insist upon sending her back here, particularly when she's so close to having the child? But be it farthest from me to question their reasons.*

Even though his musing was clear to her, Nichole ignored it. "Will you see to the animals while I get us something to warm ourselves?"

"Never mind about me, Nikki. I'll stay with the animals. You grab a quick bite and get back out here. We still have some distance to go tonight before we set camp."

At Harold Thompson's direction, Nichole sighed. She pushed away from her mount and walked heavily into the inn. Just inside the door, she paused to allow her eyes to adjust. Then she approached the counter.

Voice gruff, the innkeeper glanced over his shoulder at the gust of cold air. Setting aside the pot he had been rubbing dry, he greeted her, "Welcome to the Plucky Rakkïal. I'm Dyrlon. What'll be your pleasure?"

"A pot of warm milk," Nichole requested, "lightly laced with ale, please."

She felt his surprise. Saw it mirrored in his eyes as her voice informed him of her gender. As she shifted her weight, her cloak opened, revealing her bulging belly. He hurried down the length of the counter, one hand tugging a wisp of greying hair.

"Your pardon, lady. You wished?"

Hip supporting her weight against the counter front, Nichole pushed back her hood. His eyes narrowed now as he took in her shoulder-length hair that, even though she had been growing it out for months, was still shorter than any Fimiahri woman wore it. A deep green cloak with sleeves and deep pockets surmounted warm trousers, tunic and vest of matching russet-brown. For additional warmth, her shirt was woven from tïlkrïn winter undercoat in its natural neutral off-white hue. Hide boots, calf-high, provided sturdy, warm, waterproof coverings for her feet.

Pregnancy had instilled in Nichole more patience than she had previously possessed in her short life. Tone mild, she repeated her request. "Warmed milk with a touch of ale, please."

"Of course, my lady. There's soup on the kitchen hearth."

She shook her head. Her bearing and clothes, which were a cut above what he was accustomed to seeing, plus the manner in which she spoke, left him speculating on what a lady of obvious breeding was doing out alone in this region at this time of year. Not about to betray the presence of her partner outside, Nichole watched the innkeeper going about his chores. To her delight, he set her request to warm over coals rather than using a poker to heat the mixture.

"Please, lady." He gestured. "There's a free table close by the fire."

"Have you indoor facilities?"

With a half-wink, Dyrlon jerked his head toward the rear of the common room. Nichole made use of the tiny water closet that was, to her surprise, in nearly pristine condition given the location of the inn. Afterwards, as she settled herself by the fire, she was conscious of the polite sidelong glances that were cast in her direction by the locals at the rear of the taproom. Grateful of the opportunity to sit in a chair after riding all day, she experienced a stab of guilt.

I hope Harry's taken the ryanda into the stable so he's out of the wind at least. This may take a while.

Again the innkeeper's conscientiousness surprised her. When he returned, he brought not only the milk but also included a mug of soup with a chunk of bread as well. Not about to look a gift horse in the mouth, Nichole took a sip of the soup.

"This is good," she commended him. "Thank you."

"My lady," he said, bending to speak in her ear. "It's not wise for someone such as you to travel the roads alone in these times. Even in your condition, you won't be safe from certain types."

A small hand lifted to quiet him. "It can't be helped. There are things that prevented my kin making this journey with me. Besides, I've only a short way to go now. And, believe me, I am amply protected."

"Still…"

Again, Nichole silenced him with a movement of her fingers. With a shake of his head, he withdrew, her payment in hand. Once back behind the counter, Dyrlon realised she had given more than the meal was worth. Their eyes met across the room and she shook her head. He nodded his thanks.

Conscious of time slipping away, and of her companion waiting in the cold night, Nichole did her best to finish her small meal quickly. Conversations from the small knot of local customers washed over her. The tavern door slammed open, startling the patrons. A massive gust of frigid air swept the room and set the flames in the hearth leaping high. Sparks washed up the chimney. Loud, coarse voices and laughter accompanied the heavy thud of boots that shook the building as five men pushed up to the counter.

*   *   *   *

Dyrlon

"Drinks, innkeeper, for me and my men."

With forced humour, Dyrlon smiled and measured out ale for his new customers. All wore the rough attire of hunters. No cloaks, but rather heavy hide vests with lace-on sleeves that afforded them freedom of movement and some degree of warmth. Heavy, weatherproof, fur-lined trousers encased their legs and were lashed down the lower calf, sealing the boot tops. They jostled congenially, exchanging ribald remarks on the weather, road conditions and lack of game. When their drinks arrived, two gulped the contents of their tankards and demanded more. But one, the leader of the quintet by the actions of the other four, sipped and commenced a study of the room.

"And what bring you to my door this chill night?" Determined to keep their attention on his side of the common room and away from his special guest, Dyrlon sought to strike up conversation.

"Patrols," spat back the leader of the group. "The Usurper's got everyone running around like headless rakkïal."

"Oh?"

Conversation died. Movement stilled until only the crackle of ravenous flames biting at logs in the hearth broke the quiet. The innkeeper leaned on his elbows. News was thin in the wilds, particularly since Jikpryn's murderous incursion. Thus, Dyrlon's interest was not feigned.

"Yeah." With a sniff, the leader took another sip of his second tankard of ale, aware of his audience and clearly enjoying the attention. "Would you believe he ordered that crazy seer back for an explanation?"

"Did he now?"

Well-versed in keeping conversation flowing, Dyrlon topped up the mugs of ale, and then turned his attention to making a show of wiping the counter top. Across the room, his special guest had drawn her cloak about her and was making quick work of the small meal. For all her attire was commonplace enough, Dylon was positive she was Hynarkin. Her speech betrayed her. That made her a ready target for his present customers. Fortunately, all he had to do was keep these new customers preoccupied and she would be able to safely slip away.

"You know news is slow this year. 'Sides," the man's lewd tone inferred more than anyone present liked as he continued, "we've been tied up with business."

Coarse laughter and jostling amongst the group followed. At the upper end of the common room, one of the older men called back, "So what did she tell him?"

"Bet no one knows," countered another local. "You know how Pryni likes his secrets."

The slur against the Usurper Alaiad was not lost on the occupants of the common room, but no one objected. Rather, the leader of the group at the counter partially raised his tankard in the direction of the locals and took another slurp. After wiping the back of his hand across his mouth, he continued.

"Word slips out, my friend. Anyway, to all accounts it was much of the same."

"That black on black stuff," inserted one of his companions.

"I've been trapping all winter," said a loner closer to the middle of the room. "Who made the casting and what was said?"

"Old Triklâ was the one that originally stirred things up at the turn of last year," said Dyrlon. He quickly rattled off the words that were on almost everyone's lips since the past spring.

Intrigued, the trapper rested an elbow on a knee and stared at the group near the door. "So what did she tell him it meant?"

The group's leader shook his head. "She didn't. Just mouthed more of that nonsense."

The innkeeper prodded the man. "Which was?"

Now the group's leader turned to his companions. "What was it? Something like: at year's end will come half a ring, stars within beside and behind, sky demon above, night runner below, and half a rune borne before, guiding the destinies of all."

Heads nodded all round. The trapper frowned. "Strange."

"Yeah. And then," the leader thumped his almost empty tankard on the counter, slopping some of the contents over the rim, "she tells him to look for someone with the Great Serpent's eyes."

Someone among the locals snorted. "Ridiculous. When has there ever been anyone with green eyes?"

"Yeah, well, I'm just telling it like I heard it."

Her meal finished, the Hynarkin woman quietly rose. Hood up, she drew on her riding gloves and headed for the door. Unfortunately, her actions caught the group's attention, and although Dyrlon had done his best to keep them diverted, he belatedly realised they had merely been biding their time. The leader moved quickly to intercept her, interposing his burly frame between the woman and the exit.

"Well, well, what have we here? A little bit of something special all on its own?"

He reached for her arm but she eluded him with a nearly invisible shift of her weight. Unaware her actions had slid her from his grasp, the leader grabbed for her. This time, she twisted so that his hand clearly missed her shoulder. A shrug of her shoulders freed her right side, and revealed the swollen belly that strained trousers and tunic. Startled and concerned, the innkeeper reached beneath the counter for his short sword, but halted when a hunting knife appeared in the hand of another of the group.

"I wouldn't," Dyrlon was warned as the other leaned across the counter, blade to his throat.

Now the leader of the group bowed, his actions mocking the woman. "Your pardon, lady. Seems I was mistaken, lads. She is travelling in company."

Raucous laughter stung the ears of those present. Up the room, a young man tried to get to his feet but his friends restrained him. The leader took a step towards the woman and halted as a short sword appeared in her hand. The manner in which she drew and handled it, held it poised in readiness for battle, startled everyone.

"So," the leader hissed, "the she-blïntor has teeth."

Head slightly down, posture defensive, the Hynarkin woman responded, "Hynarkin women may not often travel openly among the Fimiahri. But when we do, we go armed. And are prepared to die for our honour."

Her words, spoken softly, carried steel and those up the end of the common room stirred. From the corner of his eye, Dyrlon caught movement in the shadows. A burly man appeared, sliding down the room and, while the attention of the group at the counter was fixed on the impending duel, he effectively disarmed the man with the knife, freeing the innkeeper. After a moment's silent exchange, the trapper withdrew and rejoined his comrades who had edged towards the altercation. The innkeeper nodded to the person who had helped him.

"My thanks, Gurran."

"Not at all, Lon," the weapons' merchant replied. "I dislike uneven odds."

The Hynarkin woman brought her attention fully to bear on the imminent duel and squared off against the leader of the band. Blade moving in tight circles, she tested him, moving left, then right. Her opponent darted in. His men shouted as she slid aside again. The point of her weapon left a scarlet trail down their leader's left cheek.

"First blood to the Hynarkin wench," shouted an old man at the back of the room.

"Five talnots on the woman," tendered Gurran.

"Five on the hunter," countered someone else.

"You'll lose that," replied Gurran.

"Everyone knows you're a Hynarkin lover, Gurran."

"Perhaps. But I know a skilled swordsman when I see one," shot back Gurran.

Meanwhile, the hunter had realised he had bitten off a trifle more than he could chew. Eyes darting about the room, he sought assistance from his men or someone else. Now the Hynarkin woman circled him, looking for an opening. To everyone present it was obvious she simply wanted the duel over with so she could leave. Desperate, the hunter lunged again. This time she dropped to the floor, her speed and dexterity wholly at odds with her condition. His sword cut the air inches above her head. She spun on one heel and came back up so quickly those about her gasped. Using his arm like a ladder, she speared her opponent's upper biceps. Curses hot on his lips, the hunter lost his weapon.

The Hynarkin woman must have seen one of his henchmen go for a knife because she lunged, cracking the man across the back of his wrist and hand with the flat of her blade. Arm numb from hand to elbow, the second hunter jerked back, slamming into the counter. The remainder of the group eyed her, wary, defensive. Instead of attempting to tackle them, she calmly wiped off her blade with the innkeeper's rag before backing towards the door.

With a flourish of his blade in her direction as she left, Gurran directed his next words at the remaining occupants of the room. "When will you lot ever learn there's good reason for the axiom: Beware the Hynarkin?"

"There's definitely far more to them than anyone ever suspected," Dyrlon observed.

Gradually a degree of normality returned to the common room in the wake of the woman's departure. It was some time before Gurran and the innkeeper realised the hunters had also left, not in a group but singly. That they planned to pursue the Hynarkin woman to exact vengeance was obvious.

Concerned, the innkeeper spoke to the weapons' merchant. "Gurran, perhaps you ought to trail them. She may need help."

"Lon," Gurran replied, "I've lived this long plying my trade because I mind my own business. Besides," he put his feet up on a nearby stool and settled further back on his chair with his mug of ale, "I rather suspect they won't find her."

"I hope you're right." Under his breath, Dyrlon muttered, "Eyes of the Great Serpent."

Suddenly unable to get comfortable, Gurran shifted his weight repeatedly. The brief seconds in which his eyes had met those of the Hynarkin woman had left him shaken far more than he would openly admit. Deep inside, he knew he had brushed prophecy.

CHAPTER 14

▼

Nichole

Tied up outside of the inn, Nichole discovered five rynada standing at the railing, tails clamped tight against their hindquarters. Rough-groomed, heads bowed, eyes half-shut, they huddled together in a vain effort to ward off the cold. Temptation suggested she loose them from the railing, but given the weather, it was doubtful the animals would go far enough for it to buy additional time.

Besides, she told herself, *you'll just piss them off more once they come out, and that'll only make matters worse.*

There was no sign of her companion. She made her way across the frozen ruts to the stable, treading carefully, fearful of twisting an ankle. Before she quite reached the building, the door opened and Harry came out leading their animals.

"Everything all right?"

"No. Let's get out of here."

Nichole took her mount's reins. He helped her step up into the saddle then flung himself onto his mount and led off down the road at an extended walk. There was no trotting or running with Nichole in her present condition. She kept an eye on him, but strained for any sound of pursuit.

"What happened?"

"It was that bunch that came in behind me."

"Ah. Rather thought they looked like trouble. Do you think they'll follow you?"

"Pretty sure, I'm afraid."

"Okay. It's not your fault. But if that's the case, we can't stick to the road."

Taking their position from the stars, Harry directed her off the beaten path into the woods. Although the Warrior had not yet risen, all three of the Maidens were up. By their light, they picked out a narrow track that took them roughly in the direction they wanted to go. Decades of decaying leaves and needles muffled their rynada's hooves. No sooner were they under cover than they heard several hard-ridden rynada racing up the road they had just vacated. Nichole and Harry drew rein, waiting while the riders swept past in the darkness. Then they pressed on.

At a seep, they paused to break the ice rimming the pool. They refilled their water flasks while their mounts slackened their thirsts. Again they moved on. Weary beyond words, Nichole swayed in the saddle. At length, Harry decided they had put sufficient distance between them and her pursuers to make a cold camp.

Rolled in her blankets and propped against a tree, Nichole stared up through denuded branches. Sight of the Warrior moon edging up the sky from behind the mountains brought back memories of a happier time.

"Dôzhik Koryn," she murmured.

Harry glanced at her before looking up at the moon. The entire colony was familiar with the havoc the 'running' had wreaked upon the Fimiahri, although the majority of the Wanderers had been unaffected. Only those born with native blood in their genes had suffered any affects. Now there was no third ring though, and he could only speculate at what had dragged that reference from her. Rynada settled, he took the first watch. Some time later, Nichole awoke to a hand over her mouth. Once certain she was awake, Harry gestured. But Nichole had already heard the snap of a dry twig. She rose. True to his training, Harry had already prepared their mounts. Something thudded close by. An oath split the air and Nichole hurriedly grabbed her mare's nostrils as her rynad started at the sound.

"Idiot," a gruff voice snarled, "With all the noise you're making, she'll hear us."

"She's probably long gone. By all the Rashordi demons, why do you want to hunt down that trader bitch?"

"She owes me."

There was no doubting the identity of the individuals in the darkness. In silent accord, Nichole and Harry began working their way quietly through the woods, heading east and south.

"I don't like this," continued the objector. "Those Hynarkin never used to carry swords. And now their women fight like seasoned campaigners, even when they're ready to drop their young."

"Shut your mouth," the leader growled back.

Their voices hushed, the hunters continued to pick their way through the underbrush. As the distance between them and their pursuers increased, Harry gestured. With a sigh of relief, Nichole clambered back onto her mare. They continued on, moving faster now along the track, certain the hunters would find their route all too soon. A branch lay across the path. Unable to see it in time, Harry swore as it snapped loudly under his rynad's hooves. The noise reverberated through the otherwise still night. He reined in.

"Take to the woods, Nikki. Keep going. You know the way. I'll try to draw them off."

"But…"

"They don't appear to know about me, so I should be able to make them think I'm you for a short time, at least. Make the best time you can, but be careful."

"Harry, if they overtake you they won't be kind."

"I'll do my best to give them the slip before that happens," he assured her.

Still uncertain Nichole hovered, but Harry raced back up the track they had been following. He cut into the forest at the bend. With a yank on the reins, Nichole urged her mare into the forest on the opposite side of the track. There she waited. Within seconds the hunters appeared, riding hard. They swerved into the woods after her companion. The noise Harry's mount made proved more than sufficient to draw them away. Nichole checked the position of the stars and realised they were off-course.

"More south," she told her rynad.

That meant cutting across the track so that she was on the same side as the hunters and Harry. Unfortunately, to continue in the direction Harry wanted her to take meant adding another day to her trip and she was so very tired.

"Going to have to risk it," she said to the mare.

Crossing the road, they angled off through the trees, moving south. Even though Harry had headed almost directly west, there were no guarantees that he might not alter direction back her way.

"Then again," Nichole mused, "it's more likely he'll attempt to double back the way we came and head for the colony."

As the night progressed, a breeze picked its way through the forest, tugging at her clothes and ruffling her rynad's mane. Still they moved forward. Dawn was not far off and Nichole feared being caught in the open, alone, at daybreak. Suddenly a rise of land threw a barrier across her path. After due consideration, she guided the mare around the base of the hill and entered the cut in the land.

Gravel crunched beneath the rynad's hooves as it encountered a dried up seep in the base of the ravine. Fearful, Nichole drew rein.

"This was a mistake," she told herself.

Too late to correct the error, she drew the mare hard against the side of the undercut. She slid from the saddle and stood at the rynad's head. From deep within the shadows she listened intently. Above, something moved then stopped. Again she heard what she was certain was the rustle of branches being carefully displaced then returned to their position. Breathless, Nichole waited. Her heart thudded so loudly she was positive it would announce her presence to the entire world.

"Forget it," someone hissed from atop the rocks. "We've lost her."

"Probably wasn't her at all," grumbled another voice. "I've had enough. I'm going back to the inn and a warm bed. Coming?"

Whatever the answer was, before long Nichole heard rynada departing. Minutes later a third followed. Caution and a suggestion of danger held her fast. Without warning a rock whizzed past her, clattering off a nearby boulder, and splattering her and her mount with stone splinters. Her mare flung up its head, but Nichole expertly twirled her cloak over its head and pinched its nostrils before it could betray their presence. Another rock, fist-size, thudded down almost on top of them. Three more landed a short distance up the defile. Two more shattered the darkness behind her. At each impact, she fought to keep her mare still. At length, a curse growled down at her. Cloth rustled against rock and foliage as someone moved away.

Still Nichole held fast, counting twice to a hundred until the last vestige of light from the racing moons vanished from the sky. Fog rose from the ground. In the grey clammy pre-dawn, she mounted and pressed on. Damp ate at her bones, compounded by the cold of late fall. She shivered and hunched deeper into her cloak in a vain attempt to keep warm. Every step her rynad took jarred her, sending pain through her weary limbs.

As yet another shiver gripped her she realised she was going into labour. The strain of the past few hours had proved too much, and she was still miles from help. Frightened, but aware there was no other recourse except to keep going, she counted the time between contractions and concentrated on breathing. Light split the sky as the sun crept up the horizon. Intervals between contractions grew shorter. Then the pain ceased altogether. At that, Nichole took a chance and dismounted at the top of a rise in an effort to get her bearings.

By presenting a readily visible target she risked everything, yet she felt her decision was justified. Beyond two ridges rose the mountains. To her left one peak resembled a jumbled mass. Recognising the remains of the main base destroyed almost two years earlier, she slipped back onto her rynad and set off once more.

She breathed a tiny prayer, "Dear God, let Harry have made it to safety."

No less tired than she was, her mount stumbled repeatedly and Nichole knew she would get no speed out of it. Instead, she let it pick its own pace, directing it along the simplest paths. They crossed a small spring. On the far side her rynad stumbled on the rime-edged rocks, throwing her forward. She slammed into the saddletree, felt a responding sharp pang through her lower stomach and into the tops of her thighs. In its wake a dull gnawing ache gripped her spine.

"No, no," she prayed, "Not here."

As her labour pains grew closer together she clung to the saddletree. Ears singing, thoughts muddled, she endured. Evening drew on but there was no cessation in her travail. A slope presented an obstacle. Unable to hold the rynad to a walk, Nichole grunted as her mount broke into a trot down the hill. They burst from the trees, crossed frozen ground and the stubble of a harvested field, and drew up outside a hold.

A hold?

The significance of the moment helped her to focus mentally as well as visually. They were on the wrong side of a fence. Beyond the railings stretched a pasture. Several dray rynada were lined up at the railing facing the main building. Four lighter saddle animals were interspersed with them. Her subconscious informed her this was important but it was so difficult to think clearly. Another contraction gripped her. She waited for it to ease before hauling on the reins and directing the mare around the pasture, onto the lane up to the cabin.

When the mare halted alongside the pack animals, Nichole slid more than stepped down from the saddle. She called for help. Nearby someone whistled a familiar series of notes. Mouth dry, it took several attempts before she was able to produce sufficient saliva to wet her lips and reply. Then she leaned against her mount, waiting for assistance.

The cabin door opened. "Who's there? Rin?"

"No," Nichole croaked back. "Marrek. Mark, please. It's me."

"Who…" He descended one step and froze as light spilled past him to illuminate her. "Great Serpent! Nichole!"

CHAPTER 15

▼

Hafrin

This fall they were later than usual returning from their expedition. Of course this was the first year since Hafrin had ridden with Marrek that Iryô had been included in their itinerary. In their single day at the capitol…

My capitol, he silently amended.

In that one day he had learned a great deal concerning trade, bartering and the vagaries of the business. Marrek seemed inordinately pleased with his foster son's abilities and had spent a great deal of the day resting in the shade, letting Hafrin handle the business. If those of Iryô had envisioned an easier time of it dealing with the son rather than the father they were sorely mistaken.

His trading acuman was equally sharp and, with his ability to sense emotions, he knew precisely when to hold his ground on a prescribed cost for an item. Like Marrek, Hafrin was politely evasive. He managed to refrain from being drawn into political gossip and made a suitable impression on everyone he encountered. Keen eyes and a sharp wit had been carefully developed and honed over the years riding the routes along the Rashordi foothills. Nor did he find the coloured lenses that transformed his blue eyes to brown a nuisance.

On departing the city they had taken their time, riding at a leisurely pace north and west. Late the second day they swung past the Demons Gathering. Without speaking, Marrek selected their campsite. Something about the area constantly disturbed his memory as he went about the evening chores.

In the past year he had discovered many of his childhood prejudices had faded, something he could trace back to the day he and Marrek had rescued two Wôbiny soldiers from a raging river. He had broken his arm that day. It still ached when the weather was cold and damp, something Marrek had informed him he would have to accept as part and parcel of such injuries.

Unaccountably weary, Hafrin had to force himself not to eavesdrop on his foster father's thoughts any more than he could help. But Marrek's rambling thoughts rose and fell like a babbling brook on the periphery of his extra senses.

E.S.P., he recalled the abbreviation. He rolled the words about his mind in an effort to tune out Marrek's thoughts. *Extrasensory perception.*

Hands paused in releasing the saddle cinch on his grey gelding, Shalinô. He never rode his black stallion, Bïzhan Koryn, on the trade routes. His stallion drew far too much attention from the local villagers near where Marrek had his wintering home. Instead, he rode Shalinô. His orved, however, seldom left his company for any length of time. At this moment she was perched on a small tree nearby.

Marrek's next thought was as clear as if he had spoken out loud. *What was I thinking? Of course, it was near here twenty years ago. So long.*

Quit eavesdropping. At times like these Nichole's gentle admonishments were ever present in Hafrin's thoughts. Nor could he bring himself to push away the memory. *Nikki.*

As if she had read his thoughts, Vrala Harz cocked her head, mantled her neck and head feathers at him and then resettled. Determined not to be distracted further, Hafrin hurried to finish stripping the animals of their burdens. Behind him, Marrek was laying out their blankets beneath a low tarpaulin so they would sleep dry if not altogether warm. The tiny fire he had lit would be banked to coals before they slept. That way if they needed to vacate the area in a hurry they need not concern themselves with the chance of a forest fire erupting in the wake of their departure.

Damp gnawed at Hafrin, sending a shiver up his spine. Patches of fog were congealing in transparent pools, shrouding trees and shrubs. It appeared to steam up through the branches. Clouds scudded overhead, moving inland. By the time Hafrin had completed his chores the three rynada were relaxing, hip-shot at their tether line. Head beneath her wing, Vrala slept.

"All done?" Marrek asked him as Hafrin joined him at the fire.

"Yes."

"Here. Eat." His foster father passed him a plate of food and a mug of mulled ale. "Then get some sleep. I want to get an early start tomorrow."

"Thanks."

"How's the arm?"

"Aching…as usual," Hafrin admitted. He rotated his shoulder and settled on a nearby stone.

Marrek nodded. They ate quickly, cleaned their dishes and belt knives and repacked all the extraneous items. In the past there had been far too many departures on the spur of the moment. Such moves had, in the past few years, been spurred as much by roving bands of disgruntled soldiers brought in from Wôbiny by Hafrin's uncle, as they had by lawless individuals looking for an easy mark. It made for uneasy travelling. Much as Marrek would have liked to leave the rynada saddled, he seldom did so.

"Better," he had once told Hafrin, "that the animals are well rested and ready for a long hard ride than prepared for a rapid departure and tired from not being properly cared for. Saddles and trade goods can always be replaced."

Ensconced beneath his blankets, feet to the fire, his boots within easy reach, Hafrin stared out into the darkness and considered everything he had learned over his twenty short years. Sometime soon, he knew, Marrek's people would begin forming an army, one that brought Fimiahri and Hynarkin…Star blood, Hafrin reminded himself…together against an enemy far more dangerous than the threat presented by his uncle, Jikpryn. At his side, he heard Marrek's breathing slow, become measured.

Wish I could sleep, he silently groused.

But sleep remained elusive. Instead, a strange restlessness invaded him. He rolled on his side and closed his eyes. Drawing upon something Piltar had taught him during one of his brief visits, Hafrin struggled to slip into a meditative state and failed. Again he shifted, rolling onto his other side. But the cold, hard ground refused to let him drift off. Rather than risk waking Marrek, Hafrin crept from his blankets and went out to the picket line.

At his approach the rynada snuffled. Shalinô twitched an ear in his direction. Something goaded Hafrin, stealing his resistance to fight off the compulsion, and fogging his thoughts. As if in a dream he picked up his saddle and reins and began tacking out his mount. Annoyed at being disturbed, Shalinô repeatedly stomped his off rear hoof throughout the process. Stirred from her sleep, Vrala Harz twisted her head from side to side. Releasing his mount from the picket line, Hafrin led Shalinô into the forest. Vrala took to the air. She coasted down the night breeze to settle on his shoulder.

Clad in dark blue, Hafrin soon merged with the night. Mist pooled and swirled about them, making them phantoms in a surreal world. Before long Hafrin had put sufficient distance between him and the camp to step into the saddle. Something compelled him onward. It drew him on a winding course that brought him to the edge of the Demon's Gathering. Driven on, he followed the edge of the awesome cleft until he encountered an animal track. He took it over the lip. Haunches drawn beneath him, Shalinô slithered down the crumbling cliffside.

Once in the bottom Hafrin turned northwest. Towering cliffs vanished against the night sky high above so that it was impossible to make out where the rims were. And like a gaping gullet the ravine yawned wider and wider, ingesting them as it broadened and deepened.

On his shoulder, Vrala mantled and hissed repeatedly, but her vocalisation failed to penetrate the mist now clouding Hafrin's mind as surely as the fog thickened to shroud the landscape. Their surroundings were indistinct. Ghostly shapes emerged and faded back into the fog as they moved on.

Eventually the fog pooled in the lowest depressions, forming pockets that made footing treacherous. Shalinô's pace slowed. Moonlight pierced the darkness, providing them some semblance of illumination. His gelding's ears pricked sharply forward until their tips aligned with the spiral horns. One ear swivelled toward Hafrin. He let his rynad have its head and it broke into an easy trot.

Again their route dipped before it levelled. Massive boulders dotted the bottom of the draw. Hafrin could hear the soughing of the wind in the forest high above. Somewhere a dislodged pebble bounded down the cliff face, clattering away into the dying night. Now the mist dissipated, ripped asunder by a rising breeze. The moons raced away the remainder of the night. Daylight gradually crept upon them. Still Shalinô pressed on, as though he was as compelled as his rider was to penetrate the length of the gorge.

Without warning Shalinô staggered, worn out. Hafrin quickly reined in. Thoughts momentarily clearing, he dismounted and checked his mount. Finding a small stone caught in one cloven hoof, he worked it loose. Vrala hopped from his shoulder to the saddletree to watch him. When he straightened she 'creeled' and took to the air.

With a start, Hafrin became wholly cognisant of his surroundings. A high-pitched scream announced the orved's dive. Wings caught back, she dove on an unsuspecting lizard and soared aloft once more, its corpse still twitching in her clenched talons. Gazing around him, Hafrin asked, "Where am I?"

But no one answered his inquiry. The mist of the previous night was gone, and a brief investigation of his surroundings told him what he needed to know.

"The Gathering. What are we doing here? Where's Marrek?"

He turned back to Shalinô. When he attempted to remount, however, his rynad tugged him onward, refusing to halt even when he dragged repeatedly on its reins.

"Shalinô, stop."

Hafrin dug in his heels and, by dint of both mental and physical exertion, finally succeeded in stopping the gelding. Nearby three large boulders provided convenient shelter against weather and intrusion. He led Shalinô into the tiny hollow, stripped off the gear and set the picket pin as deep in the ground as the rocky soil would permit. Then, wrapped in his cloak, he settled to sleep. His last conscious thought was for his orved, now hunched in the shadows on a ledge part way up the cliff behind him. Vrala Harz ripped at her catch with razor beak and talons.

Sometime later, urgent pecking brought Hafrin instantly awake. Nearby Shalinô was tossing his head and pawing in the dirt. A short distance across the floor of the rift stood two male blïntor. Neck bristles twitched as they studied him through tiny, narrowed eyes. Swirling his cloak, Hafrin leapt to his feet and shouted. Like most wild animals, they preferred to err on the side of caution and bolted.

"Which is just as well," Hafrin told his two animal companions. "The last thing we need is a battle with them. What's the matter with me? We've got to get out of here. Marrek must be going crazy with fear."

Thoroughly confused, frightened at finding himself without his foster father, and with no memory of having abandoned Marrek, Hafrin hurriedly broke camp. As eager as his rider to leave that place, Shalinô stepped out. They rounded a cluster of boulders. To Hafrin's frustration, they encountered the boars once more. This time the blïntor stood their ground. Hafrin reined in then urged the gelding to back up. But both blïntor were now thoroughly aroused and pursued them step by step. The old scar across Hafrin's ribs unaccountably tugged and tingled, as though remembering his youthful encounter.

Carefully reaching back, Hafrin loosed his short bow and slowly strung it. As he drew an arrow from the quiver hanging at his right knee, one of the boars charged. Shalinô leapt straight up, nearly unseating Hafrin. He grabbed for the saddletree just as the gelding came back down and then dodged sideways. Vrala Harz arrowed in, screaming. As his orved distracted the boar, Hafrin regained control of Shalinô, managed to set the arrow to string and loosed it. Shock of the shaft striking home staggered the charging boar. It took three stumbling steps then collapsed, its head digging into the earth, flipping it onto its side. The remaining boar chose that moment to attack. This time Shalinô obeyed Hafrin's knee commands. Whipping about, Shalinô placed several low boulders between them and the enraged blïntor. As his gelding came about, head lowered, on the defensive, Hafrin notched another arrow. The remaining blïntor appeared. Eyes red, froth flecked its tusks. At the last moment, Shalinô reared. Caught off-guard, Hafrin's arrow went wide. Flung forward, Hafrin scrabbled with both hands to remain mounted while his gelding vaulted the charging boar.

One stirrup lost, hanging off the saddle, Hafrin clung to the saddletree, giving Shalinô his head until he could recover his seat. Once properly back on Shalinô, he glanced over his shoulder. They were part way up the gradual slope on the north end of the gash now. The boar came on, unwilling to let them go so easily after the death of its companion. Bachelor boar packs could be as family-oriented and vengeful as true family herds. Hafrin hauled Shalinô about and forced the gelding to a standstill.

High above, Vrala Harz screamed defiance. Once more she descended like a bolt of lightening. This time her talons raked the surviving boar above one eye. Taking aim a second time, Hafrin loosed another arrow. This one struck true, although lower in the ribcage than he would have liked. Befuddled and in pain, the boar paused. While it shook its head, Hafrin transferred his bow to his left hand, drew his sword and sent Shalinô in. Bent low, Hafrin urged his mount on. Shalinô gathered himself. As the gelding vaulted the staggering boar, Hafrin buried his blade deep in the blïntor's spine just behind the ears. Blïntor Krel lived up to its name. The boar convulsed. Hafrin reined about just in time to see it drop to the ground, wheezing, legs twitching.

Drawing a deep breath, Hafrin slowly released it. With shaking hands, he slithered from the saddle and leaned against his mount. Shalinô was trembling as well, snorting repeatedly, no less unnerved by the encounter with the blïntor. With each quick flip of his head the gelding telegraphed his fear and displeasure. Short, sharp pains stabbed Hafrin's left wrist as Shalinô's actions jerked the reins. Vrala circled back from her last dive, back-winged and settled on the saddletree. Her beak caressed Hafrin's cheek and she chirped softly. In response to her concern Hafrin stroked her head. Then he spoke to the gelding.

"It's all right, Shalinô. Brave boy. Without you and Vrala, I'd probably be dead."

CHAPTER 16

▼

Marrek

Something brought Marrek instantly out of a deep sleep in which phantoms pursued him through a mist-shrouded landscape. For several breaths he lay motionless straining to identify what had roused him. Somewhere in the distance a twig snapped. Marrek rolled onto his back.

"Rin?"

When his soft inquiry received no response he sat up, short sword in hand. A quick inspection of the campsite revealed two things. First, one of the rynada was missing. Even as Marrek noted it was the grey gelding that was gone from the string, he realised his foster son was also absent.

"Son of a bitch."

Slowly, cautiously, Marrek drew free of his blankets, slid from beneath the tarp and placed his back against the tree beneath which he had been sleeping. Eyes darting from one patch of shadow to the next, he confirmed Hafrin was indeed gone. Now, Marrek inspected the campsite. Tracks were difficult to pick out by the dim glow of the fire's embers, yet it appeared Hafrin had left of his own accord. Marrek withdrew to the fire, rekindled it and heated some of their travel soup.

Eventually, dawn sent questing fingers through the mist. Bewildered by Hafrin's uncustomary behaviour Marrek killed the fire. He repacked and saddled up the remaining rynada before setting out on foot to track his foster son, leading his mount and the pack animal. Before long, however, despite his skill at following sign, he lost the trail. Somehow Hafrin had managed to conceal his tracks in the darkness. Why he had gone to so much trouble worried Marrek. Worse, if he did not break off pursuit now and head home, he risked missing his contacts.

"Damn!"

On the heels of that expletive Marrek mounted, jerked his mount's head around and set off at a quick trot along the final leg towards the rendezvous point. Normally a two and a half day journey, Marrek elected to press on through the night, resting the rynada at intervals, dismounting to eat and drink on the walk and halting only to relieve himself. Several times he dozed off in the saddle. Fortunately his animals knew they were headed home and were eager to get back to their wintering grounds.

They arrived at the pre-arranged rendezvous spot to find Sandi waiting for them. As Marrek rode up to the campsite, Sandi uncurled himself from his autumn-brown cloak and got to his feet. He peered beyond Marrek's pack animal.

"Hi, Marrek. You made good time. Where's Rin?"

"I don't know."

Marrek's damning declaration shook Sandi. "What do you mean you don't know?"

"Just that." Bone-weary, Marrek slithered from the saddle and leaned against his mount. Rubbery legs threatened to spill him onto the ground.

"Wasn't he with you?"

"Yes, until the night before last anyway. Then, sometime during the night, he up and disappeared."

Sandi came around the fire. "This isn't good."

"You're telling me." Marrek's next words were meant more as reflection than information. "I should have known better than to remain at that cursed campsite once I knew where we were."

"What campsite?"

"What? Oh." Marrek pushed away from his mount, took two wobbly steps forward, and lost his balance. Sandi grabbed him before he collapsed.

"Hey! Easy, Marrek. You're worn out."

Marrek mumbled back, "Rode straight through the night."

"Idiot."

Through a mental fog, Marrek let Sandi settle him by the fire. He sipped the hot drink and watched while Sandi checked over his rynada. His fellow agent loosened their girths but did not remove their tack. After watering them, he tied them alongside his own mount and two pack animals before returning to see how Marrek was doing. Assured Marrek was all right, Sandi began packing up his few things.

Over one shoulder he asked, "Are you going to explain what you meant about your last campsite?"

Resigned, Marrek told him, "Somehow I elected to camp out at a spot very close to where I originally found Rin."

"So?"

"I don't know, Sandi. I just had the strangest feeling before going to sleep. Like something was watching us."

"I realise I'm probably asking the obvious, but did you try to track him?"

Marrek nodded. "Lost him in the woods. I don't know how he did it, but his tracks just…faded out. Like something didn't want me to follow him."

Too long a field agent to ridicule the intangible, Sandi said, "He's well versed in woodcraft, Marrek. And I've seen few who could best him with either short or long sword."

And he has Vrala, Marrek told himself.

"Has he forgiven you yet for letting Vern take Nichole away?"

"Forgiven? I think so." But Marrek's treacherous thoughts ran on, *But we've lost some of the closeness that existed before.*

"I doubt it'll do any good waiting around to see if he shows up," Sandi broke across Marrek's reflection. "He's more likely to head straight home, isn't he?"

"Yes."

They extinguished the fire, buried the embers and set out together for Marrek's cabin. Sandi said little throughout the remaining three days, for which Marrek was grateful. Deeply troubled over Hafrin's disappearance, he found himself returning repeatedly to Hafrin's emotional withdrawal the spring after Nichole's departure.

Had it not been for necessity throwing Hafrin constantly into contact with Zivvoz and his family, he might have avoided everyone. But Marrek had ensured this had not happened. In fact, he had made certain Hafrin was seldom allowed time in which to brood. Although Hafrin appeared to recover, he remained quiet, introspective. It took Marrek some time to realise that almost every gift Hafrin had received at the midwinter feast had vanished into Hafrin's personal storage locker. There was little, unfortunately, that Marrek, the hold family or the traders could do to draw him out, so they left their Alaiad-in-exile to work things out for himself. When he did have free time, Hafrin took to disappearing off into the woods on Bïzhan, Vrala his ever-present guardian. Marrek allowed him his freedom, seldom asked where he went, and bit down impatience and worry over his foster son's safety.

The previous trade season, immediately following Nichole's departure, had been particularly difficult. Over time some of Hafrin's bitterness faded as he applied himself to the task of gathering intelligence and improving his trade skills. In retrospect Marrek suspected the incidents over two trading seasons with the sinkhole and the stranded soldiers had helped immeasurably. It was evident to Marrek, however, that the close father-son relationship he had so carefully built from the time Hafrin had moved in with him had been sundered, and it was unlikely he would ever recover it.

"Marrek?"

Jerked back from the past, Marrek glanced up. "Yes?"

"We're here."

Somewhere along the way he had dozed off in the saddle. It was mid-afternoon. Marrek raised his head. Before them stretched the open ground running up between two small pastures to the cabin Marrek had shared with Hafrin for almost eleven years. No light spilled from the building.

As they approached the cabin Sandi observed, "Looks like we're first in this year."

After stabling Marrek's ryanda and turning out Sandi's animals, they went inside. Marrek set kindling and wood chips in the stove and lit it while Sandi saw to the hearth. Usually that was Hafrin's chore. In the midst of setting a small pot of ale on the stove, Marrek found himself staring at the closed shutters across the room.

In the back of his mind a tiny voice called out, *Rin, where are you?*

"Here, Mark," Sandi deftly relieved Marrek of the pot. "Why don't you let me unpack while you have a seat? You're worn out, man."

At that, Marrek released his hold on the pot and wandered over to the three large packs. Listless, he tugged at the lashings on one. It came free, allowing the contents to spill out on the floor. Settled alongside it, he mechanically sorted the remaining items. Those items that did not require attention he stored, while the camping utensils and pots went into the sink to be dealt with later. The remainder of the food he put away. Silently Sandi helped where he could, moved aside when he could not. At length, they were left with a mound of dirty laundry, a few trade items, the trail blankets and Marrek's personal toiletry articles.

The trade goods went into the large chest to the right of the hearth. Linen and blankets were pushed into the corner between the chest and the wall. Amused, Sandi gazed at the mess.

"What are you doing?"

Marrek glanced up. "I'll wash them in the morning."

Raising an eyebrow, Sandi proffered a mug of warm ale. "Here. Drink."

Mug to his lips, Marrek caught the sound of a rynad. "Rin!"

From outside they heard a thin call, "Help."

Marrek whirled, adrenaline washing away fatigue as he dashed for the door, Sandi at his heels. At the railing stood a weary rynad. A small figure in homespun clothing leaned against it for support, head bowed. Habit and caution made him whistle the signal.

From behind Marrek Sandi inquired, "Who's out there? Is it Rin?"

Several seconds passed before the response came. There was so lacklustre a note to the call that Marrek knew it was not Hafrin. Then the figure looked up. It was a woman. Disappointment and curiosity warred with Marrek. He came to the top step and halted, trying to make out the features in the shadows of the hood. Then she spoke.

"Marrek...Mark, please. It's me."

"Who..." He came down one step and froze as light spilled past him to illuminate her. "Great Serpent! Nichole!"

He and Sandi leapt down the three steps as one. They closed in on her as she pushed away from her rynad, swaying dangerously. Sandi caught her arm to support her. Across her he exchanged looks with Marrek. With a nod, Marrek deftly swung Nichole up in his arms. She felt decidedly heavier than he remembered. Then her cloak fell open to reveal her condition.

"By all that's holy," he blurted.

"No time," she told him. "I'm in labour. Sorry. Tried to get here before this happened."

Each sentence emerged in a measured puff, sending steam into the cold air. Against his arms, Marrek felt muscles contract in her back. He might not be familiar with the processes of childbirth first hand but he knew enough about it to realise the baby's birth was imminent.

"Mother of space." He exploded in their native tongue, "What perverse idiot..."

No less annoyed, Sandi pointed, "Get her to bed, Marrek, then fetch Kili. I'll put water on and keep an eye on her."

"Right."

While Sandi headed for the kitchen, Marrek bore Nichole across to the loft. This was one of the few times he blessed his own foresight, having installed drop-down stairs rather than an actual ladder to the attic. Even so, the climb was sufficiently steep that he was winded by the time he reached the loft. He set Nichole down on the edge of Hafrin's bed.

"You better get undressed," he advised her, his tone unconsciously distant and cold. "You'll find one of Rin's old nightshifts in the box."

Clearly unprepared for his abruptness, Nichole stared at him before following the direction indicated by his finger. She gave a short nod and began unfastening her cloak. Before she had tugged it off he left her. He slithered down the ladder and dashed from the cabin. He paused briefly at her rynad, but it was too exhausted to go further. Marrek led it across the open ground to the pasture gate. Along the way he unfastened the breast band and loosened the cinch. Before turning the rynad into the pasture he unclipped the jaw reins and yanked away the saddle, letting the saddle and pad drop to the ground outside the pasture. He turned in the tired animal and grabbed Sandi's mount as it snuffled around the entrance looking for food. Clipping the reins to its jaw horn ring he flung himself onto its bare back before it could object and sent it through the opening. In passing, he kicked the gate shut behind them. Then he clapped his heels to its sides, sending the rynad flying down the path towards the dark woods and Zivvoz's hold.

They slithered to a halt so close to the hold house the rynad's breast actually touched the railing. Wood creaked. Oblivious to the near disaster, Marrek flung himself from the animal and leapt up the steps. The door opened even as he reached it.

"Marrek. What demons chased you here in such a state?" Zivvoz glanced past Marrek's shoulder then back at him. "Where's Rin?"

"No idea. No time to explain. I need Kili now. There's a baby on the way at my place." Marrek shoved past Zivvoz, shouting, "Kili!"

"I heard you, Marrek. Just let me grab my things."

All business, Kili went to the alcove she shared at night with her husband and began digging out such swaddling bands and baby things as she determined what would be required. While she worked, she flung questions over her shoulder. Marrek replied as best he could.

"How far along are the contractions?"

"I don't know. Fairly close, from what I felt."

"Is the infant full term?"

Now that was the one question Marrek was unable to reply to. He shook his head and Kili rolled her eyes with irritation. Intrigued, but not about to interfere, Zivvoz held out her cloak as she tied up her two bundles and stood. From beside the hearth, Indoro watched, silent and speculative.

Kili remarked, "All right. I think that's everything."

"Have you got the knife?"

To her husband's question, she nodded. "Last thing in, on top of the herbs."

He dropped her cloak about her as she went by. "So I guess we'll see you when we see you."

"I'll bring word," Marrek promised. "Or send it."

Zivvoz asked, "Where is Rin? Up at the…"

But Marrek hustled Kili down the steps and boosted her onto his mount without answering. Turning the rynad, he urged it back the way they had come. By the time they reached his cabin it was staggering. Coat matted with sweat, sticky streams of saliva trailed from the corners of its mouth, spattering them with unpleasant globs as it wobbled to a standstill. Sandi met them out front. He nodded to Kili and silently directed her to the loft. Then he joined Marrek.

Concerned for the rynad, Marrek began slowly walking it about the yard. Every so often he glanced at the house. But there was little he and Sandi could do at this point except get under foot. If Kili needed them, she would call. He glanced at his companion.

"Did you get anything out of her?"

Sandi shot him a look across the drooping rynad's neck. "Yes."

"Well? What's she doing back here?"

"They sent her back."

Irritated, Marrek snapped back, "That's obvious. Why?"

"Apparently the baby is Rin's."

A dash of ice shot through Marrek as the information sank in. He came to an abrupt halt, mentally calculating the time it would have taken Nichole, in cold sleep, to travel from Fimiah to the Academy, and back again, factoring in her time at the Academy. He met and held Sandi's gaze. Silent obscenities raced about his mind. Between them, the now recovering rynad bobbed its head, effectively distracting them. They automatically headed for the watering trough to let it slack its thirst.

At length, Marrek found his voice. "How?"

"You tell me," replied Sandi, tight-lipped with the implications. "You were supposed to be keeping an eye on them."

The little voice in the back of his mind nudged him. *When has that ever stopped young people?*

Marrek recalled the days Hafrin and Nichole had spent at Zivvoz's hold while he had been trapped at the colony by foul weather. There had been only Zivvoz and his family to supervise the pair, a family that saw nothing wrong with an alliance between their Alaiad-in-exile and the Hynarkin traders. A groan escaped him.

Damn it, Ziv. How could you have let this happen?

Wasn't his fault. A feminine voice invaded his thoughts. *Sorry, Mark. Knew you'd want to know.*

"Why, Nikki?" He spoke out loud for Sandi's benefit, relaying her explanation as she 'pathed him the information between contractions.

We fell in love. Not infatuation. Not sexual attraction, Mark. Real love. You have no idea what it's like for two telepaths. It was Sandi's turn to express his annoyance as Nichole expanded her 'pathing to include him. *It's not Mark's fault either, Sandy. He didn't know until too late about Hafrin's abilities. Rin told me that when he was younger, he simply accepted it as youthful imagination. Later, he thought at times he was actually going insane.*

Marrek retorted, "But you showed him the truth."

Had to. Once we…joined, she broke off for a long minute, *Sorry. Got to make this fast. Our thoughts merged. He knows just about everything I do, Mark.*

"Oh, great." Sandi flung up his hands, startling his mount. "So much for gradual recovery for this world."

You have to trust him, Sandy. Mark, you've taught him so well. There's so much he wants for his people, so much he's certain they've lost due to the Craneeno's incursions. But, at the same time, he realises culture shock would…

A mental scream filled their minds. Their contact with her snapped. On the heels of her silent cry of pain, a scream split the air, followed almost immediately by a wail. Thoroughly frightened, the rynad reared, nearly tearing the reins from Marrek's hands. He hung on. Sandi grabbed its mane, and between them, they brought it back under control.

"Here. Let me finish this. You get inside," Sandi ordered, and took the reins from Marrek's hands. For a brief moment, Marrek hovered, indecisive. Then, with a curt nod, he dashed back indoors.

CHAPTER 17

▼

Nichole

Fingers gripping the bedposts, Nichole strained to deliver the baby. Pain, pleasure at accomplishment, helplessness that she could not adequately control her body, filled her consciousness. Bent over her lower extremities, Kili held out a warmed cloth, prepared to catch the infant as it emerged.

"Again, Nikôla," the hold woman encouraged her. "I can see the head."

Taking a deep breath, Nichole bore down. In spite of herself, she cried out, verbally and mentally. Somehow she succeeded in breaking her contact with the men outside. At that moment, there was a sudden relief of pressure. A baby wailed. Gasping, sobbing for breath, she sought respite but another contraction insisted she push again.

"After-birth's out, too," Kili announced. "Good girl."

Slumped on the bed, Nichole gasped for breath. Relief from pain and helplessness was a dream in itself. A pleasant crooning filled the air. Humming softly, Kili wiped off the baby, cleaned out its ears, nose, and mouth and gently wiped mucus from its eyes. Then she held it up.

"There. A fine boy and you're fine as well. A few stitches perhaps, but you did extremely well for your first," she remarked. Then, as though seeing the child she held for the first time, she gasped. "By the Great Serpent. He looks like Rin."

"Yes," Nichole acknowledged, well pleased with the results.

There was no doubting the identity of the father. On the heels of Kili's observation, Marrek appeared at the top of the loft steps. He paused, and then came forward. At the sound of creaking wood, Kili slowly turned. Looking a trifle guilty, she held out the baby. Marrek accepted him. He stared down at the watery blue eyes, which he knew would darken to a near-sapphire blue as the baby grew.

Black thatch crowned the baby's head, but there was a suggestion of auburn highlights amongst the dark downy covering, legacy of his mother.

"Yes," Marrek admitted, "he does resemble Rin, doesn't he?"

With those words, Marrek also acknowledged the baby's parentage. He gazed across the infant to its mother. "So this was why you didn't want to leave."

"Actually," she told him, switching to Hynarkin, "I didn't find out until I had been at the Academy for almost a month."

"And when did they find out?"

"About the same time. I started having morning sickness. At first, I thought it was the flu because I had it at different times of the day and I had been in sleep for so long. But, about the time my brother dropped by for a visit, it was mostly in the morning and last thing at night. He dragged me off to Medical."

"And that's when it came out."

"Uh huh." She managed a weary nod. Her midwife training taking over, Kili fetched her a drink before returning to clean up the aftermath of the birth.

A stray thought spun around the periphery of Marrek's mind. *They never say anything in first aid training about how messy it is birthing a baby.*

Unconcerned by his momentary distraction, Nichole continued, "Apparently once they realised exactly who the father of my baby was, no one wanted to tempt fate."

"The sword?"

"I guess."

"But it's missing."

Nichole shrugged. "What do any of us really know about the sword's fate, Marrek?"

"True." Marrek reverted to Fimiahri. "Sorry, Kili. I didn't mean to be rude but I had to get some things straight with Nikki."

"I understand." A quiet smile slipped across her features. "Who am I to question the Star born?"

Unable to conceal his shock, Marrek almost dropped the baby. "How…"

"This, for one." Kili pointed to the infant, retrieved the baby and placed him in Nichole's arms. "How else could Nikôla carry Rin's son for over a year and still deliver it at term? Somehow, I don't believe this is normal for your women, anymore than it is for ours."

Marrek fought down the impulse to argue the child could have been the result of a liaison with someone else distantly related to the Alaiad bloodline. Something prevented him disrupting the moment with a blatant lie. Instead, he elected to ask, "What else?"

Unafraid, Kili was blunt in her assessment. "Oh, the way you have with wounds and illnesses; like that physician of yours who healed my husband and Rin. Plus, there are a lot of other small things that have just never added up. Besides, how could it not be the truth?" And she looked pointedly at Nichole and her baby once more.

"Does Zivvoz believe I..." Marrek glanced at Nichole, "we aren't Fimi-ahri-born?"

Kili snorted. "Men. You seldom see beyond the end of your nose. It's we women who have to look to the broader picture."

In spite of herself, Nichole laughed. In her arms, her son stirred and muttered. She traced the soft spot on the top of his head and a quiet smile touched her lips. Caught by the maternal scene, Marrek's heart raced. A lump formed in his throat as he remembered a soiled infant secreted beneath a bush. He looked quickly away.

"Will you tell Ziv?"

"Only when you think the time's right," Kili informed him. "Their safety's far more important to me, Marrek Lytsun. By the way, where is Rin? He should be here."

Before Marrek could reply, he was interrupted. A fluting whistle outside announced the arrival of the other traders and he wondered where Sandi was. With a sigh of resignation, Marrek gestured.

"You had better stay put Kili, while I try to explain this mess to my comrades."

Thoroughly amused, Nichole and Kili nodded to one another. Marrek ignored the silent exchange as he headed downstairs. Although she knew she should not, Nichole decided to eavesdrop on the conversation below. At the same time she rocked the newborn in her arms. She watched him as he pressed his face up against her breast, seeking her milk.

Davyn Lytsun, Marrek's brother, was first in. *Marrek, I see you and Sandi met up. But aren't you short a rynad?*

Rin's away, Marrek responded to his brother's inquiry.

Away? A pause. Nichole knew Davyn had glanced past Marrek to Sandi, and then at the open loft with the lantern light spilling down it. *Then who...*

I want everyone inside before I say anything. There have been some unexpected developments these past couple of days that need the entire group's deliberation.

Forewarned, the rest of the traders trooped indoors and, one by one, divested themselves of their cloaks and boots before taking seats about the hearth. Marrek patiently poured ale for all. Only when he and Sandi were settled, he on the hearth apron and Sandi to one side of the fireplace with one elbow resting on the mantle, did Marrek dare glance at his brother.

Feet up on the hearth apron, wriggling his toes in the warmth Piltar, the senior scout, pressed, *So what's the news?*

First, Marrek told them, *Rin took off before we were to meet Sandi and I have no idea where he went. Or why.*

"What!"

Davyn's explosive reaction needed no telepathy to hear. Kili's silent exchange with Nichole amounted to a raised eyebrow and a grin. Being closer to the loft entrance, she could hear what was being said downstairs but was unable to make out anything from the conversation as the men were speaking Hynarkin. For Nichole, however, concerns for Hafrin, his safety and whereabouts, captured a sizeable portion of her attention.

We were camped out very near where I found Rin as a baby.

You think that had something to do with his behaviour?

I don't know. I've never shown him the location, although we've ridden past there often enough over the years since we started trading again in Iryô District.

No one said anything for several minutes. Finally Piltar closed the subject. *All right. Obviously we're going to have to get word out to our people at the moon base and have them scan the area for any sign of him. He's still got the implant, doesn't he?*

Nichole sensed Marrek's nod to the inquiry. She released a tiny sigh of relief. That they had implanted a tracking device on her husband to track him in emergencies was something she should have suspected. Hafrin was far too valuable, to Fimiahri and the Wanderers.

Piltar continued, *Is that everything?*

No. I have guests upstairs.

We rather suspected that when you said Rin wasn't here but you've got the loft lit up like it was Christmas, observed Robar.

Who's up there?

Nichole felt Marrek steel himself as he announced, *Nichole's back.*

Robar blurted, *God in heaven. Are they insane?*

Ever outspoken, Davyn demanded, *Who the hell decided that?*

Sandi set his mug aside and raised a hand, quieting the room. Piltar got to his feet. *Mark, just what the hell is Patrol up to?*

It's not their fault, Sandi told them, allowing Marrek time to gather his defences.

What do you mean it's not their fault? Why would they send her back here? Davyn pointed at the cabin floor. *Not to the colony but actually here, to this place?*

She was pregnant when she arrived on the doorstep, said Sandi. Silence enveloped the room. Anticipation was so thick Nichole could have cut it with a knife.

With Rin's son, concluded Marrek.

Rin's son? Piltar sank slowly back into his chair. *Sweet Mother of God, we have an heir.*

Exactly, said Marrek. *Apparently once Academy Medical determined that, they decided they really had no other option.*

But the sword's gone.

The sword is missing, Piltar corrected Davyn. *Who rode in with her?*

That was something Nichole had failed to explain and she sensed Marrek shrug. *She came alone.*

Alone? That's crazy. Now Robar echoed Davyn's sentiments. *Have they completely lost it up at the colony?*

Unable to supply an answer, Marrek could only shrug again. Piltar rescued him. *How's Nikki doing?*

Fine. The baby's a healthy boy. I don't think she's chosen a name just yet. Probably waiting for Rin to come home. Kili's upstairs with her. And, be advised, she knows about us.

How? Piltar got to his feet. As senior patroller, he was within his rights to censor or reassign Marrek if he felt it necessary. *Have you been indiscreet again?*

Marrek shook his head, *No. She guessed.*

At her breast Nichole's son finished suckling his first milk. She held out her infant son as he smacked his lips and made small noises. "Kili, please take him downstairs. They have a right to see him."

"And me?"

To Kili's question Nichole smiled. "Marrek's told them. They'll be wary, but they're good people."

Surprised that Nichole felt obliged to add that last reassurance, Kili replied, "How could they not be?"

Now Nichole waggled a finger in Kili's direction as the hold woman accepted the infant. "Every race has its good and bad, Kili. Facts of nature as you well know. Is every rynad a good mount or a dray, every rakkïal an excellent laying fowl?"

Eyes dancing with mirth at the gentle remonstration, Kili cradled the sleeping baby in the crook of her left arm and carried him downstairs. Beneath her weight the ladder creaked and the men gathered in the sitting area fell silent. Those who were sitting down got to their feet as she appeared. Heart racing, Kili stepped into their midst, acutely conscious of all eyes on her. She held out the heir-apparent for them to see. There was no doubting the awe, excitement and, to her surprise, incredible possessiveness all of them radiated. Nichole kept track of the situation, aware of the tension rapidly seeping out of those present as they gathered about the hold woman.

He's got his father's hands, remarked Piltar, lifting a tiny hand with one of his fingers. Even in his sleep the infant responded to that touch. Little fingers curled. He stirred slightly in his wrappings.

Looks like he'll be slender like his mother, Robar observed.

Davyn remained silent, but Nichole sensed him warming a fraction. Frayed nerves slowly knit while Marrek made proper introductions employing the scouts' trader names. Piltar ushered Kili to a chair close beside the hearth. Worn out, Nichole drifted off to sleep. The conversations below slipped around her thoughts until darkness took her.

She woke in the middle of the night to the wail of an infant. Even as she pushed herself up in the bed, Kili was at her side, the baby held out for her to take. While her son suckled Nichole stared out the loft window. Kili settled on the side of the bed.

"He's wet," she told Nichole.

"Well, he can eat first."

"He'll probably wet himself again right after I change him," Kili warned her.

"Then we'll change him again," Nichole replied. One side of her mouth tugged with suppressed mirth.

To that, Kili grunted. Wood creaked. They glanced toward the stairs just as Marrek's head appeared in the opening. "How is he?"

"Hungry. Wet. What else?"

"Never thought I'd have to worry about another baby," Marrek commented. He moved the rest of the way into the loft.

"Mark, where is Rin?"

Nichole's question produced quite the opposite effect to what she expected. The manner in which all of the walls in Marrek's thoughts slammed up, shutting her out frightened her. Their eyes met and she saw fear and concern mirrored there. He shook his head.

"So what happened?"

"He...just...rode away," Marrek told her. She waited with more patience than he was expecting, allowing him to explain in his own time. "Two nights before we were due to meet Sandi, we camped near the Demons' Gathering. There was no need to keep watch. Not with Vrala on duty, so we both slept. At least, I know I did. When I woke, Rin had disappeared into the woods."

"Was he riding Bïzhan?"

"No. We leave the stallion and his dame with Ziv during the summer. You know how much attention he attracts." Before she could ask, he added, "But he had Vrala Harz with him. And the gelding he uses, Shalinô, is as battle-trained as Bïzhan."

Nichole looked away. For several minutes she stared out the window into the night. Clouds had moved in and the treetops were darker shadows against the black of night. Her son began pushing at her breast and making noises.

"I think he's finished," Kili said quietly, catching Nichole back. "Let me take him for you, Nikôla."

Wordlessly, Nichole passed her son back to Kili. Marrek moved up to sit next to her while Kili took the baby across the room to change and resettle. He touched her nearest hand as she organized her nightgown, covering her breast.

"I'm sure he's fine, Nikki."

"I know he is," she told him. "But I can't seem to reach him. There's some sort of fog surrounding his mind."

"It was foggy when we camped. Strange. You know, when I tried to track him in the morning I couldn't find any sign." Before Nichole could question him further he switched tracks. "Why didn't they send someone with you?"

It took a second before she could catch herself away from her concerns about Hafrin to understand what he meant. "Oh, they did, Mark. But we...I," she amended, cheeks turning crimson, "ran into a little trouble in Revïl."

"Oh?"

"I needed to rest so we broke our trip at the tavern. You know the one." Marrek nodded. "A group of hunters took an interest in me. I managed to get away, but we couldn't shake them. Finally Harry decided to try to draw them off. It worked...for a while."

"What do you mean, for a while?"

"Either they lost him or..." Nichole broke off, not wanting to pursue that thought. "Anyway, they came back. I managed to give them the slip. Hid out in a ravine. They couldn't find me in the dark and eventually gave up."

"What about Harry?"

"I don't know." She blinked hard, struggling to hold back tears. "If he had been a telepath, I'd have been able to find out right away. Marrek, is there any way you can contact the colony? Find out if he's okay."

"In the morning," he said. "There's little any of us can do tonight even if I contacted them now."

"Before dawn, then," she insisted. "That'll give them time to prepare a scout party to look for him if he hasn't returned to base."

"Alright." Marrek promised, aware she would insist upon riding out herself if he argued the point. "I promise I'll contact them before I feed the livestock."

As satisfied as she could be with the situation, and certain Marrek would not renege, she settled back on the bed. Marrek remained at her bedside, watching her. Across the loft, Kili gently rocked the baby to sleep before resettling herself in bed. In her sleep, Nichole sensed when Marrek returned to his own bed.

CHAPTER 18

▼

Hafrin

Much as he hated abandoning two perfectly good kills, Hafrin knew it was impossible to adequately transport the meat and hides. High overhead aerial scavengers were already circling the cleft. On shaking legs, Hafrin led his gelding away from the site. Once certain he and Shalinô were on the trail once more, Vrala took to the air.

Heat, such as late fall never should produce, built with the day, but there was little sunlight. Rather, a thin, high haze obscured the sky. The wind sent questing fingers along the draw to lift the edges of the cloak he had thrown back off his shoulders. Towards midday he encountered the suggestion of a seep. The further north they went the more pronounced it became. Eventually, he located the source; a thin thread of moisture emerged from a crack in the rocks high above and wormed its way down the precipice into a small cup just out of arm's reach. The overflow splashed down into a slightly larger pool against the base of the cliff.

Here the compulsion that had been pricking Hafrin finally faded. Shalinô tugged on the reins and Hafrin let the rynad head for the water. While his mount slacked its thirst, Hafrin took down his water skins and refilled them from the trickle of clear water that flowed down from above. His orved dropped in. Chirping, she dipped her beak in the pool, lifted it, drank then dipped again. Tired, and with a headache forming behind his eyes, Hafrin stuck his head beneath the miniature waterfall. As he straightened, something reflected in the pool caught his attention. For a moment, he doubted what he was seeing.

"A sword?" He drew the gelding away from the water. Cupping his hands beneath the flow he studied the image. "Reflection. But from where?"

Head tipped back Hafrin stared up the rock face, struggling to correlate what he had seen in the water with the surrounding scenery. After a bit he spotted a fracture in the rocks. Bent at an awkward angle, he stared up into the overhang of boulders and calcified mineral deposits. Between two large stalagmites he made out the hilt of a sword.

Drawn on by increasing curiosity, Hafrin carefully stepped onto the slick rocks at the base of the waterfall. Mist beaded on his hair and clothing, moistening his face from time to time. He ignored the irritants, drawn on by the image. Pressed against the cliff, he inspected the indentations for adequate hand and toe-holds. At some point in the past a section of the rockface had fragmented and fallen away. What had probably once been a relatively easy scramble was what Sandi once told him experienced climbers might refer to as a difficult pitch. Slowly, Hafrin inched up until he was within reach of the weapon.

"Okay," he told himself, "Now what? If I grab it, I'll only have one hand free to get back down."

Without thinking, he glanced down to check how high up he was and realised he might just be able to leap off the rocks and land safely beyond the pool. Time stretched into infinity while he considered his options. Impulse goaded him into action. Casting fate to the winds, he grabbed for the sword. His fingers encountered the hilt and he pushed away from the rocks. Twisting in the air, he landed awkwardly on the ground, lost his balance and sprawled onto his hands and knees in the sand and gravel.

Hafrin got to his feet. Breathing hard, he hobbled two steps, his ankles stinging. He was pleased to discover he had somehow maintained his grasp on the sword during his fall. Perched on the rocks above the pool, Vrala Harz released a piercing scream quite unlike anything Hafrin had ever heard her give vent to before. Shalinô reared, tossed his head and tore at the ground. Bemused by their actions, Hafrin looked at what he held.

"Great Serpent."

Light rippled along the blade. Pale blue and green twined and coiled before his eyes. Perfectly balanced, the weapon seemed to have been crafted specifically for him. Slowly, he turned the hilt in his hand. Just below the guard, scored deep into the wood grip above the leather lashings, was a fractured rune.

"Hafrön."

Whispered as a prayer, the name conjured incredible images that were not Hafrin's own. Star Given, his people had named it when first they had seen it. Now Hafrin knew the truth of that title. He sank onto the ground and balanced the blade across his knees. With his free hand, he ran a corner of his cloak across the blade surface several times, wiping away moisture and grit. Apart from the indignity it had suffered from his spill, the weapon was undamaged.

"Hafrön, hear me. I am Hafrin, only child of Fanhri and Rityöm, rightful Ala-iad of Fimiah."

Why he should make that declaration Hafrin could not say, yet as he spoke he stood and held aloft his family's hereditary sword. In response to his pronouncement a melodic hum filled the air, washing over him. The sound penetrated his body until even his bones vibrated to it. Images that could only be those of each of his ancestors at the height of their respective reigns filled his mind. Eye-blinding gold light shot straight up from the blade tip to vanish in the watery afternoon sunlight. Transparent blue light cascaded down the length of the weapon and poured across his hand before dissipating.

With another scream, Vrala left her perch. She circled Hafrin and the sword three times before alighting on Shalinô's saddletree. At some point during the experience Hafrin found he had sunk to his knees. When he came back to himself, he was staring down at the sword. Awed by his experience, he cupped the weapon in his hands for several more seconds before recovering his senses. Slowly he pushed back to his feet. From behind the saddle, he took his bedding, wrapped Hafrön inside, and lashed the roll back in place.

"I think we should go home," he told his mount and orved.

Swinging into the saddle, Hafrin urged Shalinô into an easy lope. By evening they were free of the Gathering and well into the forest. Hafrin allowed the gelding to halt and graze. While his mount cropped the sedges, Hafrin munched on trail bread and washed it down with the spring water. But he could not keep his eyes off the precious bundle behind the saddle. It was all he could do not to rip off the coverings and reassure himself of his discovery.

Once Shalinô had eaten his fill Hafrin remounted. They set off once more. They did not halt during the night. Rather Hafrin stepped down and walked at his rynad's head. When he caught himself stumbling, half-asleep on his feet, he got back into the saddle. After imprinting their destination in Shalinô's thoughts, Hafrin gave him his head and settled to doze on the gelding's back.

They made good time, even though the gelding elected to depart from the road at some point during the day, and take to the woods. Several times Hafrin woke with a start to discover he was about to lose his seat because of a low tree limb. It was Vrala Harz who nudged him awake just in time on each occasion and Hafrin reined Shalinô around the obstacle or ducked his head to avoid injury. Towards dawn Hafrin woke with a start as his rynad halted beside a brook to drink. The spot looked familiar and Vrala confirmed they were a half-day's ride from home. Stiff and sore Hafrin slithered to the ground. Kneeling by the stream, he splashed icy water in his face.

"Think I'll rest for a bit," he told the animals. "Vrala, wake me when the sun's above the horizon." She chirped back in response to the picture he 'pathed her before he fell asleep.

True to her promise, Vrala Harz roused him at the appropriate hour. Grimy from the long hours in the saddle, Hafrin took a few minutes to strip and bathe. Dry and dressed in the cleanest of his travel clothes, he mounted and set off on the final leg home. When they emerged from the tree line smoke was rising from the cabin chimney. Turning Shalinô onto the road, he allowed the gelding to break into an easy run. His rynad halted at the railing, dropping his muzzle into the small trough while Hafrin stepped down. Vrala banked in, back-winged and took her customary perch on the railing. Hafrin unlashed the bundle from behind the saddle. Although guilt pricked him for abandoning Marrek on the trail without explanation, he took the three steps to the porch in a single bound. Heedless of the inherent hazards should he trip, and eager to display his trophy, he removed the sword from its wrappings as he took the leap.

He flung the cabin door open, calling out, "Marrek."

His foster father leapt to his feet, knocking over the kitchen chair in which he had been sitting. Hafrin had just enough time to realise there were two women in the room, one being Kili, who was holding a baby. Then a bright light shot from Hafrön. Hafrin turned his head aside, his eyes tearing with pain. The infant, who had been laughing and gurgling and waving his arms in the air, let out a shriek. As Hafrin recovered his sight, he saw Kili instinctively clutch the baby to her breast. The other woman scrambled to her feet and joined her in inspecting the baby. Bewildered, Hafrin froze just inside the cabin door.

"God in heaven," Marrek blurted in Hynarkin, transfixed by what had happened. He likewise wiped at his eyes and cheeks.

But the younger woman turned in that instant. "Rin."

Hafrin's breath caught in his throat. For a moment he was incapable of speech. Then he managed to croak, "Nikki?"

She was across the room and into his arms before he had completely recovered from the multiple shocks of the sword's actions, the sight of the baby and his greatest wish come true. Hereditary sword hanging from his right hand, Hafrin clasped Nichole against him. Heart singing, he pressed his lips against the crown of her head as she buried her face in his chest. Kissing was foreign to Fimiah and he was not yet entirely comfortable with that Hynarkin custom.

Across the kitchen, Kili was staring at the puckered mark on the underside of the baby's arm. She breathed a short prayer. "Blessed Serpent."

Marrek stepped around the table to inspect the child as well. The baby continued to fuss but had quieted appreciably from his initial response to the unexpected assault. Hafrin's entire universe remained centred on the woman in his arms.

"Nikki, how?"

"They sent me home," she told him. "Where have you been?"

"I'm not sure," he replied. His gaze travelled across the room to meet Marrek's eyes. "But I found this in the Gathering."

With that declaration he raised Hafrön above his head. Nichole gasped. Incredulous, Marrek came quickly across the room. As Hafrin brought the sword back down, Marrek inadvertently reached out to touch the weapon. Too late, Nichole slapped his hand aside. His fingers grazed the blade. In response to his temerity red flushed the length of metal. Then, just as quickly the colour pulsed, switching to gold and green.

"What..." Grabbing Marrek's hand, Nichole checked it for any damage, "Why...you're okay. But I thought only the Alaiad and his heir could safely touch it?"

Bemused by his close call, Marrek considered the awesome weapon. "Apparently it recognises us as something other than Fimiahri."

"And acknowledges your right to handle it," added Hafrin.

Only then was he able to drag his attention back to Kili. His one-time foster mother was gently wiping ointment onto the underside of the baby's arm.

"Another one, Kili?"

Strangely disgusted by Hafrin's question, Kili snorted. "Just like a man to make that assumption."

Nichole, a strange look on her face, gave him a push. "Oh, Rin, he's ours."

Dumbfounded, Hafrin stared down at Nichole for a long minute. Wonder filling him, he went into the kitchen, setting the sword on the table.

"Ours. But you've been gone over a year." He accepted his son from Kili as she set him carefully in his arms. Then she lifted the baby's left arm.

"Your heir, ser," she announced, employing the honorific used only when addressing the Alaiad. "A fine healthy son, for all he's been over a year in the making."

Slowly Hafrin turned back to Marrek and Nichole. "I don't understand. How can this be?"

With a sigh, Marrek gestured. "I think we should all sit down while I try to explain."

"This should be good," Nichole muttered at him. "Just how are we going to explain this so they understand us?"

"We tell them the truth," said Marrek firmly, and led the way to the chairs grouped around the hearth.

As he settled himself in a chair, still cradling his son, Hafrin glanced around the cabin. "Where are the others?"

"Gone," said Marrek. "I'll send a message later today that you're safely home."

Hafrin blushed. "I'm sorry, Marrek."

His foster father gave a short shake of his head in response. Across the cabin, Nichole had paused by the window. "Rin, whose gelding is that?"

Hafrin swore in Hynarkin, "That's Shalinô. Oh, damn. Marrek, I have to put him away. He's worn out after our trip."

"I'll do it right now," said Marrek.

"But it's my responsibility."

"That you've learned that much is to your credit," Marrek replied. "But I think your time's best served getting acquainted with your son. Besides, this will only take a few minutes. I'll rub him down, store the tack and turn him out in the pasture."

"Now that Rin's back, perhaps you should send Ziv and Doro a message," put in Kili.

Marrek nodded. "I'll send Vrala."

"I'll write the message while you turn out Shalinô," Nichole offered.

"All right," Marrek agreed. "But you're to sit down right now, both of you. Rin, you're worn out and, whether you believe it or not, you're staggering from need of sleep. And, Nikki, you know you shouldn't over-exert yourself. I'm sure Kili won't mind fetching what you need."

On the verge of arguing the point, Nichole caught Kili's stern expression and subsided. Head ducked to one side she slid a look at Hafrin. He grinned back at her before allowing the baby in his arms to catch his attention once more.

CHAPTER 19

▼

Nichole

Once the chores were done, they settled around the hearth, the baby in his father's arms. Hafrin gently tickled his son's tiny hand until he curled his little fingers about his father's digit. When the baby proceeded to suck on it, however, Nichole took him from Hafrin and rocked him. Kili quickly fetched a bottle of tïlkrïn milk that was on the stove warming plate in a saucepan of water.

Hafrin observed, "You aren't breast-feeding."

"She was but she hasn't enough milk," Kili informed the men. She handed Nichole the bottle. "It frequently happens with new mothers. I'm sure she won't have that problem with the next."

Next? Hafrin's startled mental message caused Nichole to duck her head. But not before he caught the quiet smile tugging the corners of her mouth.

Well, she silently countered, her cheeks burning, *you don't expect him to be an only child, do you?*

Hafrin conceded, *I guess not.*

She felt an aching in his left arm and traced its source to an unusual thickness in the bone that had not been there during her previous time on Fimiah. *When did you break your arm?*

Unprepared for her question, Hafrin stared at her in surprise. *Last year, saving a couple of soldiers.*

Mingling thoughts with Hafrin after so long an absence filled Nichole with a sense of belonging as nothing else had in her entire life. As though something beautiful that had been torn apart had been seamlessly mended, she was whole, complete as never before. And so, it seemed, was Hafrin. Nichole slid a quick look in Kili's direction.

By the way, she knows about Mark and I.

What! Hafrin shot a quick look in his milk mother's direction.

It's true. Ask her.

"Kili, I understand you've developed a theory about my wife and Marrek." Hafrin dared ask his milk mother, "When precisely did you decide Nikki and Marrek were Star born? And why?"

"Ah." Amusement danced in the hold woman's eyes. "I had my suspicions for many years after Marrek first settled here. But it was his familiarity with so many things, a number of which even the most educated of our people are ignorant. There's the way in which he concealed your appearance, ser, not to mention Nikôla's garments when she first came to us. Am I right Marrek? Or is it Mark?"

"Eavesdropper," shot back Nichole.

"Sometimes it pays to know certain things," Kili responded to that remonstration.

"And sometimes it can be dangerous," Marrek reminded her. Kili admitted the truth of that with a slight shrug. He continued, "Marrek will do." He frowned. "I don't know how the...how my people are going to react to this, though."

"Marrek." Nichole shifted her son from one arm to the other and repositioned the bottle. "I really think you ought to hear my report before you start worrying about whether or not the Fimiahri know about us."

Set back by her bluntness, Marrek glanced at Hafrin and Kili, and nodded. "All right."

Without switching to Hynarkin, Nichole briefed him. "Patrol and Fleet are on full alert."

"Say again?"

"The Craneeno are on the move. Apparently we've interfered in too many of their operations for far too long for them to continue ignoring us as anything less than a real threat. From all reports, it looks like they're preparing for a full-scale offensive."

"Damn."

Relentless, ignoring Kili's frightened look, Nichole continued, "Unfortunately, intelligence indicates Fimiah will be on one of the front lines. Fleet is positive they can keep the bulk of their forces tied up so they won't get through the blockade we've set up over the years. But it also appears sufficient quantities of them have slipped through in small numbers that they can field a substantial opposition. How much equipment they've landed is anyone's guess."

"I'm sure Vern's been keeping track."

"So he won't be surprised when you tell him they've managed to build up a sizeable ground force. And we all know they've got people planted in high places influencing Jikpryn's advisors."

"Are you referring to my uncle?"

Nichole glanced at Hafrin and away. Marrek answered for her. "I suspect his move against your parents was driven as much by Craneeno influence, Rin, as by his personal motives. We know Tolbôun is an agent in their pay."

Marrek avoided Nichole's gaze but she was not fooled. There was a faint possibility that the Outsider was actually something more; a mimic, capable of going under cover disguised as a Fimiahri. One reason the Craneeno appeared to hate the Wanderers and Fimiahri was because they so closely resembled the Craneeno. Other wholly alien species such as the amoebic Shrklattr and the reptilian Uthssitssi they might despise, but their reactions towards anything remotely similar to humanoid they regarded in a xenophobic manner.

Marrek continued, "There are ways of influencing a person's behaviour that only someone with the right training and equipment would recognise as tampering, and given we know Tol's connection to the Craneeno...well...let's just say it's possible."

"Which means Jikpryn may not be entirely responsible for Fanhri's and Rityöm's deaths," said Kili. Strangely, she seemed relieved.

Unprepared to be as forgiving as his foster mother, Hafrin snapped back, "I doubt that."

Don't let your emotions cloud your judgement, Nichole silently cautioned him. *Better to give him the benefit of the doubt until events prove out which way he'll jump when given the option.*

"We don't know that," said Marrek in response to Kili's statement. Then he caught Hafrin's scowl and was alerted. He paused, studied their faces. "Are you two talking behind our backs?"

At that, Nichole went deep red from the roots of her hair to the neck of her housecoat. Hafrin coughed to cover his embarrassment. Intrigued, Kili watched Marrek rise and walk to the fireplace. He turned, leaned one arm on the mantle as he addressed his foster son.

"You both know the rules."

"Sorry, sir."

"Don't 'sorry me', Rin. And Nikki, you definitely know better."

Marrek's sharp tone caused Kili to stiffen. She raised an eyebrow. Evidently she was on the verge of objecting to the way in which Marrek remonstrated the

Alaiad-in-exile. Nichole caught her eye and gave the tiniest shake of her head. At the warning Kili subsided. Marrek turned to their guest.

"I believe I ought to explain why I'm annoyed with them, Kili." With a stern look, he pinned Nichole and Hafrin where they sat. "Nikki and Rin have a rare gift. They're able to speak to each other without the rest of us hearing them."

"Ah." Now Kili nodded. "That explains it."

"Oh?"

"Yes. There are legends of the Alaiad knowing things without being told but no one could figure out how."

Unaware he was 'pathing, Marrek mused, *That's definitely interesting. Vern will want to know about that particular legend.*

Hafrin rose, gave his foster mother a short bow and apologised. "I'm sorry we've been rude, Kili. Nikôla and I shouldn't speak like that when others are around. Unless subterfuge is necessary, that is."

"No, ser." Now it was Kili's turn to remind those present exactly who Hafrin was. "Privacy is your right and privilege. It isn't our right to dictate to you how you wish to conduct your affairs."

For a long silence Hafrin and Marrek could only stare at Kili. Then Hafrin added, "But the rights of my subjects are just as important. And manners are equally important. If I fail to conduct myself within the rules of common decency and concern for the well-being of my subjects, who am I to govern others and order them to abide by them?"

"Well said," Kili told him. "I'm pleased to see you remember your lessons so well."

Eyes twinkling, Hafrin raised a finger. "I can see I'm going to have difficulties with some of my subjects remembering their place."

"Hah!" Nichole laughed out loud. "As if you care when it comes to your friends."

"True." One side of Hafrin's mouth turned up, skewing his features slightly out of true. "Except when we're in public. If nothing else, they'll keep me from...how did you put it Marrek?"

"Getting a swelled head?"

"Which brings us back to our present situation," Kili reminded them.

"Ah, yes. The Hynarkin and the Craneeno," said Marrek. Nichole knew he wished he could put off venturing deeper into this particular quagmire. Equally, he knew he could no longer avoid it.

"Who are the Craneeno?"

In response to Kili's question, Marrek elected a roundabout route to the answer. "You're aware that rumour has it the Hynarkin live on the off-shore islands?"

"Yes."

"And no doubt you and Ziv have always wondered why I choose to live here if that's the case?"

"Frequently." Patience itself, Kili fed Marrek the appropriate responses to draw him on.

"In actuality, as you've guessed, we are Star born," Marrek told her.

"In more ways than one," muttered Hafrin under his breath. Nichole silently hissed at him to be silent and he subsided.

"Rin's right." Marrek nodded to his foster son. "We, Nikki and I, and all the traders you know as Hynarkin, are just that; descendants of parents who were star born. In fact, some of us are also star born, although there are those at our colony who were born here on Fimiah."

"Star...born?" As the ramifications of his statement sank in Kili blinked. Hesitant, she asked, "You come from the stars?"

"Yes."

"But how can that be?"

Now Nichole leaned forward, her son resting in her lap. "Every point of light in your sky, Kili is either a sun, some larger, some smaller, or massive groups of suns we call galaxies. A few of those suns have worlds spinning about them, even as Fimiah spins about its source of light. Not all of those worlds have moons, or rings. Some have nothing at all."

"Then you weren't born here?"

"On Fimiah? No. My birth world has three moons and is called Baccaria."

"And I was born and raised on Zlitterka. It has five planets in its system, as does Fimiah, but no moons."

For the first time Nichole knew something of Marrek's background. Raised among the insectoid race of the Conglomerate of United Worlds, he possessed a unique perspective when it came to alien relations. And since his brother, Davyn, was the older, it was a given that he had also been born there.

"And not all planets can support us," Nichole told Kili. About to continue with a quick lesson in xeno-biology, Nichole saw Marrek frown again, and bit back the rest of what she had meant to say. However she 'pathed several images to Hafrin and saw his startled look in response. Marrek's frown intensified, aware of the exchange. This time, however, he allowed it to slip by without remarking on it.

"And these…Craneeno also come from another world?"

"Yes."

"But what do they want with us?"

"I'm afraid they consider us," Marrek gestured broadly to include the whole group, "everyone who is not of their race, to be little more than highly intelligent animals and unworthy of possessing any world. A small group of our people fled a massive upheaval on our original home world several hundreds of years ago, Kili. We don't even know where it is anymore. The first world we found that could support us was already occupied. They were under attack by the Craneeno. Understandably, the inhabitants were suspicious of us, and of our intentions. Once talks began, however, they readily welcomed us. Over time, we've contacted seven other intelligent species at our level of technological advancement, or higher, with whom we formed an alliance to fight the Craneeno."

Gaze drifting from Marrek to Nichole, Kili prodded, "What about us? We look like you. Are we of your race?"

"No. There are certain subtle differences in your make-up, principally internal, for all the outward similarities," Marrek explained. "But we've discovered over the years that what formed all of us settled on certain types, if you will. Whether that species was intelligent or not, all seem to fall within certain guidelines. That's made it easier to expand our…bloodlines."

Marrek almost said genes, and Nichole quickly fed him the appropriate term. He nodded his thanks to her timely assistance, saw Hafrin grin at him.

"But that doesn't explain the sword's reaction," Kili observed.

"Not entirely, no."

"Did your people give it to us?"

"No. Nor do we have any idea who left it. It's even possible they're your progenitors. I wish we could find them. We could do with their help."

"If they're still around," Nichole said to Hafrin.

Kili asked, "Why?"

"Because anyone capable of fashioning so intricate and sophisticated a piece of weaponry as Hafrön would be an incredible asset to us in our battle against the Craneeno," said Nichole.

"And that is why the Hynarkin…the Star Born have been encouraging us to progress," Hafrin put in.

"Introducing innovative, new ideas and materials," said Nichole.

Marrek nodded. "By stimulating the imaginations of the Fimiahri, we've succeeded in bringing you back from the very brink of extinction."

One finger tracing her son's cheek, Nichole reminded them all, "But now the real war's just begun."

"Where do we go from here?"

Across Hafrin's question Kili said, "Perhaps we should begin with naming your son, ser."

Hafrin looked at Nichole. "Did you have anything in mind?"

"Ser," Kili advised him, "it's the Alaiad who names the heir, not the mother."

"Unless the Alaiad happens to be the Alaia," Nichole teased Kili. The older woman shook her head but grinned in spite of herself.

"There are some customs which are just plain silly." Hafrin considered his son and shrugged. "I've never considered the possibility of having a child, let alone a son, so soon. Please, Nikki, help me out."

"Well," she passed the two-thirds empty bottle back to Kili, "how about Valrin."

"Silver shield? Why that?"

To Marrek's inquiry Nichole laughed quietly. "This year is Fimirin, Fimiah's Shield, in the age of Dôzhik Koryn. And he was conceived at the turn of the age."

"Don't remind me," Marrek grumbled.

"Ser," Nichole extended the sleeping infant, "please accept your son, Valrin, heir apparent."

With those words Nichole placed the baby in his father's arms. Hafrin acknowledged his son by raising him high in the air. "Behold my son, Valrin. This is my first born upon whom Hafrön has set his seal."

CHAPTER 20

▼

The cabin door opened even as he spoke, and Zivvoz and Indoro entered the room. They took in the scene, absorbing what they had heard. Somehow Indoro had the presence of mind to close the door. While he and his father gazed at the tableau, Zivvoz moved first. Dropping to one knee, he held out his hands, palms up. Slowly Hafrin lowered his son.

"Ser," Zivvoz pledged, "behold your most loyal servants."

Indoro rapidly copied his father, but he spoiled the moment by peering up through a shock of hair that had fallen in his eyes. He caught Hafrin's gaze. Hafrin nodded to his shield brother then flashed a grin, breaking the seriousness of the moment. Both men rose at the lift of Hafrin's free hand. As they removed their boots and joined him, Hafrin returned the baby to Nichole. Zivvoz glanced at Marrek, then at the mother of the infant. For the first time he really saw her.

But it was Indoro who blurted out, "Nikôla."

"How..." Zivvoz broke off, tried again. "Where have you been?"

"Is he yours?" Indoro glanced from his shield brother to the baby and back again. When Hafrin nodded, Indoro asked, "But how is that possible? She's been gone what...a year?"

"More," said Zivvoz, wonder written across his face.

"You had better sit down," said Marrek.

When Zivvoz and his son remained standing, Kili pointed to the nearest seats. "Sit."

They obeyed her, slowly sinking into the chairs. Kili glanced at the door and frowned slightly. "Ziv, where's Dina?"

"Outside."

Nichole craned her neck. A quick glance out the window confirmed Deenala was playing near the stable. She and Kili exchanged a look. Relieved that her daughter was all right, Kili turned her attention to Marrek. Indoro continued to stare at Nichole. His inspection of her new full figure made her uncomfortable. Abruptly realising his inspection was causing her discomfort he redirected his attention.

Hafrin settled next to Nichole, while Marrek adjusted his position to a more comfortable one. There was no ducking the issue and since Kili had guessed enough to make the question moot, Marrek decided to give the holder and his son the whole truth. Quickly, he outlined what had happened, where Nichole had been and did his level best to explain in layman's terms how she could have been absent for so long and had still borne Hafrin's heir.

Only Kili's matter-of-fact expression held back the flood of questions dancing across Indoro's face. Stoic, even in the face of such earth-shattering revelations, Zivvoz studied the tableau made by Hafrin, his heir and the two off-worlders. Arms crossed over her front, Kili leaned against the kitchen counter and waited.

"Well," Zivvoz managed at length, "this is indeed news."

Indoro found his tongue, "So what do we do now?"

"That has yet to be discussed. Winter is on the way, which is a good thing for us in one way," observed Marrek. "It'll be some time before we're able to do much of anything, at least until the snow begins melting."

"We could start calling in our contacts," suggested Zivvoz.

"You might want to wait until the roads to the capital are under snow," remarked Kili. "That way you should cut down the likelihood of the Usurper's people stumbling onto us."

Zivvoz nodded. "Hmmm, you have a point, my love. There have definitely been more patrols lately than in previous years."

"Do we know why?"

"They're looking for something," Marrek told Nichole. "Or someone."

"Someone?" Face frozen, Nichole stared across the room past the others. Memory of the incident in the tavern rushed back to slap her.

Hafrin touched her hand. "What's wrong, Nikki?"

For a moment she failed to respond. When he repeated his inquiry she shook her head. "I don't know. It's probably nothing but..."

When she trailed off Marrek insisted, "Let us be the judge, Nikki."

Now she looked away from them, out the window at the pasture where the rynada were grazing. Laying fowl scratched the ground between cabin and stable, bringing back memories she had once tried so desperately to tuck away in the back of her mind. Deenala was hanging on the top railing where Zivvoz had pastured his rynada. Several limp strands of straw dangled from her fingers as she sought to coax the animals over to her. Nichole clung to the homey scene like a drowning man to a life vest.

"At the tavern, the men who chased me told the innkeeper about a new prophecy."

"A new one? That is news," said Zivvoz.

Marrek held up his hand, silencing the holder and his family. "Can you remember what was said?"

"Not specifically. But apparently the first part was something a seer had told Jikpryn at the turn of the New Year. I guess he wasn't happy about it because they said he demanded the seer explain it. Instead she added to it." Nichole paused, shook her head in regret. "I'm sorry. I was so tired I'm afraid I don't remember what they said."

"Can you recall the gist of it?"

At Marrek's insistence, Nichole scrunched up her face in thought. One side of her mouth pinched in. "There was something to do with black on black. That much I do remember."

"We've heard that much," said Marrek. Curious, to Nichole's mind, he was staring at Hafrin. Hafrin studiously avoided his foster father's gaze. Determined to recall as much as possible of the incident, Nichole struggled to summon up those anxious minutes in the tavern.

"Eyes of the Serpent," Nichole added. "The seer told them to watch for someone with the eyes of the Serpent."

Unlike those at the tavern who had snorted and returned to their drinks, her companions stared at her. Beneath their disconcerting expressions she felt her cheeks unaccountably grow hot, and she struggled to remain calm. Abruptly she realised that of all the inhabitants, Fimiahri and those Wanderers living among the planetary inhabitants, she alone had green eyes. In order to regain her composure, she was forced to drop her gaze. When she dared a glance at Hafrin from the corner of her eyes, he appeared deep in thought.

"So we may finally have what we needed to convince our proponents," said Zivvoz. His voice was surprisingly calm, despite the bright, almost feverish light in his eyes.

With a hitch of one shoulder, Marrek indicated he was not entirely satisfied with the solution, yet he was equally cognisant of time slipping away. If they did not consolidate their forces now, they stood a good chance of missing a solid opportunity of drawing in a substantial force with which to regain Hafrin's inheritance. Additionally, to let it slip by meant they risked losing everything when the Craneeno came out of hiding.

"The time for covert action is past, Marrek," Hafrin said decisively. "I'm old enough now to take what is mine and hold it without a Regent."

"You're still very inexperienced in warfare," Marrek reminded him.

"My father never fought a day in his life," Hafrin retorted.

And look what happened to him, thought Nichole. But she kept that treacherous mind whisper safely locked away. For all of that, it was obvious Zivvoz and his family were thinking the same thing. Slowly Hafrin got to his feet. Arms crossed over his chest, jaw set, he stared them all down.

"I have both of you," he announced, shifting his gaze from Zivvoz to Marrek.

After a very long minute of silence, Marrek broke the tableau. "Right, then. I'll have to include all of this in my message."

"Should be interesting considering you have to keep it short," said Nichole.

Marrek raised a finger. She grinned at him but refused to be cowed by the admonishment. With a shake of his head, Marrek let the matter drop.

Kili leaned forward. "Marrek, if Jikpryn's men are looking for Nikôla, is it wise for her to remain here?"

"This is my home as much as it's Marrek's," countered Hafrin. "I won't let any harm come to her."

"You might not be able to prevent it," said Zivvoz.

His logic raised more concerns Marrek had not wanted to deal with at this juncture. Unfortunately he could see the matter would have to be addressed. In Nichole's arms, Valrin slept, his lips puckered, almost petulant. Slowly Nichole looked up.

"I'm not that concerned about my well-being," she told them. "It's Val I'm worried about. If he's here and soldiers come…"

Her words trailed off into silence. Marrek nodded. Kili's expression turned sombre. Hafrin rested a hand on her shoulder. Their eyes met. A silent message passed between them and he nodded.

"Ziv. Kili. Would you look after our son?"

"Ser!" On the verge of objecting, Zivvoz bit back what else he was about to say in the face of Hafrin's grim expression.

Hafrin continued, "There's no one else I would trust with his care and upbringing should anything happen to me…us."

"Surely Nikôla would be safer with us?"

To Indoro's inquiry, Marrek shook his head. He explained, "I believe what Nikki and Hafrin have in mind is to divide and maximise protection." He glanced at Hafrin, saw the Alaiad-in-exile nod. "With Val at your home and ostensibly yours, or even Doro's, it's doubtful anyone would look for an infant here. Should it become necessary to defend ourselves, not having to worry about his safety would be less distraction."

Zivvoz acquiesced with a tug of his forelock. "I understand, Marrek. You're right ser, my lady. We shall care for your son as we did for you, ser."

"I couldn't ask for more," said Nichole quietly. But it was clear to all present that she was reluctant to part with the baby.

"Well," said Kili, "I can stay here for a couple of days, at least. That should give them some time together. After all, the wife of an Alaiad is not expected to feed and care for her children. That's for the nursemaid and servants."

"Our history is full of such stories as well." Marrek acknowledged her observation, his statement a gentle reminder to Nichole. She drew a deep breath and slowly released it, resigned to having to give up her child. "Now, if you'll excuse me, I have a message to compose and send."

CHAPTER 21

▼

Nichole

Messages back from the colony in response to Marrek's report advised that Nichole's guide and travel companion had failed to return. Marrek feared the worst but dared not attempt to conceal the truth from Nichole. She met the news with a grim expression. Her eyes glistened with unshed tears for the man she had known only a short time. The topic was shelved.

Vern advised Marrek that, in light of Nichole's relatively easy delivery, he would not risk anyone else on the trails. And so Nichole dealt with the results of Kili's crude episiotomies. That she was uncomfortable went without saying. Although she took particular pains to ensure against infection, she healed slowly, which meant Marrek forbade her to attempt any heavy chores.

One day ran into another. Marrek and Zivvoz rode out frequently. Disguised, they visited villages several days distance from where they lived, spreading rumour, laying the groundwork for revolution. Despite Jikpryn's efforts to maintain control of his troops, there had been sufficient incidents in the area to arouse the ire of the locals. Enough soldiers in the more sparsely populated regions had overstepped the bounds of their responsibilities, trammelled the rights of the populace, and had gone unpunished. Unrest fermented close to the surface. Talk in the taverns revolved continuously around the prophecies.

In the absence of the older men, Hafrin and Indoro drilled repeatedly, on foot and on rynadback. Nichole watched them, at once envious and frustrated, wishing giving birth had not left her so physically debilitated. Despite her initial interest concerning the prophecy, she forgot about it.

The weather held, cloudless and persistently sunny. Such crops as had survived the summer were brought in. Fields were turned. Then, almost without warning, the temperature plummeted. They woke one morning to glistening fields and rooftops. Frost whorls coiled up windowpanes and etched railings and the cabin steps. Marrek waited until after breakfast before approaching Nichole. While Kili washed the dishes and made bread, he went out to find Nichole outside watching the rynada. Fed and changed, Valrin slept indoors beside the fire in the trundle cot provided by Kili and Zivvoz.

"How are you doing?"

Hands resting on the railing, Nichole glanced over her shoulder. "Fine. Still a bit sore."

"That's to be expected out here."

A nod of her head indicated she accepted life on the fringe: a step back in time to the way in which their ancestors had probably lived. Marrek recalled her upbringing. Even though Baccaria possessed advanced technology, its farmers and ranchers maintained the basic skills and household appliances. Wood stoves and fireplaces were commonplace due to frequent power outages when some of its fiercer storms blew in off its seas. Undoubtedly she had been taught to cook in stoves heated with dried sectambulator droppings. Archaic as this seemed where methane stoves could as easily be employed, it was a common practice on the plains. Trees were found only in the alpine reaches, the arboral giants husbanded with an eye to the ecology. Droppings were easily renewed and stored, and plentiful on the grasslands. If a traveller became stranded, fuel for heat and cooking was readily at hand, unlike trees, which took generations to replace.

Marrek joined Nichole. Perched on the railing, he wrapped one hand around a support pole and stared off across the field. Stubble left over from the hay he, Hafrin, Zivvoz and Indoro had mowed just days earlier now glittered with melting frost. Tiny gems of moisture winked where the early light caught it.

"Was there something you wanted, Marrek?"

Forthright to a fault, Nichole caught him back to the present. He drew a short breath and nodded. "I think it's high time we sent Val down to Ziv's. Every day we delay we risk discovery."

A shadow flickered across her face. She turned away, head tipped to one side. Then she looked up. Again she nodded, this time just once, a short dip of her head. He tried to catch her eye but she evaded his gaze.

"Would you like to accompany me?"

Before he had finished his question she was shaking her head. With a sigh, Marrek slipped from the railing and went inside. Minutes later, Nichole followed. Silent, expression pinched, she moved about the cabin putting together clothing and such other items Kili would need for Valrin's care. Before long she had two neat bundles. She set them on the kitchen table.

"I think that's everything."

Now their eyes met. Marrek studied her, struggling to sense what she so carefully guarded. Unable to get a definitive reading from her, he made a mental note to ask Hafrin to watch for any signs that she was under stress or suffering from the separation.

I shouldn't have let him take off with Doro yesterday, he considered. Unfortunately, they were short on meat, fresh and smoked, and winter looked to be severe. There was no telling how soon the pair would be back.

"It's all right, Marrek," Nichole told him. "Val and I have had enough time to bond, and it won't be long before I can start riding over to see him."

There was a trailing thought from Marrek, one that she knew he meant her to catch. *Not for a while yet. At least not until you've been seen by the Medic.*

Resigned, Nichole inclined her head just enough to let him know she had heard. "Anyway, it's not that far, after all. I could probably walk down. The exercise would do me good."

To that Marrek nodded. They each took a bundle and, side by side, walked to the door. Outside they found Hafrin standing alongside Bïzhan. Not altogether surprised to find him there, Nichole passed her husband one of the bundles.

Marrek looked past Hafrin to his companion. "When did you get back?"

"Just now."

Along with Indoro was Zivvoz, leading a spare mount. No one said anything. Hafrin vaulted onto the stallion and sat, lightly controlling the black with his knees and thoughts. His own thoughts tightly shielded, Marrek mounted Shalinô. He knew his expression told his charges that he felt they were far more prepared for this moment than he was.

Before Marrek could say anything, though, Kili emerged, carrying the still sleeping Valrin. She paused, allowing Nichole to tenderly touch Valrin's cheek before she headed purposefully down the steps. Zivvoz lifted his wife onto the spare rynad he had brought up from the hold.

"You'd better take the crib back with you, too," said Nichole. "I've appreciated its convenience, but you'll need it now Val's going to be staying with you."

Zivvoz nodded and went inside to collect the cradle. Nichole helped him position it across his rynad's withers, then lifted a hand as the party turned away and headed off in the direction of Zivvoz's hold. Just as they reached the trees, Indoro clapped his heels to his mount and shot into the forest, his mount going all out. Between two breaths, Hafrin released Bïzhan. Tail arched on the breeze behind him, the black took off, a tightly coiled spring given freedom.

Abandoned on the cabin stoop, Nichole wrapped her arms about her as though suddenly conscious of the cold. After a quick look about the empty yard, she stepped back indoors and firmly closed the door behind her. Aromas of baking bread and spices greeted her, partially easing the ache in her heart.

*   *   *   *

Winter pressed in upon them with an abruptness that took Nichole by surprise. When she spoke of it to Hafrin, he told her the previous year had been surprisingly mild, with scant rain and even less snow. That this winter came in fast and cold had not entirely surprised him. But, once again, there was little moisture on the rock-hard ground.

Marrek and Hafrin continued to ride out, almost as frequently as before the cold. Safety and security foremost in his mind, Marrek took his communication equipment with him, but only contacted Vern at the community once they were well away from civilisation. Neither of them spoke to Nichole about what was entailed in each expedition, and to Nichole's irritation, Hafrin kept the information carefully secure in the back of his mind where it would not accidentally leak out. In her absence he had obviously received training to refine his talents. She knew she should be grateful to Vern for sending someone to instruct Hafrin, yet at the same time she missed the openness they had shared before.

Five weeks after Valrin went to live with Zivvoz's family, snow began falling, a light dusting barely boot sole deep. Still, the promise of more to come lay foremost in their thoughts, and was eagerly awaited. To ease Hafrin's mind Nichole stayed with Zivvoz's family in his absence. Despite the cold and her slow recovery from the episiotomies, Nichole made the effort to trudge up to Marrek's cabin to feed the animals. Although she thoroughly enjoyed the opportunity to visit her son, Nichole knew she was using every excuse available escape the cabin.

Cabin fever, she mused, recalling a phrase from a story she had once read. At the time she had failed to comprehend its meaning. Now she knew what it meant all too well.

A second, heavier snowfall insulated the fields, much to Zivvoz's pleasure. He had made no secret of his fears for the next spring. Before long, however, he prepared to once more accompany Marrek and Hafrin. While Zivvoz gave Indoro last minute instructions in the sitting room concerning the women and Valrin, Nichole vented her frustration at yet another separation as she pulled journey loaves from the oven. Her wordless expression of dissatisfaction was not lost on her husband.

"Nikki."

Without looking up she asked, "Why, Rin?"

"Because it's necessary," he responded, evasive as always.

"How long this time?"

The plaintive note in her voice caused him to grin. He put his arms around her. "Only four, maybe five days."

With mock severity she drew out of his arms and turned to confront him. "So this time I'll stay here, at Marrek's cabin."

"Are you sure?"

"Yes."

"Bet you don't make it past day two," he parried.

With a snort, Nichole turned away once more, just in time to catch Marrek sneaking a pinch from the edge of one loaf. She smacked his fingers with the flat of the wood spatula.

"Quit it, Marrek."

But his actions drew a faint smile to her lips in spite of herself. She wrapped up the last of their meagre travel rations and thrust the packet at Hafrin. Wordless, he accepted it. Equally silent, she followed them out onto the porch, remaining there while Indoro accompanied them down the steps. After they disappeared into the woods, he turned to Nichole.

"Ready?"

"I'm staying here this time, Doro."

Clearly he had not expected that response. "Are you sure that's wise, Nikôla?"

"Perhaps not," she told him, "but this is what I want."

"Did you tell Rin?"

"Yes."

To that, Indoro could only grunt. He leapt onto his mount and rode away with only one glance back. Abandoned, Nichole returned to the cabin. She banked the fire in the hearth to husband the embers, washed the dishes and tidied up around the cabin preparatory to returning to Zivvoz's hold to see Valrin. But before she left she fetched down Hafrin's short sword from the chest at the foot of their bed in the loft. For several minutes she turned it back and forth. Then, she began marking out the paces taught her, first by Zivvoz, and then at the Academy. Slowly she wove back and forth, finding the rhythm.

A day passed, then a second. Twice a day she worked with the sword at the cabin, careful not to over-exert herself. On the third day, as she was preparing something to eat, she caught the sound of rynada approaching the hold. Eagerly she pressed to the frosted windowpane. What greeted her eyes sent fear washing over her. Seven men in Wôbiny mauve rode up the road and drew rein at the railing. As one soldier dismounted, Nichole instinctively glanced in the direction of the loft. She backed toward the ladder, too late. The door crashed open.

A voice outside demanded, "Who's in there?"

In reply, the soldier in the door responded over his shoulder, never letting eyes leave her, "Just a woman, sir."

"Bring her out."

There was no denying the authority in that voice. There was something about it that sent shivers up Nichole's spine. She instinctively sprang for the ladder to the loft. The soldier lunged for her as she scrambled up the rungs. Somehow she eluded him and made it to the top. Her belt knife lay on the pallet. She dove for it. Her fingers curled about the hilt and she rolled onto her back. But the soldier was there, reaching for her before she was prepared. The wild slash of her blade tip caught his cheek and sent him reeling back. Now Nichole scrabbled back until wood pressed against her spine. She used it to push to her feet. Arms outstretched, the soldier moved in on her. To her chagrin, he ducked her next defensive move, grabbed her knife hand and squeezed. His grip numbed her fingers and the knife clattered to the floor. Nichole bit back a cry of pain.

"Bitch," he cursed her. One hand still gripping her wrist, he grabbed a handful of hair with other and dragged her back across the loft. "I ought to cut you for that."

Strangely, he did nothing except direct her towards the ladder. Unable to wriggle free, Nichole gritted her teeth as he forced her back downstairs. Still dabbing the cut on his left cheek, the man maintained his hold on her, the fingers of his left hand twisted in her hair. Tears started in her eyes.

Another soldier was picking at Nichole's food, clearly enjoying the contents of her plate. Lips curled in a leer, he crossed the room to examine what his companion had found.

"Well, what have we here?"

Infuriated by their proprietary behaviour towards her and their invasion of what was her home, she lashed out, knocking the plate and the remnants of her meal from the other man's hands. He stared at her stupidly, startled by her unexpected act of daring.

"That was mine," she growled, twisting in her captor's grip so she was turned sideways to both of them. Her actions caused her additional pain but she refused to be cowed. From outside, the soldiers' commander bellowed again.

"Do you have her?"

With a brief stutter, the man holding Nichole responded, "Yes, lord."

"Well," returned the speaker, "where is she? Bring her out here."

"Yes, lord." At that, the soldier pushed Nichole across the room, using her hair to govern her direction. "Move."

She stifled another cry of pain as she was forced, unwilling, out the door and onto the porch to confront the rest of the troop. Behind her she could hear the other soldier turning over the cabin. Her secret fear was that they might stumble upon Bînlârâ's sword. From Hafrin she had learned that it was stored in a secret compartment in the bottom of the chest in the loft. With that in mind, Nichole decided it was unlikely the soldiers would find it unless they decided to smash the cabin furniture.

Once on the porch, Nichole had the opportunity to study the troop and their leader. Most of the soldiers were typical stocky build. Two were above average height. All had the light skin and dark hair and eyes common place among the Wôbiny. But their leader was an entirely different matter. Almost abnormally slender by Fimiahri or Wanderer standards, there was something about his hatchet features and piercing eyes that sent an involuntary shiver up Nichole's spine. Intent upon their captive, the man kneed his rynad forward.

"Do you know who I am, woman?"

Beneath his contemptuous stare she gathered her tattered courage about her and responded smoothly. "No. Should I?"

The soldier holding her yanked her hair, giving her head a sharp jerk. "Watch your manners, bitch."

But the object of her scrutiny merely raised a hand. "Leave it, Oryl. I admire spirit."

Nichole felt there was a certain lack of sincerity behind his words. At the same time, there was grudging approval for her determination not to be cowed. It permeated the other soldiers and because of it this person was cautious not to act in a manner that might cost him his control of them.

"I am Tolbôun," he told her.

Slowly Nichole straightened, though not through any show of respect for his person. Emotions frozen within, she continued to meet his gaze. This was the Fimiahri who had betrayed his people to the Craneeno. Something no Wanderer would ever consider.

How can anyone stand to be in close proximity to a Craneeno?

Unaware of the track her thoughts had taken, he nodded. "I see my fame has spread before me."

Were I you, she silently retorted, *I wouldn't be so proud of such fame.*

Now the Outsider gestured. "Come here, wench. Closer. Someone as proud and spirited as you must be life-mated. Are you?"

Nichole nodded. Unwise, she knew, to deny the obvious with the lump of the armband visible through the taut sleeve fabric. Her captor released his grasp on her hair but added a grip on her wrist as they descended the steps.

"Where's your husband?"

Even as Tolbôun glanced about the yard, Nichole informed him, "Out. Hunting with the neighbours."

There were sufficient fresh tracks about the yard to back up her declaration. Tolbôun turned back to her. "Personally, I wouldn't be such a fool as to leave a wife as lovely as you alone."

"He loves me well enough," countered Nichole, wondering why she let herself get dragged into defending Hafrin's actions. At the same time, she thanked fate for taking him and Marrek away before the soldiers' arrival.

Laughter barked from Tolbôun's lips, startling the laying fowl, and causing the rynada to throw up their heads. In the pasture, the small tîlkrîn herd bolted across the field. For the first time she locked gazes with the Outsider. An oath burst from his lips.

"Serpent slime."

An involuntary yank on the reins made his rynad rear and spin on its hocks. As its forefeet touched the ground, he brought his fist down hard between its ears, staggering it. Nichole winced at the viciousness of his actions. Stunned, the rynad allowed itself to be hauled about so that its rider once more confronted Nichole. Tolbôun slipped from his rynad and forced Nichole's chin up. Then he addressed the troop.

"So my friends, fate has indeed been kind this day. We came to ask the holders where we might find someone with Serpent eyes and look what we've stumbled on."

Shocked by that announcement, Nichole's captor jerked his hand away as though her flesh had suddenly burned him. Cold worse than midwinter invaded her. Trapped, she could only wrap her arms about her. The Outsider walked slowly around her, inspecting her like she was a new mount he was preparing to purchase. Inexplicably, the hairs on the nape of her neck crept. Her flesh prickled beneath his examination.

"Oryl, bring up one of the rynad and see if there's any tack in the shed."

"Lord."

"Worrek."

"Lord!"

"Get down here and take charge of this woman. I want her dressed to ride by the time Oryl fetches her a mount."

Stunned, Nichole failed to react until the soldier on the porch came down and grabbed her arm. Galvanised into action by their high-handed behaviour, she glared at them.

"And just where do you think you're taking me?"

"To Iryô," was the response. Tolbôun gestured. "See she's dressed in something appropriate. And put together provisions from what's in the cabin. I won't have our own supplies strained by an additional mouth to feed."

"Yes, lord."

CHAPTER 22

▼

Fortunately, the soldier allowed Nichole a measure of privacy in which to change for the journey, but only after the loft had been thoroughly searched and anything that might even remotely be used as a weapon had been removed. They failed to find the sword in the chest.

In the time it took to prepare for the trip under their supervision, Nichole reached the conclusion that it would be sheer suicide to attempt to escape. Fuming, she took down her below shoulder-length hair and properly braided it for the trip. Then she dressed in her travel clothes: an undershirt, a wool outer shirt, a vest with its tilkrin wool turned in against her body, split skirt and lined boots were designed to provide a measure of warmth when riding. She tucked the hem of her ankle-length skirt into the tops of her knee-high boots, grabbed down her sleeved cloak and stomped down the ladder.

She discovered they had selected Neranïl for her to ride. Several soldiers grunted appreciation at her choice of clothing when she emerged from the cabin. She hid her irritation over their selection of mount. Too old to outrun the soldiers' trail-hardened rynada, yet young enough to keep up with them, he was an excellent choice. Nichole concealed her irritation as she tugged on her cloak and fastened the front. Oryl held Neranïl's head while she swung up onto the old rynad's back.

While she had been dressing, Worrek had been busy in the kitchen and larder. The two sacks he tied behind her contained more than enough to see her most, if not all of the way to the capitol. The minute she was seated on Neranïl, however, Nichole knew she was not going to be able to maintain the pace these men undoubtedly would wish to set. She shifted her weight in the saddle, trying to get comfortable. When that failed to work, she tucked several folds of her cloak beneath her. Someone snickered. Nichole ignored them and reined about as Tolbôun gestured and led them off down the road into the forest.

A brief glance behind told her the cabin door was shut. When she failed to visit the hold today, she felt certain Indoro would ride up to find out what was wrong. She prayed he would find the note she had left beneath the pillow in the loft. Even though Hafrin was still within mental range, Nichole dared not attempt to contact him. As familiar as she was with him, she knew he would come racing after her before Marrek and Zivvoz could develop a plan to rescue her. And that would prove fatal.

Before long she was aching all over and requested a brief halt so she could dismount and walk for a while. They kept moving, mending their pace to accommodate her, which surprised Nichole. Further adding to their leader's irritation, she needed to take frequent breaks to relieve herself. Eventually Tolbôun selected a campsite and ordered a halt. Undoubtedly he was annoyed by their slow progress. Rather than speaking to anyone, he settled himself on his riding blanket beneath a nearby tree. From there he glowered at everyone as they went about their assignments.

While all the soldiers, with the exception of Nichole's guard, went about setting up camp, she walked and stretched in an effort to work out the stiffness formed from hours in the saddle. Then she settled. Her guard shackled her ankles to prevent any escape attempt in the night. Cold and damp ate through her clothing and she slept poorly.

The next two days on the trail were much the same. Nichole's suffering increased. Each time she dismounted to relieve herself she checked for signs of bleeding, fearful that her pain meant something serious. Her fears proved unfounded and she decided she was merely suffering from readjusting to riding after an extensive absence from the activity. By the middle of the third day, however, she felt she could go no further. Stepping down, she settled on a rock at the side of the road. The Outsider reined back and glared at her. Instead of complying with his silent command, she defiantly crossed her arms.

"Look," she snapped back at him, "I can't keep on like this, okay? I've been…ill."

At her slight hesitation Oryl stared at her intently. Something, she was uncertain what precisely, appeared to alert him to exactly what she was alluding. Perhaps it had been the manner in which she padded the saddle-pad beneath her. Or it might have been her numerous breaks to relieve herself. He barked a laugh.

Tolbôun snarled at him. "Stop braying, you idiot."

"Sorry, m'lord," said Oryl. "But we should have realised the first day."

"Realised what?"

"Why, lord, it's obvious. She's recently dropped a child."

Head snapping up, the Outsider stared at the soldier, and then back at Nichole. "Is this true?"

Lips compressed, Nichole kept silent. The last thing she wanted was for them to ride back to the hold and attempt to locate Valrin. Uncertain what to expect, the soldiers milled about. Their rynada grunted and shuffled, heads bobbing as they awaited direction from their riders. Nichole's silence in itself appeared to answer Tolbôun's question.

"Where is it?"

Chin tipped down, Nichole fought against rising fear. If they returned and found Val, they would undoubtedly force her to bring her son, using him as an additional hostage. At the moment, an attempt at escape was difficult but not entirely beyond her abilities. With the baby it would be impossible. Compounding her anxiety was her concern for the safety of Zivvoz's family and the young woman they had employed to nurse Valrin.

Caught by the truth behind her refusal to respond, Tolbôun weighed the problem. Stray thoughts flitted across Nichole's mind as he considered the feasibility of returning to find her infant against making the best time possible back to the safety of the capitol. Eventually, to her immense relief, he jerked his head.

"Walk, then, if you must, but we keep moving."

They made their third camp at a site used by numerous travellers. There were several old fire pits and stones on which to rest cook pots. Stumps and logs were arranged about each hearth. Some were so old they were crumbling to dust from weather and insect infestation. Two copses of trees provided natural corrals for the animals, the trunks and branches cunningly trained so that there was only one opening between the grove exterior large enough through which the drays and mounts could pass. A rope across the opening provided sufficient deterrent to keep them inside.

As with the previous nights, Nichole was tethered to a tree and her ankles shackled against any escape attempt. This time, she was fortunate enough to have a patch of ground beneath a large tree that was bereft of snow and with sufficient mulch from rotting needles and other plant refuse to cushion her body. As one of the soldiers fastened the shackles she watched, mildly amused by their efforts. Given the opportunity to escape she knew she could easily pick the locks. Unfortunately, the rynada were well guarded and, in her present condition, she was better off waiting for assistance to arrive.

Stretched out on her back, she glanced across the fire to discover the Outsider was propped on his elbow, studying her. Something about him sent a shiver through her once more. Unlike the soldiers whom she merely disliked, what she experienced in Tolbôun's presence was so adverse that her emotions baffled her. She forced herself to meet his gaze before turning her back on him. Although she suspected her calculated move annoyed him, Nichole was not about to let him think she was afraid of him and his men. At the same time, she wondered if she was making a mistake, if appearing fearful of them and cowed would have been the better option.

Too late now, she told herself.

Nikki?

Rin! It was all Nichole could do not to start at how loud his thoughts were. During her absence his ESP ability had definitely matured and grown.

Thank the Serpent. Where are you? Are you all right?

I'm fine, Rin. We're about two day's ride north. I'm not sure where we're going. I thought they were taking me to Iryô, but if they are, they're certainly taking a roundabout route.

They who? What happened?

Jik's advisor arrived at the cabin two days ago with a fighting tail. The minute he saw me he ordered me to accompany them to meet your uncle. Didn't you find my note?

No, and I'm afraid you're not very clear.

Sorry, but I have to abbreviate this. There isn't much time.

Thought as much. Vern told Marrek the Craneeno are gathering their forces south of here. They've got some pretty impressive weaponry but your people are going to try something that they hope will incapacitate much of it.

What about me?

A twig snapped. Nichole rolled onto her back. Tolbôun stood over her. A silhouette with the fire behind him, he was at once unreadable and terrifying. Skin prickling, Nichole pushed up on one elbow.

"What do you want?"

"Still awake?"

"Yes."

Nikki, Hafrin called to her again, unaware she was preoccupied, *Marrek says to tell you not to do anything to antagonise them. Go along with them. We'll catch up with you before you reach the city.*

Still pinned by the Outsider's gaze, Nichole responded, *When?*

I don't know specifically. Just…watch yourself.

I will.

Something dark and vile moved behind the Outsider's eyes. Before she could react, Tolbôun reached down and yanked her to her feet by her vest front. Uncertain of his intentions, but suspecting the worst, Nichole simply reacted.

Voice high-pitched with fear, she shrieked, "Leave me alone!"

Squirming, she struggled to free herself. She lashed out, her work-ragged nails raking his flesh. When he tried to gag her cries with his free hand, she bit him. A roar of pain escaped Tolbôun and he flung her against the trunk. Pressed against the tree, slightly dazed from bashing her head against it, Nichole watched him, wary, waiting for his next move. Those soldiers at bivouac stirred and sat up. One of the duty guards emerged from the shadows.

"What's wrong, lord?"

Oryl glanced from Nichole to his superior and back again. Teeth gritted, her eyes flashing Nichole confronted the Outsider. With a grunt, the Outsider stepped back.

"I thought she had somehow freed herself. When I went to check, she attacked me."

It was evident from Oryl's expression he did not believe the Outsider. At the same time, he was not about to argue with his superior. Cautiously he approached Nichole. She allowed him to check her restraints, and then she resettled herself. All the while, she watched Tolbôun and wondered what could have possessed him to attack her.

My God. Her breath caught in her throat. *Could he possibly be a latent? But I didn't think the psi talents could be passed…what am I thinking. Rin's a telepath, but that would mean Tolbôun's also got Wanderer genes in his bloodline!*

Tolbôun withdrew to his bedding once more. This time, he turned his back on her. Grateful for small favours, Nichole forced herself to lie down. But what sleep she got was fitful and she woke feeling groggy and strained.

To make matters worse, the night's incident seemed to have put Tolbôun in a particularly foul mood. Nichole's continued slowing of their progress only served to further acerbate the situation. Ignoring the soldiers' stares, the Outsider got them moving at a faster pace than the day before. He cut down on the number of halts they made, too. And when Nichole insisted upon dismounting to walk, he forced her to move more quickly, so that in the end she realised she could either exhaust herself trotting to keep up with the rynada, or risk injury riding at an extended walk. Given the choice between the two, she opted to ride. To her surprise, the soldiers did their utmost to surreptitiously mend their pace whenever possible.

Forest began giving way more and more frequently to fields that were fenced and tilled. Dry-stone walls formed field perimeters. Domestic livestock grazed in pastures, pawing aside the snow to reach the stubble and sedges underneath. Very little hay was evident even where there was clearly scant forage for the animals. Most of the stock appeared far too lean. In the distance, the sound of an axe rang clearly on the crisp air. Before long, they all heard rending wood give way to the crash of a forest giant measuring its length upon the frozen ground.

Mounted once more, seated on a pad one of the soldiers finally contrived despite Tolbôun's foul temper, Nichole shrugged her shoulders and resettled her cloak, striving to find a measure of warmth. Despite lined boots and gloves, her extremities were fast growing numb. She might blow on her hands to warm her fingers and stuff them in her armpits, but her feet remained a problem. The only solution was to continue to dismount whenever possible and walk to stir up circulation in her feet.

"Tonight we'll spend indoors," one of the soldiers informed her. She glanced at him. "There's a posting station not far ahead and I suspect he," the soldier gave a jerk of his chin in the direction of their leader, "will want warmth and a proper bed as much as we do."

At that remark, Nichole caught movement from the front of the group. The Outsider glanced back, a scowl on his face. He drew rein, waiting for Nichole and her escort to come alongside.

"Take point from Gwyrn."

In the face of that thinly veiled chastisement, the soldier went stone-faced. With a nod, he reined away from Nicole, galloped forward and relieved his comrade-in-arms. As tempted as she was to comment on Tolbôun's actions Nichole bit back the words and stared forward. From then on she would remain courteous but do her best not to be overly friendly with her captors.

Unaffected by the cold shoulder, the Outsider snapped, "You will refrain from engaging my men in conversation. Is that understood?"

"Perfectly," she replied without glancing at him.

As promised, the route they followed brought them to a posting station. Unfortunately, it was just past noon and Nichole knew Tolbôun would not permit them to halt yet. However this was a major thoroughfare. From her studies she was aware there should now be such posting stations at regular intervals, approximately half a day's ride apart. At once buoyed and depressed by that knowledge, she slithered from the saddle and leaned against her mount until she had recovered sufficiently to walk unaided. Then she made her way to the bench against the outside wall of the nearest building and gingerly sat.

Nearby, the senior officer at the posting station spoke with Tolbôun, his voice too low for her to eavesdrop. Or so he believed. Unashamed, Nichole touched the periphery of his thoughts.

An orved flew in yesterday, my lord. One of the Alaiad's own service.

What was in the message?

We were to watch for you and tell you to make haste to the capitol. Two informants came to him five days ago with news of a woman with green eyes.

An impatient wave of Tolbôun's hand cut off whatever else the officer was about to say. *I know. We have her.*

With an involuntary start the officer glanced in Nichole's direction. She stared back at him, unabashed. Wide-eyed, the man turned back to the Outsider.

How is it possible, sir?

That is for the Alaiad to determine when he's had the opportunity to speak with her, not us. Now both men stared at Nichole. Slowly, deliberately, she turned her gaze away, across the compound. *Serpent's breath! Do you suppose she can actually hear us?*

Abruptly there was a blank where earlier the Outsider's thoughts had been plain to read. Nichole stiffened and fought an urge to look around. Every fibre of her being suddenly screamed at her to flee but there was nowhere to run. Somehow he knew she could read minds. Trapped, she could only fight the unexpected rush of fear coursing through her.

"We're leaving."

The voice so harsh in her ear made her jump and turn. Expression unfathomable, Tolbôun stood just out of arm's reach. No longer able to appear unaffected, Nichole flinched as she got to her feet. He gestured and a soldier brought a fresh mount. She was sorry to see Neranïl go. Despite his years, the old rynad's presence had been strangely comforting. She stepped into the saddle of the strange rynad, which was, to all intents, as old as Neranïl. The troop fell in around her while the Outsider mounted up. They set out once more.

CHAPTER 23

▼

Hafrin

All around them the familiar hubbub of Revïl's market washed over them. Hands running across the strip of cured and dark blue dyed blïntor hide, Hafrin tested for imperfections that might be detrimental to long wear. Across the stall Marrek watched him from the corner of his eye, likewise preoccupied with a potential purchase. Between them they kept the merchant hopping.

"You won't find any better," declared the merchant from the other side of the stall.

There was just a touch of anxiety in the man. Again, Hafrin examined the piece of hide. About a third of the way along the length, his fingertips finally detected a slightly thicker piece of skin. He kept his fingers moving as though he still detected nothing. After one more test, he set it down.

"How much?"

The merchant named an exorbitant price, much as Hafrin had expected. He countered with a disparately low bid. Thinly veiled disgust emanated from the merchant as he countered Hafrin's insulting offer. To that Hafrin folded his arms over his chest. Marrek put aside the merchandise he had been looking over.

"Problems?"

Hafrin shook his head. "No. Personally, I think we can do better ourselves."

"Are you sure?"

"Positive."

With a shrug, Marrek started out of the stall, Hafrin at his heels. This was a game they had perfected over the years. Now the merchant hurried after them. He called out, aware he was about to lose a sale.

"Hynarkin, I'll take off a third." When Hafrin snorted the man hastened to add, "And I'll give you the name of someone who does excellent work for a discount when you purchase from me."

"Probably a brother or cousin," countered Marrek with a sly grin. It was all Hafrin could do not to laugh outright.

Out-matched, the merchant replied, "I swear on my honour and the Great Serpent, Hynarkin, that I won't cheat you."

Hafrin softened. "All right then."

To his credit the merchant was true to his word. The trip to the hide smith was not wasted. Rather, the smith proved sincere in striking what even Marrek agreed was a decent price for the work they brought him. He promised to have the job done by the time they had eaten a late afternoon meal.

Pleased, Hafrin barely contained himself upon commenting on his good fortune. Marrek quickly brought him back to earth. "Undoubtedly their arrangement is an extremely lucrative deal. Between the two of them, I'll bet they corner almost all of the market for the surrounding area."

"Spoil sport," countered Hafrin. He grinned when Marrek cuffed him in the shoulder. "So, are we going to leave right after supper?"

"I'm not sure. We could do with one more night here to make certain of our contacts." Hafrin dropped back two paces and fell in behind Marrek while they worked their way through the press of customers crowding the square around the food sellers. Once he was able to catch up with his foster father, Marrek continued.

"What did you contract the smith for anyway?"

"A sword belt."

"For Nikki?"

"Yes. I hope she likes it."

"Well, the proof will be in the pudding," commented Marrek as they approached the tavern. "Or so my mother maintained."

"Pudding?"

"Never mind, Rin."

They ordered supper. Before they were finished, a child appeared with a small package for Hafrin. Hafrin made the delivery boy wait while he opened the wrappings and checked the finished product.

"What do you think?"

At the question, Marrek studied the belt. He took it from Hafrin and tugged it firmly to check its suppleness. Then he turned it slightly. Light caught the delicate rynad head and rune for good fortune embossed on either side of the buckle and at the centre back.

"Pay the boy and let him get his supper."

Hafrin dug out a tip and tossed it to the boy who grabbed it out of the air and raced off through the crowded tavern in the direction of the door. Marrek passed back the belt and Hafrin wrapped it up once more. He set it between them on the bench and sipped the dregs of his ale.

"Is Ziv meeting us on the trail?"

"No. He'll be going directly home."

Hafrin stifled a yawn. "I'm for bed, sir."

On the trail Hafrin was respectful of his foster father, taking great pains to maintain the father-son relationship and appearance of Hynarkin trader. He continued to wear the contact lenses that altered his eyes from blue to brown. Over the past year he, Marrek and Zivvoz had continued to carefully sounded out the locals, villagers, trappers and roving merchants, locating the dissatisfied whom they felt they could trust. Those that professed a desire to return to the old days when Fanhri had ruled under the blessings of the Great Serpent with the guidance of Hafrön were carefully investigated at great depth. Hafrin acted as final approving authority, employing gentle mind-touch to ascertain the absolute truth behind each respective individual's statements.

Hafrin admitted to himself that he still could not figure out how Marrek and Zivvoz, or the other Wanderer agents, knew which men or women could be trusted: who to select as the nucleus of their future army, and who to watch as potential enemy to their cause. Yet, they always seemed to pick the right people, a knack that was particularly important since they were not telepathic like he was.

Marrek pushed aside his empty mug. "You're right. We could do with an early night."

And an early morning on the trail, Hafrin silently finished. He caught Marrek's eye and grinned, aware his foster father knew exactly what he was thinking. With a shake of his head, Marrek rose and headed for the stairs.

The rising sun found them well down the trail, heading home. Vrala Harz had left ahead of them, winging off to the Wanderer community with a message from Marrek. Unlike other orved, she knew exactly where to go, even if it was somewhere she had never been before. There were no set departure and arrival points for her, as with others of her kind. She went where Hafrin sent her, dropped off or picked up information as was required and then found him again even when he was on the trail, even flying at night when circumstances necessitated it. Their mental rapport was incredibly acute, so much so that all the traders, including

Marrek, remarked upon it. Yet Hafrin's rapport with Vrala was nothing compared to the one he shared with Bïzhan. And that was something he kept from everyone except Nichole, who knew almost all of his secrets.

The light dusting of snow did little to muffle the shod feet of the rynada. By the time the sun had risen and was beginning to lend a measure of warmth to the morning, the scream of an orved split the air. Without being instructed to, Bïzhan halted. Hafrin raised his arm just in time as Vrala Harz dropped from the sky. Her weight, combined with her forward speed, threatened to tear him from the saddle. But Hafrin was accustomed to her antics, and had braced himself in time.

"One of these days she's going to catch you off-guard," observed Marrek.

Hafrin shook his head. "She won't."

"You're so sure of that."

"You forget, sir."

"No, Rin," Marrek shook his head. "That I can't. Still, I suspect with a little more speed upon landing…"

A raised eyebrow from his foster son caused him to break off and chuckle. Vrala cheeped, not her usual greeting but something that set every nerve in Hafrin's body twitching. He locked eyes with his orved. The intensity of their union alerted Marrek.

"Is something wrong?"

To Marrek's question Hafrin raised a hand, stilling his foster father in a manner the older man would usually not have accepted gracefully. This time he froze, watching Hafrin drop into full mental rapport with the orved. As his surroundings melted into middle-distance, images blurring, Hafrin slipped into Vrala's mind. There was nothing definitive in the orved's unrest, nothing from the community out of the ordinary. Nor had she seen anything amiss during her flight back. Yet Hafrin could not overlook the fact that something was, indeed, wrong.

For the space of two breaths he considered another reason, then he reached out across the intervening distance toward home. And met a blank, a wall that should not have been there. Again, he attempted to contact Nichole, and again he was blocked out. He snapped out of his trance.

"Marrek, something's wrong at home."

"Nichole?"

"I'm not sure, it's just…I can't make contact with her."

"Right. Send Vrala on ahead and have her report back. We'll keep riding, but head for where the transmitter is hidden instead."

Even as Marrek gave him instructions, Hafrin passed along the information. Vrala took to the air, her battle cry acknowledged her awareness of the importance of this mission. Before she was out of sight Hafrin and Marrek put their rynada at the slope. They left the road, moving into the forest, cutting across country. Anxious, they pressed their rynada, but the pack animal slowed them more than either of them liked. In spite of that, and not knowing what they might face the other end, they did not turn it loose.

Out of necessity they paused for a midday snack, loosened the cinches and walked the rynada about to ease their limbs. Marrek ran his hands over the pack animal and then his mount while Hafrin checked the stallion. Bigger than the rest, the trail hardened Bïzhan Koryn stood the course far better than the other rynada. As soon as the rynada's breathing had eased they watered them. Then they tightened the cinches and started out once more. This time the riders walked and led the animals.

Anxiety goaded Hafrin. Driven by his inability to contact Nichole he considered riding ahead. But each time he thought to step into the saddle and leave Marrek, logic restrained him. Finally they remounted and put the rynada into a ground-eating trot. Mid-afternoon, Vrala returned. She refused to land. Instead, she circled overhead, conveying her message to Hafrin. He touched the reins and Bïzhan skidded to a halt.

"Marrek!"

At his shout, his foster father glanced back. He reined down to a walk and brought his mount and the pack animal around in a wide circle to where Hafrin waited. "What's wrong?"

"Vrala says there's no one at the hold. The herd animals and the other rynada haven't been fed yet. Nor have the rakkïal."

"That's not like Nichole."

"It's worse." Hafrin stared up at his orved still circling over the tiny clearing where they sat. "Vrala checked down at Zivvoz's hold."

"Nothing?"

"No. She tried to contact Nikki but can't reach her. Unfortunately, their connection isn't as good as mine so she's limited to a finite area. I get the impression Kili's frantic, though."

"Send Vrala for Ziv. We'll reach the transmitter site by mid-dark if we don't stop for the night."

"We keep going, then."

Now Hafrin fully understood what Zivvoz had taught him and Indoro in theory; this was campaign speed. They rode until the weakest of the animals, the pack rynad, began to wheeze. Then they dismounted and walked. Marrek employed the homing device built into the hilt of his belt knife to guide them towards their objective. Darkness slowed them further. The going was rough, the ground frozen iron hard. And still Marrek refused to unburden the pack animal.

"It's entirely likely we're going to need some of those supplies," he told Hafrin.

Unable to argue the point, Hafrin fell silent and concentrated on maintaining the pace Marrek set. All too soon, the pace took its toll. Eventually he had to admit defeat. He was far more accustomed to riding than he was to walking, unlike his foster father. When he remounted, Marrek refrained from voicing an opinion. He simply ploughed on. But when Marrek took a wrong step and twisted his ankle, Hafrin was abruptly conscious of how weary his foster father was. Hafrin bit back a comment. It was evident Marrek was furious with himself for pushing too hard. Silently he remounted.

Again Hafrin tried to contact Nichole and was gratified with a response. "Marrek. She's okay."

Marrek immediately halted. "Where is she?"

Hafrin held up a hand as he received the information from Nichole. "A group of soldiers rode in two days ago led by the Outsider. They were looking for someone with Serpent eyes."

"Son of a bitch," Marrek swore in Hynarkin. He hurriedly considered the situation and felt compelled to ask the redundant question. "Where are they headed?"

"She thinks they're going to Iryô," responded Hafrin, confirming Marrek's worse fears, "but they seem to be taking a circuitous route to get there."

"Tell her to do as they say…within reason, of course. She's to use her judgement, but no heroics. No trying to escape. We're on our way."

"She understands." Abruptly Hafrin shook his head. "Ouch."

"What?"

"Nothing. She just cut me off too fast." Frowning, Hafrin considered what might have led Nichole to do something so severe. When he met Marrek's gaze, he realised his foster father was equally concerned. "She's alright, though."

"You're certain?"

Hafrin nodded, determined to assuage Marrek's fears where he could not entirely soothe his own. "We better get moving. How far are we from the transmitter?"

Consulting the tracker, Marrek gestured. "We're close, that's the best I can say right now. Can't make out the usual landmarks at night."

They pressed on, husbanding their animals' remaining strength now, conscious that they might well have need of it for longer than they had originally estimated. Even Bïzhan was blowing hard by the time they reached the site shortly before dawn. While Marrek located the communication device, Hafrin saw to the rynada. He stripped their gear, walked them then rubbed them down. Finally he threw blankets over all three.

Once the animals were taken care of he built a small fire. There was a seep nearby. He drew two large pots of water and set them to warm. All the while he kept watch on his foster father. Seated on a fallen tree, Marrek spoke earnestly into the transmitter. Voice pitched low, he set the receiver volume so it was impossible for Hafrin to catch what was being said. He knew better than to eavesdrop. Instead, he finished warming the water and took it to the rynada so they could quench their thirst. As he set the basins where all three animals could drink, a scream overhead announced Vrala's return. Close on the heels of her cry, the sound of weary rynada caught their ears.

CHAPTER 24

▼

Marrek broke off his transmission at that same moment. Apparently he had concluded his report, for he stored the transmitter and joined Hafrin by the fire. Zivvoz staggered into view leading his mount and a pack animal. Both rynada were blowing hard. Their chests and necks were lathered, with strings of saliva trailing from their mouths. Shocked that the old campaigner would drive his animals so hard, Hafrin dashed forward and took their reins from Zivvoz's hands.

"Thank you, ser." Zivvoz tugged his forelock in respect. "I'm sorry I pressed them so hard but when I got your message, I knew I had to come as quickly as possible."

Speechless in the face of his old friend's apology, Hafrin could only nod. He took the rynada away, stripping the gear from them as he went. After allowing them several slurps of water, he took the rugs from Bïzhan and Shalinô and threw them over Zivvoz's animals. While he worked, Marrek took care of Zivvoz. From her perch on his saddletree Vrala watched them all, her head turning from side to side. Once certain his charges were going to recover, Hafrin returned to the fire.

"Right, now we're all together," began Marrek, "I'll bring you up to date."

"You spoke to Piltar?"

To Hafrin's inquiry, Marrek lifted a hand. "Let me do the talking, Rin."

Chastised, Hafrin mumbled, "Sorry."

"That's alright. I know you're concerned. We all are. Ziv," Marrek turned to the holder, "this has pushed up our timetable, I'm afraid."

"Tell me what to do, lord."

Bemused by the unexpected bestowing of the title, Marrek blinked then quickly collected his thoughts. "I've spoken to my people. All of the traders will make best speed to meet up with us, either at my cabin, or en route to overtake the soldiers and Nikki."

"Then you want me to round up some of those loyal to my lord?" Zivvoz nodded in Hafrin's direction.

Marrek shook his head. "No. I want you to ride down with us. You'll have to brief Indoro and see to it Kili, Val, Deena and the wet-nurse are sent to safety."

"Lord, at the moment, with winter coming on, there's nowhere safer than my hold."

That gave Marrek and Hafrin pause. Time stretched away. Hafrin's heart raced, desperate for Nichole's safety, as well as concerned for his son and heir. He could not protect both. He looked at Marrek, caught his eye and nodded.

"He's right, Marrek. Besides, we can always leave a couple of the loyals at the hold along with one of the Wanderers. And equip the Wanderer with a transmitter so he can let us or the community know the minute there's trouble."

"That's just it, Rin," said Marrek, "We won't be able to use that form of communication. The community is shutting down everything at dawn."

"Why, my lord?"

Marrek glanced at Zivvoz. "There's been far too much Craneeno activity in the area. Too many transmissions would mean running the risk of drawing them to where we are. We've lost one colony already and don't plan to lose another. Nor do we," he pointed at his companions, "want them on our trail."

"So how do we keep in touch with your people?"

Hafrin picked up the explanation before Marrek could finish. "Orved. There's enough at all of our communities to utilise them. It'll slow communications but ought to be adequate for the time being."

"Yes. In short," Marrek amplified on Hafrin's brief explanation, "we keep the equipment for emergencies only."

"Do we have a chance of defeating them?"

"Yes. A chance."

Although Marrek replied positively to Zivvoz's question, Hafrin picked up the suggestion of something Marrek was holding back. Fear that not every weapon would be disabled. And that would still leave the Fimiahri and their Wanderer allies at a disadvantage. Hafrin fought the urge to dip into Marrek's thoughts, to find out exactly what his foster father feared. Before he had quite wrestled down the urge, Marrek caught his eye. In that instant Hafrin knew Marrek was aware of what was going through his mind.

Still holding Hafrin's gaze Marrek said, "Leave that for the future. I think we should all get some sleep."

"Is that wise, lord?"

"It'll give the rynada time to recover," Marrek explained.

"Which means we'll make better time tomorrow," concluded Hafrin.

On that, they finished the meagre meal then curled up around the fire. Hafrin asked the jesset to wake them as soon as the sun hit the trees at their backs. He was asleep almost before he knew it and woke all too soon to Vrala's beak tapping his cheek. Daylight was edging the treetops, but there was no sun. Instead, a high thin cloud cover had moved in overnight. Shivering, he tossed back his covers and built up the fire. Meanwhile, Vrala set about stirring Marrek out of his bed as well.

"Rin," Marrek caught his foster son's attention.

"Sir?"

"Draft notes to our closest allies. Have them meet us at the cabin. I'll do the chores."

"You want Vrala to deliver them?"

"Yes."

It took time for numb fingers to pen seven notes, keeping them short and concise. Marrek brought him a hot drink and what remained of the travel bread and dried fruit.

"Sorry it's not more, Rin. Are you almost done?"

"Just finishing now, sir. Do you have the tubes?"

"Ready to go." Marrek produced the lightweight tubes.

"Thanks."

It took less time to roll the notes and slip them into each tube than it did to relay to the orved where she was to take them. By then the rynada were saddle. With the load from the Wanderer pack animal evenly distributed between their pack rynad and the one Zivvoz had brought, they were ready to go. Bïzhan pawed the ground in his eagerness to be on his way. Hafrin vaulted onto his stallion but, by unspoken accord, it was Marrek who set the pace. Just before midday they reached the cabin. By then, Hafrin had been in contact with Nichole once more. He had done his best to reassure her they were on the way without explaining what they planned to do. In truth, he was still very much in the dark. Only the appearance of five of the expected seven traders on the cabin porch as they rode into the yard went any way to allying his fears. But Hafrin recognized Davyn, Piltar and Robar.

"Marrek, Rin." Piltar greeted them. He nodded to Zivvoz. "Zivvoz. So this is it."

"Well, the start of it anyway," replied Marrek as he slid to the ground. "When are the others due in?"

"They'll meet us on the way. What did you have in mind?"

"A moment, please, Pete." Marrek addressed Zivvoz. "How quickly can you and Doro be ready to ride, Ziv?"

Zivvoz glanced at the sky where the sun was barely visible as pale ball through the clouds. "Before the sun's halfway from where it is now to the trees. But only Doro's mount will be capable of keeping up. These are worn out."

"Don't worry," said Piltar. "We've brought fresh animals, plus remounts. Take one now."

Grateful for the offer, Zivvoz turned to Marrek. "Can I leave mine here?"

"Of course, Ziv. They should be okay until they can be returned to your hold. See you shortly. Get Palor ready for Nikki then wait for us. We'll collect you on the way by." Due to the mare's fine lines she, like her son invited theft. That was why Marrek left her at Zivvoz's hold when he was away.

With a nod, the holder stripped the riding gear from his mount and the pack animal. To Marrek's surprise it was his brother who hurried to assist the holder. Davyn picked up the packsaddle and three of the satchels belonging to Zivvoz and followed him down to the pasture now full of rynada. Bïzhan tugged at the reins, informing Hafrin he would very much like to join the other rynada.

"Okay, Bïzhan. Just let me get your gear off," said Hafrin out loud.

The two traders who were strangers to Hafrin glanced at one another. Their expressions ranged from raised eyebrows to bemusement. Ignoring them, Hafrin unclipped the reins, pulled the saddle pad from the stallion, and gave him a parting slap. With a flick of his heels and toss of his head, Bïzhan took off down the slope. He passed Zivvoz and Davyn, cut toward the pasture, and soared over the top railing.

"Rin's a level five esper," Marrek explained.

"Just as well," observed one of the two men, intrigued by the Alaiad-in-exile, "given that beast of his can clear the fence."

The entire group pitched in, removing tack from the other rynada, sorting what remained of the trail supplies in the packsaddles and grooming the mounts and pack animals. While they worked, Zivvoz left on his fresh mount, making time but keeping his rynad to a respectable pace.

"How far does he have to go?"

Marrek glanced up at the question. "Only a short distance."

Hafrin asked, as they stored the last of their travel things indoors, "What now, sir?"

Marrek glanced out the window. Piltar and another man were turning the trail-weary rynada out to pasture. Tail held high, old Dintan circled the strangers, snorting and tossing his head in an amusing display of feigned fierceness. Someone else was scattering food for the rakkïal now turned loose against an extended absence.

"We grab a bite to eat and get ready to leave. Go take your contacts out. And shave."

"Yes, sir."

Marrek put together the makings of a meal for them and their guests. Heart pounding, nerves on edge, Hafrin removed the contacts and diligently stored them in their cleansing container. Then he set up the mirror and began shaving. He was running his hand across a bare chin and cheeks that he had not seen in years when Robar shouted a warning.

"Marrek! Rin! Riders coming!"

Hafrin dashed to the chest where he had stowed his sword, removing it from its hiding place. Quick as he was to the door, Marrek was ahead of him. They stood, side by side on the porch, watching the first of their Fimiahri fighting tail arrive. Two local holders and a trapper rode up to the fence. The flick of their eyes took in everything: the unusual number of rynada in the pasture, the strange men who were undoubtedly Hynarkin, and as they drew rein, the young man at Marrek's side.

Slowly all three dismounted. In their initial greeting, they acknowledged Hafrin as Marrek's son. Then Hafrin caught and held their eyes. Unconsciously he shifted Hafrön to the fore. Diffused daylight spilled down the blade. Blue and green rippled along its length. Transfixed by the sight of the weapon, the newcomers immediately dropped to one knee at the foot of the porch steps.

"Ser, we are yours to command," one managed to choke out.

"I thank you for responding to our summons," said Hafrin. Shoulders back, his head high, he gestured. "Come. Get up. We're all friends here. You've known me since I was a child. Blorik, you taught me the fine art of skinning and curing hides. Alenul, didn't you chase Doro and me off your property when you caught us stealing from your orchard?"

At his side, Hafrin felt Marrek stir. But it was the approval radiating from his foster father that warmed him and informed him that he had read the moment correctly. Embarrassed, tugging their forelocks, the three men got to their feet. Piltar rescued the awkward moment by calling the men to assist him in bringing up fresh animals, plus the string of spares. Marrek quickly and concisely outlined the events that had led up to the in gathering. Upon hearing of the kidnapping of Hafrin's wife, the men muttered rebelliously.

Alenul cursed and spat on the ground. "Knew it would come to this, Siyon."

"Aye. Never thought they'd be that foolish myself," averred Siyon. "Stealing womenfolk. That's just plain crazy. You lead, ser, and we'll take our lead from you and yon traders."

"Thank you," said Hafrin.

They rode down the trail to Zivvoz's hold shortly after midday. Everyone was well fed, with fresh supplies for the journey ahead. Despite the hard ride behind him, Bïzhan refused to permit Hafrin to leave him behind. Instead, he joined the spare string and slowly recovered his strength, preparing for what was to come. Scale mail and weaponry jangled with each bouncing stride of the trotting rynada. Behind the last three men trailed the spare mounts and pack animals, grunting and muttering complaints. Piltar and Robar rode in the vanguard, Marrek and Hafrin immediately behind them. Hafrin chafed at not being in the front rank but Marrek's expression stilled his tongue. In so much, Marrek wordlessly reminded him that no ruler ever led on the trail, except under extreme circumstances. Accustomed as he had been to taking lead from Marrek on the trade routes, Hafrin now realised all that had changed.

They emerged from the woods and slowed to a quick walk up the hill to the hold, passing between the fenced fields. Before them, gathered in a knot at the foot of the house steps were Zivvoz, Indoro and three more men. Indoro raised an arm in salute as the party halted.

Zivvoz came forward, tugged his forelock and announced, "Ser, these men will be remaining here to watch over my family."

He did not add 'heir' to that statement, which made Hafrin glance up quickly to where Kili stood. With her was a young woman whom Hafrin did not recognise, but because she was cradling Valrin he realised she was the wet nurse Zivvoz and Kili had brought in to care for his son. Hafrin quickly redirected his attention, not wanting to betray his relationship with any one person at the hold.

"There are five more joining us along the trail before we reach the crossroads."

"Good," Marrek responded for Hafrin.

Zivvoz and Indoro quickly mounted and drew into the column. With something between a grin and a smirk, Indoro held up a long shaft with some fabric wrapped and tied about the upper third. Ignoring Hafrin's puzzled expression, he fitted the butt of the shaft into a cup attached to his stirrup. In unison, the company whirled and headed back down the road. At the forest edge, Hafrin paused to look back as they turned northeast. Then, he set his face forward and rode in earnest along the rutted road.

CHAPTER 25

▼

During their first night on the road they broke long enough to feed and water themselves and their animals and stretch out the kinks. Several of the party had not ridden much in a number of years and Hafrin feared they might become a burden on the rest of his company. When exactly he had begun to think of them as his own he was not certain. Perhaps it was when Marrek had pulled a deep blue, almost black shirt from his saddlebag immediately after they had set temporary camp. Picked out in real silver thread, the symbol for the Wanderers glittered in the firelight. An equally dark blue cloak lined with wool and edged in blood red followed.

"Wear these," Marrek told him, and tossed them to him.

Shivering with the cold, Hafrin quickly changed. Men's eyes followed his every action. All movement in the camp ceased, however, the instant he raised his arms to tug on his shirt. Revealed for the first time to the strangers was Hafrön's brand. Where once there might have remained some doubt amongst their allies as to their actions and to the wisdom of following this green youth and his companions, it was dispelled once and for all. Those who were not his closest companions now drew together. In subdued tones they remarked upon what they had seen and speculated. Feeling alienated for the first time in his life, Hafrin sought out Indoro. At his approach, Indoro rose and bowed.

"Oh, cut it out," Hafrin softly snapped, peevish and flushed with sudden notoriety.

"Dad said I must," countered Indoro. But he settled back on his chosen spot with a mischievous grin when Hafrin glared at him. Before he could settle next to his shield brother, the cry of an orved pierced the dusk.

One of the holders glanced up and casually remarked. "Just a wild one."

Quietly amused, Hafrin raised his arm and braced himself. Vrala Harz dropped from the sky, settling on his forearm with more than her usual grace. Undoubtedly as conscious of their audience as he was, she flipped her wings neatly into place and chirped at him. No message tubes adorned her legs. She caught his eye and bobbed her head, conveying information quickly and precisely. The image in Hafrin's mind was crisp and clear.

"Marrek," Hafrin called to his foster father across the clearing, "the troop has swung north towards Pûdornâ instead of heading straight for the capitol. They must expect us to try something."

"Possibly. Or they may simply be playing it safe," said Piltar.

Marrek frowned. "Regardless we'll have to risk cutting straight across country. Give Vrala a message for the men who are expecting us at the crossroads. They should be able to catch up with us before we encounter Tolbôun and his men."

"If they turn south once they hit the main road, there's a spot we can use if we can get ahead of them," said Davyn. His expression was studious as he considered their next move. The men drew in around him. He went to one knee and with a stick rapidly traced out a crude map on the ground. "There are plenty of fences here and here, lined with berry shrubs."

Someone muttered, "Just what I wanted was to spend a day lying amongst the brambles."

Another jostled the grumbler, "Shut up, Raxel."

"Was only jesting," Raxel replied defensively.

Hafrin found the man who had spoken and grinned at him. "It does indeed look like a prickly proposition. Davyn are there any good points to this spot?"

"The ground dips just here." Eyes twinkling at the intentional puns, Davyn Lytsun pointed with the stick. "If we can make it to the top of the rise and be on the other side of it before they come through, we should have the advantage."

"Depending upon how good their outriders are," put in Zivvoz pragmatically.

"There's always that," Marrek agreed.

"Since we have no choice, I'll send the message and we should get moving. I think we're all sufficiently rested," declared Hafrin.

The diplomacy and immediacy with which Hafrin dealt with the situation drew looks of approval from the oldest men in the group and a nod from Marrek. Hafrin withdrew to pen the message, no easy task on the road, using a solid ink block that had to be wetted and then scraped to produce enough ink with which to draft the missive. Once the ink on the slip of paper was dry, and the message rolled and stowed in the metal tube he attached it to one of Vrala's legs.

"My sweet lady of the air," he addressed the jesset, "take this to the men at the crossroads."

From memory he drew the image of the road. Vrala chirped. After a bob of her head, she launched into the air and winged away. Hafrin turned to find the rest of the party mounted and waiting. He swung up onto his spare mount, opting to continue keeping Bïzhan as a spare until the last possible minute. Zivvoz led off with Robar alongside. They pressed on across country.

By late afternoon they were in a fold of the land. Davyn, now in the van, raised his hand and the column halted. They dismounted and grouped around him. Off in the distance, Hafrin picked out another party approaching across the fields. The presence of his orved overhead supplied the information he needed.

"It's okay. It's the others we've been expecting."

"Good," said Marrek.

Once the remainder of the party joined them, they squatted amongst the stubble. While the rynada pawed through the thin blanket of snow in search of edible sedges, Marrek and Piltar briefed the men.

"Most of you already know the primary reason why we've asked you here." He glanced about the gathering, then pinned the newest members. "We're making our first stand now."

"To what end, trader?"

Eyes never leaving the group, Marrek responded, "You've met Rin, Loek."

"Sure. A fine lad, Marrek, one I'd be proud to call son."

"But he isn't my son," replied Marrek. To that Loek appeared startled. He glanced at Hafrin. "In fact, I found him as a babe hidden beneath a bush a day's ride from Iryô."

Indignant, Loek exploded, "What mother in her right mind would abandon a child?"

"One with no other choice when her life and the life of her child are at stake," said Piltar.

"How so?"

Rather than beat around the bush any further, Marrek cut to the point. "When his mother is Rïtyom."

"Great Serpent!"

"Just so."

Slowly, Loek straightened. Unsurprised by Loek's reactions, Hafrin gave him full marks in that he refused to take the statement at face value. "What proof do you have?"

At a nod from Marrek, Hafrin slowly drew his hereditary sword from its scabbard. Light danced along the blade, blue and green mingled with flecks of red. All eyes fastened on the sword. Even Marrek felt his breath leave him. Since Hafrin's recovery of the weapon it had always shown blue or green, or a mixture of both. The red sparks near the tip were wholly unexpected.

Alenul spoke up. "Leave be, Loek. We've all seen the mark he wears. No one can fake that."

Feverish light in his eyes, Loek drew his sword and placed on the ground between him and Hafrin. "Ser, I'm yours to command. We've all heard rumours that Fanhri's heir lived, and then there's the prophecy. I thank the Great Serpent that I've lived to see this day."

Hafrin managed the formal acceptance. "We thank you, Loek for the offer of your blade and your assistance."

Prophecy and fear mingled with anxiety and excitement, curdling the air and unsettling Hafrin's stomach. Uncomfortable with the honours despite all of his training, he looked to Marrek for support. It was Robar who rescued him.

"I think we should try to get some rest," Robar suggested. Piltar nodded.

With their rynada picketed nearby in the fold of land, the men curled up in their cloaks and blankets in pairs on the cold hard ground. Back to back, they shared such body warmth as they could muster. High above them, Vrala Harz maintained a patrol, constantly circling.

All too soon she screamed a warning. Hafrin woke with a start at the cry. Rolled onto his back just as Marrek tossed aside his blanket, Hafrin launched to his feet.

"We're out of time, gentlemen." Marrek gestured. "Ser, we must deploy now or risk losing the advantage."

Hafrin nodded. "I bow to your experience."

Marrek thought back, *Thank you.*

He rapidly sketched out their plan of attack. Departing the camp, each man leading two rynada apiece, they split into three groups. The bulk of the party deployed on either side of the road under the command of Zivvoz and Robar. On command, their mounts knelt. Heads drawn low by their riders they were concealed behind the bushes. Hafrin shifted to Bïzhan now and joined Marrek, Indoro, Piltar and another Hynarkin whom Hafrin did not know. Mounted, they rode through an open gate onto the highway.

At Marrek's signal they halted just below the crown of the hill. There were a number of deciduous trees lining either side of the road. Hafrin sent a request to his orved. She responded by settling on the bare tip of a weather-damaged evergreen. From there she kept him apprised of the approaching column's progress. As the troops and their prisoner started up the slope Hafrin nodded to his foster father. With a wave of his arm, Marrek ordered the tiny group forward. When they crested the hill and halted in plain view, they discovered the distance of only five fence posts separated them from the troop. Wind whistled across the open fields. It lifted their cloaks, setting them billowing across their rynada's rumps. Oblivious to the cold, Hafrin stared down the road at the advancing soldiers and their prisoner.

✳   ✳   ✳   ✳

Nichole

Despite layers of lined clothing supplied by the posting station's senior officer, Nichole continued to shiver as the temperature dropped. Worse, the threat of snow was sending damp fingers through every gap and seam to chill her flesh. She ducked her chin and breathed down the neck of her shirt in a vain effort to warm up. Somewhere off to her left lay the sea. At this point in her travels, she was closer to the Neranik Sea than she had thought possible when first she had arrived on Fimiah almost three years before.

"How are you holding up, lady?"

"I'm okay," she replied as she turned to see who had spoken.

One of the younger soldiers had ridden up alongside her. "I pray you are well, lady."

"I'm fine, really," Nichole insisted. "And please, my name is Nikôla."

"Lady Nikôla, I am Corporal Tynnim."

That he was determined to carry on a conversation with her disturbed and distracted Nichole. She was acutely conscious of his presence, sensing he was developing an interest in her that went beyond professional. Tolbôun's instructions echoed in her thoughts.

"This is unwise, Corporal. He," she jerked her chin in the Outsider's direction, "doesn't approve. I wouldn't want to see you in trouble."

"Surely not, lady. After all, you bear the name of the double-clustered star flower that grows only in the Rashordi alpine meadows, and they're said to bring good luck."

Before she could respond a bright flash of light caught her eye. She stared down the road. Something manmade occupied a distant rise. Again there came the blink of light.

"A distance viewer," Tynnim informed her.

She nodded, but refrained from commenting. Forwarned by that display, she suspected they must be very close to Iryô now. Tynnim proceeded to explain how the long-range viewers were positioned along the primary thoroughfares between Iryô and other primary centres of habitation. Spaced at half-day intervals, they transmitted signals far more quickly than an orved could fly. Unfortunately, their effectiveness was limited by the weather. Further complicating matters, there were presently no craftsmen in Jikpryn's service with the ability to construct more of the devices. All of the original ones had held allegiance to Fanhri. Most had died within days of the true Alaiad's passing. The remainder had vanished into the wilds.

Which means whatever Rin and Marrek are planning, they better act fast because troops at the next station will know what's happening, Nichole thought.

"Look there."

Caught by Tynnim's gesture, Nichole glanced up. An orved wheeled across the sky. It banked to rest in the top branches of a tree alongside the road. Tynnim observed, "No jesses. Must be a wild one. We seldom see them this far from the mountains. A good omen, do you think?"

It was all Nichole could do to duck her head so he could not see the smile tugging her lips. Even though Hafrin had closed her out of his thoughts, kept her from knowing he was this close, she knew Vrala Harz on sight.

A shout went up from the front of the column. Tynnim grabbed her rynad's reins and halted it. Nichole redirected her gaze. The column came to a standstill. Five men blocked the road. Even with bare heads, helms at their knees, there was no doubting they were fully prepared to fight.

Unperturbed, Tolbôun ordered them, "Move aside."

"Not until you return what is rightfully ours," replied Hafrin.

Nichole tried repeatedly to catch his gaze but his attention fixed on the Outsider. On either side of him sat Marrek and Indoro. Piltar and another person she did not recognise covered Hafrin's back. When Tolbôun remained unaffected by the demand, Hafrin slowly drew his sword and laid it across his knees in plain sight of everyone. Several soldiers started, causing their rynada to rear slightly. Behind Nichole someone cursed.

"How is it possible?" Tynnim whispered to no one in particular. "The Captain threw it into the sea."

"Apparently not," responded Nichole softly.

For a moment Tynnim looked at her before turning back to the tableau: Hafrin, dressed in dark blue and black, mounted on a black rynad. Words whispered from his lips. "Black on black."

"Come, sir," said Hafrin, maintaining a conversational tone of voice. "Is it wise to start a war over a woman?"

Nichole bridled at his choice of words. Marrek caught her eye. With a tiny shake of his head he commanded her to be still. She fumed, but her emotions caused her rynad to jib several times before Tynnim brought it under control.

Finally Tolbôun responded. "I'm afraid I can't do that. I have my orders from the Alaiad. He wishes to speak with her. Of course, you're always welcome to accompany us to court. Perhaps he will let you have her back when he's finished with her."

The nasty edge to his words sent a shiver up Nichole's spine. What Tolbôun inferred was picked up by Vrala and Bïzhan and conveyed to Hafrin. The orved took to the air. Hovering just out of range of bowshot she only waited the signal to attack. Expression set, gaze as cold as the wind picking up across the fields, Hafrin declared his intentions.

"I think not, sir." Without shifting position, his voice lifted. "Now."

From behind the brambles hedging either side of the road appeared a number of men. Grim-faced, all were armed with drawn swords or bows. Nichole started at the sight of two crossbows, and what was euphemistically referred to by scouts as a re-bow; a bow that bent back upon itself.

There's going to be hell to pay over that breach of techno security, Nichole mused. *Nikki*. For the first time in more than a day, Hafrin 'pathed her. *Behind you.*

Now Zivvoz appeared behind the rear guard, leading Palor. Thankful for the change, Nichole pulled on her mount's reins and tightened her knees. She urged it around. For a second, Tynnim refused to release her but she caught and held his gaze. In the face of her determination, and the unknown quantity of the unexpected force of arms, he jerked his hand from the reins. After a moment, he acquiesced and Nichole rode back to meet Zivvoz. She slid from the troop rynad and struggled onto Palor.

"Here, lady." Zivvoz handed her a pad that had clearly been designed to ease her discomfort.

"Thank you, Ziv."

Hafrin touched a finger to his brow. "Thank you, good sirs. You're free to continue on your way."

He touched Bïzhan. As the black answered to his command, Tolbôun slammed his heels into his mount. Sword drawn, he bore down on Hafrin.

Indoro shouted a warning and drew his sword. In the same instant, he released his grasp on the material wrapped about the pole he held. The wind caught it, snapping the banner with the force of a whip: silver on dark blue, the rune of the Alaiad cut the air above his head.

From Hafrin's reactions, however, he had been expecting Tolbôun's response. Hafrön rose to the challenge. At that same instant, Bïzhan reared on his hind legs, pivoted and came down, horns levelled at the advancing threat. Hands clapped to her mouth, eyes wide, Nichole could only wait. No one else moved, trapped by the impending combat. Time slowed.

Red light flared. Rynada screamed. Blinded, Nichole jerked her face aside. When she was able to see again the sound of a running rynad caught her attention. The Outsider's mount vaulted the fence and raced away across the field, empty stirrups flapping. How it avoided tripping over the jaw lines she could not understand. She looked quickly around.

Measured in the snow dusting the frost-hardened ground, Tolbôun lay face down on the road. For several breaths no one moved. Then Tynnim steeled himself and rode forward. He swung down. On one knee, he checked on the Outsider's condition. Fingers sought a pulse. Shaking his head, he looked up.

"He's dead," Tynnim announced. Then he rolled the body onto its back. As the face came round Tynnim swore and leapt to his feet. "Serpent preserve us!"

"By the Rashordi demons," exploded another, "He looks like he's been thrown into a fire."

"Or struck by lightning," Indoro observed. That he maintained the dispassionate tone of a distant observer amazed Nichole. Tynnim scrubbed his hands on the thighs of his breeks as though proximity to the corpse had stung him.

"I'm sorry it came to this," said Hafrin. Bile burned his throat and made speaking difficult. It took every fibre of his being not to spew his morning meal. Several men gagged. Trapped by her husband's emotions, Nichole had to look away.

"Not your fault, sir," declared the senior officer in the troop. "He provoked you when you would have let us leave unharmed. We'll take him back to the…" About to say Alaiad, the soldier paused, eyes fixed on the banner. Slowly his gaze travelled back across Hafrin's face. "To our lord…ser."

This time he tugged his forelock, the extent of his acknowledgement of Hafrin's identity. If any of the Troop had thoughts of dismounting and paying homage to the rightful Alaiad, they reconsidered their actions. Until this stranger and their leader met, under whatever circumstances might arise to bring them together, it was unwise to declare a change of allegiance. Particularly as those with the long-viewer would undoubtedly note whatever happened. And they were less than a half a day's hard ride away.

CHAPTER 26

▼

Jikpryn

Seated on the high seat in the audience chamber, Jikpryn twisted his goblet around on the left arm. Rings of moisture dampened the top of the carved claw. He was not the first to do this. Time worn grooves in the wood testified to predecessors' actions much the same as his.

"One more day," he muttered, then glanced to his right to see if his page had overheard. Still perched on his stool, the boy, Krysp af Althiön appeared bored. *Why is it taking them so long to get here?*

Two days earlier a mysterious malady had struck a number of the fortress staff. Noble or commoner, soldier or servant, its brutal affects were scattered indiscriminately amongst his people. It had even struck him. One minute he had been sitting at his desk, pouring over petitions. The next, he had been retching out the window. Searing pain at the base of his skull had temporarily blinded him. He had spent a day and a half in bed, assaulted by bouts of nausea, the brutal agony in his head threatening to explode his brain. A tender spot remained just behind his left ear even now. Reports were filtering in that similar incidents had occurred in the surrounding provinces. Wôbiny had been particularly hard hit by the strange affliction.

Since then dreams...no, he corrected himself...nightmares had pursued him whenever he closed his eyes. Each vision had forced him to relive his actions throughout more than twenty-one years. Every time he had lurched awake, sometimes five times a night, sweating, pulse racing. So much bloodshed, much of which he now regretted, especially his sister and her baby. And, he forced himself to admit, Fanhri.

Movement at the side entrance to the hall caught his eye. Captain Hilcaz gestured urgently. He, too, had been afflicted by the malady. Now his eyes darted about the hall to ensure no one else had witnessed his furtive actions. Conscious of his nobles and their ability to read things, erroneous or otherwise, into his actions, Jikpryn casually stretched and stood. His page started from a daydream but Jikpryn gestured the boy to remain where he was.

"I'll return shortly, Krysp. Keep note of anything you believe worthwhile."

The boy nodded. Well-versed in what was expected from him, he knew precisely what to watch for. Satisfied, Jikpryn eased from the hall before anyone among the gathering was aware. His captain waited in the passage. Jikpryn glanced past Hilcaz but aside from the guard outside the exit they were alone.

Jikpryn spared the guard a glance, noting with approval how his gaze remained studiously fixed on the far wall. "Well? Have they returned?"

"Yes, my lord. But," Hilcaz appeared strangely disconcerted, "I think you should come with me, my lord."

"What is it?"

Hilcaz remained strangely resolute. "Please, ser."

For a moment Jikpryn was inclined to snap at Hilcaz, but reason prevailed. The Captain of his personal Guard was not given to requests over inconsequential matters. Instead, Jikpryn nodded. As he started to accompany Hilcaz, the door guard moved to fall in step at his back. Jikpryn lifted a hand. Halting the guard, he silently ordered him to remain where he was. Then he continued down the corridor and out through a side door into the stable yard.

They crossed the cobblestone yard quickly. Scent of hay, mingled with the detritus of stable waste, and blended with the pungent aroma of hot metal and coals from the smithy. A group of exhausted rynada stood steaming in the afternoon cool. Grooms hovered nearby, waiting for permission to take charge of the mounts.

"Here, my lord."

Hilcaz drew Jikpryn around to the far side of the rynada to where the riders were clustered. At Jikpryn's approach, the men drew back in a half-circle. On the ground at their feet was a body wrapped in a blanket. Upon seeing the man they served, one of the Guards bent to flip back the blanket. Jikpryn halted. Sight of the crisped and blackened skin roiled his stomach and he nearly disgraced himself in front of the soldiers. He took a deep breath, which proved a mistake. The stench of scorched flesh assailed him. His stomach heaved. He fought to regain control. Suddenly the eye-stinging odour of urine filled his nostrils. Eyes watering, Jikpryn gulped for fresh air and felt his stomach settle. Hilcaz slowly lowered a piece of urine-soaked rag.

"Sorry, my lord, but it helps."

"It does indeed," Jikpryn acknowledged. "Thank you, Captain."

"There's more, ser. Prepare yourself. I suggest you breathe through your mouth. It makes it easier to stomach."

On that cautionary note Hilcaz toed the corpse. Strips of burnt skin sloughed away to reveal pallid grey flesh. Where it had stuck to the blanket, it peeled back like fruit rind. The entire face flapped from the throat in ragged strips. Beneath it lay wholly unrecognisable features. A mouth with over-thin lips drawn back in a silent snarl conveyed a malevolence that set all Jikpryn's nerves jangling. Eyes the shape of the tip of an armour-piercing arrow possessed the flatness of those belonging to deep-sea provender. Beneath them were skin flaps over slits that Jikpryn assumed were this creature's version of a nose. There was little more than vestigial flesh to infer ears on either side of the skull. An oath burst from Jikpryn. That this obscenity had been his advisor since his coming of age went beyond all reason.

Hilcaz nodded. "When the men saw this, ser, they felt the body should be returned for your inspection."

Bile burned Jikpryn's mouth again. He turned his head aside and spat into the nearest pile of manure and straw. "Get rid of that…thing, Captain. See to it personally then report to me in my study. And Captain?"

"Ser?"

"Make certain it's buried somewhere far away."

"Aye, ser."

It took all Jikpryn's restraint not to flee the scene. Where panic urged him to run, training dictated he turn on heel and walk slowly back across the yard. He paused by the smithy to speak to the senior blacksmith concerning shoes being fitted to one of the Guard rynada. The stench of scorch hoof and hot metal went far to settling his stomach. He re-entered the fortress. Inside the door, he slumped against the wall. Head resting against the cool stones, he concentrated on recovering his composure. A door opened nearby, closed with a muffled thump. Pushing away from the wall, Jikpryn headed for his quarters. Along the way he ordered a servant off to locate his page and send the boy upstairs.

Back inside his private office Jikpryn went to the window and flung wide the horn pane windows. Hands on the sill, he leaned forward to inhale fresh air. It seemed to take forever to clear his lungs. Behind him the door opened.

"Ser?"

He turned at his page's tentative interruption. Jikpryn gestured the boy in. Then he closed the window and settled at his desk. His page waited across from him, eyes wide and dark.

"Fetch me some wine, Krysp," Jikpryn instructed, feeling once more in control. "And some of the best cheese."

"Bread rolls, ser?"

For a moment Jikpryn considered the question before nodding. Krysp put the fingers of his hand to his temple and departed. Jikpryn's thoughts spun, skittering this way and that as he struggled to countenance how he could ever have fallen under Tolbôun's sway. Vague memories flickered about the periphery of his conscious as he fought to piece his past together in such a way that he could understand and justify his actions over the past twenty-five years.

Fortunately his page returned with food and drink before Hilcaz reported to Jikpryn's study. Halfway through a tankard of wine, Jikpryn sat with his feet up, staring at the watery scene beyond his study windows. Hilcaz's knock gave him sufficient time to drop his feet to the floor.

"Come."

The Captain of his Guard stepped into the room and closed the door behind him. He saluted then slid a glance toward the alcove where Krysp sat working over figures. Jikpryn signed him to sit.

"Report."

Not unduly surprised by the sharp edge of his superior's voice, Hilcaz sat on the edge of the chair, back straight. His gaze firmly fixed on Jikpryn, Hilcaz delivered the report he had just received from his men. His steady tone belied the emotions that were flitting through the depths of his eyes.

"Ser, the troop was making inspections of several holdings to the northwest. At one of them, they found a young woman who may be the person mentioned in Triklâ's prophecy."

"Female?"

"Aye, ser. Young and life-mated. And she's had a child recently, although the men found no evidence to that effect at the hold."

"Any information on whose hold it was?"

"No, ser. The locals are close-mouthed about their neighbours and the men saw no reason to pursue the information through methods more conducive to intelligence gathering."

"Not when they had the woman. A wise decision," Jikpryn muttered. He flapped a hand, ordering Hilcaz to continue.

"She put up only token resistence when they ordered her to accompany them back to the capital."

"Yet the troop arrived without her. Instead, they returned with that…abomination."

Jikpryn could not bring himself to say his one-time advisor's name. Nothing about the corpse in the courtyard had endeared itself to his memory of Tolbôun. Indeed, that thing, which had been the Outsider, put his own actions into question.

Just how many of my decisions were influenced by him? I never liked the Deccötti, it's true, but I can't remember ever feeling such a hatred for them as I did after Rityöm married Fanhri. Why did I do what I did? Could he have been responsible? And if so, how could he have made me do it?

"Ser, there's more to this." Hilcaz waited until certain he had his liege-lord's complete attention. "Two days out from Iryô the troop was intercepted by a party of men they believe to be outcasts or hunters and trappers who live in the Rashordi wilds."

Cradling the last of his wine, Jikpryn raised an eyebrow. "Oh?"

"Although their dress was rough cut like most peasants, it was not of the same style seen on those living close by the cities."

"Interesting. What else?"

Hilcaz shifted his weight, uneasy with his role of messenger. "The party was led by five men, three older, two barely into manhood. They displayed the Alaiad's banner, and several of my troops swear one of the younger men was Fanhri."

Abruptly, Jikpryn set his tankard aside. The desire to slap a hand on the desk or blurt an explosive denial was tempting. For once, Jikpryn did not deny the possibility. Instead, he recalled Hilcaz's return from pursuing Rityöm. The lack of any conclusive evidence of the infant's demise now loomed before him.

"What do you think, Hilcaz?"

Eyes fixed on his lord, Hilcaz answered with extreme care, putting Jikpryn's thoughts into words. "Ser, given my men were unable to find any physical evidence of the heir that day, there's always a possibility."

To his credit Jikpryn succeeded in keeping his own thoughts buried. "As you say. Tell me more about this young man."

Hilcaz's eyes darted to Jikpryn, then away to a point beyond his lord's shoulder. "He was dressed in black and dark blue, and rode a black rynad stallion, ser."

Prophecy. The treacherous thought threatened to slip from Jikpryn's lips. He pressed them together, fought back the urge and asked, "Who killed Tolbôun?"

Amazed by the directness with which he voiced his question, Jikpryn watched his Captain carefully. It was evident Hilcaz was fighting a variety of emotions from shock to disgust as he replied. "It was the young man, ser. Or, more precisely, the weapon he held."

For several breaths the only things moving were the flickering flames in the two sconces lighting the darker corners of the room. Then the page twitched. Aware Krysp had given up all attempts at subterfuge and was shamelessly eavesdropping on his superior's conversation. Jikpryn stood.

"Krysp, come here."

Slowly Krysp slid from his stool and entered the study. "Ser?"

"You will report to the Weapons Marshall and undertake two study periods in arms."

Startled, Krysp managed, "Yes, ser."

"And know that if I discover you have made free with this information to which you have been privy I shall see you are sent home in disgrace." Now Jikpryn held up a finger. "After having you thoroughly thrashed. Do I make myself understood?"

A hesitant nod from the boy reflected his fear. Jikpryn gestured and Krysp fled. The minute the door closed behind his page, Jikpryn turned back to Hilcaz.

"I believe you were saying something about this young man's weapon, Captain."

With a nod, Hilcaz explained. "The men say he drew his sword and rested it across his knees so they could all see it."

A betraying thought crept through Jikpryn's mind. *Can it be?*

"This young man and his people insisted the troop turn over the woman, which my men did, although reluctantly. They had no other recourse, being caught unprepared by such an audacious act, outmanoeuvred and outnumbered."

"Were they in any danger of attack afterwards?"

"No, ser. In fact the leader of the ambushers insisted my men were free to go as long as they made no attempt to retake the woman. But your advisor chose to attack. Before he could close on this young man, the sword spat fire."

Hafrön. The sword's name whispered through Jikpryn's brain. He quickly addressed himself to Hilcaz. "I know what you're thinking, Captain. The same thing I am. Yet you swore to me you had thrown it into the sea."

Fearful for his life, Hilcaz responded, "In truth, ser, I believed I had. However, there's much rumoured about that infernal weapon, and less known in truth."

"You're suggesting you were enthralled by it?"

"I don't know that, ser. But if this young man does indeed carry the sword of the Alaiad…"

When Hilcaz's words trailed away Jikpryn finished for him, "He must be of the bloodline. May be, in fact, the last of the line."

Exhibiting great daring, Hilcaz asked, "You think he could be Fanhri's heir, ser?"

"There's that," Jikpryn admitted. Once put into words, the fear gnawing at him eased considerably. He massaged his temples with his fingertips for a minute, grateful when the pain he had suffered for so many years when under stress, failed to assault him. "Hilcaz, it's come to me that over these past years I've acted the fool."

"Ser." Mortified by such an admission, Hilcaz stood. "Never that."

A weary smile tugged Jikpryn's lips. From his Captain's expression, it was evident Hilcaz was struggling to recall when he had last seen one. Staring into middle-distance, Jikpryn considered the news Hilcaz had imparted and what the future held for all of them. The path ahead was muddy. Numerous branches offered a plethora of choices.

"At this juncture, one misstep, an inability to correctly read a situation could lead to disaster for all of us." Caught by his superior's admission of fallibility, Hilcaz could only listen as Jikpryn outlined their forthcoming actions. "Send out orved to the various garrisons. I want to know what's happening on the frontiers. Also send out messengers calling in all of the lords, and quickly. There's a storm coming that shall, I fear, effectively curtail our investigation until winter's end."

"Aye, ser. And your son?"

"He stays where he is. I can think of nowhere safer than Wôbiny at this time. Those who rode with him and his nurse, as well as my uncle's soldiers, will protect him."

"And if they cannot?"

Head down, Jikpryn responded heavily, "If there's no safety for him in the north, there certainly isn't at the capitol."

"What about this man? How can he be Fanhri's heir?"

How indeed? Jikpryn pressed a finger to the desktop. Fear warred with curiosity and, he admitted, anger that he could very well lose everything he had fought so long to attain. Dangerous thoughts intruded. *And yet, it's not mine to begin with.*

"I don't know. For now, we wait," Jikpryn finally said. "And gather such intelligence as we can."

"What should I tell my men to do should they encounter the woman or this man again?"

"They're to avoid all confrontations for now."

"And later, ser?"

Now Jikpryn's head rose. His gaze pinned Hilcaz where he stood. "Do you know the place where your men found the woman?"

Hesitant, Hilcaz nodded. "I believe I can find it."

"When the time comes you shall act as my emissary," Jikpryn informed him, "Always supposing this young man and his men don't descend upon us first."

"Best pray the weather holds, my lord."

Jikpryn shook his head. "Rather pray for a multitude of storms, Captain. I suspect foul weather will prove a far better ally at this time."

For a long minute Hilcaz hovered, unable to determine whether or not he had been dismissed. Then he asked, "Do you wish me to approach the Temple again, ser?"

To that, Jikpryn shook his head. "Such portents as they would give us now would undoubtedly prove to be chancy things at best. Given what's happened and what little we can deduce, I'd rather trust to my own judgement."

"Then what would you have me do in the interim, ser?"

"Look to your men, Captain. See that the arsenals are well stocked, the men on high alert."

"Aye, ser."

"And ensure they are aware I will not tolerate any further harassment of the population. However much they...we," Jikpryn forced himself to amend his statement to include himself, "may dislike the southerners, we are on the brink of great change. I would not see this situation dissolve into civil war if at all avoidable. Once the garrison has been briefed, send replacements to our outposts with those instructions."

"Ser."

Snapping a smart salute, Hilcaz left the study. In the wake of his departure Jikpryn returned to the window. Directly to the north of the tower housing him was the aviary. A short time later several orved flashed past heading south. One inbound orved approached the fortress. It circled the aviary once before back-winging to rest on a sill.

"It begins," Jikpryn muttered to himself.

CHAPTER 27

▼

Hilcaz

Back in the stable yard, Hilcaz found the troop that had ridden with the Outsider were waiting for him. They had not yet been dismissed although their mounts had been removed. As he crossed the cobblestones they slipped off railings and grouped nervously before him. Tynnim appeared particularly pale and anxious. Hilcaz nodded at each in turn as Tynnim made his report.

"We disposed of that...thing as directed, Captain, deep inside the forest and off the beaten track."

"Well done. Our lord is pleased with how you've performed these past few days." Slowly he caught each man's gaze before returning to the Corporal. "Tynnim."

"Captain?"

"I want you to convey our lord's instructions to the lieutenants."

"Yes, Captain."

"Tell them the Guard and rest of our standing force are to be briefed accordingly. Our lord instructs that the men be made aware there is a possibility of an uprising in the countryside."

"Then we're to prepare for war, Captain?"

Hilcaz shook his head. "Not against our own people. Rather, I fear against demons."

"Sir," Tynnim displayed far more daring than Hilcaz had accounted him capable of to that point, "if the demons can hide amongst us, as did that one in the guise of the Outsider, how do we know there aren't more?"

"We don't," Hilcaz replied honestly. "That's why no one is to do anything that might cause further disruptions amongst the people, in particular the Deccötti."

"Understood, sir."

"Lord Jikpryn wants the lieutenants to select replacements to ride out to the outposts with his instructions. Contingents will be rotated over the next two weeks."

"Given we have the time," someone in the rear rank muttered. Hilcaz ignored the man. It would benefit nothing to chastise his subordinates for voicing what was on all their minds.

"Keep what you know of this matter to yourselves." Now Hilcaz's voice took on an edge that boded ill for anyone who disobeyed his orders. "Understand that I will know who is responsible should word get out of what's happened."

"Sir."

"Dismissed."

But if either he or Jikpryn thought a call to arms would be required within days, an uprising failed to materialise before the winter storms returned. Reports arrived almost daily from outposts, garrisons and major centres but there was little news. On the other hand, Iryô's markets became a hive of speculation all too soon. Before long there was a noticeable drop-off in fresh furs and other rarities that ought to have been trickling in from the wilds. Nor did any of the Hynarkin ply their trade late into the fall as in previous years. Snow fell, blocking access to the wilds, and the troopers were forced to rely largely upon orved message traffic. This was highly limited due to weight restrictions on the avian messengers in cold weather.

Hilcaz's spies brought back to him whatever they could scrounge, and he reported to Jikpryn on everything, no matter how trivial or inconsequential the morsel of information. Even more curious was the lack of seers. Although those who served the Great Serpent made themselves available at Temples throughout the provinces' major centres, they no longer wandered the countryside.

As each day passed, Hilcaz grew increasingly apprehensive. The feeling that they were marking time grew appreciably more pronounced. Jikpryn made no attempt to conceal his own uneasiness whenever Hilcaz briefed him on troop matters. Twenty days following the return of the dead demon spy, Krysp slipped into Hilcaz's study at the rear of garrison mess hall.

"Captain," the boy did not wait for Hilcaz to acknowledge his presence, "Lord Jikpryn requests your presence immediately."

Hilcaz rolled up the pay document he had been perusing and asked, "What is it boy?"

Krysp responded as they left the office, "An orved just arrived from the Revïl garrison, sir."

"News?"

Now Krysp ducked his head. "He didn't say, Captain."

Krysp's evasiveness only served to heighten Hilcaz's uneasiness. They hurried through the side passage nearest the troop quarters, passed the duty guards and took the back steps two at a time. For all his lack of stature and age, Krysp beat Hilcaz to the landing. He slipped through the door to Jikpryn's office just ahead of the Captain, announcing Hilcaz's arrival even as he entered the room behind the boy.

"Captain," Jikpryn gestured to the chairs across the desk from him, "sit, please."

"Thank you, ser."

Hilcaz eased into one of the two chairs, settling on the edge. Unaccustomed to this new, more genial Jikpryn who had emerged since Tolbôun's death, he could not help wondering when and if the more familiar, acerbic lord would return. It was equally evident Jikpryn was conscious of the changes within himself. Unlike his subordinates, however, he was adapting to them. More relaxed, able to produce more objective assessments of situations, his new personality appeared to be having a positive affect on his page and the servants.

Which is a good thing, Hilcaz thought. *Not only is the quality of food improving but everyone is unwinding.*

"I've just had word in from Revïl, Caz." Jikpryn rested a hand on a tiny message roll. "Reports are coming in that bands of demons have been seen gathering along the Rashordi foothills."

"Where, ser?"

"There's a deep valley here." Jikpryn flipped a map roll across the desk. Hilcaz caught it and opened it. With the tip of a finger Jikpryn indicated the area where, over a year earlier, Tynnim had reported there had been a skirmish between some demons and Tolbôun's people. The Outsider's faction had come out on the losing end of the battle when the entire side of a mountain had exploded in flame and collapsed. Hilcaz looked up.

"Ser, that incident two years," he began.

"Precisely my thoughts, Caz. It could well be our assessment of the situation was wrong. Those we initially thought were demons may indeed be quite the opposite."

"Outside help, ser?"

A slow nod affirmed his inquiry. "It's a genuine possibility."

Thoughts whirling, Hilcaz cast back over the previous years, reports of odd incidents that no one had followed up on. He leaned forward. "Ser, do you suppose it could be the Hynarkin?"

Fingers forming a steeple, elbows resting on the desk, Jikpryn tapped his fingers against his lips. Then he settled back in his chair and ran a hand through his hair. Far too much grey coloured the thick brown thatch. Years of adversity, combined with the weight of taking and holding sovereignty through force of arms, had worn him down more quickly than might otherwise have been the case. Deep creases lined his face, marred his brow and drew down the sides of his mouth.

"Whether or not they were involved, we shall have to find some means of contacting them."

"Ser?"

A wry smile tugged one side of Jikpryn's mouth. "Given their innovative ideas, Caz, they would prove advantageous allies, don't you think?"

Not entirely surprised by Jikpryn's declaration, Hilcaz added his own thoughts. "Aye, ser. And there may be a way to locate at least one of their contacts in lieu of actually waylaying one of the traders."

A hand rose. He went silent as Jikpryn straightened. "Tell me later. For now, I want you to gather the troops."

"All of them, ser?"

"Leave back two companies to protect the fortress and send out heralds to round up all able-bodied men in the nearby towns and villages. We shall pick up more en route."

Troubled, Hilcaz countered, "Ser, the population have not been drilled in arms since you took control. It's doubtful they'll willingly follow your orders."

"Well thought. Have our company commanders set up training sessions. I won't risk the capitol. It would be a fool's move to leave Iryô unprotected in our absence."

"Yes, ser."

"Messages are even now going out to the provinces ordering them into the field."

"Where are we going, ser?"

"Two days' easy ride this side of Revïl there's a series of valleys. Once the snows recede I plan to settle us on the hilltops in that area."

"Won't that split our forces, my lord?"

"I have my reasons," replied Jikpryn. "See to my instructions, Caz. I want to ride out of here before first light tomorrow to inspect what we have to fall back on should circumstances necessitate a defensive position."

"Tomorrow, ser?" Shocked, Hilcaz stared at his superior.

Head tipped to one side, one corner of his mouth caught up in a wry smile, Jikpryn responded. "I thought you could work miracles, Caz?"

Trapped, Hilcaz af Oril gathered his scattered wits and slowly nodded. "As you command, my lord."

He rose and headed for the door half-expecting Jikpryn to call him back. But he stepped into the passage without being recalled. Campaign requirements surged through his brain as he trotted down the steps to the main floor. There he paused to consider his next course of action before heading for his quarters.

CHAPTER 28

▼

Nichole

Veneration directed towards her and Hafrin forced Nichole to guard her tongue. Acutely conscious of her elevated status, every sentence was carefully considered before she spoke. No one in the party doubted Hafrin's right to command, not after Hafrön had demonstrated its powers. Nor was anyone inclined to investigate what had happened to the Outsider. That he was dead was evident. How Jikpryn would react to the news was problematic. At their first camp they drew together around two small fires.

"Nikki."

Hafrin touched her shoulder. She started and looked up. In spite of their connection he had succeeded in creeping up on her. He looked particularly tired, his features drawn, a reflection of her weariness. Their shared bond made them both all the more conscious of just how tired they were.

"Here. You may need this, and Marrek says you probably know how to use it."

A sword identical to his was pressed into her hands. Nichole turned it carefully in the firelight. "What is this? It's not Hafrön, but it sure looks like it."

"It belonged to Lord Binlâra. Marrek bought it for me almost two years ago. Remember me telling you about it? I named it Blintor Krel."

"This is what was hidden in the loft?" When Hafrin nodded, Nichole allowed its tip to sag against a nearby tree trunk. "I can see why you wouldn't want your uncle's men to find it. Thank you."

Under the watchful eyes of the men, Nichole stood and moved into a clear space away from her audience. While they watched, she moved through a number of practice paces. Several of the strangers in the group nodded approval of the skill she demonstrated wielding the weapon. It was responsive if heavier than what she was accustomed to. But she was positive that, if she strengthened her shoulders and arms, she should be able to manage it without too much difficulty. Presently, she felt worn to the core, as though a hard puff of wind could blow her from the forest to the mountains.

"Thanks."

"How are you holding up?"

Her rebuttal surprised even Nichole as she blurted in Hynarkin, "How do you think? I'm stiff and sore, I've been insulted and hauled across hell's half acre with little or no regard for my well being..."

She broke off. Hafrin read her silent apology. With a nod, he settled next to her. One of the men quietly passed around travel rations and a strong spirit. When the man on her left offered her the flask, Nichole raised a hand and shook her head.

"No, thank you," she deferred. "I'd rather not. Does anyone have some water?"

Marrek passed her a flask of chilled spring water. From the taste, she suspected he had dropped a water purification tablet in it at some point. It was all she could do not to make a face. She glanced around the fire as she swallowed, and caught Piltar's eyes on her.

Better the bad taste than risk some bacterial infection.

His mental message, however well meant, also caught her unprepared. Cheeks flushing, Nichole ducked her head away before Marrek could pick up on the silent exchange. Hafrin passed her some dried meat.

"Here. You need your strength."

Alenul leaned forward. "What now, Hynarkin?"

Twig in hand, Marrek met Alenul's gaze. "This has necessitated pushing our timetable forward."

"They," Raxel jerked his head in the direction of Nichole and Hafrin, "won't be safe where they've been living up to now."

"We don't know that," countered Indoro. Zivvoz placed a hand on his son's arm to quiet him.

Piltar rubbed a finger along the side of his nose. "I'm afraid given the way matters are progressing, Nikki and Rin won't be safe anywhere."

Except maybe off-world. The errant thought rambled through Hafrin's mind.

Catching that, Nichole gently mentally nudged him. *Even out there, we're at war. Better to be on the ground with somewhere substantial to hide than in the vacuum of space.*

Their eyes met and Nichole 'pathed him an image of space and what happened to anyone unfortunate enough to wind up outside of a ship without a spacesuit. His eyes darkened and his complexion turned pale. Across the fire a twig snapped. Their connection broke and Nichole turned her attention back to Marrek. He scowled at her. She mouthed 'sorry', and saw him shake his head.

Unaware of the undercurrent Alenul continued, "So what do you propose, trader?"

Marrek and Piltar exchanged looks. Piltar leaned forward. "We," he gestured to Marrek and himself, "have our orders. We're to collect those loyal to our Ala-iad-in-exile and prepare for war."

"Then you're planning to move against the Usurper."

Piltar shook his head. "No. We've larger concerns than Jikpryn."

"How's that?" For the first time Siyon's attention centred on Piltar.

"There's a bigger game afoot," Piltar explained. "One that involves the destruction of both our peoples."

"Demons," said Indoro.

"Just so," said Piltar.

"Demons?" Raxel laughed. "Now who's been listening to fables?"

Marrek slowly stood. "I'm afraid the rumour of demons is closer to the truth than any of you realise."

Hafrin got to his feet and moved to join his foster father. "Marrek and Piltar are telling the truth."

Silence greeted his announcement. Now Indoro, Zivvoz and Nichole also stood. As a group, they faced the other men in their party. On a branch just outside the ring of firelight, Vrala Harz flipped her wings. The rustle of feathers blended with the hiss of burning sap.

Raxel found his tongue once more. "You say the rumours are close to the truth, Hynarkin. What exactly are they, if not demons?"

Okay, Hafrin 'pathed to Piltar and Marrek, *Now you've dragged us in this far, just how much do you plan to tell them?*

Piltar frowned at him. Marrek caught his superior's eye and shrugged. "In for a penny," he said in Hynarkin.

Drawing a deep breath, Piltar looked at each of the men in front of him. "What I'm about to tell you may seem a wild story told by someone suffering brain fever. However, I swear by all you hold dear that it's the truth."

"And that is?"

"The ones you've called demons all these years are actually a race of beings who come from off-world."

"The Star people."

Raxel jumped to the conclusion Nichole feared all the Fimiahri would. It was Hafrin who shook his head. "No. Like the Hynarkin, they are Star people, but neither of them are the ones from our legends. Although they also come from off-world, the Hynarkin are here to help us against the demons."

"As Rin has said, we are not the original Star people," said Marrek.

Not about to let the matter drop without an answer he considered satisfactory Raxel pressed him, "Who, then, were these others?"

"We," Marrek gestured to Piltar, Nichole and himself, "are not entirely sure. Part of our research on Fimiah has been an attempt to discover that information. Unfortunately, the arrival of the Craneeno...your demons...put a halt to our studies."

Raxel stood. He stared at Hafrin. "Ser, no one among us denies who you are. The Star-Given declares you the true Alaiad."

"Thank you."

"But what these say...ser, will you swear by your murdered parents that what the Hynarkin say is truth?"

"By my murdered parents, by Hafrön and by my ancestors, I swear that the Hynarkin are indeed travellers from beyond our world," Hafrin readily solemnly swore. Light flashed from the pommel of his sword, once, twice. "It was Marrek...Mark who found and raised me, his people who protected and trained me in everything I should know. Things that go beyond what I would have learned had I been raised only by my own people."

"We whom you refer to as Hynarkin have no wish to see the Fimiahri destroyed as the Craneeno have done to untold other races," said Marrek. "To that end, we've been slowly reintroducing different things you've lost over time due to the machinations of the Craneeno."

"So what you're saying is that you want us to fight the traders' war against these demons."

To Alenul's accusation Hafrin shook his head. "No. This battle isn't just between the Hynarkin and the Craneeno. In fact, from everything I've learned, the demons were here long before the Hynarkin discovered our world. It's the demons who have been stirring up violent unrest among our people for a long time now. I suspect they are responsible for holding back our technological advancement. And you all know the Hynarkin have been doing quite the opposite."

Several of the Fimiahri nodded. The others remained doubtful so Piltar added, "That's how they work. Everything they do is conducted behind the scenes, using spies trained to infiltrate and impersonate the inhabitants."

"Maybe the Outsider was one," put in Indoro.

Zivvoz gave his son a gentle cuff to quiet him. Indoro ducked and scowled at the admonishment. He looked to Hafrin for support but received an uncustomary short negative shake of the head instead.

Hafrin wished he could share with Indoro his knowledge of Tolbôun's activities, but knew that was out of the question at this time.

"We don't know that," said Zivvoz firmly.

"We...I need you," Hafrin told his people. "No matter how we may feel about being caught in the middle of all this, the time has come when we Fimiahri are going to have to fight or die. Personally, if I have to die, I'd rather go down fighting."

Even Nichole was amazed at how Hafrin's impromptu speech stirred those around the fire. Every one of the men nodded. A tiny smile flickered about Marrek's lips. He settled himself on the ground and Nichole sat next to him. Piltar sat more reluctantly. When Indoro would have taken his place with them, Zivvoz pointed to the rynada.

"Check the animals. We won't be staying here longer than it takes for the lady to recover."

Now Hafrin took complete control of the briefing. "We want you to ride out of here going your separate ways. Speak to the loyal. Bring in everyone you can. Ensure they're well armed but leave no township unprotected. Be careful. It could prove disastrous if any of you are caught and questioned."

"That's understood, ser." Alenul asked, "But how can we protect our own and still fight the demons? And what about your uncle? Suppose he also raises an army against us?"

"We deal with each problem as it arises," Hafrin told him. "The demons...the Craneeno," he nodded to Marrek and Piltar, "are the priority. I am given to understand that once we are prepared to go against them, the Hynarkin...the Wanderers, will make certain they have to fight us on something closer to our terms, rather than using their superior weapons to defeat us. I suspect we will also be able to rely upon those Wanderers who live on Fimiah to help us. And once the enemy find themselves reduced to fighting as we do I think they'll discover we're more than a match for them."

"And the Hynarkin?"

Hafrin nodded to Piltar for him to answer. "Those of us that are permitted will definitely fight with you. The rest of our people will be dealing with the Craneeno who are out there, beyond your reach."

"Out where? There?" Raxel pointed to the sky where cloud cover obscured the stars.

"Yes."

Apparently satisfied at long last, Alenul asked, "Where should we meet, ser?"

Using a sharp stone Marrek gouged rough lines in the frozen ground. Hafrin squatted next to him adding to the drawing. "Are any of you familiar with the mountain that exploded last year?"

Heads around the fire nodded. Alenul added, "I was running my traps near there, ser. It was a terrible thing to see, even at a distance."

"You were lucky to survive," said Nichole. "There were Craneeno and Wôbiny troops in the area as well as the Outsider."

"Aye." A wry grin set Alenul's eyes dancing in the light of the flames. "I know about the troops all too well, lady."

An image flitted across the periphery of Nichole's mind and her eyes widened as she realised just how close a call the hunter had had. Only through his skill at tracking game had he eluded detection. She looked at Hafrin, saw him give a mere suggestion of a nod confirming that he too had picked up the image.

Marrek continued, "That was our doing, I'm afraid. Hafrin and I were pursued by some of the enemy. We took refuge in one of our colonies. Unfortunately, the net result was we were forced to blow up our home rather than risk it being overrun. We took a number of them out when the place went, but we lost a lot of important equipment, as well as some of our people. The rest of the survivors are dispersed throughout the remaining communities."

"So there are more of you here than just the traders?"

"Lots," said Nichole.

Hafrin laughed softly. "In fact, I would never have met Nikki if it hadn't been for that incident."

"You were at this colony, lady?"

Nichole nodded. Marrek raised a hand. "We're getting away from the matter at hand."

Raxel apologised. "Sorry, lord."

"Not a problem." Marrek smiled to take any sting out of his words. At the same time he was bemused that another individual had arbitrarily granted him a title he did not feel he had earned. "We'll gather here. On the ridge overlooking the valley below Veran Pindkol."

"Why not in the valley itself, lord? There's a lot of ideal ground for setting camp."

"And a great place for a trap," said Hafrin. "If I've learned nothing else about battle strategy, it's that one should always hold the high ground to maximise the advantages provided by the terrain. Marrek." He turned to his foster father. "Perhaps it would be prudent to settle our people on the flank of the mountain instead. There are innumerable folds and crevasses in which to hide, plus we have three definite escape routes for a large force. It'll give us the ability to send out scouts and recover them with a minimal risk of discovery, as well as more room to accommodate individuals and small groups with less risk of discovery. Where you propose, over here," he rested a fingertip on the ridge, "we run the risk of either being surrounded or, at the very least, infiltrated behind our lines. Too many gaps to cover."

"Well thought, Rin." Hafrin blushed as Piltar praised his foresight. Around the campfire the older men nodded. Indoro caught Hafrin's eye and raised an eyebrow. Piltar continued, "He's right, Marrek. The mountainside would be a better spot, strategically speaking."

There was no denying the wisdom of his charge. Ruefully, Marrek admitted his foster son was rapidly growing beyond any requirement for further fostering or rudimentary instruction. "Now that's decided, I suggest we all try to get some sleep."

"Right, then, we move out before dawn."

On that, everyone agreed, to Nichole's relief. She was beginning to shiver with fatigue and the cold. And she was stiff and sore all over from the past days of strenuous activity. A hand settled on her arm.

Stay there. I'll bring the blankets, Hafrin told her.

Grateful for his attention, she complied. All the men dug through their meagre travel supplies to draw out blankets. Marrek and Piltar rummaged in their packs and pulled out not only blankets but also thermal ground sheets. To Nichole's amazement, there was more than enough to supply the entire party. From Piltar's studious expression it was evident he was responsible, although how he had convinced Vern to cough up such precious commodities amazed her. As she settled on the covers she would share with her husband she watched their companions examining the ground sheets they had been given. There was no denying the astonishment that something so thin could provide so much comfort. Before long, however, they were content, esconced in pairs about the fire. Curled up, her back against Hafrin, Nichole felt their shared body heat rapidly build. Before long, she dropped off to sleep.

CHAPTER 29

▼

Three days later, seated before Zivvoz's hearth, Nichole basked in the warmth indoors. With Val cradled against her breasts, she watched those around her. Studious and silent, the young nursemaid, Annarek, sat at her side. Word had reached the hold just ahead of their return, and the men left to protect Kili and the children were understandably anxious to ride on. Only Marrek's insistence that they be properly briefed had kept them at the hold. Kili bustled about the kitchen putting together food for the returning party. Zivvoz brought up ale from the cellar. Hafrin and Indoro disappeared below as well to inspect travel rations. Marrek cornered the holder as he emerged from the cellar. Curious, Nichole shamelessly eavesdropped on the conversation across the room.

Ziv, we need to talk.

Aye. Went without saying, replied Zivvoz and settled the small cask he had brought up from the cellar on the counter. He leaned on its top. *You're worried about them.*

Not surprising, Zivvoz surreptitiously jerked his head toward Nichole. Marrek slid a look in her direction. She kept her head carefully tipped so he could not see her face.

In part, Marrek admitted. *Nikki's combat-trained. All of our operatives are expected to be. Once she recovers from that impromptu expedition with the soldiers, she'll be more than capable of protecting herself. I just don't want to risk Deena, Annarek, Kili and Val.*

You were thinking they should move into town.

Might be advisable. There's a stockade there. I doubt anyone will concern themselves with three more women and a couple of young children taking refuge there.

What if the enemy over-runs the village?

It's a risk we'll have to take. Revïl's relatively far north of where we're likely to encounter the Craneeno.

For a long minute Zivvoz said nothing. Then he looked up. *I've still got contacts in Iryô. We could send them all there.*

"No." Unable to keep silent, Nichole left off all pretence of being absorbed in the tiny sleeping baby. Her explosion startled the complacent Annarek, who stared in wide-eyed amazement at her. "I'm sorry, Marrek, but you're not arbitrarily sending me away again."

"Nichole."

Marrek's warning failed to faze her. She passed Valrin to Annarek, stood and crossed the room, halting in front of the men. Behind her she heard the door open. A blast of cold air washed around her. Flames in the hearth roared up the flume and her riding skirt wrapped around the backs of her legs as the door closed. The charged atmosphere in the kitchen drew Hafrin across the room.

"What's wrong?"

"Marrek wants Nikôla and your son to accompany Annarek, Kili and Deenala to the capitol. We," Zivvoz nodded toward Marrek, "agree they'll be safest there with some friends of mine. Sirken is an old campaigner like me. He was loyal to your father, ser."

A frown twisted Hafrin's brow as he considered the problem. "Marrek, didn't you say you thought the townsfolk would be mobilised if there's civil war?"

"Yes."

"So this Sirken is likely to be drafted to protect the city when the army rides out."

"Yes. And that works in our favour since he'd be staying in Iryô," said Marrek. "Nikki?"

Puzzled by Nichole's stubbornness in the face of logic, Hafrin silently asked her to be reasonable. Kili had ceased all pretence at disinterest in the conversation. Behind her, the two men who had remained to guard the hold listened intently, amazed by Nichole's behaviour. It went against everything they were accustomed to. Annarek's expression emulated theirs: women were expected to defer to males in most things.

Unperturbed, Nichole dug in her heels. "Rin, I've spent months being trained in warfare. I'm more than able to fight. In fact, I probably know a few things you don't."

"The battlefield's no place for women," countered Zivvoz.

To the surprise of all the Fimiahri present, Nichole laughed out loud. "You don't know my people, Ziv. Every able-bodied person, male or female, is entitled to sign on for field operations. Even those who don't make the grade and are confined to office work are expected to qualify at combat arms."

Shocked, Zivvoz asked Marrek, "Is this true?"

Marrek nodded. "With our people, women outnumber men five to one, Ziv. Which makes sense, if you think about it."

It only took Zivvoz a moment to make the connection. "You only need one stud to breed a herd."

"Right. And, after all, aren't females the more dangerous and unpredictable of most species?"

Being discussed as though she was nothing less than breeding stock, Nichole took umbrage. Before anyone could respond to Marrek's rhetorical question she said, "Speaking of which, shouldn't we decide what to do with the livestock, Marrek?"

Effectively distracted, all of the men considered the problem. Ullavin, once a stonecutter by trade in one of the major centres, had lost his business when an opponent had resorted to malicious slander and underhanded tactics. The ensuing trial had nearly cost Ullavin and his family their freedom. The story was well known throughout the wilds. Adaptable, he and his family had settled north of Revïl where he had taken up live-trapping tïlkrïn to enhance domestic stock. Unsolicited, he offered assistance.

"Ziv, you can load the rakkïal in cages and put them in the wagon. There's more than enough room for those."

"And we can use four of the rynada," Kili added, "which means we'll be able to take at least some of the furniture."

Ullavin continued, "And Popiôl and I can drive the rest of your stock over to my pastures. I've four sturdy lads of my own, plus several nephews to protect them and my own animals. If push comes to shove, we know a few places to secure them against thievery and anyone conscripting for the enemy, demon or otherwise."

"That's an excellent option. And if the lady is set against accompanying us, we can definitely take Annarek," said Kili, and slipped an arm around her husband's waist. Nichole glanced at the wetnurse. Rather than being alarmed by the course of the conversation, Annarek appeared relieved.

Zivvoz nodded. "Aye. You'd have to take her anyway, to keep the little one fed."

"How soon would you be wanting us to leave?"

"That's something we'll have to discuss," Marrek deferred. The problem now was a general consensus on what ought to be done. "At the moment there doesn't appear to be any apparent need to close up and steal quietly away."

At that inference, Nichole caught his eye and grinned. Humour was infectious and the mood soon lightened. Kili quickly passed out food to everyone. There was little conversation over the late morning meal. Immediately afterwards, Ullavil and Popiôl departed after giving Marrek and Zivvoz information on where they would be going. Both were determined to pull in the best rynada stock available for use by the new army of their Alaiad-in-exile. While they sorted out last minute arrangements, Nichole put Valrin to bed. Leaving Annarek to keep watch, she crept off to the loft to sleep.

*   *   *   *

Hafrin

Head tipped on one side, Hafrin 'listened' as Nichole undressed and slipped into bed in the loft. He was acutely conscious of her weariness and that she was in more pain than anyone else realised. At his side, Marrek stirred. Hafrin hastily transferred his attention, bidding a formal farewell to the departing men. Piltar hovered in the background, holding the reins of a sturdy rynad. He came forward once the others were gone.

"So, young Rin, how's our Alaia?"

A wry grin twisted Rin's lips. "Asleep finally."

"That's good," said Marrek sombrely. "It's been a rough few days for her."

Out of the corner of his eye, Hafrin saw his orved mantle briefly on the porch railing. Age was catching up with Vrala Harz. She had been less inclined to search out a mate this past spring. Of all her offspring only two had ever voluntarily remained to be trained, and those were at the colony, employed to convey messages whenever using transmitters was out of the question.

Orved were long-lived, as fowl went. Domestic ones had been known to survive to almost twenty, unlike ryanda who lived to thirty or thirty-five. Vrala was close to twelve, past her prime. That had not, however, diminished the ferocity with which she attacked when needed. Nor did she appear to be slowing down in flight. Still, Hafrin realised time was growing short in their relationship. Their eyes met. She blinked once, slowly, unconcerned by his train of thought and turned her attention to the activity of the rakkïal across the yard.

Thought of age reminded him that Marrek was in his late forties. Zivvoz, who had bought his way out of Fanhri's service at thirty-one, was now in his fifties, while Kili was forty-three. He took a long moment to consider just how short time was for some of his Fimiahri friends and acquaintances. Unlike the Hynarkin, most Fimiahri seldom lived past their mid-sixties.

"Rin?"

Hafrin gave himself a mental shake and returned to his surroundings. "Sorry, sir. What did you say?"

"You certainly seem miles away." Marrek grinned at him. "I asked how Nikki was doing, since you can tap into her inner thoughts."

"Well, truthfully, sir, I wish we could get a healer down from the colony to look at her."

Now Piltar frowned. "Is she in much pain?"

"Some. I just can't tell if it's from the long days in the saddle to which she's no longer accustomed, or if she suffered an injury during the trip. She's so tired right now."

"I'll ask Kili to check on her," said Marrek. He yawned. "I think we should all get some rest."

"Aye." Piltar tugged at a lump of fluff on the cuff of his riding glove. "And I'll head home as well. I'm glad the men thought to check on your place, Marrek."

"We've been fortunate over the years in collecting a solid group of supporters," Marrek reflected.

To that, Piltar nodded. "I'll speak to Vern as soon as I can. Unfortunately, with the Craneeno in the area, all transmissions are being kept short. We're going to have to move locations after each use as well. Can't risk them triangulating on our position. Once I've sent news to the colony, and got what information I can, I'll close up my place and come back here, if that's alright with you."

"It might be for the best. They'll suspect something's up anyway," remarked Hafrin.

"That they will, lad." Piltar flung himself onto his mount. "You two take care. Look for us in five to six days. We won't be alone."

"Will do. Look after yourself," said Hafrin.

"Go with God," said Marrek in Hynarkin.

The image of a benevolent, yet stern elder father figure flashed across Hafrin's thoughts.

So that's how they see the all-powerful one. Curious

It was definitely a strange contrast to that which his people venerated: a symbol that was two runes combined rather than an actual image of any particular individual.

The minute Piltar was into the trees Marrek placed a hand on Hafrin's shoulder. "Come on. We should get some rest, too."

"All right. I'll have Vrala keep watch."

"Good thought. Wouldn't want the enemy or your uncle's people catching us unaware."

There was no sign of Zivvoz when they returned to the house. Annarek was also missing. In the kitchen, Kili was kneading dough for bread. Deenala stood beside her, watching the process intently and trying her hand with a bit of dough. As Hafrin and Marrek entered, Kili glanced up and smiled. Seated by the fire, Indoro thrust his feet out before him. A mug of mulled ale rested on the arm of the high-back seat.

"So you've decided to come in." He jerked his head toward the downstairs bed alcove his parents used. "Dad's sleeping."

"I'm for that," said Marrek. "Where do you suggest, Kili?"

"Use the loft. We partitioned it into three chambers over the summer, so you'll all have a measure of privacy."

Indoro caught Hafrin's eye and grinned at him. Refusing to rise to the bait, Hafrin hung his outdoor things on the pegs behind the door before heading for the loft. Marrek held back for a few minutes to speak with Kili.

Upstairs it was warm. Heat from the oven kept the loft at a bearable temperature throughout the cold months. On hot summer nights, Deenala slept in the sitting room by the hearth, while Indoro generally retired to the stable loft. Hafrin knew his shield comrade preferred the privacy of the stable, for more than one reason. He also knew that, for all his friend's efforts, his attempt at subterfuge was wasted on his parents. Both were well aware of his antics. Hafrin just could not bring himself to tell Indoro.

A massive yawn caught him unawares. Stripping off his clothes, he gave himself a quick sluice over with the water in the large basin kept in the alcove for that purpose. Ever mindful of guests, Kili had fashioned a curtain. This could either be looped back or dropped to provide the person inside privacy from prying eyes. Then, dressed in his undershirt and carrying the rest of his things Hafrin slipped into the room where Nichole slept. After softly setting his clothes on the floor in one corner, he crawled under the covers. Nichole stirred briefly. She rolled onto her side with her back to him. Another yawn caught Hafrin and he fell asleep.

CHAPTER 30

▼

If Nichole had any thoughts that they would be going into battle immediately, time proved her wrong. And for that, Hafrin was grateful. They had enough to keep them occupied, rounding up the last of the stock and driving it down to Zivvoz's. Ullavil, two of his sons and a nephew did not arrive for another seven days to take the herds. This gave the animals time to settle in together and sort out pecking orders. Now Nichole was back, Annarek no longer spent the night. She arrived shortly after first light and left soon after the evening meal, a cousin dropping her off and returning promptly as escort.

Kili, Nichole and Deenala went to work turning the mass of tïlkrïn milk into curds and cheese that could be safely stored indefinitely and easily transported. In between daily chores, Nichole also helped the family sort out what they would require during a drawn-out campaign, then pared it down.

Deenala made repeated attempts to take all of her toys. Limited as her supply was, there were simply too many. Each evening after she was asleep, her mother patiently pulled out half of them and returned them to the loft chest. By the end of the second week they were all on edge. To combat rising tempers, Zivvoz brought in a master swordsman. Between them, they kept Hafrin and Indoro busy.

Days flew by, one following the other so quickly Nichole felt they would never be ready. Winter closed in, partially alleviating their fears. Yet they all knew the weather patterns were no longer reliable. A thaw could easily reopen the roads at any time. Whenever Nichole could make time from helping Kili she joined the men in the yard or stable working on sword drills and perfecting her archery and knife fighting. Their instructor, Albîon af Elten, watched her carefully the first couple of days.

"Marrek," he confided one afternoon, "I must admit I thought you were mind-touched when you insisted I teach her. In all honesty, I never thought any woman could hold her own in combat. But this one would make any tutor proud."

"Because she's a woman?"

Marrek's jest caused Albîon to chuckle. "You caught me there, Trader."

"Well?"

"Truthfully? She's exceptional as a woman. Her gender aside, she's more than able to make a stand in battle, although why you would let his wife," now Albîon jerked his head at Hafrin who was sparring with Indoro using knife and sword, "risk herself that way is beyond me."

"You don't know Nikki," Hafrin countered as he and Indoro broke apart. Before he could say anything else, Zivvoz let out a shout of surprise. Everyone turned. Flushed with success, Nichole held her wood training sword at the holder's throat. The old campaigner's weapon stood, point first in a stack of old hay several feet away.

"By the Serpent, lady," Zivvoz gasped, "how did you...where did you learn to do that?"

Stepping back and lowering her training sword Nichole glanced at Albîon. "I've had a number of teachers, Master Albîon, some of whom would challenge your sense of reality. They were determined I be prepared for whatever lay ahead before I returned."

"No easy task for someone carrying a child," reflected Zivvoz. "Perhaps you or Marrek would be good enough to teach Doro and me that move."

Nichole glanced at Marrek. "Marrek would be a far better teacher. Besides, I think it's time I checked on Val."

She passed her sword to Hafrin and left the stable. Albîon scratched his head and Marrek grinned. Hafrin shrugged. "Can't argue with that."

"She certainly has a knack of arriving and leaving in such a way as to make you remember her," remarked Indoro. "Are we done?"

"Aye," said Albîon. "Got anything to lubricate a throat, Ziv? This is thirsty work."

"I'd be surprised if Ziv didn't have something set by," said Marrek.

With a throaty laugh, Zivvoz gathered up the training tools and stacked them in a corner on top of some hay. Then he led them across the yard to the house. As they had all feared, the weather was warming once more, melting much of the snow on the roads and the open fields. Pockets and drifts remained for now beneath the forest's sheltering arms. Along the mountain slopes, the lower ridges were rapidly appearing as well. A concern for all of them, which no one had as yet, voiced out loud.

Inside the cabin, they found Nichole standing in the kitchen discussing spices with Kili. Deenala leapt up from where she was playing with her toys by the hearth and flung herself at her father before Zivvoz could get out of his jacket and boots.

"Heyah!" The holder picked her up, tossed her in the air and caught her again. Now darkened from gold to a warm nut brown over the past year, Deenala's curls bounced merrily. She laughed and demanded more but he shook his head and put her down.

"Ziv, you best be careful," Kili cautioned him. "I swear one of these days she's going to hit the ceiling."

"No fear of that, Kili," Zivvoz responded as he unfastened his coat. "She's getting too heavy for these old arms. Before long, I won't even be able to pick her up at all."

Kili snorted and ordered, "Well, don't just stand there in the doorway. Come inside and get your things off. You're letting in the cold. I've made a pot of stew. If you'll bring up some ale for the men, Ziv, we can eat."

To Nichole's amusement, the men commenced good-natured pushing and shoving as they all tried to be first to the kitchen for the food. In the end, Indoro won the battle for the front of the line. Only Hafrin deliberately hung back in the sitting room. Nichole glanced around the room, before performing a quick mental sweep. She located Annarek in the loft changing Valrin.

While Kili and Zivvoz passed out food to the rest of the crowd, Nichole put Valrin to bed. Then she brought Hafrin a bowl of stew, a couple of slices of bread and some cheese. She settled next to him on one side of the hearth.

"Aren't you hungry?"

She shook her head. "No. I snacked while I fed Val."

"Well, ser, my lady," Albîon, who had elected to sit on the floor in front of them, spoke in between mouthfuls. "How soon do you see us moving against the Usurper?"

"Ah." Expression grave, Hafrin replied with a frankness that surprised Nichole. "That is indeed the question. And one I'm uncertain how to answer, Sword Master."

"But surely it must be soon. At the next break in the weather, certainly, otherwise we'll have to wait until spring and lose the element of surprise."

"That isn't the problem, Albîon," Hafrin told him. "Marrek, please explain. You're better versed in the overall situation than I am."

Although he had been taught to respect the privacy of others' thoughts, that it was the most singular important tenant amongst all the races, Marrek knew Hafrin needed to know exactly where they stood with Albîon. While Marrek explained about the Craneeno and the impending battle between the Wanderers and this intergalactic enemy, Hafrin tapped into the Sword Master's thoughts. Astonished by what he was hearing, Albîon nonetheless appeared receptive. This was something they kept encountering. An unexpected thought provided an explanation.

Star Born! Serpent be praised. And here I never thought there was any validity behind that legend. Now what they're saying confirms there is a grain of truth in them. We did come from the stars.

"Marrek." Hafrin broke across his foster father then apologised. "Sorry, Albîon."

"Not at all, ser. I'm gratified you and your kin have found me worthy to be included in your confidences."

"It's more than that, Albîon. As Sword Master, you have every right to be included in Council. I must admit the willingness with which you and the rest have accepted the information my foster father and his people have imparted has continually amazed us."

"Amazed? Aye, I suppose they might expect us to consider them outsiders almost as bad as demons. Meddling in our affairs, however well meaning their efforts." Albîon grinned at Piltar and Marrek. "But there's the legends, you see."

"Legends?"

"Aye. Most don't hold by the stories, thinking them nothing more than yarns made up to amuse children. The tales are seldom told anywhere north of Ekôzav, but there's the Star-Given sword. I saw it for the first time when I was a bit younger than you are, ser. And even then I could tell it wasn't of this world. Now, what you say," he nodded to Marrek and Piltar, "confirms we came from a world beyond Fimiah. 'Course I could never figure out where that other world was or how our ancestors got here from there. Ships, though. That makes sense. I'd really like to see such ships."

"Perhaps when this is over."

Piltar's reply was ambiguous. Even though it was obvious to everyone Albîon saw it for what it was, he appeared satisfied. Intense images washed over Hafrin as the Sword Master attempted to make sense of what sort of ship might sail between worlds. Having been educated on such matters by Nichole, it was all

Hafrin could do not to laugh out loud at the thought of vessels designed for an ocean, moving between worlds in the vast voids of space. A sense of urgency bordering on panic blanked out everything else.

"Rider coming," Hafrin quietly announced.

Albîon grinned, caught Marrek's eye and jerked his head. "Got orved ears, has he?"

Before Marrek could reply, everyone heard Bïzhan whistle a challenge. Chairs scraped as the men headed for the door. Hafrin gestured Nichole to remain near the rear. At first, she bridled, but he 'pathed his concern to her regarding the children and Kili. Realising he was relying on her to cover the rear flank, she acquiesced. The men gathered on the porch as a rider burst from the trees on a sweat-flecked rynad. The rynad staggered up the path and stumbled to a halt in front of them.

"Marrek Lytsun."

"Siyon." Marrek leapt down the steps as the trapper slipped from the exhausted rynad. "What's wrong?"

"The Usurper's troops are on the march. Was heading into Iryô when they forced me off the road. Dumped m'load with a friend and came back 'cross-country as fast as I could get fresh remounts to warn you. Spread the word on the way. Our men will meet us along whatever route we decide upon."

"Which way is the army headed. Here?"

"Looks like it, but I could be wrong. This general direction anyway. There are a number of routes they could take between where I met them and here. You know the roads as well, if not better n' most of us, Lytsun."

High above an orved called. Vrala Harz responded from the cabin roof peak and Hafrin realised what he thought to be a wild orved was one of Vrala's offspring who had been gifted to the Wanderer community when it was still a fledgling. Now the young orved wheeled slowly in, clearly seeking someone specific. When Hafrin stepped away from the group, the orved promptly folded its wings and dropped. He raised his arm. At the last moment, it back-winged. Anyone else might have been staggered by that unprecedented act, but Hafrin was accustomed to it.

"Well, Keen Eye," he addressed the avian messenger as he recognised the newcomer, "what have you brought us?"

Keen Eye dipped his beak and tapped the slender metal cylinder fastened to his left leg. Marrek detached the tube. Along the length of it was incised a series of letters from the Hynarkin alphabet.

"It's from Vern."

"Let's get it back inside," Nichole urged from the doorway. "You can read it as easily in here as outside and it's cold out here."

Since Keen Eye appeared in no hurry to depart, Hafrin gave the orved a ride indoors. Vrala left her perch and flew past the men into the cabin. Nichole scolded the jesset for her audacity. Unperturbed, Vrala settled on a chair back. Flipping her wings neatly into place she chirped at her son. Keen Eye launched himself onto the opposite chair.

"Looks like some of us will have to stand," Nichole observed, and took a place on one side of the hearth apron.

Wiping her hands dry on her apron Kili joined the group. "What is it, Ziv?"

"Message from the Hynarkin community," he told her.

Marrek opened the tube and slipped out the film roll that had been stored inside. Aware of his company's avid interest, Marrek reluctantly undid his belt and removed the miniature player/recorder from its secret pocket. Siyon and Albion grunted in appreciation but refrained from questioning Marrek. He inserted the strip and quickly read the Hynarkin script running across the device's tiny screen.

"Craneeno."

"Where?"

"Right about where we thought they'd be," Marrek replied. "Both here and out there."

"What are we up against, sir?"

To Hafrin's question, Marrek glanced quickly around. In the past three years, Zivvoz and Indoro had properly finished the interior cabin walls and white-washed them. Recorder turned so its tiny lens pointed at the far wall, Marrek activated the play sequence. Zivvoz, Siyon and Albion jumped in shock as images played across the white surface. Indoro released a grunt in amazement.

Kili gasped. "Great Serpent, how do you do that?"

Hafrin's lips twisted briefly in a smile. "This is nothing. You should see what else they're able to do up at their communities."

"Rin."

Piltar's sharp reminder only made Hafrin grinned more broadly. "Sorry, Pete, but the time for subterfuge is past. I'm afraid my people are about to receive an exceedingly rude and abrupt education into advanced technology."

"That's something we're going to minimise wherever possibly."

"You may certainly make that effort. But what about the enemy?"

"He's got a point, Pete," said Marrek. "Let's brief them. Ziv, you're going to have to pack up Kili, Annarek, and the children, and get them out of here as quickly as possible. I don't want to be caught sitting here like a prize wild rynad in a snare."

Hafrin pointed at the image on the wall. "Continue with the briefing, please, Marrek."

After a quick glance around the room to ensure he had everyone's attention, Marrek plunged into the briefing. Accustomed as he was to passing along information, of keeping things brief and concise, he was forced this time to pad out his report with explanations. It took far longer than usual. Fortunately, everyone present listened attentively and kept questions to a minimum.

"So, what exactly is this pulse thing supposed to do that your people plan to use against these demons?"

Albîon's question was not entirely unexpected. Piltar explained, "We use machines that operate on a specific current. The closest approximate I can give you is controlled lightning."

"You've harnessed storm power? Wonderful."

Piltar held up a hand. "It's like lightning, but not exactly. We have machines that create this energy, and the pulse will disable everything that's not shielded, especially if it's powered up."

"And your people will shield their weapons?"

"Some of them. In any event, we'll do our best to minimise the damage by temporarily shutting down. We've been trying to keep an extremely low profile here over the past year. Very few vessels have arrived, but each has been packed with what we need and has removed all non-combatants."

"Ah. So not all of your people fight?"

"No. We have children, as well as older people who are no longer physically able to keep up in hand-to-hand combat, and there are specialists whose jobs don't require them to fight except over great distances. Where possible, we prefer to keep them away from the war zone. They're far too valuable to risk."

"Then what about the Alaia?"

Hafrin laughed and rested a hand on Nichole's shoulder. "Enough, Albîon. My wife is a trained combatant. As such, she is entitled to join us. She won't be in the vanguard anyway."

Nor will you, Nichole silently informed him. Their eyes met and he smiled at her.

Of course not, Nikki. Unless the enemy overruns our position, that is.

Their eyes met. She responded, *In which case, we shall all be in trouble.*

CHAPTER 31

▼

By mid-afternoon Keen Eye had been sent back to Vern with an update. Annarek's cousin had been summoned to take her home so she could pack her belongings. In short order, the hold wagon was loaded with provisions and such other things Kili wished to take. Siyon offered to escort Kili and her companions as far as Albîon's hold, along with a message for his family to pack up and form a caravan. Troubled, Kili watched as Nichole, Marrek and Hafrin gathered their things and prepared to leave for Marrek's home.

"Are you sure you won't come with us?"

Arms wrapped around Kili in a farewell hug, Nichole found herself repeating an earlier refusal. "My place is with Rin, Kili. If I could, I would keep Val with me, too. But he must be kept safe."

"The road's not safe these days," countered Kili as she stepped back out of Nichole's embrace.

"It will be this time," declared Hafrin. He hugged his foster mother. "You're going to find a lot of people on the move to Iryô. Some of them, I'm sure you'll know."

"Enough, woman," Zivvoz scolded as he lifted his wife into the wagon.

With Indoro at his side, he watched her lift the reins. The two dray rynada surged forward. Seated next to her, an unusually solemn Deenala cradled Valrin who slept, oblivious to the tearful parting. In cages strapped to the wagon's sides between the water barrels, the rakkïal huddled, silent, their feathers fluffed out against the cold. Two more dray rynada trailed the wagon, their leads tied to the tailgate. The tiny wagon, with its precious burden, rumbled and lurched through the ruts down the road into the forest, its smoke-stained canopy rocking unevenly. Along the way they would pick up Annarek and her relatives, all of whom had been alerted via orved message the previous day.

"All right," said Zivvoz, as soon as he was certain his family was well on its way, "what now?"

Expression grave, Marrek gestured. "Time you and Indoro closed up house and joined Rin, Nikki and me at my place. Bring what you'll need for a winter campaign, Ziv. I trust you in this. In fact, I rely on you to show the rest of us what we'll need."

"You're expecting a long campaign?"

"If it's against just the Craneeno," Marrek replied, "it'd better be short. They'll have the advantage over us if the weather turns cold again."

"And if my uncle gets involved?"

Marrek glanced at Hafrin. "You better hope not, Rin. The last thing we need is a war on two fronts at the same time. That's something we can't hope to win. And it'll accomplish exactly what the Craneeno have wanted all along."

In short order, they had packed up everything Zivvoz considered necessary, doused the fire and dropped the exterior locking bar in place. Nichole, Marrek and Hafrin helped Zivvoz and Indoro load the packs onto the rynada, distributing everything evenly between Marrek's two drays and Zivvoz's remaining one. As they swung into the saddle, Vrala took to the air. She cleared the tree line, her cry piercing the wintry air.

"Rider coming," said Nichole.

"Another?"

"I believe it's one of the trappers," Hafrin told them just as Raxel emerged from the woods.

They mounted and rode down to meet him, leading the pack animals. Raxel slowed his rynad as they approached him. At the last minute he dropped to a walk and swung in alongside Hafrin, tugging at his fur hat.

"Ser, our people are ready. Most have sent their families to the capitol. The rest are making a move south toward Ekôzav and Nûhykar. We've set up messengers to spread the word to each group gathering to await your summons."

"Fine," said Hafrin. "Ride with us. We're heading up to Marrek's cabin. I'll draft the necessary missives so we can get them out immediately. And I'll send Vrala out to the farthest ones. That way, they'll receive the word more quickly."

Conscious of Nichole in their midst, they urged their rynada on at an extended walk. Disgusted, Nichole put Palor Orved into an easy lope along the path leading to Marrek's home. The men all looked at Hafrin. With a grin, he released Bïzhan. The black easily overtook the mare and from then on they ran, side by side, weaving through the trees. Behind them the rest of the men encouraged their rynada onward at a faster pace.

"She sits that mare well," Raxel observed with a glance at Nichole. Marrek nodded but refrained from letting Raxel draw him out.

When they reached the cabin they found the rest of the traders waiting for them. They had brought extra remounts and pack animals, as well as several messenger orved. One was from Vrala's clutches. With a minimum of discussion, everyone except Hafrin and Nichole sorted out supplies so each person received a fair share of food, clothing and sundries. Two of the pack animals carried grain for all the rynada. While the others worked, Hafrin set to drafting the messages to be sent out to his army. Once he and Nichole had agreed upon the wording, she helped him pen them. He signed each and, using a seal ring created for him in silver by Vern, Hafrin set his seal in wax firmly on the bottom of each tiny slip of paper. Then he and Nichole hurriedly rolled the messages and inserted them into tubes for Vrala and the other orved to carry.

"I hope this works," muttered Nichole as she tapped the seal onto the end of the last tube.

"If it doesn't, we're all going to be in for a nasty surprise," reflected Hafrin.

For a long moment they sat at the table, his hand covering one of hers before she suggested, "Guess we better get a move on."

Everything was ready to go when they emerged. Marrek and Robar helped them distribute the messages between the orved. Raxel took a couple as well. With a flourish, he took off to begin calling in the army. Meanwhile, Hafrin impressed upon Vrala where he needed her and the other orved to take the messages. One by one, the orved took flight. Vrala went last. Her route took her in the direction of the colony so that her return trip would be shorter.

"Ready?"

To Marrek's inquiry, Hafrin nodded. He flung himself onto Bïzhan's back and swung around. Davyn and Albîon took the lead. Marrek and Zivvoz rode on either side of Hafrin, while Indoro dropped in behind with the standard firmly locked in its cup in front of his left stirrup. For now he kept the colours furled. Nichole and Piltar rode side by side behind Indoro. The rest of the company brought up the rear.

They set out north and west. Overhead, clouds were moving in. A breeze crept up from behind them. It took Nichole a couple of minutes but she soon realised the weather was changing. She glanced up and then over her shoulder.

"Something wrong?"

At Piltar's question she shook her head. "No, it's the weather. It's almost as though it can't remember the season."

"What do you mean?"

"Haven't you noticed? The wind is out of the east. And it's warmer. The rest of the snow will probably melt."

"Could be worse. At least we won't freeze."

Piltar grunted at Sandi's remark. "Unfortunately, there's a down side to all this. It'll be slower going if the ground thaws too much. And it'll get slippery. I don't like the thought of that during a cavalry charge."

"Be miserable sleeping, too," said Zivvoz over his shoulder.

"There speaks an old campaigner," reflected Marrek.

Shoulders hunched against the weather, Zivvoz sniffed and peered down the road. Before he could say what was on his mind, two of the Hynarkin, Davyn and Piltar, took off at a light run into the woods on either side of the road. Hafrin silently commended his foster father's friends. However green they might be in first-hand battle experience, they were aware of the need for scouts. As traders who had been forced to rely upon no one else for protection over the years, they were all well versed in woodcraft and subterfuge.

Robar returned all too soon. "Riders coming."

Hafrin call back, "Whose?"

"Ours, I believe."

They rounded a bend and discovered a motley group of local men. Some were armed and mounted on drays or crossbred rynada. Many carried farm implements. Only a few had anything that resembled armour. There were, to Hafrin's relief, a number of archers in the party. Hunters, he suspected. Marrek and Zivvoz quickly organised the men and, in short order, they were on their way once more.

With the day rapidly advancing toward dusk, Hafrin began searching along the side of the road for an adequate site to pitch camp. Eventually he turned to Zivvoz and Marrek.

"Do either of you know the area well?"

Zivvoz shook his head. Marrek pursed his lips for a moment, then swivelled in the saddle and shouted back down the train. "Sandi."

"Ho." Waving his arm, Marrek urged him to join them. As Sandi approached he asked, "What's wrong?"

"We need somewhere to camp for the night," Hafrin replied. "Do you have any suggestions?"

Without hesitation Sandi said, "Sure. There's an excellent spot just up ahead. We should be there shortly and the foot soldiers will make it by dusk. It's big enough to set the tents for everyone."

"Which side of the road?"

To Zivvoz's question Sandi gestured. "Both sides have water and an adequate supply of deadfalls year round. I'd suggest splitting the group evenly between the two areas."

High above them the scream of an orved alerted them to Vrala's return. She dropped from the sky, landing on Hafrin's saddletree. Bïzhan turned his head and snorted at her, ruffling her feathers. Vrala chirped back. Hafrin laughed at the exchange.

Sandi asked, "What's so funny?"

"Oh," Hafrin rested a gloved hand on Vrala's back, "Bïzhan told her to stop showing off. He doesn't like it when she lands so hard."

Zivvoz stared hard at Hafrin. "Ser, do I understand you correctly? You can hear the animals?"

"Well," suddenly aware he had committed a dangerous indiscretion Hafrin flushed as he admitted, "yes, after a fashion. It's actually more images than words."

"And the lady?" Hafrin nodded. Zivvoz's eyebrows rose and he blinked hard. "That does indeed explain some things. Too bad you didn't use it against that boar."

"Unfortunately," Hafrin explained, "at the time, I thought I was making things up in my head."

"Thought he was going off his nut," put in Piltar. He cuffed Hafrin in the shoulder.

"And that's why he and Nikki are so suited for each other," finished Marrek.

"Thank you for your confidence," said Zivvoz, "but, ser, you must take more care. There are some as would not accept such a thing from you."

"I'm aware of that, perhaps more than most," Hafrin told him.

Ahead of them the land rose. Their route led between the folds of several low hills to surmount another. Below them stretched the campsite Sandi had told them about. They immediately reined to a halt.

"Looks like we've got company," said Hafrin.

"Aye. What do you make of them?"

"Can't say at this distance." Piltar dug in the small saddlebag at his knee and pulled out a distance viewer. "Ah, more of our people on the other side. And there're some of our people amongst that unfamiliar lot, by the looks of things, Marrek."

"Allies. Good."

Without visible cue, Hafrin urged Bïzhan down the slope. The vanguard broke into a light run, putting some distance between them and the rest of the cavalcade. Ahead of them, their scouts broke from the trees and fell in with them. Zivvoz dropped back next to Indoro.

"Doro, break out the Alaiad's colours."

Between them, father and son unfastened the ties. Catching the following breeze, the standard snapped out, boldly displaying itself to everyone in the vicinity. A ragged cheer went up from those ahead. More men poured from the trees to line the road. Cheeks hot, Hafrin rode with his head high, conscious that Nichole's embarrassment was no less intense over the accolades they were receiving. Suddenly she was next to him, stirrup to stirrup. They exchanged a brief glance. Marrek, Piltar and Sandi fell in behind. Indoro spurred ahead then turned aside into an open area. Their entire mounted party turned into the glade behind Indoro and halted.

Someone, probably one of the Wanderers, had ensured there were sufficient three-man tents to house roughly a hundred men. Hafrin realised that, at a pinch, each could probably hold five men. They would be cramped but warmly housed. The tents had been raised in groups of approximately five to a fire pit and at the centre of those on the left side of the road, directly in front of him, was a large pavilion that could easily hold ten or fifteen people.

"That would be our headquarters," said Marrek quietly.

Someone ran forward to take the reins of the vanguard rynada. With a snort and lift of one forefoot, Bïzhan indicated no one was to touch him. The would-be helper backed up and Hafrin stepped down, unassisted. Alongside him, Nichole nodded her thanks to the man holding Palor steady and slipped to the ground. Her divided skirts lapped about her boot ankles. Giving a shrug, she settled her fur lined cloak more snugly around her and stepped up beside Hafrin. With Zivvoz, Piltar and Marrek at their heels, they headed toward the largest tent.

CHAPTER 32

—————— ▼ ——————

Hafrin

As though he had been trained to this duty, Indoro planted the banner firmly to the right of the entrance and took up position next to it, his sword drawn. Rixon bracketed the opposite side. Two more Wanderers, whom Hafrin did not recognise but whom Piltar and Marrek greeted warmly, stationed themselves just inside the entrance. At Marrek's gesture, Hafrin ducked his head and entered the pavilion. Nichole followed close behind. They moved into the interior, stopping only when there was sufficient room behind them for the rest of the entourage to enter.

"Now this is more like it," said Nichole.

Before them stood a large collapsible table set on a rug. Capable of accommodating twelve at a pinch, a number of folding-chairs were set around it. Approximately five paces beyond the table hung a dividing fabric wall with three openings. Battery-powered lights provided illumination. These were hung from the support poles at the peak, as well as from the exterior poles.

"It's warm," Zivvoz observed as he stripped off his gloves.

Hafrin caught Marrek's thought. *They've hidden a heater in here somewhere.*

"Maybe there was a brazier in here earlier," Albion suggested.

"Perhaps." Zivvoz sniffed and Hafrin knew the old campaigner suspected the heat came from another source. There was, he concluded, a decided lack of the betraying odour of burning charcoal inside the pavilion.

Before anyone could get sidetracked, Hafrin asked, "Council now?"

"That might be best," said Piltar. He glanced at the rest of the group inside the entrance. Someone had thoughtfully dropped the hide door into place. "Is this everyone, or is there anyone else the rest of you think should be included?"

"Perhaps we should do a walk-about first," suggested Marrek. This, Hafrin knew, was a term for getting out and meeting the people one-on-one. "Meeting the men should give us a better feel for their temperament. And we could do with a look at what we have in the way of resources in manpower and armament."

"It should also give us good idea of what sort of experience we have to draw on," added Albîon.

"Alright." Hafrin turned to Nichole. "Nikki, why don't you get some rest? We've a long road ahead of us yet, and I know you're tired."

For once, Nichole did not argue with him. "I'll ask someone to have food and drink ready when you come back."

"That would be fine."

"Wake me when you're going to start deliberating on tomorrow's plans." When Hafrin started to shake his head, she insisted. "Rin, please. I've spent months training and studying at the Academy towards this moment. I'll have fresh thoughts on the matter. You know me. Even if my suggestions seem outlandish, at least they'll challenge everyone to think outside the obvious."

"There's that," he reluctantly admitted. "Okay, but only if you promise me you'll go to bed as soon as we leave."

"As soon as I've ordered food and drink," she agreed.

Satisfied, Hafrin gestured. "Gentlemen, shall we?"

Davyn quickly drew aside the door and bowed to Hafrin. Cheeks hot, Hafrin took a deep breath to steady his nerves and stepped from the tent. He paused long enough for his entourage to assemble. Indoro took up position immediately behind him, but it was Marrek who led the way into the camp. Intent upon remaining close to Hafrin, Vrala Harz dropped to his shoulder from the pavilion roof. With her keen eyes to warn him of any threat, Hafrin stepped out.

Several of the troops had unpacked the rynada and were apparently awaiting permission to place the baggage inside the pavilion. Robar paused to have a word with them as the entourage moved off. Alenul appeared at that moment, and Robar assigned the fruit grower the task of overseeing the Alaiad-in-exile's household. Even with his back to Alenul, Hafrin felt the man swell with pride at the prestige such a position gave him.

"Remind me to speak with Alenul when we return," Hafrin told Marrek.

His foster father nodded. Men around the campfires came to their feet as word raced ahead of Hafrin's approach. Most simply appeared mildly curious to see the young man to whom they had sworn their allegiance, sight unseen. Others were genuinely eager and pressed forward so that guards were forced to order them back. Hafrin made a point of pausing to speak with a person here, another there. To his horror, he realised some had brought their wives and chldren.

"Marrek," he said softly, "I don't like this. Is there anything we can do to separate them from their families? I'd rather not have to worry about non-combatants."

"We can try," Marrek told him. "Unfortunately, this has always been the case, at least throughout the ancient history of my people as recorded in the chronicles our ancestors brought with them when they took to space."

"Do what you can."

As Marrek nodded, there was a stir of bodies ahead. Men abruptly parted. Before Hafrin and his party, a blood brown rynad stallion almost as massive as Bïzhan trod slowly forward. On its back sat an elderly man dressed in full battle panoply. Someone behind Hafrin gasped.

"It's Lord Baryan of Nûhykar," murmured Robar.

Without turning his head, Hafrin demanded confirmation of the identification. "You're certain?"

"Positive. He used to come into the market personally to barter at least once a year. Occasionally, he visited my stall."

Uncertain which way this encounter would go, Hafrin's supporters closed in about him. While still some distance away, Lord Baryan reined in his mount. They stared at each other. That Hafrin had chosen to go bareheaded rather than wearing his war helm on his walk-about granted everyone an unimpeded view of his face. After a long minute holding Hafrin's gaze, Lord Baryan swung down. He came forward at a measured pace. At a predetermined distance he slowly, carefully drew his sword. Around Hafrin, men drew their weapons. But Lord Baryan went to one knee and rested his weapon across his raised knee.

Hafrin acknowledged the noble. "Greetings, Lord Baryan."

Looking up, Baryan stared past Hafrin at Robar. "Ser, you have excellent advisors."

"That we do," Hafrin agreed, electing to employ the royal address. "What can we do for you?"

"Many have believed me loyal to your uncle, the Usurper," said Baryan making no effort to couch his words with diplomacy. "I have only done what I must over the years to protect my people. Had I known of your existence things might have been different."

"That is understood. We do not hold this against you as we hold the well being of our subjects…all of our subjects, paramount."

"Thank you, my liege." Baryan took hold of his weapon by hilt and blade, bowed his head and extended his sword toward Hafrin. "I give you my life and the lives of my men. We rode at your uncle's summons. When word reached us of your army gathering in the area, we reached a decision by general consensus to come here to await your arrival."

Hafrin reached out, touched the sword hilt and stepped back. "We thank you for your generous gift, Lord Baryan. Please get up. It embarrasses us to have our loyal subjects kneeling in the mud when it isn't necessary. We're certain we shall all have recourse to be knee deep in muck all too soon."

Chuckles rose from those men within hearing. Around them, tension visibly eased as the exchange was passed on through the gathering. When Lord Baryan's head rose, he was grinning broadly. He slid his weapon back into its scabbard.

"You have your father's wit, sire."

Hafrin extended a hand and helped Baryan to his feet. "Thank you, my lord."

"Ser, your uncle is on his way from Iryô even as we speak. He's not yet aware of you and your men, that I know of, being more concerned with reports of demons massing along the Rashordi foothills."

"So that's what drew him out at this time," said Zivvoz.

"Aye." Baryan nodded. "I understand that he was going to wait until spring. But this early thaw must have..."

With a lift of his hand, Hafrin silenced everyone. "My lord, sirs, we pray no more of this. We shall hold a briefing in my quarters shortly. For the moment, we wish only to meet our subjects. Lord Baryan, we request you and your entourage accompany us."

Heads bowed, acknowledging his command. The group, now stronger by five...Lord Baryan accompanied by his son and three of his senior soldiers...moved on through the camp.

The further they went the more amazed Hafrin was by the calibre of the people drawn to him. Many had prior combat experience, being retired from service under his father years before his birth. Most had somehow armed themselves with swords and lances. Those who could not were well supplied with bows and an abundance of hunting points. Several fletchers were hard at work producing more arrows. There were even two smiths. From amongst them Hafrin and his advisors selected another three men to join the council of war.

At length, Hafrin drew his group back to the pavilion. They had found one more lord amongst the cobbled-together fighting force, an exiled noble who had with him a son, two nephews, a cousin and several retainers, all of whom were well versed in war theory.

"Theory's all well and good," observed Albîon to Hafrin. "Experience is better."

"And a fresh eye is even more important."

To those observations Hafrin shook his head. "Each has its merits, but without a clear head willing to examine all sides of a problem, they are useless."

A dip of Baryan's head conceded the point and they entered the pavilion. During their walk-about full dark had fallen. Somewhere in the camp someone was playing a musical instrument. Voices rough and melodious, young and old chimed in words to the tune. Within the pavilion, the temperature was comfortable. They stripped off their outerwear. Even as they settled about the table, Marrek prepared to unroll a large map of the area. Outside, someone called a request.

"Ser, permission to enter."

Davyn opened the flap and three men entered bearing food. The aroma of roast meat set Hafrin's mouth watering. He glanced over his shoulder.

"I should wake Nikki."

"I'm already up," she informed them.

She emerged from the left cubical, head high. Dressed in a fresh riding skirt, her now shoulder-length hair brushed out, she made an immediate impression on those who had not previously met her. Lord Baryan produced a low bow, and his retainers all dropped to one knee.

"Nikki," Hafrin made quick, informal introductions, "this is Lord Baryan, his retinue and heir."

"Please, my lord, gentlemen, none of that," she deferred with an accompanying lift of one hand. "We're all warriors here, after all."

"My lady?" At that, Lord Baryan suddenly realised there was a sword at her left side, a long blade dagger on the right. From the manner in which she moved, it was evident to all that the weapons were not merely for show. He turned to Hafrin. "Ser, be it farthest from me to question your decisions, but is it wise for the lady to be here?"

"My wife is more than capable of defending herself," Hafrin countered.

"But the risk..."

"Is nominal," said Marrek. "There is an heir."

Exclamations greeted the announcement. Hafrin cut them short with a more formal introduction. "Gentlemen, I present my wife, the Alaia-by-marriage, Nikôla Terrient of the Hynarkin."

One by one, the men bowed to Nichole. Face flushed with pleasure and embarrassment, she pressed more closely against Hafrin. He quietly drew out a chair for her and saw her seated, before taking a chair next to her. Davyn summoned the servants. Having quickly distributed the food and placing flasks of drink nearby, the impromptu servers withdrew.

Somewhat bemused by the entire affair, Marrek asked, "Where were we?"

"About to call a council of war, I believe," said Piltar.

"Food first, discussion later," announced Hafrin.

*   *   *   *

Once the dishes and remnants of the meal were removed, Marrek unrolled the map he had brought. Sight of a Wanderer topographical map literally took everyone's breath away. Hafrin glanced from his foster father to Piltar. It was evident from Piltar's expression that he was responsible for this particular gift.

"This is amazing," Baryan exclaimed. "Why, you can see exactly where the ridges and folds are. I never realised there were so many streams or ravines in the area."

"Aye," said Zivvoz. "The place is rife for a trap. We're going to have to be extremely careful about moving through there, ser."

"Which is why we're going to split into four companies. Zivvoz."

"Ser?"

"You'll head up my immediate command."

"Thank you, ser."

"Albîon, I want you to take charge of one company of mixed archers and lancers."

"Ser." The Sword Master tugged his forelock respectfully.

"Lord Baryan."

"Ser?"

"I realise you are unfamiliar with the terrain so I shall be assigning a party of Wan…" Hafrin caught himself, "Hynarkin under Piltar Darryk and Davyn Lytsun."

Piltar and Davyn straightened so Lord Baryan would recognise those with whom he would be riding. Baryan nodded. Marrek traced a line along the rift valley between the foothills and the mountains. Baryan examined the valley.

"So this is where you plan to meet your uncle."

"No, my lord," countered Marrek. "He's actually the least of our concerns, whatever everyone else here may have thought otherwise. There is another, much more dangerous enemy out there to be tackled."

"We know this force as Craneeno." Now Hafrin had everyone's undivided attention. "Our scouts, Hynarkin scouts, place them approximately here." A stab of his finger indicated a distance north of Revïl. "That's roughly a day's ride south of Brïtfin."

Baryan interrupted him. "This word you used, Craneeno, it's unfamiliar to me, ser."

"Undoubtedly you've heard rumours of demons in the mountains, my lord?"

"Yes. In children's tales."

"Not so. These demons are actually a race of people. I use that term loosely with regards to them," said Marrek. "They come from beyond your world."

"Star people?"

"Yes, but not ours," Hafrin told him, clarifying, "Not the Star people of Fimi-ahri legend."

"Meaning no disrespect, ser, but how do you know this?"

"Because our Star people are among us right now."

"Here? In this camp?" Baryan's son, Nevion snorted. "I've seen only trades-men and townsfolk."

"Try looking beyond the end of your nose," snapped Blorik.

Voices rose in argument. Nevion leapt to his feet, sending his chair over back-wards. His father attempted to restrain him but Nevion yanked free of Baryan's grip and took a step down the table. Nichole caught Hafrin's eye and he nodded. They stepped forward, placing themselves between the potential combatants. Hafrin raised his arms and bellowed.

"Enough!" Silence fell. He looked at each man in turn as he spoke. To his credit, Blorik had not moved from his place throughout the entire verbal alterca-tion. "It is true there are Star people among us. In fact, many of us have had deal-ings with them."

"Really?" Intrigued, Baryan stared at the gathering. "Where are they, ser? I would meet them."

"They're here." Hafrin gestured to the Wanderers, one hand coming to rest on Nichole. "My wife is, in fact, one of them."

"Father, this is ridiculous," Baryan's son scoffed at Hafrin's declaration. "They're no more Star Blood than I am."

How true. Nichole fought back the laughter threatening to explode from her lips. There was Wanderer blood in Baryan's line from his wife's side.

"Quiet, Nevion." Lord Baryan commanded his son. Beneath the reprimand, Nevion sulked as his father continued, "When will you learn to hold your tongue? The signs are all here. Anyone with half a wit can see that. The demons have returned as legend predicted they would. The Temple seer has foretold the coming of the Star blood and return of the true Alaiad."

"But Dad." In his refusal to obey his father, Nevion slipped into common Fimiahri, winning him further disapproval around the table. "It's also said we would know the Star blood by the sword. And everyone knows the Usurper ordered Hafrön thrown into the sea."

Before Nevion could finish what he was saying, Hafrin slowly drew Hafrön from its scabbard. The scraping of metal slipping from its sheath silenced everyone. All eyes turned to Hafrin, only to be captivated by what he held. Blue light skittered up and down the weapon's blade. Silver flecks glistened in the depths of the crystal-like metal. Light reflections rippled across the top of the collapsible table and flickered from everything metal. Among those around the table who had seen the weapon at Fanhri's investiture, there was no doubting the identity of the sword.

"Serpent preserve us, you have it," Baryan gasped. "How?"

"I found it," Hafrin told him. "Or it drew me to it. I'm not sure which."

Determined to get the meeting back on track, Nichole asked, "Can we finish the briefing now?"

"Aye, my lady. I think that would be an excellent idea," Baryan agreed. "Nevion. Pick up your chair and sit down. And this time, listen."

Nevion complied, but his sulky face soured Nichole's stomach, so that she avoided looking at him whenever possible. Grunts from others around the table indicated everyone else was in agreement. They set to working out strategy for the following day. Into the plans Hafrin included contingencies for several problems they might well face. The worst was the possibility of what they might encounter should they face opposition from his uncle. That was something no one at the table was eager to consider. Eventually the men headed off to their billets leaving Hafrin, Nichole, Marrek, Zivvoz and Piltar alone in the pavilion. At some time during the night, Zivvoz and Piltar made the rounds. They checked the other bivouacs and the guards. When Hafrin would have joined them, they insisted he and Nichole get as much rest as possible against the impending battle.

CHAPTER 33

▼

Two days later they were in the foothills. Throughout the morning, Hafrin sought any form of landmark that might tell him precisely where they were. Except for fleeting glimpses of snow-capped peaks through the trees, however, he failed to find anything reassuring. To his credit, he had succeeded in persuading the bulk of the women and children to leave the army. A number of campfollowers…a term he learned from Piltar…persisted in accompanying the army, but Zivvoz informed him this was to be expected and permitted. Most of those who left turned southeast in an effort to avoid running into Jikpryn's troops who, according to Vrala's reports, were now somewhere roughly two days behind Hafrin's forces.

Someone in the vanguard shouted back, "Hold."

A scout emerged from the trees and raced toward them. At the last moment, he reined his rynad in a tight circle, slowing it to a walk as they came about to face the army's leaders.

Hafrin asked, "What news?"

"We've only one more set of hills between us and the great vale, ser."

"Excellent." Hafrin turned to Marrek. "Would you check with Vern? I need a status report."

While Marrek rummaged in his saddlebag for his communication device, Hafrin took the opportunity to check on his army. He found it exceedingly strange referring to this motley assortment of men and dubious choice of arms as an army, much less that it belonged to him. Just the thought of commanding such a force kept him awake for hours at night. Strung out along the road, the rear of the baggage train was nearly half a day behind the cavalry. Nichole rode forward.

"How are you doing?"

"Fine, love," he reassured her as best he could. "And you?"

"Good," she replied. Her tone and expression were sufficiently buoyant that he knew there was no need to check more deeply.

"I think tomorrow will be the day." His quiet announcement shook her.

"So soon."

"Soon?" He shook his head at that. "I was just thinking how long it's been in coming."

"Rin." Marrek called to him.

"Duty calls," he told her. She forced a smile and returned to her place in the marching order.

While waiting for Hafrin to join him, his foster father drew off to one side. From one saddlebag, he removed a communications headset and donned it. When the rest of his command would have also halted, Hafrin ordered the remainder of the cavalcade to proceed. Under Albîon's direction, the army resolutely continued on. Zivvoz, Piltar and Hafrin grouped around Marrek. The old campaigner kept his curiosity in check at the sight of the device. To Hafrin it resembled two curved pieces of shiny black wood. In reality, it was fashioned from a resin compound, with a wire coming off one side and running down to a battery pack and transmitter. One piece fitted over Marrek's head. A second, which could be swung up out of the way or down in front of the mouth, was presently in position for him to speak.

"Field Force Prime to Force HQ. Come in HQ." After a pause Marrek's fingers tightened on the battery pack. "Yes, Vern. We should be in position by this evening." Again, Marrek paused. "They're where?" Pause. "When?" Pause. "All right. I'll let the others know. Thanks. Use the orved for any emergency communications. Right. Prime out."

Marrek stripped off the set and stored it. Gathered around him, the others waited patiently. He looked up after sealing the saddlebag. Hafrin muttered to himself. Since discovering Hafrin and Nichole were telepaths, Marrek had been exceedingly careful about keeping his thoughts shielded. Now he appeared to be doubly cautious.

"Well," Hafrin urged. "What did he say?"

"The Craneeno forces massed in the valley not far from here two days ago. Yesterday they began pushing north toward our nearest remaining patrol base and our primary breeding colony, transporting their personnel in machines. Consequently, our people have been packing up and retreating further into the mountains. To our advantage, our fleet has arrived."

"That's good."

"Unfortunately, the Craneeno managed to get some of their mechanised vehicles on the ground. We can't hope to match that sort of firepower with hand-to-hand combat weaponry and rynada."

"Okay, so what do we do? Skirmish?"

Marrek shook his head. "Not possible. Their technology, like ours, can pinpoint someone even in the dark of night or during a storm. Hopefully it won't come down to that. Patrol is preparing a power burst. That should effectively disable everything on the ground that hasn't been switched off and properly shielded for several hours. It won't affect hand weapons, I'm afraid. Nor will it completely immobilise the Craneeno. They've not been entirely slow in seeing the wisdom of employing domestic animals for transportation."

"So, apart from the weapons, the footing will be even."

"Don't discount those weapons. They will definitely be a drawback," Piltar mused.

"Highly polished shields would be an asset," said Marrek. "From what I understand, those beam weapons of theirs have a tendency to reflect at right angles when they hit brightly polished metal or crystal."

"It's doubtful they'll bring many of them to bear if they're reduced to foot or rynadback," replied Piltar. "They're too bulky."

"We plan for what we can and improvise where we can't," declared Hafrin. His expression and thoughts turned grim. "I want the companies to take cover along the ridges and in the crevasses. Camouflage every piece of baggage and make sure the animals, healers and physicians are well away from the line of fire, but within reasonable reach."

"That means we'll have to scramble if we're forced to make a run for it."

"We will anyway," said Hafrin.

"There's this," put in Marrek. "Those light hand weapons of theirs do have a limited range."

Hafrin caught on that. "How limited?"

With a grin, Marrek told him, "A good archer can shoot further."

"Now that is indeed interesting," muttered Albion almost to himself. Then, "Ser, I suggest we muster our best archers as quickly as possible."

"I leave that in your capable hands, Sword Master," Hafrin deferred. "Zivvoz, go with him. If we have sufficient numbers, I want them split into two companies to cover left and right fields of fire."

"And the others?"

"We'll distribute them amongst the other two companies."

Albîon stared at the Hynarkin seated at the table. "Who trained this boy…begging your pardon, ser?"

As he tugged at his forelock in an effort to excuse his verbal blunder, Hafrin laughed aloud. "No offence taken, Albîon. Compared to most of you, I am a boy."

Marrek rested a hand on Hafrin's shoulder. "I found him. I raised and trained him, with Zivvoz's help."

"So," Baryan leaned forward in the saddle as though really seeing the Hynarkin for the first time, "I was right. I always thought there was far more to you traders than met the eye. In all honesty, however, I never thought your expertise ran so deep. Are you all trained in the art of war?"

"Only those of us who are employed in exploration and the military," Nichole said.

"Women as well as men?"

"Of necessity, yes."

"Gentlemen, we digress."

With that, Hafrin drew them all back to the matter at hand. Behind them, the foot soldiers marched stoically onward. A lancer company followed the pike bearers; both were small groups. Hafrin had yet to decide where to employ them to his best advantage.

"Where did these Craneeno come from?"

Marrek readily responded, "Their primary Fimiahri base is on the Kandyn Islands. And that's definitely on our fleet's list of targets."

"Marrek, exactly when was that discovery made?"

"Last summer," Marrek told Hafrin.

Which explains why no Fimiahri vessel that dared explore or attempted to fish in that area ever returned, thought Hafrin.

For days now, he had been operating in something of an emotional vacuum, but with this knowledge anger flared deep inside. "All right, divide the companies now and make your way to where we discussed. I want everyone in position as quickly as possible. If the Craneeno are retreating, they will undoubtedly return the way they came since it's the quickest route."

Baryan voiced the question that Hafrin knew was on everyone's mind. "What about your uncle's army?"

"I haven't forgotten about them," said Hafrin. He held Baryan's gaze. "In fact, I'm hoping they arrive before the Craneeno."

Nevion sniped, "You're planning to sacrifice them to wear down these Craneeno."

To that Hafrin all but snapped back, "Not if I can help it."

"Then…"

"If my uncle's force arrives in time, and he is agreeable, we should be able to catch the Craneeno unawares between our two armies."

"A masterful plot," Baryan commended. Still, he appeared somewhat unconvinced as to any compromise on Jikpryn's part.

"But one that relies heavily on luck," Marrek reminded them.

"Everything we do from hereon in will be up to chance."

In that, Hafrin flatly informed them that he had no illusions concerning what the future might hold for them. He raised his voice as the infantry passed their impromptu council. The baggage train was only a short distance behind the foot soldiers and he wanted the discussion over with before it caught up with them.

"As I've said before, we plan where we can and improvise where we must."

"And pray to the one who guides us all that we prevail," said a voice behind them.

They all turned. Bïzhan reared and pivoted on his hind feet to bring Hafrin around to face the author of that statement. A thin whip of a woman sat an eager mare. Aged, her seamed face reminded Hafrin of an orved. She appeared an extremely capable rider despite her years. On the left breast of her cloak was embroidered the symbol of the Great Serpent. Hafrin bowed low over Bïzhan's neck. All around him the others were also saluting the old woman.

"Madam," Hafrin greeted her, "you are most welcome here."

"Hafrin af Fanhri, Alaiad Presumptive." She returned his greeting. "The Serpent has held you very close these past years. Indeed, you are favoured to have drawn such an auspicious gathering to you in so short a time." Her mare flung its head up and down, and bared its teeth when Palor snorted at its impudence. "I am Triklâ."

Indoro blurted, "Iryô's seer."

"Aye. My years are drawing to a close, but I thank him whom I serve that I have lived long enough to meet the Star Blood. I would ride with you the rest of the way."

From the corner of his eye Hafrin saw his foster father staring at the old woman as though certain he knew her from somewhere. Hafrin considered her request. "We would be honoured, Seer, but wouldn't you be safer with the healers?"

"Safer perhaps." Laughter cackled back at his concern. "But at my age every day is just another spent in this life rather than with him whom I serve. Besides, I can be of some use to you."

"Begging your pardon, Seer, but beyond the obvious," said Marrek, "how can you help us?"

On the periphery of his thoughts, Hafrin caught a hint of shock. Marrek had remembered where he had seen the seer; an image of an evening at a tavern filled his mind. Surprise nearly shattered Hafrin's composure as he realised Triklâ had prophesied for Marrek a day before he had discovered Hafrin beneath a bush.

"Hynarkin, I've watched you for years. You're the one he chose to care for these special children." She looked from Hafrin to Nichole and back to Marrek. "But, in answer to your question, the Temple has asked that I document everything that happens here."

Fascinating, thought Hafrin. Catching Nichole's eye, he realised she was considering the same thing.

I'm pleased you find it so, a strange voice insinuated itself into his thoughts.

Shocked, Hafrin jerked around and stared at the seer. From the corner of his eye he caught Nichole's expression. She was as dumbfounded as he was by the revelation. Expression serene, the old woman nodded just once.

Oh my God, Nichole's exclamation whispered through Hafrin's thoughts. *She can read minds!*

Nikki, Hafrin hissed back at her mentally.

She clamped down on her thoughts, but her cheeks burned. As Triklâ casually returned her attention to the rest of the party, Hafrin realised there were far more surprises in store for him and his people than he had ever envisioned. He nudged Bïzhan and the black swung back.

"Let's move out. We've wasted far too much time."

At his command, company commanders and their seconds saluted and took off down the line. The Sword Master and Zivvoz sped off to ferret out the best of the archers. Meanwhile, the remaining commanders and Hafrin's entourage broke into an easy run past the rear files of the army. All too soon, this curious interlude would end and the dirty business of war would begin, and violent death of his own kind was something he had yet to experience.

How many of us will survive? To that question, however, there was no answer.

CHAPTER 34

▼

By midmorning of the following day, Hafrin's army was well distributed along the east face of Veran Pindkol. Hafrin had to admit he had been startled that his advisors had selected this particular area. Since the collapse of the caverns where the Wanderers had previously established their colony, the mountainside was a jumbled maze of massive boulders. The most recent aerial cartography showed them where escape routes lay, both those that could be used by the baggage carts and riders, and those that were accessible only to someone on foot. Most of the small dells created by the fall provided adequate or excellent cover. The main camp hugged three large cul-de-sacs in the cliff face. With campfires beneath overhangs and green branches fastened to the rocks above to dissipate the smoke, they cut down on the likelihood of betraying their position. Fortunately, Weather Devil remained quiescent, in contrast to its usual disposition of drawing storm clouds.

Flat on his stomach atop a massive chunk of rock, Marrek inspected the rift valley below, before turning his viewer on the ridge east of his position. Having located his foster father, Hafrin scrambled up the rocks behind him, dropped flat and wormed the rest of the way up alongside.

"Anything?"

"Shouldn't you be briefing the troops or something?"

"Or something," replied Hafrin.

Marrek set his viewer down and looked at his foster son. Hafrin grinned back at him. Suddenly Marrek unintentionally dropped his guard. Through his foster father's eyes, Hafrin realised just how far they had come in the past year. For the first time, Marrek was seeing him as a man, capable of making his own decisions and accepting his failures. Loss loomed, forming a massive gulf between them. There was no attempt to disguise the pain Marrek felt at Hafrin's anger and sense of betrayal over the incident with Nichole and the decision to send her off-world. Unable to hold back tears, Hafrin quickly turned his head away. A hand settled on his shoulder.

"You've made me very proud these past few years, Rin. I'm sorry we chose to cause you so much pain, you and Nikki. As long as I'm able, I will be here for you to use as a sounding board. To support you when you need it and to council you when I think you've lost direction. That's if you want me."

"Thank you, sir."

Suddenly visibly uncomfortable, Marrek picked up his viewer and scanned the scene below once more. This time he stopped mid-way through his inspection. Somewhere overhead an orved screamed. Down in the camp, Vrala Harz responded and took to the air. Marrek turned his viewer skyward to scan the other orved.

"It's wearing jesses," he announced when he found it.

"Probably belongs to my uncle's men."

"Undoubtedly."

"There they are," Hafrin said, pointing toward the ridgeline.

Even without a viewer, the troops were visible, moving amongst the trees. Hafrin watched as his uncle's men deployed along three separate ridges. Blue and gold surcoats of Iryô troops mingled freely with the white trimmed maroon of Wôbiny. A few forest green and brown could also be detected; those of Lord Baryan's men who either had not received word in time to avoid joining with Jik-pryn's force or had decided to back the larger, more experienced army. Russet and ochre appeared as well.

"So they're all here," Hafrin murmured, even though no one had any difficulty identifying the rest of the Fimiahri nobility with their colours clearly designating them and their entourages.

Several more orved took to the air, loosed by members of the opposition. Vrala Harz began diving at them, driving them away from the mountain. Reaching out mentally, Hafrin called to his jesset but she ignored him. He could see men pointing at the aerial assault. Someone loosed an arrow but Vrala remained well out of range.

"You have to admire her determination," said Hafrin after several minutes, "even if it's misplaced."

"Perhaps you should call her in," Marrek suggested.

"I've tried." Hafrin explained, "I'm afraid she's pretty worked up right now. She'll come when she's decided they've had enough, or when she's too tired to keep it up."

They returned their attention to Jikpryn's army, which continued to emerge from the forest and deploy down the slope. As groups formed, their billets were assigned and men began rapidly setting up camp. Recalling the nights of organised chaos to which his own force had devolved each night on the road, Hafrin could only marvel at the orderly fashion these seasoned troops displayed.

Of course, he considered, *the bulk of my men have spent most of their lives, if not all of them, farming, trapping or mining. A lot of them are tradesmen, too. Only a few, like Ziv, have any actual experience as soldiers.*

Out loud, he asked, "Now what?"

"We wait," said Marrek. He replaced the viewer in its case and slithered down the rock into their camp. Hafrin followed him. The minute he landed next to Marrek, his foster father declared, "I could do with something to eat."

Reminded of how long it had been since they had broken their fast that morning, Hafrin concurred and they headed for the headquarters pavilion. Security at the forefront of his thoughts, Hafrin had ordered a separate, six-man tent set up nearby to house Nichole, Marrek, Piltar and him. Those who had brought the pavilion were disappointed at having the grand structure relegated to nothing more than a weatherproof area for meetings, but Hafrin pointed out that any sneak attacks would be aimed at that particular structure. And he refused to risk lives unnecessarily. While they ate, Hafrin and Marrek scrutinised a topographical map of the immediate area.

Part way through their meal, Nichole asked, "Do you suppose he knows we're here?"

"Undoubtedly," Marrek responded.

"They sent up orved," Hafrin explained.

"Was that what upset Vrala?"

Hafrin laughed. "I wish you could have seen her trying to drive all five back to the woods."

"I'm surprised they didn't try to shoot her down."

"They did," Hafrin said, "but Vrala's smart enough to remain well out of range."

"Thank God for that," Nichole murmured.

"Ser!"

From a ledge above, someone called down into the camp. Hafrin leapt to his feet and backed out to where he could just make out the guard. The man waved to indicate he could see Hafrin. Then he signalled and gestured.

"What is it?"

To Marrek's inquiry, Hafrin replied, "Rider coming."

"One rider?"

"Apparently."

Leaving their meal half-finished they raced to the lookout. Piltar and Zivvoz joined them. More troops gathered below their position as Hafrin and his companions scrambled up the rock. Beyond their position, they caught sight of a rider clad in mauve already halfway across the rift valley and proceeding at a fast pace. In his free hand was a standard from which trailed a serpentine green banner.

Curious, Nichole asked, "What's that?"

"That," Zivvoz informed them, "is a truce flag."

"I'd say they know where we are."

"But not how many of us," countered Hafrin, "Nor where exactly all of our troops are."

"Might as well stop trying to hide," said Piltar.

Hafrin nodded and rose to his feet. The rest of his party stood. Zivvoz gestured behind him, selecting several levelheaded older men with combat experience to form a guard for their Alaiad-in-exile. Nichole wisely elected to remain where she was when they made their way down the rocks to the frost-burnt grass to await the rider. Marrek raised his viewer as the rider approached. Even at this distance, it was evident from his panoply that he was an officer.

Marrek exclaimed, "Rin, that looks like the Captain of your uncle's personal guard."

"Hilcaz?" Piltar peered at the rider as the man slowed to a walk over the remaining distance. Now Nichole slithered down the rocks to join the rear of the party.

The officer reined in at a respectful distance. His mount threw its head up and down, tossing strands of foam from its jaws. He brought it to order. There was no avoiding the torrent of thoughts from Hilcaz as he used the opportunity to inspect the group before him. Hafrin took two steps forward. When Nichole would have accompanied him, Marrek put out a hand. She halted but remained alert.

"Ser." The officer saluted and formally introduced himself. "I am Hilcaz af Orïl, Captain of the...your uncle's personal guard."

"Captain." Diplomatically ignoring the stumble, Hafrin returned the greeting. "We are Hafrin af Fanhri. What brings our uncle and his army here?"

He sensed the Captain bridle as he employed the royal 'we' and heard Hilcaz's thought, *Got a bit of a nerve when he hasn't even been invested as Alaiad.*

But, out loud, Hilcaz replied with civility. "There are demons massing north of here, ser. The...my lord can only assume from this gathering of people that you also have heard about them."

Hafrin dipped his head. Now he gestured to Marrek. His foster father came forward. "Greetings, Captain. We've met in passing, I believe. I am Marrek Lytsun."

Hilcaz went pale. Hafrin caught the concern that here and now he might well be called to answer for his crimes against the Hynarkin. The Captain's eyes darted across Hafrin's entourage to alight on Nichole. Tension was so thick Hafrin was surprised Hilcaz's rynad failed to respond to the charged atmosphere. High above, Vrala Harz screamed defiance, refusing to come to rest. Then Hilcaz's gaze darted beyond Hafrin's party. Images flickered through his thoughts.

Concerned by what he was reading, Hafrin slowly turned and looked back toward his base camp. All along the rocks directly behind him were lined archers and swordsmen all of whom stood ready for combat. Hafrin raised his arms.

"There's no fight here," he shouted to his people. "Stand down. Now."

Slowly, reluctantly, swords were sheathed. Most of the archers retired along with the other fighters. Finally, only three remained and Hafrin knew there would be no dismissing them. He turned back to Hilcaz.

"In answer to your earlier question, Captain, we are quite aware of these demons. My Alaia's people refer to them as Craneeno, and they are indeed the principal reason for our men massing here."

"Ser," Hilcaz touched two fingers to his helm, "my lord commanded me to hand you this message."

Reaching carefully into his surcoat, Hilcaz gingerly withdrew a roll of paper. He extended it, not directly to Hafrin but rather to Marrek. With a nod, Marrek accepted the missive. He glanced at it before passing it to Hafrin.

"I believe you were present when this was written," said Hafrin after a cursory examination of the contents. "As such, we would have the gist in your own words, Captain."

Surprised by Hafrin's move, Hilcaz stared at him for a moment. Then he found his voice. "You're correct, ser. I was with my Lord Jikpryn when he wrote the message. In essence, it requests you join forces with him. He also promises no harm will come to you or your people before, during or after the battle by any order of his. In fact, he has commanded a group of my men to ensure no one among his army attempts violence against any of you."

"Well," Marrek observed, "this is definitely something to reflect on."

Still making no effort to properly read the message, Hafrin nodded to Hilcaz. "You have our thanks for your forthrightness, Captain. Please tell our uncle that we shall send word shortly concerning this matter."

In spite of himself, Hilcaz glanced skyward then back to Hafrin. "How soon should we expect delivery of your answer, ser?"

A grin tugged Hafrin's lips. "Soon. And please inform our uncle to expect an orved."

The Captain nodded, touched his helm once more and wheeled his rynad about. Once certain Hilcaz was well on his way, Hafrin gestured to his entourage. They returned to camp well protected by the archers. He settled at the pavilion table. Marrek and Nichole hovered at his shoulders as he unrolled the message and inspected the contents at length.

Without looking up he asked, "What do you think, Marrek?"

"Truthfully?" Marrek shrugged. "I'd say we have to take your uncle at face value for the time being."

Zivvoz countered, "You aren't suggesting we agree to this?"

Head rising, Hafrin stared at him. "We have no choice. He has the larger force. Even with everyone we've mustered along the way, we can only field a third of his compliment, Ziv. And, given what we're up against, I'd say we need all the expertise we can draw on. If we attempt this piece-meal, as it were, we risk a fiasco. In that event, the only winner would be the enemy."

"Particularly since the Craneeno have better weapons."

"But there's more of us than them," Zivvoz argued.

"Aye." Piltar nodded. "But it'll take some doing for our men to overcome the initial shock of seeing the opposition up close and personal."

Hynarkin heads nodded. Recalling his experience, Hafrin nodded in accord. Marrek reinforced their opinon. "They're like nothing you've ever seen before, Ziv. Even hardened fighters amongst our people find it difficult to react instantly the first time we run up against them face to face."

"We have visual images of them to show our people," put in Nichole. "This evening all of the senior staff and company sergeants and officers will have to be briefed. That should help a bit."

Zivvoz bowed his head briefly. "If you're set in this then I suggest we get it over with."

"Marrek." Hafrin turned to his foster father. "You're the best person to pen a response. Would you please put together something suitable while I see if I can convince Vrala to come in?"

To that, everyone grinned. Marrek nodded and settled at the table with pen, ink and paper. After a minute's reflection he called across the interior. "Seer, would you mind lending me your expertise, as well?"

Triklâ joined him. Nichole at his side, Hafrin left the pavilion. Lord Baryan had arrived, drawn by news of the meeting with Jikpryn's Captain. Now, on Hafrin's request, he waited while they sought to summon Vrala. It took Hafrin and Nichole combined to convince the irate jesset to leave off harrying the other orved. When she did come in, she elected to settle on one of the pavilion ridge-poles before finally condescending to land on Hafrin's arm.

"Begging your pardon, ser, but I'm surprised you allow her to get away with that sort of behaviour," commented Lord Baryan. "Did you train her yourself?"

Hafrin shook his head while Nichole explained, "She's not trained, Lord Baryan. Vrala comes and goes as she wishes."

"She's wild?"

"Yes."

Voice dropping, Lord Baryan muttered, "Amazing."

Employing gentle mind touch, Hafrin explained to Vrala what he needed of her. She dipped her beak twice and shifted her weight from one foot to the other. By rustling her wings, she conveyed her eagerness to be off. Throughout their silent exchange, Hafrin could hear Lord Baryan's thoughts running on. Amazement at the control Hafrin exerted over the wild raptor was foremost in his mind. Marrek appeared.

"Here you go, Rin."

"Thank you, Marrek."

Between them, they secured the message. Then Hafrin raised his arm. Once more he impressed upon Vrala where she was to go, including the image of Hilcaz. Bobbing once more, Vrala launched herself skyward.

"Now we wait," said Marrek.

CHAPTER 35

▼

Jikpryn

With the coming of night, fog rose from the ground. Anyone experienced in warfare knew that meeting an opponent under such conditions was ill advised. But Jikpryn was determined to display complete confidence not only in his men's ability to protect him, but in his nephew as well. He was impressed with this young man who, despite his youth, had managed to bring together a formidable force. Nerves jangling, he left his tent. Outside, Hilcaz waited with a handpicked group of guards and two of the nobles who they could most rely upon. Jikpryn nodded to Hilcaz and stepped into the stirrup. His rynad attempted to rear but the handler kept Origan firmly in place until his master gave the signal to release him. Then Origan did rear slightly. His rider called him to order. With a lift of his hand, Jikpryn ordered his party forward. They rode slowly through the forest, down the slope and into the open.

Before and around them mist swirled, pooled and frayed. Rynada hoof falls rang loud nearby, while being muffled a short distance away. Had there been any scouts out in the valley, it was unlikely they would have spotted anything, unless they were right on top of the party. The piercing scream of a raptor alerted them, out-of-place as it was with the night. They halted. Jikpryn gestured to Hilcaz.

"Captain," he said as soon as Hilcaz approached, "ride forward and see if you can make contact."

"Ser."

"And, Hilcaz."

"Ser?"

"Be careful. I have no desire to lose you."

*　　*　　*　　*

In response, Hilcaz touched his fingers to his war helm. Heartened by Jikpryn's words, he wheeled and rode off into the mist. Every instinct told him what he was doing was foolish. It went against everything he had been taught and was contrary to all common sense. Yet he continued on, holding his rynad to a walk while he listened to the repeated cries of the orved that he was certain belonged to the young Alaiad-in-exile.

"Hold."

A voice in the mist caused his mount to shy and rear. He quickly brought it to order and forced it to stand as another group of men emerged from the forest. Clothed in dark blue and black, and mounted on a magnificent black rynad, the young man appeared before Hilcaz. His helm hung at his knee. Before him rode another young man. This one wore full battle armour. A topknot of tïlkrïn hair streamed from his helmet.

"Captain."

That the young Alaiad recognised Hilcaz immediately won him points with the Captain. Hilcaz touched his fingers to his helm. "Lord Jikpryn requested I ride out to meet you, ser. He's waiting just up ahead."

"We're aware of our uncle's presence," the Alaiad replied. "Please, lead on."

Spine contracting, Hilcaz forced himself to turn his mount and lead the parley party back to where Jikpryn and the rest of his men waited. In a small forest clearing, they broke free of the mist. On the far side waited Jikpryn and his party.

*　　*　　*　　*

Jikpryn edged his mount forward. He studied the young man who rode, bareheaded, in the midst of the well-armed party. "Black on black," he murmured before he could stop the words in his throat.

His eyes widened at the sight of a woman in the entourage. Equally incredible was her attire; she was as well armed and armoured as the men. And then prophecy drove home. A magnificent raptor dropped to rest on the young man's saddletree.

"Vrala," the young man ordered, lifting his arm, "please."

Jikpryn waited only until the orved had launched itself onto a nearby tree branch before saying "You call her demon."

"Vrala Harz."

"Sky Demon." Trapped, Jikpryn forced himself to delve for confirmation of his worst nightmare. "And the night runner would be?"

"Bïzhan." With a gentle slap of a hand to his mount's neck, the young man indicated his rynad.

Jikpryn cleared his throat. "And the Star blood?"

"My wife and he who raised me," said the young man as he pointed to the woman and then to one of the men flanking him.

"My captain tells me you hold the sword."

With a dip of his head in assent, the young man urged his rynad forward. For a moment Jikpryn wondered at his motives, what action he might pursue next. His spine tingled. A chill settled about him that had little to do with the elements.

Hilcaz moved between them to make formal introductions. Even Jikpryn marvelled at his Captain's careful diplomacy. "My Lord Jikpryn, this is Hafrin af Fanhri. Sir, my lord Jikpryn af Kinhar."

"Thank you Captain." Hafrin dipped his head and Hilcaz reined his rynad into Jikpryn's party. Now Hafrin addressed Jikpryn frankly, "Uncle, there's much that needs to be discussed between us. As such, matters of state must take second place at this time. A greater peril threatens our people than internal strife and squabbles over who should rightfully rule. I believe...as do my advisors...that it is prudent we put such matters behind us and concentrate on what endangers our world."

That this young man, uncannily resembling his late lamented sire and dam, could so readily set aside blood debt amazed Jikpryn. Of all the things he expected to hear, this prompt dismissal of family matters in favour of their people as a whole left him adrift. Thrown off-balance, Jikpryn struggled to regain his composure. Behind him, his guards and entourage murmured amongst themselves. As though aware of the turmoil within him, Hafrin edged his huge black forward until they sat, knee to knee. Jikpryn's hand prickled in close proximity to the hereditary sword. He flinched from it.

"My apologies," said his nephew. "I've heard rumours that you were injured by Hafrön."

With difficulty, Jikpryn cleared his throat and managed, "My fault for discounting legend as falsehood."

"We both have much to learn," said Hafrin. "Sir, we need to meet now. Our intelligence advises us that the enemy will descend on us, if not tonight then as early as tomorrow. Time grows increasingly short and we must be prepared for what's coming."

"Aye," Jikpryn acknowledged. "Come…if you would…ser."

That he could bring himself to admit his own failings and Hafrin's authority over him drew louder murmurs from his men. A hand rested briefly on his arm. In spite of himself, Jikpryn started. He looked up. Blue eyes, clear of guile, met his. Nerves wound tight abruptly released. He took a deep breath.

"Please, uncle. Lead on."

Side by side, they rode into Jikpryn's camp. All around them men leapt to their feet. Mist swirled around the rynada, ghostly blue where damp torches guttered fitfully. Before long, a mass of men enclosed the party of riders, barely leaving room for the animals to move forward. Irritated, Bïzhan suddenly reared. Horns tossed, scattering the men.

"Zhan!" Hafrin admonished his mount with a sharp word and a slap from the flat of his hand.

The sharp report caused a number of those about them to jump, and the men who were pressing in around them rapidly drew further back. On the heels of that, Hilcaz bellowed a command. Jikpryn's personal guard promptly thrust forward as one. Facing the crowd, they turned to form an avenue with swords drawn.

Jikpryn nodded to Hilcaz and they rode on. Their progress over the remaining distance to his pavilion was unimpeded but Jikpryn saw his nephew glance repeatedly across the crowd. Occasionally his eyes would narrow as he picked out an individual here and there. Yet Jikpryn was unable to ascertain what had alerted Hafrin to potential problem spots, nor who, in most instances, had caught his attention.

As one, the group reined in and stepped down. When Jikpryn turned to his nephew, he discovered Hafrin standing, eyes locked with his rynad. After a few seconds, the black bobbed its head. It was evident to all that the stallion was reluctant to obey whatever silent command had been imparted. Servants stepped forward to take the rynada. For a moment Jikpryn thought the black would refuse to accompany its handler, but then it moved off. Tail swishing, horns tossing, the stallion reflected his annoyance.

"Quite the handful," Jikpryn commented. He lifted the tent flap, allowing Hafrin to preceed him.

"Sometimes," his nephew agreed. He paused and grinned. "But there are few who have his trust, so I don't need to be concerned about losing him."

Inside, they found the tent brightly lit. Several braziers warmed it. Partitioned in three, the tent's forward portion was the largest and clearly meant for holding council. Lanterns hung from support poles. A small table to one side held several goblets and a flask. Central to the front area was a large folding table and a group of chairs. On the verge of sitting, Jikpryn hastily reminded himself that he no longer held claim, however tenuously legitimate, to the high seat. He gestured. Hafrin smiled.

"Thank you, uncle, but I think we should forego protocol. If you would summon your senior officers and lords, we had best get to the problem at hand."

Relieved by this second adept step around the leadership problem, Jikpryn nodded. "Hilcaz, send for the rest of the council."

"Ser."

How he accomplished it, Jikpryn was uncertain. Yet, somehow Hilcaz managed his salute so that it encompassed both Jikpryn and Hafrin. The minute he left, Jikpryn went to the table and hefted the flask.

Uncertain how his nephew wished to be addressed, Jikpryn asked, "Wine?"

Hafrin shook his head. But there were others in his company who came forward to help themselves. Such a relaxed gathering was not something Jikpryn had expected. The deference his nephew's followers held for Hafrin was openly evident to everyone. At the same time, Hafrin granted them their due by rank and experience. While they waited on the rest of the council to arrive, Hafrin seated his wife near the head of the table. Then he elected to sit next to her rather than at the head. Startled, Jikpryn silently inquired about his decision.

Flashing a quick smile, Hafrin explained, "Uncle, this is your tent and your camp. Aside from that, you have far more experience in these matters than I do. For now, I defer to that."

Nervous once more, Jikpryn slowly settled into the chair at the head of the table. With Hafrin on his right and the Hynarkin, Marrek Lytsun, at his left, he urged the rest of the gathering to sit. To their credit, Hafrin's men seated themselves in such a manner as to allow Jikpryn's men room between them. When his people began arriving, Jikpryn ordered them to grab the nearest available chair. The last to arrive was his uncle.

Kizrun af Olnaer entered with all the caution of one familiar with court machinations; worn by the years of governing his province while his nephew made hard and fast work of controlling the unruly. Stress and care lines heavily ingrained his features. He paused before taking the remaining chair, which coincidentally was directly opposite Jikpryn. Hard dark brown eyes inspected the gathering, noted Hafrin's position to Jikpryn's right. His eyebrows shot up in surprise. Hafrin caught Kizrun's gaze and nodded a wordless greeting.

Jikpryn offered Hafrin the opportunity to speak first. "Ser?"

His demeanour frank before the gathering, the young Alaiad squeezed his wife's hand as he stood to address the assembly. He looked slowly around the table. Where men attempted to avoid his gaze, he waited until they looked up before his eyes moved on. Jikpryn made note of the two who scowled when caught unprepared. At his shoulder he felt Hilcaz stiffen and knew his Captain had noted something perhaps far more sinister.

There will always be those who will dispute his right to rule, Jikpryn told himself, watching the expressions on his men's faces as he relinquished authority to his nephew.

But will you back him, a voice whispered through his mind, *or will you attempt to undermine his rule?*

It took all of Jikpryn's self-control not to look wildly about the table. The question in his mind was not his own. That much he knew. There was a distinct flavour to it, almost feminine. Slowly he allowed his eyes to drift to his right. The young Alaia made no effort to avoid contact.

"Gentlemen," said Hafrin, unwittingly breaking the tableau, "many of you are, I'm certain, here under the belief that my uncle and I are about to discuss the terms of his surrender. I wish to make it perfectly clear that this is not the case. We're gathered here to prepare for war, a war that is not of our choosing, but one we most assuredly cannot avoid. This is a war thrust upon us by a race many Fimiahri refer to as demons. The Hynarkin...Wanderers as they call themselves...or Star Born, to give them their correct title, know them by another name: Craneeno. It's possible some of you here have already encountered the enemy disguised as our people. We don't know for certain. To all of you, I tell you now they are not a threat to be taken lightly."

Jikpryn stiffened at that. Conscious of the importance of not breaking across his nephew's address to this war council, he caught the Alaia's eye and thought hard. *It's important I speak to him once this meeting breaks.*

Not entirely to his surprise, she slightly inclined her head, acknowledging she understood. Kizrun rose. Leaning against the table, he glared at Hafrin. "What right have you to tell us what we shall or shall not do, boy?"

"By my birthright," said Hafrin quietly. With that, he carefully drew his sword and laid it on the table before him.

Jikpryn commanded, "Uncle, please sit down and listen."

Startled by his nephew's sharp tone, Kizrun demanded, "Are you going to let this...child...tell you what to do?"

"I remind you, Uncle, that this child, as you call him, is your grandnephew and the rightful Alaiad." Hands resting on the table, Jikpryn squared his shoulders and made his declaration. "What I took by force, I now return to the one whose right it is to sit on the high seat in Iryô. And I solemnly tell you all now that I will back him against anyone...anyone," he repeated, "who would try to take that from him."

"Thank you, uncle," said Hafrin. "Would you please coordinate the direction of this meeting? I defer to your experience. My people will provide the up-to-date intelligence we require to pull off our offensive."

"Thank you...Hafrin."

"Call me Rin, please. At least for the duration of this campaign."

There was no denying the overall easing of tension in the room. The unfortunate altercation with Kizrun had provided the necessary opening for Jikpryn to declare his personal intentions. Those who envisioned rebellion now realised that, if they elected such a route, they would do so without his support. It was a foregone conclusion that Nûhykar would follow the new Alaiad. So would the bulk of Ekôzav's population. How his own people in Wôbiny would react was a given as they were intensely loyal to his bloodline. Most would comply with his edicts. He suspected there might be trouble from his uncle, but to what degree was anyone's guess.

Hafrin reached out to retrieve his sword. Before he could sheath it, however, it began to hum. Blue and green roiled along the blade. Frozen in place, Hafrin stared as light spilled from the sword and writhed along the table. Transfixed by what was happening, everyone watched the light crawl toward the seat at the end of the table and its occupant. Unable to move, Jikpryn waited for whatever was to come. The light swept over his fingers. It curled about his hand, crept up one arm, crossed his shoulders, and slithered down the other. Nerve endings twitched and tingled. Hairs along his arms and on his head stood on end. As quickly as the sensation had assailed him, it passed. The light winked out.

Uncertain what to do next, Jikpryn raised his crippled hand. Something was different. Stunned, he whipped off his glove. His fingers were straight although pale and shrunken from lack of exercise. Otherwise, they appeared perfectly healthy. He wriggled them, unable to countenance what he was seeing.

"Behold the justice of Hafrön," declared Marrek. Even though his voice was steady, Hafrin could see from his expression that his foster father was shaken by what had transpired.

Jikpryn slowly sank into his seat. Hafrin hurriedly sheathed his sword and sat down. Jikpryn found he could not stop marvelling at his return to complete health. Amplifying his astonishment, the young Alaia reached out to rest her hand over his restored limb. Her fingers briefly covered his without the hesitation other women had demonstrated.

"Sir, as you can see, my husband is a generous and caring person."

To that, Jikpryn could only nod. He was relieved when Hafrin brought them all back to the reason for their meeting.

"Gentlemen," said Hafrin, his resolute tone drawing them back to more important matters, "it's time to consider our resources, the geography of this region and what we're going up against. Uncle, your assessment please."

CHAPTER 36

▼

Hafrin

From a low rise on the flank of Veran Pindkol, Hafrin sat next to Marrek. He studied his men as they prepared for the battle ahead. Two Wanderer physicians and their three assistants, who were trained Field Medics, moved purposefully about the camp below. Each man was outfitted with a device designed to pick up foreign devices; specifically those that operated on Craneeno frequencies.

Already they had scanned the senior staff and discovered implants used by the Craneeno in several members. Hafrin's uncle, Hilcaz and two of the nobles who had accompanied Jikpryn were among the affected. Fascinated, Hafrin had watched the removal of the objects and was gratified to hear that they were malfunctioning.

"Do you suppose Hafrön was responsible for that?"

Nichole's question had elicited considerable conjecture, but Marrek insisted such speculation be left until later. Now, watching their limited Wanderer Medical Staff at work, Hafrin knew his foster father was far more worried than he had let on to anyone else in their party.

"You're thinking there are more implanted men in the army than we'll be able to account for, aren't you?"

Marrek glanced at him. "You really shouldn't do that, Rin."

Hafrin shrugged off the admonishment. "It doesn't take a mind reader to see what you're thinking, sir. Have you any idea how many might escape the inspection?"

"No." Marrek picked up a loose fragment of rock and casually inspected it before tossing it over the far side of their lookout, away from the camp. "But that's why Pete insisted we check all of the senior staff, as well as the archers, before anyone else."

Ever present was the thought that one of his crack bowmen might launch an arrow at him while he was preoccupied with battle strategy or in the midst of combat. Unsettled, Hafrin frowned. Below, one of the Medics had separated out a man from his companions. Discussion was rapidly turning into an argument. Hafrin stiffened. Marrek put out a restraining hand.

"Leave it, Rin. See." He gestured to where Zivvoz and Hilcaz were making their way to the hot point. "Let them deal with it."

"And the others? The ones we miss? How will we deal with them in the heat of combat?"

Marrek shook his head. "There's no side-stepping this issue, is there?"

"No, sir." Hafrin waited. When Marrek maintained his silence, Hafrin prodded him. "So what have you and Pete decided?"

"We've advised the senior commanders of the problem, explained what to expect and told them to deal with the situation if it arises."

"Deal with the situation." Hafrin's frown turned to a scowl. "You mean, kill them."

"If necessary." Witnessing Hafrin's rising opposition to that decision, Marrek stopped prevaricating. "In the heat of battle, Rin, there's no time for niceties. If your best friend turns on you with a weapon, you do what you have to to survive."

However logical the explanation, Hafrin was unable to justify the decision to his subconscious, even though Marrek saw the validity of the situation. He got to his feet. Marrek looked up at him. What he read in Hafrin's face kept him where he was. Scrubbing his hands down his hips, as much to brush off the grit and chaff as in an attempt to erase the knowledge of what might well occur the next day, Hafrin swept the campsite once more. Then he nodded and left, carefully picking his way back down to the canyon floor.

It was unlikely any of the control devices had been active when the Wanderers had generated the pulse to disable all electronic equipment on the ground. So they were stuck with the unknown factor of how many moles…a word Nichole had explained…were still active, unwitting agents for their enemy. One side of Hafrin's mouth tugged in at the thought of tiny creatures that would fit in the palm of his hand presenting a serious threat to his army. Humour died as he considered what Nichole had said next.

"And knowing all this, how much of Jikpryn's antipathy toward your father was Craneeno induced, amplifying his discontent to murderous fury?"

To that, and in light of his uncle's revelation after the meeting, that Tolbôun had been a Craneeno agent, Hafrin had no answer. Thrown into close quarters with Jikpryn, unschooled in adequate thought control, Hafrin was acutely conscious of his uncle's personal doubts and self-castigation. With that in mind, Hafrin continually strove to put his uncle and his great-uncle, Kizrun, at ease. Again, one corner of his mouth caught in mirth at the image of the mole Nichole had 'pathed him the previous evening.

"What amuses you, ser?"

Caught back to his surroundings, Hafrin found the seer standing in front of him. Still entertained by the notion, Hafrin quickly explained. Triklâ was equally intrigued.

"There is this, however," she cautioned him. "Even the smallest, unexpected obstacle can destroy the best laid plans of any person."

There is that, thought Hafrin, aware the seer heard him. She nodded and moved aside to let him pass. Hafrin joined Nichole in their tent. She was lying on the mound of rugs, snug beneath a Wanderer thermal cover.

"Not asleep?"

"Neither are you," she countered.

He stripped off his jacket, vest and boots, and set them aside. As he settled on the edge of their camp bed, Nichole took his nearest hand in hers.

"It'll be alright, Rin."

"I wish I was as confident as you are."

"Someone has to be," she replied. "Now, come to bed. We're both going to be up extremely early, and somehow I don't think Marrek's going to be particularly forgiving of either of us if we don't meet his expectations in the morning."

"You've got that right."

Hafrin caught Nichole's gaze. Mirth twinkled in her eyes. Rolling his eyes, he stripped off the rest of his things and slipped under the covers. It took considerable doing, but following a measure of what Nichole referred to as 'slap and tickle', they both succeeded in dropping off to sleep after a couple of hours.

*   *   *   *

Light was just tinting the horizon above the trees. All around Hafrin, ryanda shifted their weight, grunted and pawed restlessly at the ground. Riders adjusted their weight in the saddle. A number of Troops, mounted and on foot, repeatedly checked equipment. Everywhere, any piece of armour or tack that might make a betraying sound was muffled with rags or hide strips. These would be ripped away if there were time before combat was engaged. And if they could not, they would not impede warriors or animals. There was the occasional repeated 'snick' as someone nervously slipped a belt knife or sword part way out of its sheath and then replaced it.

Tension was so thick Hafrin could not maintain his mental shield. In spite of the instruction he had received the previous year, the thoughts of those surrounding him continued to leak through his guard. Soon the seepage became a torrent. He was able to sift them, monitor those he considered important and push aside the rest. In spite of his best efforts, the constant barrage proved wearing. He envied Nichole's ability to shut it all out.

But she's had the benefit of proper training. When this is over, I'll have to get her to teach me.

He glanced behind him to where she sat Palor Orved, surrounded by a trusted guard. Alongside her, making notes on a scroll, the seer sat her steady mount. Hafrin caught Nichole's attention as she scanned the rank-and-file immediately in front of her. A wan smile twisted her lips. When the time came, her party would withdraw to the camp below to await the first casualties. Satisfied, Hafrin turned his attention back to the battlefield.

In the darkness along the ridges on either side of the rift valley, verlanik…archers…prepared their bows. Amongst Hafrin's archers were Wanderer bowmen. Each was equipped with the curiously shorter weapons Marrek had informed him were called rebows. Their peculiar construction doubled their effectiveness and power over greater distances than Fimiahri weapons.

Something else my people are undoubtedly going to take note of, thought Hafrin. *More unauthorised technological advancement.*

Where the land rolled south, the forest halted. Here the ground dropped away slightly, an ideal spot for an ambush. Behind it were clusters of thick brush. Hidden amongst the shrubs were Kolbrian…lancers in Wanderer terms…armed with blintor spears. Beyond them, in the woods to the south were massed Emiarl…foot soldiers. The foremost carried long pikes. Up either slope, held back in clefts and folds, were the Derynada…Cavalry.

From his vantage point on the mountainside, Hafrin considered again the strategy the council of war had worked on until the early morning hours. They had all managed to snatch desperately needed sleep while their forces were rising and preparing for impending battle. Then Hafrin and his men had raced pell-mell into position on opposite sides of the rift. While orved were dispatched with messages to his commanders, Hafrin met with the arrivals from the Wanderer forces. Most were scouts who had flanked the Craneeno force to join up with the Fimiahri armies. Two were telepaths, sent with specific instructions to position themselves where they would be most useful in relaying intelligence to

Hafrin and, through him, to the army. To back up their intelligence, Hafrin dispatched Vrala with orders to perch in a treetop far enough into the forest to provide adequate warning of the enemy's arrival.

What amazed everyone, particularly the men in the forests along the three hills, was Jikpryn's decision to turn immediate command of his army over to Lord Adosô. Even Hilcaz questioned that decision. For his part, Jikpryn was strangely determined to see out the conflict alongside his nephew. Only in that manner did he feel he could quell the bulk of the dissenters among his men who might see the battle as a means of removing the last obstacles from their lord's path to unquestioned rule. The last thing their people needed was to lose a potentially strong leader to a malcontent's envy and ire.

Hafrin glanced at his uncle. Their eyes met. Jikpryn's helm-covered head nodded. Again Hafrin swept the ground they had chosen for this battle. Light crept across the forest, pallid wintry fingers that drove away the fog below and caught on dewdrops. Farther up the mountainside, above where they waited, night's moisture had formed pockets of frost. Although the sky had been clear most of the night, a hint of cloud was edging in from the sea in the east.

At these temperatures the snow will return, Hafrin considered. *I could do with a Wanderer weather report right now.*

Through his tie with his wife, Hafrin felt Nichole shiver. Knew when she blew on her fingers before tucking them in her armpits to warm them; a fighter's trick taught at the Academy. Alongside her, Gurran, the Weapons Merchant smiled briefly at Hafrin as his eyes passed over him. Between him and Nichole, Triklâ remained outwardly oblivious to the uneasiness of those surrounding her.

I still wish you'd let me fight beside you, Nichole projected to Hafrin.

Nikki, we've been through this until it's deader than a week old carcass, he replied.

But you know I can fight almost as well as Doro.

Which is why I want you back there with Gurran protecting the seer. Besides, he applied logic, *you've got more medical skills than most Fimiahri surgeons have. The Medics Vern sent down will need all the help they can get.*

Snort, she responded and withdrew, willing to admit defeat. A rare capitulation on her part, for once it was genuine.

Someone within the ranks cried out. "Look!"

Others around the perpetrator hushed him, but murmurs raced through the ranks. Picking up what the startled soldier had seen, Hafrin stared at the sky. Between patches of thin haze, faint flashes of light were just visible against the dawn sky.

"So it's begun out there," murmured Marrek.

"Ours?"

"Yes."

"Ours?" Jikpryn stared at the flashes. "What do you mean?"

Hafrin explained, "Those are Wanderers fighting demons, uncle."

"In the sky?"

"Beyond the sky."

"Mother of he who protects us," Jikpryn breathed a prayer. "What are you saying?"

"That the legends are true," replied Zivvoz from behind them. "We came from out there, beyond this world. Even as do the Star blood, whom we've referred to as Hynarkin all these generations."

"I wouldn't go that far," stated Marrek. "Your ancestors were the original Star blood. From what world, we have no idea."

"But if we're different races, how can we look alike?"

A wry laugh from Marrek surprised Jikpryn. "That's something that's got our scientists…learned men and women…spinning to understand. By rights, we shouldn't be able to inter-marry, even with help."

"Yet my nephew and your kinswoman have a son."

"Yes."

"They're coming," said Hafrin as Vrala projected images of grey clothed figures flitting through the forest. Silence fell across the army.

Flashes of light were now visible through the trees. As they drew closer, explosions became audible. Rynada reared and men muttered at the unholy sight. Then, the enemy emerged into the meadow below. In spite of his hatred for the Craneeno and what they were intent upon doing to Fimiahri and Wanderer alike, Hafrin granted grudging approval of the orderly manner in which the enemy was retreating.

"Why south, Marrek?"

"They have," Marrek corrected himself, "make that, had a base in Nûhykar near the headwaters of the Karid; an easy route for their sub-surface craft to use to pick up and drop off their people from here. We eliminated it yesterday evening. They won't know that because their communications, like ours, is down. And…"

When Marrek paused, Hafrin verbally nudged him. "You were saying?"

A tip of Marrek's head indicated his concerns were not completely eased by news of the destruction of the Craneeno base in the south. "We think they're on the continent beyond the Kandyns as well."

Below them, the Craneeno had withdrawn, as expected, into the dip where their pursuers would not see them until the last minute. Here, they re-grouped, forming skirmish lines.

"There's a lot more of them than I thought," said Marrek.

"How many do you figure?"

"Close to four hundred."

At the centre of the enemy lines, several aliens appeared to be conferring on whether or not to take to the high ground presented by the mountain flank. Hafrin clapped his helmet on and adjusted his shield once more. Beneath him, Bïzhan Koryn tensed briefly, relaxing only when certain his rider was not yet ready to move out.

At the forest's northern perimeter, Hafrin picked out Wanderers flitting from one piece of cover to the next. As they neared the edge of the wood, several fell, picked off by Craneeno sharpshooters. Hafrin passed the order.

"Uncle, if you would please."

Jikpryn lifted a banner-topped lance and waved it in the air. Kolbrian rose from their hiding places and charged, bellowing at the tops of their lungs. To their credit, the Craneeno whirled en masse to face the new threat. One party continued to cover their rear. There was no evidence of panic as they methodically laid down fire on the lancers. As man after man dropped, Hafrin cringed. All around him, soldiers cursed the accuracy of the aliens. As they had hoped, the Craneeno broke, retreating toward the mountainside.

"Archers, Rin," Marrek reminded him.

The order raced along the mountainside. Piercing whistles heralded the ensuing deadly hiss as bolts arched through the air, volley by volley. Craneeno dropped beneath the unexpected onslaught. They whirled, still deadly and calculating in their actions, and headed toward the hills across the opposite side of the rift. Again, they encountered the deadly rain. Once again, they halted. Now indecisive, disorganised for the first time since emerging from the woods, they turned and headed directly for the kolbrian's position.

Now!

In response to Hafrin's mental yell, a flock of orved, some thirty-five strong and led by Vrala Harz, rose from the trees. They descended on the Craneeno. Talons and beaks raked unprotected flesh, tore at the weapons raised against them. Even in the diffused light of rapidly gathering clouds, they proved an awesome spectacle.

Cued by the raptorsi assault, the derynada simultaneously surged forward. Breaking cover, they poured from clefts in the mountainside, yelling at the tops of their lungs. Across the valley, the remainder of the army also emerged. Wanderers at the north end went to one knee. With deadly accuracy, they picked off the Craneeno.

Undaunted, the enemy met the ambush with silent determination. The Craneeno continued to take out their assailants with their handweapons. Unexpectedly, a massive explosion shook the left flank. Another created a hole in the middle of the charging cavalry. As deryanda went down, many men and mounts literally torn apart by the devices, Hafrin swore out loud. Everywhere, rynada reared and screamed in terror. Lord Baryan somersaulted over his mount's head as it flipped into the earth and came down. He rolled, barely escaping being pinned. Two soldiers swerved toward the dazed noble as he stumbled to his feet. Another explosion on the right and the charge wavered.

At that moment, at three locations along the lines, Fimiahri soldiers turned on their comrades. For several moments, those around them were caught unprepared and struck down. Then their companions reacted, rounding on the enemy within with deadly precision. Hafrin could only watch, helpless to intervene. Unfortunately, the resulting confusion had the desired effect for the Craneeno. The Fimiahri lines wavered and bowed as his men's resolve crumbled.

"We're losing it," Hafrin observed.

Before anyone around him could react, he released Bïzhan. The great stallion lunged forward, eagerly thundering down the slope, his steel tipped horns levelled and ready. For a moment, his startled uncle and companions failed to absorb what he was doing. Then his bodyguard raced after him. A short pace behind them, Jikpryn and his personal guard laboured to catch up. Flanked by Marrek and Indoro, with Zivvoz covering his back, Hafrin drew Hafrön.

Battle yell exploding from his lips, Hafrin flourished his sword over his head and drove straight for the front lines. It was a mad thing to do; a choice that Marrek was even now cursing him for making. But Hafrin refused to see everything lost when they were so close to a victory. Men drew aside, shouting and cheering as he and his company swept past. With renewed heart, the Fimiahri converged on the enemy.

"You were going somewhere without telling me?"

Jikpryn caught up with him at last. In response to his question, Hafrin threw him an icy smile. "All you had to do was ask."

Then they were in the thick of it. Craneeno weapons attempted to target Hafrin, but a blue aura rose from his slashing blade, appearing to absorb the beams. Within moments, his sword was covered with blood, yet its radiance refused to dim. He lost track of the number of pinched, grey faces he cut down. Of those

Bïzhan trampled or skewered. Blood spattered him as Bïzhan flicked his horns in the air, tossing bodies left and right. Everywhere was chaos. The battle deteriorated into a one-on-one melee, sometimes two and three Fimiahri to one Craneeno.

There was, according to the Wanderers' intelligence reports, no word for surrender in the Craneeno vocabulary; no phrase or word for mercy had ever been translated from their dialect. No quarter was asked and none was given.

Throughout it all, the orved somehow maintained their assault. Hafrin lost all track of time. Surrounded by his comrades and troops, Hafrin fought on while his muscles wearied and screamed for rest. Numbed by the carnage, his mind shut down to everything except the immediate. Instinctively reacting as required, he trusted to his companions to protect him. Far in the back of his mind he was aware of Nichole. He forced her from his thoughts and concentrated on what he had to do.

Wherever Craneeno beam weapons struck, men dropped. Silent death, the only mark upon their bodies was a strange burned hole. In contrast, Fimiahri weapons hacked, slashed, battered and stabbed. Blood splattered everywhere. Craneeno went down; some were silent as death caught them quickly and cleanly. Many more, however, emitted high, piercing screams or bubbling whines. Bïzhan staggered, his hooves momentarily fouled by the bodies of ally and enemy alike. Hafrin lurched forward against his black's neck. He clutched wildly at his rynad's mane and somehow recovered his balance.

Senses returning at long last, Hafrin forced Bïzhan to a halt. Gradually cognisant of his surroundings, Hafrin took stock. They were far down the field, almost into the tree line at the south end of the extensive clearing. Between where he sat Bïzhan and where his cavalry had struck the Craneeno lines, there stretched such carnage that his stomach abruptly heaved. Unable to control himself he managed to lean far left as he vomited his breakfast on the mass of churned soil and indescribable detritus. Using the back of his left sleeve, he wiped away bile and stared about him. Uninjured soldiers and those with flesh wounds stumbled wearily about, dazed and unsure of where to turn next. Hafrin reached behind his saddle and found only one of his water flasks had survived the fray. He drew several mouthfuls of water, sluiced it around his mouth and spat it out. The second mouthful he swallowed, letting the tepid fluid trickle slowly down his throat.

At the tree line combat continued, but it was evident the bulk of the enemy were dead. Those that remained had broken and were fleeing south, hotly pursued by vengeful Fimiahri and Wanderer soldiers. Someone wavered towards them through the dead and injured. Bïzhan threw up his head as the man put out a hand for support. For once, the black made no effort to evade the soldier.

Hafrin started and stared down at his shield brother. "Doro. Are you hurt?"

Indoro tugged off his helm. He stared blankly at where the tïlkrïn topknot had once waved so bravely. Only a charred stump remained, a chilling reminder to just how close the enemy's weapons had come. To Hafrin's question he replied, "No. Don't think so."

"There's so much blood on you."

"Yeah? Well, you should see yourself," Indoro countered. He rested his sword point on the ground and sagged against it.

"Have you seen Marrek or your father?"

"No, not recently. Lost them somewhere back in that direction."

A limp hand flapped back north and east across the battlefield. Indoro looked to be on the verge of collapse. Short of another assault, there was no getting him motivated to move. Scanning the field and surrounding hills, Hafrin searched for his foster father and Zivvoz, but there was no immediate sign of them. A few Temple acolytes were moving through the chaos, checking for the living, accompanied by some women.

Overhead, a high-pitched whine broke the strange stillness that had settled over the brutal scene. People stared up. Terrified screams rang out. Several soldiers broke ranks and dashed madly about seeking cover until others tackled them. A strange shadow skimmed across Hafrin. He fought to keep his seat as Bïzhan reared and whistled a challenge at the massive intruder as it passed over them, headed for the mountainside where his primary camp lay. In size, Hafrin estimated it was large enough to hold half the royal entourage.

Fear shot through him. Hafrin lifted the reins and yelled, "Heyah!"

Indoro stumbled clear just as Bïzhan launched himself after the flying contraption. What threat it posed, Hafrin could only guess. Slowed by corpses and the wounded, Hafrin cursed. His eyes never left the ridge as the device settled beyond the crest where his headquarters lay.

CHAPTER 37

▼

Nichole

Hands red, the front of her surcoat a collage of blood and vomit, Nichole and one of the Fimiahri surgeons settled the most recent patient on a blanket in the far corner of the headquarters tent. Only the most seriously wounded were laid out inside. The remainder dotted the landscape around the campsite. She wiped her hands on a nearby rag, placed them in the small of her back and stretched.

"Are you all right, my lady?"

A wan smile on her lips, Nichole nodded to the Fimiahri surgeon. There was little they could do for most of the patients surrounding her. Her companion checked the pressure bandage then glanced over his shoulder.

"Why don't you take a break, my lady? Get some fresh air."

"I'm okay," she told him.

"My lady, please."

His tone brooked no disobedience. After a moment, she nodded and left the tent. Apart from the occasional groan or cry from the injured, the cleft was strangely still. Everything was surreal. She desperately wanted to contact Hafrin for reassurance, but not knowing his status she maintained a tight shield rather than risk distracting him at a crucial moment.

In the past two days, more Temple members had followed Triklâ's entourage in joining both armies, evenly dividing their most skilled between each force. The degree of experience and expertise they displayed quite frankly surprised and pleased Nichole. Additionally, they had commandeered the more sensible and steady of the camp followers to assist them. Many now worked at removing the dead and laying them out in preparation for the burial details. Others cared for the injured. Their presence was proving a boon Nichole had not thought possible.

A cry went up from the lookout above. "They've broken! They're fleeing!"

Closing her eyes Nichole breathed a quick prayer, "Thank you, God."

"You invoke the one above."

With a start, Nichole opened her eyes. Triklâ stood in the shadow of a nearby tent watching her. Cheeks burning, Nichole nodded. The seer smiled. Her age-seamed face crinkled about her eyes.

"It's good someone remembers who is responsible for victory."

Before Nichole could respond, a familiar, yet out of place whine drew her attention. Several men cried out. A couple of pages looked frantically for somewhere to hide. The seer stared at the contraption rapidly bearing down on them, awed but refusing to retreat. Nichole called out.

"It's okay. It's one of ours."

People froze where they were as the flier's shadow undulated across the landscape. Above and slightly ahead of it, the shuttle banked over the battlefield, arrowed towards the cleft and halted. For a minute it hovered above the headquarters pavilion. Those inside who were not preoccupied with the wounded stared fearfully out of tent openings at the alien shape. Then, it shifted sideways towards a bare patch of ground.

Expectation a tight knot in her midriff, Nichole moved forward. Landing gear was extended. Within minutes the shuttle was on the ground. The engines whined down to idle. Metal hissed and popped as it adjusted to the cool air. With it came the familiar sharp tang of the propulsion units. Someone sneezed and Nichole suddenly realised the seer had accompanied her. As they reached the shuttle, the hatch opened. A group of armed men and women in Fleet Patrol deep blue emerged. Evidently the personnel had been fully briefed for their leader saluted Nichole.

"My lady, we were told to come as soon as the pulse dissipated. We've brought fresh Medical supplies, three surgeons and several Medics. We understand you only have two field-qualified surgeons. No doubt they're experiencing problems keeping abreast of the situation."

Now that's an understatement, thought Nichole.

She struggled not to smile at the heavily inflected Fimiahri the man spoke. At the same time, she stared past him at the mass of men and women grouped in the doorway and responded in her native tongue, "You are most welcome. If you would, please, the worst of the injured are in that tent."

One of the older men nodded and the staff began disembarking. Each person carried either a stack of cases or two carryalls. Nichole moved to help but her assistance was refused. It was Triklâ, her dark eyes gleaming with excitement and curiosity that led the Medical staff to the headquarters tent.

"Looks like you could do with some hospital tents too," said someone behind Nichole. Surprised by the unexpected, she turned to face the author of the statement.

"Victor!"

As she flung herself into her brother's arms, her mental shield dropped. Victor caught her, swept her off her feet and spun her around once before setting her back on the ground. Laughter bubbled from Nichole's lips for the first time in days. All around them Fimiahri paused in the midst of their duties to stare at the unguarded enthusiasm of their greeting. Just as quickly a wave of fear swept over her.

Rin! She stiffened. Conscious of the change in her demeanour, her brother released her.

Nikki!

In her mind's eye she could see him tearing up the grassy slope toward the entrance to the cleft. From his right, a mounted figure moved to intercept. Marrek.

Concerned for his safety, she projected calm and an image of her surroundings. *Rin, it's okay. It's my brother, Victor. He's brought additional Medical staff and supplies.*

Even before Hafrin reacted to her information, Bïzhan was slowing to a halt. Marrek caught up with him and Nichole lost contact with her husband. Someone cleared his throat. Caught back to earth she turned to her brother.

"Oh, sorry, Victor. My husband was a bit concerned when he saw the shuttle. I had to explain before he went off at half-cock and did something stupid."

"No problem. Understandable."

More than you could possibly know, she thought, the memory of her departure from Fimiah foremost in her mind.

"So, how are you doing?"

"Good."

"And the baby?"

"Growing."

"Boy or girl?"

"A boy. We named him Valrin. Silver Shield. He's with Rin's milk mother."

"Ah, too bad. I was hoping to see him."

"Well, depending upon how things shake out after the battle, and whether you have to return to the fleet right away, maybe you will." She checked on the

Medical staff then slowly started toward the headquarters tent. "How does it look up there?"

"We drove them off, destroyed two of their largest cruisers and devastated their fighters. I doubt they'll be back this way in a hurry."

"That's good," she said.

Her brother shrugged. "Maybe. Problem is we've never known exactly how large their fleet is. Patrol's preparing for a possible retaliatory strike."

"Where?"

"Don't ask me. I'm just a lowly peon."

"Yeah. Sure you are," she nudged him, adding, "Lieutenant."

As she reminded him of his fleet promotion since their last encounter, he retaliated, "You should talk, Madam Alaia. No wonder they wanted you back here on the double. How the hell did you manage that?"

"It was wholly unintentional," she countered.

"Sure it was." He nudged her back and winked.

Scandalised by what he was implying she gave him a push, "Victor."

"Nikki."

"Cut it out," she hissed, once more snapping at him for using her nickname.

"What? Can't have the troops seeing their Queen clowning around with us lesser beings, is that it?"

"No," she responded as they reached the headquarters tent. "It's not that."

With a smile, Victor relented. "Never mind. I promise I won't tease you further. A word of warning though; Bertie was quite put out when the news reached him. And our cousins...well, what they had to say when I spoke to them was unprintable in polite company."

"Really?"

"Really."

On that note, Nichole ducked into the tent. Inside, she discovered a hive of activity. Old-style intravenous drips were everywhere. Two of the rear rooms were being rapidly altered into surgeries. The minute the first was ready to go, four Medics carried two patients into it and set to work. Several more Medics were examining the remaining patients. On composite strips they noted what was wrong with each person, who the most seriously injured were, and which patients could wait to be seen once they were stabilised. To one side of the entrance, a blanket draped a solitary figure. Nichole heaved a sigh.

"Looks like they've got everything under control in here," Victor said. "Why don't we go back outside?"

Exhaustion landed on Nichole's shoulders all at once with the weight of a stallion. She allowed Victor to lead her outside. They found a spot across the cleft to sit and there she sagged against the rocks. He left her briefly, returning to the shuttle to retrieve two canteens and some rations.

"Here." He passed her the canteen, waited for her to drink then pressed a package of rations on her. "Eat. I'll bet you haven't had anything since before first light, have you?"

Numb, Nichole shook her head. She ate mechanically, knowing she needed the sustenance but wanting sleep even more. At length, Triklâ appeared. With a crook of her finger, she gestured to Victor then pointed at the tent Nichole shared with Hafrin. Victor dipped his head in thanks. Between them, her brother and the seer got Nichole to bed.

When she woke some time later, it was still light. A clean change of clothing lay across a nearby stool. She pushed back the covers, groaning as muscles caught and complained. Persevering, Nichole got to her feet. After dashing through a quick sponge bath, she dressed, belted on her sword and dagger and left the tent, her cloak over her arm.

Before she had gone three steps from the tent, a wash of mental agony swept over her. Silent screams from the wounded battered her. Animals cried out against their injuries, unable to understand why they had been assaulted. She clamped down her shield and resolutely covered the rest of the distance to what had been the headquarters tent.

Toward the rear exterior, bodies of the deceased had been neatly laid out and covered with whatever tarps and blankets were available. Inside the tent, all was quiet. The most seriously injured lay, drugged unconscious so they would not move and reopen the wounds that had been meticulously sutured shut. Two Medics sat at the field table now set up in a makeshift office that had been the third cubical at the rear of the tent. They glanced up as she came in. The nearest nodded a silent greeting.

"Have you seen my husband?"

"Ma'am?" The Medic straightened.

"The Fimiahri Alaiad, Hafrin," she repeated. "Have either of you seen him?"

Both men exchanged glances. One shrugged. The other replied, "No, ma'am. Sorry, but I don't believe they're back from the battlefield yet."

"Oh." Nichole looked around the tent once more. "What about the seer? The old woman who was helping here?"

"She went with the cleanup squads to the battlefield."

"Thank you."

Concerned that Hafrin had not returned, Nichole attempted to contact him. Pain, anguish; an overwhelming miasma that marked so much violent death washed across her, blocking out all of her attempts. She pushed from the tent and walked part way across the churned up field. Abruptly, she altered direction. Her aimless wandering brought her at last to the rynada pickets. Someone had thoughtfully moved the uninjured animals upwind of the field hospital. Even so, they were restless, snorting repeatedly and throwing their heads about. All were cross-tied so they could not break free. She found Palor after some searching. The mare, along with several of the special Wanderer crossbreeds, had been picketed a short distance from the rest of the ryanda. Emotionally exhausted, she settled on the ground next to Palor. Warm breath puffed the loose strands of Nichole's hair as the mare snuffled about her head and shoulders.

Nichole reached up. "Yes, Palor. I know you're there. It's quite a mess, isn't it?"

Perhaps it was her presence amongst them, but whatever it was, the rynada gradually quieted. Some settled down, snorting and grunting with mild contentment. Others picked at the feed that, until that moment, they had been ignoring. Eventually, the pleasant crunching of hay and grain lulled Nichole until the world faded to the periphery of her perception.

"My lady?" An unfamiliar voice drew her back from the edge of sleep. "My lady."

She looked up at the soldier hovering just beyond the picket line where she sat. He held the reins of a battle-worn rynad. "Yes?"

"My lady, would you please come with me." The soldier glanced around, looking for someone, she thought. "You'll need your rynad. Do you need help saddling it?"

Bewildered, Nichole clambered to her feet, unconsciously dusting off the bits of grass and hay clinging to her clothing. "What's wrong?"

"It's…my lady, I really think you should come with me."

Fear drove a spear through her midriff. "Is it my husband?"

"Please, my lady."

Driven by fear of the unknown, Nichole yanked at the reins holding Palor at the line. Without bothering to wait to saddle the mare, Nichole threw herself onto her bareback. She whirled Palor around to face the soldier. The man was already mounted.

"Which way?"

At her question, the soldier spun his mount and headed away from the picket line and out of the camp. From behind them, someone called a question. Nichole ignored it, intent upon finding Hafrin. Goaded by her now silent guide, she commanded Palor to keep just behind him. They descended the slope at a fast walk then turned south along the lower ridge. Once on realtively even ground, the soldier urged his rynad into an easy run.

Again, from behind Nichole, someone shouted. She glanced back and caught sight of Jikpryn racing toward her. He shouted again. "Lady, where are you going?"

"Rin," she yelled back to him, and pointed in the direction her guide was headed.

She turned back and missed what Jikpryn said next. Just as they reached the tree line, something dropped from the sky. With a flurry of wings and harsh scream, Vrala Harz startled Palor. Dropping out of a headlong run, Palor twisted sideways and reared, all in one motion. Thrown forward, Nichole grabbed at the mare's mane as Palor rose on her hind legs. From the fringe of the forest a red beam pierced the mare's forehead. Beneath her, Nichole felt Palor contort. She kicked herself free and pushed off just as they crashed to the ground.

CHAPTER 38

━━━━━━━━━━ ▼ ━━━━━━━━━━

Hafrin

At the southeast end of the battlefield, Hafrin stood next to Bïzhan Koryn. Head down, his stallion snorted repeatedly at the churned up soil and grass. Blood and other indescribable remnants of the battle made what remained of the wild hay unpalatable. Bïzhan's upper lip curled. Metal tipped horns scythed the air, describing small circles as the stallion silently expressed his disgust over the situation.

It's all right, Bïzhan, Hafrin reassured his mount. He did his best to wipe away the worst of the battle splatter with a scrap of rag someone had given him. *There's plenty of fresh feed and grain back at the camp.*

From the black came the impression of a disgusting pall of nauseating odours: death and bloody wounds, along with all that such implied. It left Hafrin in no doubt as to Bïzhan's impression of trying to eat near the hospital tent. It did not help matters that none of the riders had been able to change their clothing, which was splattered with Craneeno blood.

I believe the picket lines have been moved up wind, he told Bïzhan.

Marrek broke in across their conversation. "Rin."

Caught back to his surroundings, Hafrin flashed his foster father an apologetic grin. "Sorry."

Beyond Marrek, Kizrun sat a weary gelding that was different from the one he had ridden into battle. "You seemed to be worlds away."

It was his turn to grin, and Hafrin heard the follow-on thought. This old warrior, who had for so long felt the Wôbiny had been left out of the mainstream of Fimiah politics, wanted to see what lay beyond the confines of this world. Sight of the shuttle was fermenting a plethora of fantasies. Upon reflection, Hafrin realised that he, too, would like very much to explore beyond Fimiah.

Unlikely, said a voice in his mind. *You're too valuable to risk on flights of fancy, Hafrin af Fanhri.*

He glanced over his shoulder, but the author was preoccupied with a wounded man and was not looking his way. That there were members of the Temple with psi abilities went far to explaining many apparent inconsistencies and curious anomalies throughout Fimiahri history with regards to the survival of Temple personnel during times of crisis.

I can hope, he countered. *You never know.*

"Rin." Again, Marrek distracted him, but this time a faint scowl marred his usually congenial expression.

"Sorry," Hafrin muttered.

"Lord Kizrun was suggesting we ensure all of our walking wounded have been removed to the camps. Teams of my people have been seeing to those wounded who weren't picked up in the initial sweep."

"Did we pick up any prisoners?"

Approval radiated from Marrek as he answered. "No. Craneeno fight to the death, Rin, and the wounded usually commit suicide. If cornered, they can be particularly deadly."

Images of explosive bobby traps purposefully directed his way shook Hafrin. He blinked hard, twice, and mentally shook off the horrific visions of what encounters with a wounded enemy generally resulted in.

"Any sign of more spies amongst our troops?"

"None, ser," said Kizrun. "But then, during the battle, no one was really looking for any."

A sour laugh escaped Hafrin. Memory of the free-for-all clash into which the struggle had devolved made any thought of looking for infiltrators all but impossible. Marrek picked up on that.

"But now would definitely be a good time to keep our eyes open for their people."

"Aye," put in Jikpryn. He arrived, still seated on his stallion. Respect and approval radiated from him as he studied Hafrin. "No doubt they'll be anxious to be rid of any rallying factors amongst our people."

Marrek and Kizrun stared at Hafrin. The intensity of their scrutiny and the underlying concern emanating from all three made Hafrin extremely uneasy. He turned away to stare back across the field.

"With your permission, nephew," Jikpryn interrupted his introspection, "I'll head over to your camp and check on my men. I understand several Hynarkin physicians have arrived and are creating quite a stir amongst mine...sorry, ours."

"Certainly."

While Jikpryn turned his stallion away and headed out across the corpse-strewn valley, Kizrun considered Hafrin. To Hafrin's chagrin, it was clear the man possessed a natural shield. Short of probing, which Marrek had strictly forbidden, there was no way Hafrin could discern what his great-uncle was now thinking. Since the battle, the man was mellowing toward the grandnephew he had initially disliked intensely. How much of his apparent change of heart was genuine, and how much was diplomacy, remained to be seen.

Hafrin turned away and found his gaze drawn toward the cleft where Nichole was. He yearned to contact her but emotion and death spilled across the area, dyeing their surroundings, and he was unable to make contact. Strangely, he could touch Vrala Harz hovering high above. She informed him she was hungry.

"We have patrols out scouring the surrounding forest for stragglers," Kizrun advised them. "I'm hoping we find at least one…who's that?"

Hafrin turned, stared at the riders who had emerged from the cleft where his camp was. "The rear one's Nikki. Where is she going?"

He glanced at Marrek. His foster father shook his head. Hunched against Palor's neck, riding bareback, Nichole raced after the soldier who, evidently, was leading her toward the forest at the south end of the field.

"Marrek, what's she doing?"

"I don't know," Marrek repeated. "Can you contact her?"

"No."

There was no need for him to say more. Such training as Marrek had been given as a Wanderer meant he was undoubtedly far more informed on what exactly it meant to be psi-talented. Kizrun stared from Marrek to Hafrin and back again, intently curious. Marrek stiffened.

"Something's definitely wrong, Rin."

Hafrin had reached the same conclusion. Even as he threw himself onto Bïzhan, he summoned his jesset. Vrala had already sensed something amiss and was in flight toward Nichole. Picking up his command, she increased speed. Ahead, Hafrin spotted his uncle a short distance away where he had paused to speak with a member of one of the recovery details. He shouted. Jikpryn turned in the saddle. Hafrin gestured in the direction of his wife. In the space of three breaths, the shrewd warrior assessed the situation, spun his stallion and took off after Nichole. They rapidly closed the gap. Hafrin glanced back. Kizrun and Marrek were riding hard on his heels. Kizrun, a proficient archer, was unlimbering his bow. Vrala dropped, a thunderbolt from the sky. Palor slammed to a halt as the orved crashed past her nose. Unprepared, Nichole was thrown hard against the mare's neck. Palor reared and slithered in the muck. Something red flashed from the trees and the mare crashed down.

Marrek yelled a warning. "Craneeno."

Beyond Nichole, the rider she had been following swerved aside. He reined in, flung himself from his rynad and went prone behind a bush. At first, Hafrin assumed the man was protecting Nichole. Then he realised the soldier was on the opposite side of the bush. Even as he caught onto that anomaly, a red beam struck the ground next to Nichole. She squirmed around, putting the mare's body between her and her assailant. Only then did Hafrin realise Palor was dead.

There was no time for regrets. They were rapidly approaching the ambush. In a flurry of feathers, Vrala Harz swooped and soared again, barely avoiding a snap shot. Suddenly, Bïzhan stumbled and went to his knees. Thrown forward against his mount's neck, Hafrin grunted at the force of the impact of his chest against the saddletree. Somehow the stallion recovered. Instead of somersaulting, he lurched back to his feet. Before them the disguised alien emerged briefly from cover to inspect the scene. He ducked down then bobbed up again, intent upon his target. In that instant, an arrow snarled past Hafrin. It took the enemy agent in the chest, the force of impact throwing him back out of sight.

Now more Hynarkin and Fimiahri riders and foot soldiers appeared, converging on the portion of forest from which the original attack had been launched. The body over which Bïzhan Koryn had tripped now rose off the ground. Instinct took over. Hafrön seemed to leap from its scabbard into Hafrin's hand. He swung, severing the alien's head. It bounced away amongst the bodies strewing the field while the torso toppled to the ground alongside Bïzhan. A shout drew Hafrin back to the altercation at the edge of the forest.

Jikpryn was down, pinned by his stallion. His mount screamed, more in terror than pain as it lunged repeatedly in an effort to regain its feet. It took a moment before Hafrin saw that its hooves were tangled in a mesh. Where the netting had come from Hafrin could only guess. Nichole scrambled forward on her hands and knees, her sword hampering her movements. She threw herself against the stallion's neck, quieting it. Two more red beams pierced the air around her. More shouts went up from the forest. A thunderous explosion heralded further death beneath the cold winter sky. Blowing hard, Bïzhan came to a halt next to Nichole and Jikpryn. Hafrin dropped from his mount.

"Nikki, are you okay?"

"Yes. Just bruised," she replied. "You had better see to your uncle."

While she continued to hold the stallion still, Hafrin bent over Jikpryn. A now all too familiar aura emanated from the man whom he had once despised, and now had merely neutral feelings for. He went to one knee.

"Sir. Uncle?"

His uncle reached out a hand. Hafrin returned his weapon to its sheath and took Jikpryn's gauntlet in his. Their eyes met. Neither was about to lie. Too much death lay about them to attempt to deny the obvious. Jikpryn coughed. Blood spattered from his lips across his chin and chest. Seeing that, Nichole turned her head and screamed out.

"Medic! We need a Medic now!" But even as she shouted in desperation, she knew it was unlikely anyone would reach them in time. Anguish was an unrelenting knot tightening in her throat.

"I'm sorry, Rin. Ser." Now Jikpryn finally acknowledged Hafrin's heritage. "I ask your forgiveness."

Pain gnawed at Hafrin's chest as he opened himself to his uncle's appeal. Voice choked with emotion, he replied, "You have it, sir."

"You're a good lad." Extricating his hand from Hafrin's, Jikpryn patted him on the shoulder. "Sorry I made such a mess of things. Wish I hadn't. Can't take back what's past, said and done. At least I can go to the Great Serpent with my sins forgiven. Couldn't ask for more."

Chest hurting where her ribs had been bruised, Nichole slowly sat up. Eyes blinking, the stallion watched her but made no further attempts to get to its feet. She joined Hafrin. Side by side, they knelt in the frozen mud, blood and grass.

"Look after my son, ser."

"I promise," said Hafrin.

"Thank you." Jikpryn's gaze went to Nichole. "Lady, I'm pleased to have met you. Wish we could have had more time together."

"Sir…"

A weak smile caught the side of Jikpryn's mouth, twisted his lips briefly. "Star blood. Who would…"

And he was gone with a snap that was a physical wrench. Tears spilled down Nichole's cheeks unchecked. Hafrin caught her to him and held her while she wept. Someone approached. Quietly, the newcomer helped the stallion get to its feet. Then he waited patiently for them to recover. Nichole looked up first.

"You'll have to take care of Jikpryn's rynad," Marrek told her quietly. "Like Bïzhan, he's too close to his rider. If you don't speak to him, he may turn rogue."

"I'm sorry about Palor," Nichole said between gulps and sniffles. She drew out of Hafrin's grasp.

"Nikki," Marrek took her arms in his hands. "Palor had a full life. She dropped nine magnificent foals, not to mention the genes we spliced at the colony. Of course, the others can't hold a candle to Bïzhan, but they're incredible breeding stock. She went quickly. I doubt she even knew what hit her. The beam took her between the eyes."

At that news, Nichole looked away from her husband and Marrek. Bïzhan's head swung. His muzzle pushed against her, gently at first. She touched the bridge of his nose absently. But he pushed again, shoving her back three steps into the flank of Jikpryn's stallion. Its head swung. Their eyes met. Slowly, carefully, Nichole reached out a hand. The stallion sniffed her fingers, eyes dull with loss. A gentle 'wiffle' blew warm breath across her fingers. She reached out mentally. A name appeared in the stallion's thoughts.

Origan.

In response, she extended a tentative inquiry. The stallion adjusted its weight so that it stood four square rather than appearing about to bolt. Gently, Nichole took its head in her hands and pressed her forehead against its cheek. For a long moment rynad and human exchanged the ache of sadness and loss. Gradually Nichole insinuated her thoughts into Origan's mind. Several more minutes passed. Then she released the stallion and curled one hand through the nearest rein.

"Well?"

To Hafrin's inquiry, she nodded. "His name is Origan...Defiant. He'll accept me."

"Good."

Beyond Hafrin, Nichole spotted Kizrun watching the tableau with intense interest. He slipped from his mount and came forward. "Excuse me, ser. My lady." He tugged off his helm and stuck it under his left arm. "Would you please explain what you just did? Origan never let anyone except my nephew and two of his most trusted stable hands touch him. In fact, until my nephew tamed him, I was of a mind to destroy him, he was that unpredictable."

Cheeks flushed, Nichole and Hafrin exchanged looks then glanced at Marrek. "Well, now," said Marrek, "it's a gift they have, Lord Kizrun."

"A gift, is it?" One eyebrow rose. Kizrun considered his grandnephew, his expression shrewd. When no one explained further, he nodded. "All right, if that's how you want it to be. But know this. There are certain things my studies of your lineage have uncovered, ser. And it might be wise to permit certain of your closest advisors to know exactly what your...gifts...entail."

With a nod, Hafrin wordlessly accepted the advice. Kizrun nodded again to each of them, remounted and rode away across the field in the direction of Jikpryn's camp. Two rynada approached at a run. Their riders bounced about the saddles, evidence they were inexperienced at this mode of transportation. As they slowed to a halt, Nichole recognised the nearest as one of the Wanderer field surgeons. He glanced at them as he dismounted before bending over Jikpryn's body. It took only a few moments to confirm what they already knew.

Face devoid of emotion, the Medic rose and shook his head. "I'm sorry, sir. Ma'am."

Several Wanderers and a number of Fimiahri foot soldiers emerged from the forest at that moment. A cry went up at the sight of Jikpryn's body. Troops came forward. Someone among them located a shield on the battlefield, and they placed Jikpryn on it. Two to a side, they bore him from the field with Hafrin, Nichole and Marrek riding escort behind.

CHAPTER 39

▼

Nichole

Over the ensuing five days before the army moved out, Wanderer injured were shipped off-world as quickly as was practical, along with Craneeno remains. These would eventually wind up at one of Fleet's numerous laboratories for indepth study. Fimiahri commoners were buried in a mass grave while the wounded were moved out the last night via Wanderer automated transport. Medics, and those Fimiahri physicians brave enough to attempt the flight, accompanied them. Nobles, along with those ranking soldiers who had died during the battle, were placed in stasis to preserve their bodies. Along with Jikpryn's body, they were loaded on board one special transport, which, coincidentally, was piloted by Victor. Although tempted by the offer of a ride back to the capitol, Triklâ opted to return with the army.

The trek to Iryô encompassed more than ten days. Orved were sent on ahead with news of the outcome of the battle. Hafrin and Nichole insisted upon riding with the army despite the injuries both had sustained on the day Jikpryn had died. Nichole's tumble from Palor had resulted in four broken ribs and severely scraped hands. Hafrin had bruised his kidneys when Bïzhan had tripped. Both spent the first four days in a wagon. Bïzhan and Origan kept pace one to each side of the wagon, refusing to be moved back to the spare string. Zivvoz drove the wagon while Marrek, Kizrun and Indoro took turns riding tail. Travel in the wagon afforded the pair a measure of privacy they had not experienced since Nichole's return.

On the fifth day, they were back in the saddle. Once they were out of the wagon, the cavalry wanted to make better time back to the capitol but Hafrin stubbornly held their pace down. He made a point of spending some time in each village they passed through, further slowing their progress. Some of his new council grumbled that a journey, which ought to have taken a mounted company riding from dawn to dusk fifteen days to reach Iryô, was taking them far longer than they liked. Hafrin stubbornly held his ground.

"The people are entitled to see us," he explained at their first evening camp-site, and gestured to include those nearest to him so they were aware he was not simply employing the royal possessive. "They've been through hard times. Most were ardently loyal to Fanhri. It's only fitting they know of my existence."

One day out from Iryô, Hafrin insisted they pause for a full day to rest. Here, they made preparations for a proper entry into the city. Foot soldiers washed, shaved and polished their weaponry. The women in the baggage train saw to cleaning everyone's clothes. Leather was soaped until even the most worn tack and jerkins gleamed. Armour was polished to a high gloss and banners brought out of the baggage train. People from nearby communities arrived within short order, bringing fresh food. This further cheered the surviving troops.

Day dawned, overcast and with a threat of rain. Under Hafrin's orders, the baggage train left early, accompanied by the foot soldiers. It was almost midday before the cavalry mounted up. Zivvoz could not stop grinning at Hafrin's strat-egy. Even Kizrun smiled repeatedly. To those who demanded a reason, they were quick to explain to objectors that they should catch up with the foot soldiers just outside Iryô.

At the edge of the forest, they encountered five Wanderers. Three were mounted while two sat the seat of a burial wain. On the flatbed, laid out with all honours and draped with the banner of Wôbiny, was Jikpryn's body.

And so they entered the city. Indoro went before them, bearing the unfurled and now somewhat tattered banner of the Alaiad. Flanked by Marrek, Piltar, Kizrun and Zivvoz, Hafrin rode knee-to-knee with Nichole. People poured from dwellings and shops to line the main thoroughfare. Cheers rose as they wound through the city, swelling as they passed and crossed the bridge, four abreast. Crowds lined the street all the way up the winding hill and dried flowers littered the weather-slick cobblestones.

But the shouts and revelling quieted as Jikpryn's bier passed by, escorted by an honour guard of Fimiahri troops and Wanderers. At their head rode Hilcaz. Head bare, his face was drawn with sorrow for everyone to see. That the Usurper's personal guard and the Wôbiny troops still bearing their arms rode freely amongst the young Alaiad's men raised considerable speculation within the local population. Sight of Triklâ, as well as a Temple Priest and three acolytes, furthered speculation. The murmurs followed the company up the hill.

Outside the gate to the fortress itself, the company turned and swept around the summit, heading for the fields behind the fortress. There the troops would be billeted until formal disposition was made for their placement. Only the core of the nobles and their retainers, along with the funerary bier, accompanied Hafrin and his people inside the massive stone pile.

In spite of herself, Nichole discovered she was staring at everything. Thick grey stone, flecked with black and white, surrounded the bulk of the fortress. As they passed through the portcullis, Nichole considered that, by their thickness, they could well conceal passages. High above, guards patrolled the walks behind the niches. Torches sputtered from sconces at regular intervals inside and outside of the fortress walls.

The exterior ring encircled an outer area that housed local and visiting nobles, their retinues and bodyguards. However impressive the housing was, none of the buildings stood taller than two stories. All were spaced well apart, with walled forecourts and small back yards. As well, there was evidence of stable yards. To the left and right, the main route around the outer ring was wide enough for two small wagons to pass, hinting at markets further on. But they were riding on towards the hilltop and Nichole knew she would have to wait to explore further.

Lifting her head, she stared at the inner wall rising high above the nobles' houses. Here and there, she picked out the head of a soldier staring down at them. Then they were through the second portcullis and entering a huge courtyard. To their left stretched the guards' quarters and training yards. On the right were stables. She knew from questioning Marrek that the fortress-refuse middens lay below the rear walls. From there, garbage and manure could be hauled away by those employed at such duties without compromising the security of the fortress.

But Nichole's attention was fixed on the main building directly before them. Something out of myth, it rose, a many turreted construction, each tower squared rather than the round ones of childhood stories passed down through the generations of her people. Still, the whole structure was incredible, awe-inspiring and, she considered, somewhat overpowering in the murky light of a threatening winter storm. Wan light filtered out through the watery glass of numerous windows.

High overhead, orved circled several towers, their cries piercing the air. Vrala Harz, who had ridden in on Hafrin's saddletree, rose into the air the minute the riders dismounted. A brief flurry ensued. Hafrin paused. Head tipped back he watched the aerial battle, concern for the old huntress paramount. But order returned in short order. Satisfied, his raptor settled on the roof peak directly above the main entranceway.

"Ser?"

Kizrun recalled them to the business at hand with a soft query and a partial gesture toward the entrance. Led by Kizrun, the party went up the steps. Before accompanying them, Indoro swiftly captured the banner, pinning it against the standard so it would not flare when he walked and strike those about him. They passed through a four-person wide entrance. Two doors, crafted of wood and banded in metal, barred their way. Two servants held them ajar to receive the young Alaiad Presumptive and his companions. Down a long passage they marched, boots thudding on the stone flooring. Glancing down, Nichole cringed as she equated the time and cost of the stonework against their apparent careless-ness as they left clumps of mud in their wake. Worse, metal caps on the heels and toes of riding boots scarred the surface.

Ahead, another set of great doors barred their way. No guards were posted and Nichole felt a peculiar thrill race through her. With a glance at the group, Kizrun indicated they should wait. He went to the doors. Raising a mailed fist he pounded rhythmically on the right-hand one. Slowly, majestically the doors swung out. The Lord of Wôbiny stood aside and bowed low.

"My lord, your throne awaits you."

About to step out once more, Hafrin unexpectedly halted. He tugged off his gauntlets and stuffed them in his belt. Fingers brushed his wind-tousled hair. This, Nichole knew, was indicative of her husband reining in his enthusiasm to press forward. As he considered his next course of action, she caught his gaze. A quick smile tugged his lips. He turned to the others.

"My lords, this isn't right. I may be hereditary Alaiad, but I have yet to be con-firmed by the Temple. If I enter that hall and sit on the high seat now, without their approval, it would be an insult to them and to my ancestors."

Caught on the very threshold of the great hall, several members of the party raised their voices in argument. Each one expounded Hafrin's virtues and their firm belief in his right to take the throne. He lifted a hand. Silence fell. Marrek considered Hafrin's statement and nodded.

"Gentlemen, he's correct. His ancestry may not be in doubt with us, but only the Temple can officially declare his legitimacy. We must abide by the laws of the land."

"Ridiculous," retorted Kizrun. "Even the most witless fool can see the lad's the only remaining legitimate heir by direct lineage. Hafrön's mark is on him and he carries it, bare hand, without harm."

"Even so, I won't sit on the high seat until the Temple confirms me," Hafrin firmly countered. "There're plenty of chairs. We can make ourselves comfortable around the perimeter of the room. Would someone please see if the kitchen-staff has something for us to eat? I know it's past midday. Even though it's too early for supper, none of us has had a decent meal since breaking our fast this morning."

"I'll see to it," announced Zivvoz.

"Thanks, Ziv. Marrek, would you give him a hand?"

For a moment, Marrek hesitated. Clearly, he was loath to abandon Hafrin and Nichole. Beyond her husband, Nichole saw Piltar give a slight tip of his head to reassure him. From the dubious expression Piltar received in return, Nichole knew without breaking the cardinal rule of telepaths that Marrek did not like this at all. Still, he did not argue with Hafrin, thereby reinforcing the young Alaiad's right to give orders. Without thinking, Nichole drew closer to Hafrin's side as he walked around the perimeter of the hall. Their actions drew their companions to a long table set against the wall near one of the two huge hearths. For that, Nichole was grateful. The hall was damp. Winter's chill permeated the place outside of the reach of the heat of both hearths.

Several of the nobles' retainers gathered up chairs along the way and set them next to the table. By the time everyone had reached the table and settled themselves in a casual group, a number of servants were emerging from two side doors. Some, accompanied by Marrek and Zivvoz, brought trays and platters of food, flasks, plates and goblets. The second group produced more chairs. These were set nearby so the retainers could now dispose themselves. A rustling overhead announced the arrival of guardsmen. When Nichole looked up, she was startled to note that every one of the soldiers arrayed above were Wanderers.

"We thought it best," Piltar quietly informed Hafrin when the young Alaiad raised an eyebrow at the sight of so many of his wife's people. "We can trust them implicitly where, unfortunately, your own people are still suspect, especially given what transpired on the battlefield."

Foremost in Hafrin's thoughts were the control devices. All of the devices had been surgically removed from the senior staff that had been on the battlefield. However, he was certain there were still a few with which they would have to contend. Rather than raise that problem, he nodded to indicate the nobles.

"I understand. I just hope they will too."

A noise at the upper end of the hall caught their attention. Several courtiers and their ladies were filtering into the hall, entering through a doorway at the far upper-left, beyond the throne. These, Hafrin suspected, had avoided riding to war either for legitimate reasons or personal ones. It was the 'other reasons' that he would have to have Zivvoz investigate. The group approached Hafrin and his men, curious and wary of the battle-weary party. In their wake followed several of the household guard whom Jikpryn had left behind.

"Lord Kizrun, please speak to them. I...-we," Hafrin determinedly switched to the royal designation, "have no wish to hold court today."

"They'll want news, ser," said Kizrun.

"When we have something comprehensive to tell them, they'll hear it."

"As you wish ser."

Under Hafrin's orders, Kizrun met the courtiers before they could close the distance. Accustomed to his presence, they gathered around him, listening attentively to what he said. Throughout his conversation, the courtiers cast furtive glances in Hafrin's direction. Then, with two guards to escort them, the courtiers who had remained behind at the fortress after Jikpryn's departure, politely withdrew. Several among them sketched proper obeisance before exiting. From the sidewash of thoughts, Hafrin discovered they would vacate their fortress apartments and move back into their respective villas beyond the inner circle of the fortress walls.

He was conscious of Nichole's gaze following the departing courtiers. Their immediate plans and stray thoughts on a variety of inconsequential matters floated after them. When she turned back to the gathering, Hafrin indicated he wanted her to accompany him.

"Gentlemen," he addressed the group, "my lords, we wish a private word with Freedman Zivvoz. Please wait here."

"Ser."

Kizrun responded for the others. Taking Nichole's hand in his, Hafrin drew her away from the group, across the hall to where they could find a measure of privacy. Zivvoz followed, at once curious and confident. Beyond his shoulder, Marrek raised an eyebrow. Hafrin gave a slight shake of his head. The minute Zivvoz joined them he turned the freedman and Nichole so their backs were to the group.

"Ziv," he said, his voice low, "two things. Find out why those particular individuals failed to join my uncle's forces in the field."

Zivvoz shrugged. "There are always those who aren't fit to fight, ser. And there is always a need for administrators to remain behind to oversee matters in the Alaiad's absence."

"That's understood," said Hafrin. "Just humour me, okay?" When Zivvoz nodded, Harin continued, "And do you have anyone besides Indoro and Marrek that you trust implicitly? Someone whom you can send to bring Kili, Deena and Val to the fortress?"

"So soon, ser?"

"Yes."

"Is this wise?"

"It's the best thing. I want them installed in the nursery where we can guard them."

For several moments Zivvoz considered Hafrin's request. From his expression, it was evident he felt the authority behind it and measured it against the boy he had known from infancy. Images flickered through his unguarded thoughts; Hafrin and Indoro wrestling in the straw, Kili watching anxiously, her distress not so much for the bruises and scrapes, as for the risk of Hafrin's identity being betrayed. And, again, there was the memory of Hafrin dropping from a sapling onto the back of a huge blïntor. His weight momentarily flattened it in his effort to protect Zivvoz. He nodded.

"Aye. I know someone. Best you not know who or when I send for them, though, ser."

"Just one person, Ziv. They can go and return via the kitchen entrance. I'll see they have a chit…"

A shake of Zivvoz's head stopped him. "No, ser. Let me handle this. I'll see it's done discretely. After all, Kili's my wife. Let me speak to the Senior Cook and the Chatelaine. I'll ask them if they have employment for her. I like my family close to me. It might also be best if we hold off settling the heir in the nursery just yet. Better to wait until Marrek and I have organised your personal guard."

Nichole touched Hafrin's arm. "Rin, Zivvoz is right. Let him choose the best means of bringing them here and when to introduce our son to the people. After all, Zivvoz took care of you for years. Surely we can trust Valrin to his care a bit longer."

Eyes twinkling, Hafrin acceded. "Alright, Nikki. Ziv, I trust you to do what is best for my son."

CHAPTER 40

▼

Hafrin

Two days passed before Zivvoz brought Kili, Deenala, Valrin and Annarek to the fortress and throughout that time Nichole and Hafrin yearned to see their son. As forewarned, Valrin and his wet-nurse were not immediately installed in the nursery. Rather, Kili took up lodgings in the servants' quarters in a tidy apartment. This provided separate small sleeping chambers for each of the children and the nurse, plus a larger one for Kili and Zivvoz.

Indoro moved into the barracks, invested into the position of Hilcaz's Second-in-Command. Spaces that had previously belonged to troops who had fallen in battle were now assigned to the rest of the Fimiahri commoners in the entourage. For the Wanderers, there were apartments in one of the outlying fortress wings. In the years following Fanhri's death, the building had been woefully under-occupied, so considerable cleaning was required, and that initiated the hiring of additional staff.

Meanwhile, Hafrin took over a suite of rooms, which in past generations had housed the adult offspring of the Alaiad. Unlike previous Royals and nobility as a whole, he insisted Nichole share his apartments. It flew in the face of tradition but he remained firm. For her part, whenever Nichole overheard gossip and titters amongst the staff, she summoned the Chatelaine. Quickly, efficiently and quietly, the matter was put to rest.

Throughout it all, people migrated in from the surrounding countryside. Noble and commoner alike anticipated the pomp and circumstance surrounding the investiture of their new ruler. Pavilions and tents went up on the fallow fields to house those who arrived too late to secure proper lodgings. Before long, a second mobile city sprang up around Iryô, and Hafrin requested Wanderer assistance to oversee the problems. Medics and field engineers toured the various sites in the company of Temple personnel. Troops set up proper sanitation facilities in short order, and regulations and guidelines were posted where everyone could read them. Violators were permitted the grace of one warning before being heavily fined.

Iryô merchants did a brisk business in food and merchantile goods such as had not been since since Fanhri's death. From his turret room overlooking the city, Hafrin watched the now constant press of bodies that filled his capitol's streets, straining its capacity and trying the patience of the permanent residents and patrols.

"What a time to give up the trade," Marrek ruefully reflected.

Glancing over his shoulder Hafrin asked, "Would you really rather be down in that madhouse?"

"Better that than this insane asylum," countered Marrek. "Have you considered what Pete said last night?"

"About fire pickets in the camps?" To Marrek's lifted eyebrow, Hafrin nodded. "The patrols have been doubled already. There's an early curfew in place until after my investiture. Law-breakers will spend time under lock and key until after the ceremony and then sent home. The indigent are being put to work cleaning the city streets, and anyone caught breaking the law will be dealt with."

"So you've thought of everything."

In response to Marrek's challenge, Hafrin shook his head. "Hardly, sir. Truthfully, all I can do is lay down the law and rely upon my troops and the present judicial system to act accordingly. Afterwards…well, we shall see."

"And that's about all that can be expected," Marrek concurred. A smile touched his lips and he rested a hand on Hafrin's shoulder. Through that touch, Hafrin felt his foster father's sympathy and support. Ruling Fimiah was definitely not as easy as history had made it appear.

Four days after their return Jikpryn was laid to rest in the Royal vaults at the Temple. Hafrin made certain the ceremony was carried out with all the honours due an Alaiad, much to the amazement of the population at large. Out of respect for the fallen, he insisted upon a three-day official mourning period.

All too soon for his liking, the day came when Hafrin walked the streets to the Temple. Bereft of weapons and mail, head bare, he relied upon the good will of his people as the procession wound its way down into Iryô. The night before, one of the senior priests had arrived to drill him in what the ceremony would entail. Since a part of it required he claim Hafrön in the sight of the Temple personnel and his court, he had briefly visited the Temple where he had left his hereditary sword in front of the altar.

Behind Hafrin walked Nichole and the rest of his immediate entourage. Nobles from outlying communities accompanied the senior officers of his army. The families of some had actually managed to reach the capitol in time to take part in the procession. Surrounded by Wanderer and Fimiahri guards, with archers from his provincial army on the rooftops and fortress walls to guard against possible assassination attempts, Hafrin followed in the footsteps of his ancestors. Unlike Hafrin and his companions, the rest of the cavalcade was mounted. Alongside Nichole paced Bïzhan Koryn and Origan, all in full panoply. Vrala Harz perched on the black's saddletree. Eyes bright, the orved uttered tiny cries at irregular intervals and flipped her wings, as though ensuring everyone knew who it was walking the streets to the Temple.

Citizens lined the streets. They hung over balcony railings and were even perched on rooftops in efforts to achieve the best, unimpeded view of their prospective new ruler. The crowd was strangely quiet, speculative. Their rampant curiosity concerning this young man who had survived a brutal insurrection washed over Hafrin and Nichole. Tales brought back from the market squares by Hilcaz's spies were rife with rumour. Hafrin af Fanhri had been raised by unknown individuals…commoners. That was whispered amongst the populace, some inferring his foster parents had been of respectable means. Many wondered, privately and out loud, how he would deal with his people, especially the wealthy, and whether or not claiming his throne would alter the manner in which he dealt with the common and merchant population.

Inundated by their concerns, wonder and possibilities of manipulation, Hafrin struggled to contain himself, to concentrate on the immediate. His unique upbringing had granted him a perspective no previous Alaiad in recorded history had possessed. A sympathetic and conscientious attitude toward the poor and those of limited means was something the poor hoped he would impress upon his Fimiahri councillors once he was confirmed Alaiad. From Zivvoz's contacts, he knew he would meet with considerable opposition on all fronts to any changes he might wish to instigate.

At length, Hafrin stood before the entrance to the Temple compound. His guards drew aside. By law, no one barred his path save two priests. They awaited him beneath the archway. Carefully, Hafrin approached. Unlike his ancestors who undoubtedly would have arrived attired in clothing cut from sumptuous fabric richly embroidered and encrusted with gems, Hafrin had elected once again to turn tradition on its ear. While his nobles might wear their best in an effort to draw attention, he was clothed in plain dark blue fabric delicately etched with silver. In contrast, his dark gold shirt was cut from a lighter-weight cloth.

Now, in the chill early winter air, he was forced to remove his cloak, jacket, vest and shirt. Marrek stepped forward to take them, draping them over his left arm as Hafrin passed each to him in turn. At a gesture from the elder priest, Hafrin raised his arms over his head. Both priests approached. Taking turns, they examined the mark beneath his left arm. Their inspection was detailed, right down to testing the sigil with several liquids. No word or look passed between them, but eventually the younger one signalled Hafrin to get dressed.

Lips tightly pressed together, his hands shaking with the cold, Hafrin quickly redressed. From somewhere a horn blared a summons. Now the priests silently led the way inside. The entire procession moved forward, entering the Temple compound at last. Acolytes took charge of the lead rynada. For once, Bïzhan suffered a stranger's hands on him without protest.

The entourage mounted the steps at Hafrin's heels, entering the vaulted interior. They turned left into a side chamber. This, Hafrin and Nichole knew from Kizrun's instruction, was the Hall of Ascension. Here, everyone halted.

Never having been to so large a structure, not even during his trade trips with Marrek, Hafrin surreptitiously inspected what he was able to see of the inside of the building as his entourage passed through it. He knew the Wanderers had avoided interfering with Fimiahri religion, so they were no more familiar with the precepts of it than the average Fimiahri.

If that, he thought.

In the Rashordi Wilds, the nearest centres of worship were in the larger townships where the priests oversaw tutoring of local children. Living on an isolated hold, Hafrin had had little interaction with the Temple and its priests except when on the trade routes. It had fallen to Zivvoz and Kili to instruct him in his people's religion. Now, he drank in his surroundings.

Diffused daylight streamed through long narrow windows. Between each were set torches that flickered in the disturbed air of the chamber. They augmented the otherwise diluted illumination. There were no seats. Nor was there a colonnade, which, apparently, the Wanderers half-expected. Unadorned walls rose to the ribbed ceiling supports on either side. In direct contrast, the finely worked wood panelling and ceiling was delightfully patterned with different hues to form intricate, geometric designs.

From his studies, Hafrin knew the Hall of Ascension was equally unadorned, a design emulated without fail by the smaller temples in outlying communities. At the far end of this hall, however, stood the statue of a man, which was slightly larger than life. Around the base were several oil lamps. There were flecks of something reflective in the stones of the wall behind the statue. Magnifying the light in that area of the building, it illuminated the carved figure. Engraved in the stone at the statue's feet was the rune for the Great Serpent, plus a name.

Shock almost took Hafrin's breath away as he realised this representation was actually the Great Serpent. Having spent most of his life in Marrek's presence, Hafrin had expected a creature of some sort. This wholly unexpected representation was that of an elderly man.

No less shocked, Nichole's silent gasp of astonishment reached him. *Oh, my God! They don't worship a snake!*

On the heels of her mental exclamation, a voice boomed through the hall. "Who stands before the great Sijerpant?"

For a single heartbeat, Hafrin was unable to react. Behind him, the combined mental tumult of the Wanderers washed over him as each realised the name of the Fimiahri deity had always been so badly mangled by the bulk of the people with whom they had contact that they had misunderstood. Only now were they wondering why the original scouts had thought the word for the Fimiahri deity was identical in both their language and the native dialect. That it had referred to a serpent, a legless and wingless creature similar to something drawn from the Neranik depths, rather than being the name of an individual.

In the silence gripping them in the wake of the inquiry, Hafrin managed to shake himself out of his momentary stupor. Clearing his throat, Hafrin announced his name, following with a declaration of his lineage as Marrek had instructed him. It took a long time. More than once he had to pause to remember the next ancestor, since there were several occasions when inheritance had passed to a side-branch of his family. Each time he faltered, he caught the correct name from Marrek's thoughts and resolutely pressed on. Eventually, he was done. Again, they waited.

Something stirred in the shadows to one side of the statue. A small, slightly built man of indeterminate age emerged to stand in the light of the lamps. Again following tradition, Hafrin went forward. He halted, head bowed, awaiting recognition.

"Hafrin, son of Fanhri and Rïtyom, the Temple welcomes you. Alaiad Presumptive, lift up your heritage."

At a gesture from the priest, Hafrin looked beyond him. For the first time he saw, lying across the upraised hands of the statue, his hereditary sword. Heart racing, he squared his shoulders.

Slowly, Hafrin moved forward. Halting before the statue he stared at the enigmatic visage that was curiously like his own, and yet, in some alien fashion, possessing features wholly unlike any he was familiar with, Wanderer or Fimiahri.

There was a low step at the base of the statue's pedestal. He stepped up, reached up and picked down Hafrön. At the priest's gentle direction, Hafrin turned and raised the sword high above his head. Everyone present, save the priests and acolytes, went to one knee. Light rippled along the blade at his touch. It poured from the tip to stream down his arm and head, covering him from head to toe in a brilliant olio before fading away.

Somewhere outside, trumpets blared to formally announce his elevation to Alaiad. Even through the Temple's thick stonewalls the tumult of cheering was clearly audible. The eruption of sound drew Hafrin out of his daze and back to his surroundings. Gently, the priest turned Hafrin around to face the chamber. His tone was sympathetic when he spoke.

"Rule well, Alaiad Hafrin af Fanhri."

"I shall endeavour to do my best," Hafrin solemnly swore.

Now the priest said something Hafrin had not anticipated. "You will be expected to take a wife and provide heirs."

Hafrin hesitated. Then he announced, "I already have a wife."

He transferred Hafrön to his left hand and held out his right. Cued, Nichole stood and walked sedately forward to take his hand. Eyes narrowed, the priest studied Nichole. She remained steadfast at Hafrin's side, her chin slightly raised, determined not to be cowed. Hafrin felt amusement emanating from the priest.

"What name do you have woman?"

"I am Nichole Trent of Baccaria." Fearless, she openly declared both her name and her world of birth. "As with one of the Alaiad's ancestors, I am also Wanderer, those whom you know as Hynarkin."

"Star blood, you are most welcome. Ser," the priest addressed Hafrin, "what ceremony was conducted to hand fast you?"

Cheeks flushed, Hafrin explained, "We declared our alliance before my shield brother, Indoro son of Zivvoz."

"Indoro af Zivvoz, stand forth."

To that summons, Indoro scrambled to his feet with less ceremony than Nichole had managed and reluctantly approached the priest. Even more embarrassed than Hafrin, he mumbled an explanation of where and when the declaration had taken place. Throughout the recital, the priest remained expressionless. He nodded and gestured Indoro to return to his place.

"Hafrin af Fanhri and Nikôla of the Star Blood, here and now receive the official blessing of the Temple and the great Sijerpant." The priest raised his hands and they dipped their heads so he might touch them. "Nikôla, do you swear to provide Hafrin af Fanhri with heirs?"

"With all my heart."

Before she could say anything else, Triklâ appeared. "Ralhar, High Priest of Sijerpant, I wish to speak."

Startled, the High Priest turned. Two paces behind Triklâ trailed an over-awed Kili cradling Valrin against her breasts. Ceremony interrupted, the priest waited for the seer and her companions to approach.

"Triklâ, what brings you to this hallowed place at such a time?"

"High Priest, I present to you the heir of Alaiad Hafrin."

A lift of Triklâ's hand urged Kili to place Valrin in Nichole's arms. She raised Valrin's arm to expose the mark on the underside. To Nichole's amazement, their son remained silent.

"This is their first-born, acknowledged by the sword."

"You've been busy," commented the High Priest. In spite of the solemnity of the ceremony, his eyes danced with mirth. Even so, he managed to maintain a neutral expression. "How have you named him?"

Saliva suddenly clogged Hafrin's throat. He swallowed it with difficulty and managed, "His name is Valrin."

With a nod, the High Priest took Valrin from Nichole and raised the now squirming, irritated infant high above his head. "Behold the son of Halfrin af Fanhri, Valrin af Hafrin, Alaiad heir. May he prove a shield for our people in his time."

A resounding shout rose from everyone present. "Behold the heir!"

On that note, the ceremony concluded. The High Priest deposited Valrin in Nichole's arms just as nobles and Wanderers pressed forward to congratulate Hafrin. They praised him for his choice of wife and inspected the baby. Kili quickly took Valrin and wrapped him up once more. As Annarek came forward from the shadows to retrieve Valrin, he stopped crying, much to Nichole's relief.

The High Priest gestured and moved off through the gathering. They parted before him then fell in behind, Hafrin immediately on his heels. Nichole took up her position a half pace behind him. Accompanying them and a cavalcade of silent acolytes, the entire group surged from the temple. At the bottom of the stairs waited the guards and handlers.

Bïzhan reared slightly at the sight of his friend but made no attempt to break free of the acolyte hanging onto his reins. From Hafrin, he read the necessity of behaving and complied. Once everyone was mounted, the temple gates swung wide. They headed back up the main thoroughfare to the fortress. Wildly cheering throngs of merchants and poor people lined the route, many hoarse from yelling at the top of their lungs. Hafrin carried his sword across his saddle in plain view and, for a time, it held their undivided attention. Then, someone realised Nichole was riding knee to knee with Hafrin, in the position traditionally given to the Alaia. Immediately behind them, in a small cart, rode the nurse, cradling Valrin. At the sight of the baby, the population's enthusiasm knew no bounds.

GLOSSARY

Hynarkin (also: Wanderers or Gypsies) wandering traders

(intergalactic agents)

Mark Warder	Marrek Lytsun
Sandy North	Sandi Daryk (Peter's cousin)
David Warder	Davyn Lytsun (Mark's brother)
Robert Talon	Robar Telan
Peter North	Piltar Daryk
Vern Parsons	colony manager on Fimiah
Martin Anson	Nichole's sleep-teach tutor
Bertho Parsons	Records' Mistress at the colony
Nichole Trent	Nikôla
Albert Trent	Nichole's oldest brother (member of Settlement—presently on Farthom)
Victor Trent	Nichole's second oldest brother (in Patrol)
the Barlings	cousins of Nichole and her brothers
Dean Bartlett	Chief Herder at the colony
Alex	one-time colony stable hand
Bob Mackenzie	colony Quartermaster
Harold Thompson	Nichole's guide on her return to Fimiah

Major Lothar	senior medical officer at the Academy
Tom Drillian	Patrol Academy Commander

Fimiahri (planetary natives: homeworld—Fimiah)

Hafrin af Fanhri	Alaiad-in-exile (half a ring) (son: Valrin—silver ring)
Zivvoz	free man and land holder (wife: Kili/ son: Indoro/daughter: Deenala)
Berhan af Norlatzïn	Iryô merchant
Binlâra	a Ekôzav lord owns a sword that resembles the Star Given—Blïntor Krel (blïntor's death)
Fanhri	Alaiad—Hafrin's father (wife: Rityöm)
Adosô	Rimtöm controller
Baryan	Vyhal controller
Ablîon	Sword Master
Jikpryn af Kinhar	Rityöm's brother (wife: Niôfa (d)/son: Larnzan)
Tolbôun	also known as the Outsider, Jikpryn's advisor
Hilcaz af Orïl	Captain of Jikpryn's personal guard
Krysp af Althiön	Jikpryn's page
Oryl	a soldier—lieutenant
Tynnim	another soldier—corporal
Worrek	another soldier
Gwyrn	another soldier
Gurran Myrivor	weapons' merchant
Triklâ	Temple seer in Iryô
Blorik	taught Hafrin how to skin & cure hides
Alenul	fruit grower
Siyon	trapper

Raxel	trapper
Loek	silversmith
Aklarisz	great Fimiahri scholar
Pryni	a bandit, (also: slur against Jikpryn)
Annarek	Valrin's nurse

Natural Features

Deccöt	central province/capitol: Iryô
Wôbiny	northern-most province/capitol: Pûdornâ (ruler: Kizrun)
Nûhykar	province northwest of Deccöt/capitol: Vyhal (ruler: Baryan)
Ekôzav	west of Pûdornâ/capitol: Rimtön
Brïtfin	village in northern Nûhykar
Revïl	a small town in the wilds near the Rashordi mountains
Demons' Gathering	massive fault south-west of Iryô
Veran Pindkol	the mountain where the a Wanderer colony was located until the Craneeno discovered it
Hycöt River	
Wob River	
River Iny	
Rash River	
River Karid	
Kandyn Islands	
Dôzhik	largest of four moons, has rings (the Warrior)
Zhi	smallest of the Maidens

Dôa	Zhi's twin
Ihô	
Warrior Maidens	also: Mad Maidens—three smaller moons

Miscellaneous

Alaiad	ruler (fem: Alaia) last female Alaia was Nerajai—an Hynarkin wife of an Alaiad was Kristyn Carruthers)	
talnot	coin	
lasz	one-quarter of a talnot	
Hafrön	the Star Given sword	
Fimiah	inhabitants: Fimiahri	
Rashordi	mountain range	
Neranik Sea	ocean	
Plucky Rakkïal	a tavern north of where Mark and Rin live (owner: Lon af Dyrlon)	
orved	a raptor Vrala Harz	(def: Sky Demon)
rynada	(pl: rynada)	
	Dintan	(def: Stupid)
	Palor Orved	(def: Lady Bird)
	Bizhan Koryn	(def: Night Runner)
	Shalinô	(def: Shadow)
	Neranil	(def: Sleepy)
	Makalli	(def: Trouble-maker)
	Lasier	(def: Shifty Eye)
	Mortimer	
	Rampage	

	Fluster
	Menace (sorrel)
tïlkrïn	like a deer but domesticated for its milk, meat and hide
blïntor	porcine creature
rakkïal	egg-laying fowl
sectambulators	native to Baccarian (also: ditherer)
vavik	evergreen tree
noyavin	tree with sap akin to latex
verlanik	archers
kolbrian	lancers
emiarl	foot soldiers
derynada	cavalry
F.I.C.P.S	Fleet Inter-Colonies Patrol and Settlement
Dawn Star	space ship
Upper Load Vieran	a supply crawler
Frissth	race: Uthssitssi (lizoid)
Baccaria	another planet
Craneeno	intergalactic enemy
M'bracni	race: Shrklattr (amoeba)
Zkritlac	race: Zkrixtalc (insectoid)
Zlitterka	Zkrixtalc homeworld—Davyn & Marrek birthworld
Lanolií	presumably original name of the race that settled Fimiah
Vyrk'ælffa	world from which the Fimiahri immigrated
Parakol	spacefarer's oath

FIMIAH CALENDAR

Year	Age
Cur	Cur
Tïlkrïn	Tïlkrïn
Orved	Orved
Sea Snake	Sea Snake
Blïntor	Blïntor
Rynad	Rynad
Dôa	Dôa
Zhi	Zhi
Ihô	Ihô
Dôzhik	Dôzhik

Every two hundred fifty years the last age, Dôzhik becomes Dôzhik Koryn (literally: Night of the Warrior's Run(ning)) At this time a rare planetary conjunction illuminates the Warrior's third (silver) ring. On the first two nights all young male mammals, including Fimiahri under the age of thirty, go into uncontrollable rut. Many dramatic and strange events are recorded as happening at this time.

www.caryconder.com

0-595-33758-9

Printed in the United States
25738LVS00003B/86